HM I

GINA WILKINS

8000 331892

MILLS

All the characters in this book have no existence outside the imagination of
the author, and have no relation whatsoever to anyone bearing the same name
or names. They are not even distantly inspired by any individual known or
unknown to the author, and all the incidents are pure invention.

All Rights Reserved including the right of reproduction in whole or in
part in any form. This edition is published by arrangement with Harlequin
Enterprises II B.V./S.à.r.l. The text of this publication or any part thereof may
not be reproduced or transmitted in any form or by any means, electronic or
mechanical, including photocopying, recording, storage in an information
retrieval system, or otherwise, without the written permission of the publisher.

This book is sold subject to the condition that it shall not, by way of trade or
otherwise, be lent, resold, hired out or otherwise circulated without the prior
consent of the publisher in any form of binding or cover other than that in
which it is published and without a similar condition including this condition
being imposed on the subsequent purchaser.

® and ™ are trademarks owned and used by the trademark owner and/or its
licensee. Trademarks marked with ® are registered with the United Kingdom
Patent Office and/or the Office for Harmonisation in the Internal Market and
in other countries.

Published in Great Britain 2013
by Mills & Boon, an imprint of Harlequin (UK) Limited,
Eton House, 18-24 Paradise Road, Richmond, Surrey TW9 1SR

BABY FOR THE MIDWIFE
© by Harlequin Enterprises II B.V./S.à.r.l 2013

The Midwife's Baby, Spanish Doctor, Pregnant Midwife and *Countdown to
Baby* were first published in Great Britain by Harlequin (UK) Limited.

The Midwife's Baby © Fiona McArthur 2008
Spanish Doctor, Pregnant Midwife © Anne Fraser 2009
Countdown to Baby © Harlequin Books S.A. 2004
Special thanks and acknowledgment are given to Gina Wilkins for her
contribution to the MERLYN COUNTY MIDWIVES series.

ISBN: 978 0 263 91035 3
ebook ISBN: 978 1 472 01615 7

05-0913

Harlequin (UK) policy is to use papers that are natural, renewable and
recyclable products and made from wood grown in sustainable forests. The
logging and manufacturing processes conform to the legal environmental
regulations of the country of origin.

Printed and bound in Spain
by Blackprint CPI, Barcelona

THE MIDWIFE'S BABY

BY

FIONA McARTHUR

Northamptonshire Libraries & Information Services KK	
Askews & Holts	

A mother to five sons, **Fiona McArthur** is an Australian midwife who loves to write. Medical Romance™ gives Fiona the scope to write about all the wonderful aspects of adventure, romance, medicine and midwifery that she feels so passionate about—as well as an excuse to travel! So now that the boys are older, her husband Ian and youngest son Rory are off with Fiona to meet new people, see new places, and have wonderful adventures. Fiona's website is at www.fionamcarthur.com.

To The Maytone Girls, friends indeed,
who inspire me.

CHAPTER ONE

THE chapel floated like a snowflake against the backdrop of the lush Hunter Valley Gardens and the string quartet drifted silvery notes out over the waiting guests.

Max Beresford stood tall and straight at the front of the church and realised that despite the romantic venue he'd condemned himself to the type of loveless marriage his parents had.

Give me a sign, God. Am I a fool for going through with this?

The procession music started. Too late.

Max tilted his chin slightly as he watched the matron of honour walk haltingly towards him in some screechingly fashionable apricot material.

There was something about the dogged yet vulnerable expression on the woman's face that aroused his sympathy because he'd approached the altar with just such a halting advance.

Max frowned. Was there a problem or was his new cousin-in-law-to-be unbearably nervous?

Embarrassed didn't make sense because she looked gorgeous—fertile with her baby bump bulging beneath the shiny fabric—but gorgeous nonetheless.

She paused again and seemed to suck air in through gritted teeth before she raised her chin and resumed her approach.

Max knew Tayla had been reluctant to include her midwife cousin, Georgia, in the wedding party but he'd thought that had been because of Georgia's unfashionable pregnancy and some vague hint that she was depressed. Maybe there were other reasons.

Before he could ruminate on that thought his non-blushing bride staged her spectacular entry and the gasps from the congregation drew Max's eyes towards his future wife.

Max could do nothing but stare as feathers rippled and parted in the breeze and held him spellbound.

He blinked in disbelief. Tayla seemed to have been devoured by a white duck.

Framed against the door for an extended moment, his bride's shapely arms and legs stretched from beneath a strapless froth of feathers that only just covered her thighs at the front and fell in a frothy tail to the floor at the back.

A large apricot bow around her tiny waist matched the rose in her father's lapel.

Good grief, Max thought, and suppressed a smile. He'd fallen into *Swan Lake* and he had never felt less like a prince.

His bride floated up beside him, as did one of the feathers that had come unstuck and drifted just ahead of her in an eddy, and went to hand her feathered fan to the matron of honour.

Cousin Georgia was not having a good day as she missed the one cue she'd been assigned. He could see Tayla remained seriously unimpressed with her attendant.

For Georgia Winton, being matron of honour had assumed the nightmare proportions she had hoped it wouldn't.

The first unexpected labour contraction had hit her as she'd entered the church at the precise moment the whole congregation had noticed her entrance.

The next contraction had grown to such intensity she almost dropped the bouquet as her cousin handed it to her.

When she was able to, Georgia offered an apologetic glance at the bride and groom, which neither acknowledged. Tayla had tossed her head in disgust and Max had continued to stare, bemused, at Tayla's dress.

Georgia clutched the bouquet like the dead duck it resembled and forced her shoulders to drop as the pain eased away. Distraction, distraction, distraction, she reminded herself. There was plenty of that.

Max Beresford, the groom, was pretty distracting. She'd known of him, but until now not by sight as he'd missed rehearsals because of some crisis at the hospital.

The real Max was tall, broad-shouldered and far too handsome for his own good, but his kind eyes had surprised her with their warmth.

Though younger than she'd expected, he looked every inch the new department head of obstetrics for the North Coast Region of Hospitals—a position he was taking up after Tayla's and his honeymoon—and she was surprised how much she instinctively felt that Tayla had chosen well.

After her baby was born, Max would apparently find her a midwife's position in the region, so she really did hope she wouldn't ruin his wedding.

Max's brother, Paul, who had played groom each time they'd practised the wedding service, seemed pleasant enough but not a warm person and he stood beside Max now as a paler shade of his brother.

Unfortunately Paul's eyes were fixed a little too intently on his brother's wife-to-be.

Meanwhile Tayla, gloriously aware of everyone's attention, proceeded to lift her eyes theatrically towards the stained-glass window and shimmy her feathers.

Georgia could see no softness or devotion or anything redeeming from her cousin despite the perfect setting and the man beside her. Though she had adamantly said to Georgia that of course she loved Max.

On the groom's part, even the smile Max gave his fiancée seemed strained and disconnected.

Georgia ached with disappointment. Weddings shouldn't be like this. What was wrong with everybody? Except for her parents, who had remained blissfully in love until their deaths, she had begun to despair that all marriages were destined to be travesties.

Tayla she could understand. Tayla had always wanted the extravagant white wedding and the rich husband, topped off by the bridal magazine shoot currently in progress.

While her cousin would enjoy being married to a handsome consultant as she flew in to join Max briefly for social occasions in whatever city or town he visited, Tayla didn't intend that her marriage would markedly change her life.

A tiny worry line drew Max's thick black brows together even further and Georgia glared at him for not savouring the moment. Didn't he realise the sacredness of marriage?

What was in it for Max if he didn't have some affection for his bride?

Romantically, Georgia had hoped this wedding would restore her faith in true love. She'd hoped there would be a incandescent joy between these two as they stood before God and declared their troth.

Then the third contraction gripped her belly and all else was forgotten as the searing pain snatched her breath at the peak. This time the intensity drew a stifled gasp she couldn't contain. Even the minister looked across at her with raised eyebrows.

It wasn't fair. Labour was supposed to start with gentle regular contractions, gradually increasing in intensity. She should have been supported by her midwife friends at home, with birdsong playing. Not the Wedding March.

The only thing bird-like about these pains were that they flew straight to a pain score of ten.

When the contraction finally eased she accepted that it was likely the wedding would go on without her.

Georgia chewed her bottom lip and tried to focus on the glorious blue-green stained-glass window until the minister began to speak again. In the lull before the next pain, she could almost believe she could wait at least until the man-and-wife part of the service.

Tayla was going to kill her and when she looked at the bride she wanted to cry. Pregnancy hormones, of course—but, then Tayla had always made her want to cry.

She tried to concentrate on the ballet of the shooting fountains in the artificial lake below— surely the next contraction would be further apart— until a tiny clicking pop sent the trickle of warm fluid down her leg and forced her to call it a day.

'Excuse me,' she whispered to the minister as she edged away from the altar towards the side door of the church.

'You're not going anywhere,' Tayla hissed, but this time Georgia didn't hear.

Please, God, she prayed silently, don't let anyone notice the tiny rivulets of fluid in her wake. She could feel the eyes of the congregation on her back.

Suddenly the trickle became a gush and her baby kicked and squirmed in an agitated dance that evicted any thought of who was watching and sent prickles of unease down Georgia's spine.

This didn't feel right and her baby's panic was communicated to Georgia even though she had never experienced labour before. At work she'd seen labour go wrong and she tried not to allow those memories to intrude.

She remembered the words of her Calmbirth midwife—listen to your body. Listen to your instincts. Her belly heaved as her baby twisted again. Her instinct said she needed to go to the hospital and her baby demanded speed.

She lifted her eyes in panic. She needed help, and suddenly help was there. The steady gaze of Max grounded her panic with calmness and a strong, reassuring hand on her shoulder.

She swallowed the lump of fear in her throat. The last time she'd seen him he'd been at the altar with Tayla. She darted a look to the front of the church and her cousin glared with real menace towards both of them.

'Your waters have broken?'

She nodded, still stunned that Max had left his bride. Georgia didn't have the mental space to go there. Tayla would have to get used to being married to a doctor, but not yet—at least not until after the wedding.

'You've been having contractions.' His voice was

gentle and she looked back at him because it was better than looking at the gaping assembly.

Her baby twisted and turned like a fish on a hook and she cupped her stomach and grabbed his hand as the next contraction squeezed.

'Hard and fast. Something's wrong.' It was difficult to get the words out through the pain. 'Something else came out with the water. I'm thinking cord prolapse.'

Cord prolapse was one of the true obstetric emergencies and they both knew it.

If a baby hadn't 'dropped' or engaged its head in the pelvis, a loop of cord could fall between the baby's head and the bottom of the uterus when the waters broke. With four weeks to go in Georgia's pregnancy her baby hadn't dropped yet so it was dreadfully possible.

Any contractions she had after that could force the hard head of the baby onto the presenting cord and cut off the flow of oxygen from mother to baby. With no oxygen her baby would die.

If that was the case they needed to try to keep Georgia's baby's head from coming down onto the umbilical cord. Minutes counted.

'I'm scared, Max.' She'd never met this man in her life and suddenly it felt OK to call him Max.

His eyes softened and he nodded once. 'I know. We need to get you to the hospital ASAP.'

He flipped open his phone and spoke briefly into it. 'Let's get you outside to the car. An ambulance can meet us on the road if we don't beat them there.'

He scooped her up in his arms and she cringed. 'Your beautiful suit.'

'It's only a suit.' He grinned down at her and incredibly his eyes were golden and caring and she suddenly felt her baby had a chance, even though the odds were stacked against them.

Another contraction coiled viciously through her and she moaned. This was terrifying.

Max carried her swiftly to his black limousine. White ribbons fluttered on the long bonnet and the JUST MARRIED placard sat proudly on the boot.

Georgia shifted in his arms as she twisted her neck to see. 'Not this car, Max. The seats.'

'To hell with the seats. At least we have room and the windows are tinted.'

Max's chauffeur's usually impassive expression faltered as Max deposited the wrong woman in the wedding car.

'Newcastle Hospital ASAP. I'll pay the speeding fines,' Max said over his shoulder as he climbed in after her. He pulled shut the door before he sat opposite Georgia and shrugged out of his jacket.

The car accelerated away from the kerb and Georgia fell back in a heap. Max leaned across from the facing seat to help her balance.

'Can you check and tell me if you can feel the umbilical cord?' He smiled sympathetically at her and suddenly it was OK. They were a team working together to help save a baby—her baby.

With difficulty she knelt on the soft leather seat, closed her eyes mortified as a rivulet of pink fluid disappeared down the back of the seat, and hitched up the wet satin creation designed by a leading Sydney fashion house.

That morning, when she'd struggled with clipping her thigh-high stockings to the garter belt, she'd thought it a shame no one would see the pretty lace of the belt. What a joke. Once she got to the hospital, everyone would be looking at her.

As she slipped her hand down into her panties she knew what she would find—she could feel it beating like her own heartbeat except slower. Sure enough, a loop of umbilical cord fell into her hand.

Before she could confirm her finding to Max, the next contraction was on top of her and with this pain the urge to push was overpowering. It couldn't happen this quick! They were supposed to stop the labour until they could get her to operating theatre and do a Caesarean section to save her baby.

'Ma-ax,' she wailed and she grabbed his hand, put her chin on her chest and pushed, unable to stop herself.

Still calm, his voice was kind. 'There's no time for modesty. You know that, don't you, Georgia? Let me see.'

Max's face was composed but in that moment she saw the stressed beat of the vein in his temple and she knew he doubted her baby's chances despite his calm voice.

The look of surprise on his face made a tiny shaft of hope slice through the pain to imprint on Georgia's thoughts.

'First baby?' His eyes met hers in question.

'Absolutely. Probably last,' she gasped.

He smiled at that and sat back. 'Well, your baby is ready to come and is almost here. Let nature finish the job, Georgia.'

That was all she needed to find the rest of her strength and with the next pain fast on the heels of the last she concentrated from deep within herself and willed her baby to fly out into the world before the lack of oxygen from the compression of the cord could take away her life.

When she opened her eyes Max was unwinding the cord from around the baby's neck and lifting her towards Georgia, and incredibly a miniature angry red face screwed up to emit a bellow that almost lifted the roof off the car.

Max laughed and she blinked and looked again at this tiny roaring child of immense determination and began to shake in shock.

'My God.' Max wiped his eyes on his upper arm and then grabbed his suit jacket and rubbed her baby dry before he leant forward to slip the bodice strap off Georgia's shoulder to allow one side of her dress to fall to expose her skin. 'Here, keep her warm.'

Still chuckling, he placed the baby against Georgia's bare skin, flipped the jacket over to the dry side and tucked it around them both.

'Congratulations,' he said, and shook his head in disbelief. 'I'm afraid her father missed her arrival.'

Georgia shuddered. 'We didn't miss him.' Her

baby was still slightly wet and slippery and still roaring her head off and Georgia soothed her little round head that hadn't even had time to change shape for the journey through her pelvis.

'Poor baby.' She ducked her head and kissed her downy cheek. 'Do you have a headache from your quick trip?'

Max listened to the soft maternal whispers from a woman he barely knew and felt incredibly touched by a scene he'd seen so many times in so many circumstances—but never like this.

'I think you might be right about her headache.' Max shook his head again and the smile on his face felt bigger than any he'd had in the last few years. This birth brought back the notion that there could still be immense satisfaction in his chosen profession.

He'd known he needed to get back to the grass roots of it all and away from the consultancy, and board meetings, the constant demand for more high-tech medical apparatus and the financial headaches and heartaches that being head of the obstetric department left him with.

This new position promised exposure to the real world of obstetrics again. While a percentage of his duties would remain administrative, there was an expectation he would work in each hospital to gain insight into the obstetric viability of each facility.

If he was honest, that was the carrot that had got him into this marriage mess in the first place. This moment in time had proved how much more rewarding hands-on obstetrics was for him but he'd have time to think of that later.

Georgia's baby finally quietened and after a quick glance to ensure all was well he suggested to his driver that he slow the car to a reasonable pace as they finished the forty-minute drive to the hospital.

This Georgia, she was something special to have come through this with a calmness and serenity that should have been shattered, especially as, being a midwife, she'd known the complications that could ensue.

Unexpectedly the loud sound of rhythmic sucking could be heard and Max felt the smile widen on his face again.

'Umm. Isn't breastfeeding supposed to be noise-less or does this child of yours do everything spec-tacularly and with high volume?'

'I think she's loud. I should call her Thor—or Thoreen.'

'Speaking of "thor", are you?'

'Very funny.' She shook her head at him and for the first time in many years he felt like a child rebuked by an adult and his lips twitched.

She got over it quickly, though. 'Now you mention it, what are we going to do with the disaster down here ruining your upholstery? I don't suppose you have two cord clamps and a pair of scissors?'

He stripped off his elegant neckpiece. 'I do have a cord tie.'

She giggled and then covered her mouth. 'I'm

sorry. I'm feeling light-headed with relief and I'm being silly.'

He pulled a snowy white teatowel from the bottle compartment and folded it. 'Pop this between your legs.' He handed the towel to her. 'Let's just settle for that one knot in the cord with the tie and we'll bundle it all up still connected and they can sort it out at the hospital. Are you bleeding?'

She shook her head. 'Not since she started to feed.'

He marvelled at the wonders of nature without the usual drugs given at the end of labour. 'Thor looks about five pounds. How early is she by your dates?'

'Four weeks and two days.' He'd hazard a guess she was counting days from conception.

'Did ultrasounds confirm those dates?'

She lifted her chin at him. 'Ever the doctor. Why do so many obstetricians think ultrasounds know more than the mother?'

He chuckled at that. 'True. Sometimes ultrasounds can cloud issues that don't need clouding. And other times an ultrasound can clarify things.'

'Hmmph,' Georgia said. 'You can't beat good clinical skills. Technology is one of the things I won't get bogged down in when I start to practise again.'

He couldn't remember the last time he'd heard someone hmmph. 'We won't get into that discussion or maybe we'll save it till later.'

'And my baby's name is not Thor.'

'Wowser.' He settled back into the seat as all the chores that could be done had been done. The rest could wait.

He was a mess and her dress had seen better days too. His shirt was unbuttoned at the neck from when he'd pulled his tie off. The long sleeves had been hiked unevenly up to his elbows and he cupped his hands on one knee and decided he'd definitely have to throw out the suit.

He looked across at her. Actually, she looked pretty good. 'So what are you going to call her?'

She laughed at that and he loved the way she threw her whole face into the laugh. No attempt to save on laughter lines and she did have a lot to be thankful for.

'What do you call a child that arrived like this and roared so vigorously at birth?' She looked down at the now content baby. 'I could call her Maxine.'

She was delightful and with a thud he remembered he was almost married. 'That would really set the cat among the pigeons,' he drawled.

He saw the moment she remembered Tayla. 'Oh, my God. Your wedding. I'm so sorry.'

'Later. It will be a drama in due time. No use thinking about it now.'

CHAPTER TWO

TAYLA'S wild eyes were slitted shafts of fury in her narrow face as she stormed into Georgia's hospital room. Anger vibrated off her in waves and even the baby stirred in her sleep with the malevolence emanating from Tayla.

Max thought it all lost a little credibility with the feathers.

Normally Tayla was a very attractive woman but in this instance he decided he might have had a lucky escape. He stayed motionless, leaning up against the wall with his arms crossed, and waited for his fiancée to see her cousin was not alone.

Tayla saw no one except Georgia. 'You had to do it. Had to ruin everything. If anyone could do it, it would be you! I knew you shouldn't have been my matron of honour but my father had to have his way. Well I'm not the only one who's a laughing stock. Serves him right.'

'I'm so sorry, Tayla.' Georgia wilted against the pillows and closed her eyes, and Max realised that the ridiculous behaviour of Tayla was upsetting the new mother.

'You will be!' Tayla spat, and Max stepped away from the wall.

'That's enough.' His voice was very quiet but sliced off Tayla's words as if he'd swathed his arm through the air like a conductor. Tayla froze before turning slowly to face him.

'Max?' She stamped her foot and another tiny white feather puffed into the air. 'I knew you must have stayed with her.'

'Obviously,' he drawled, and then regretted his provocativeness for Georgia's sake. Outside work interference it was probably the first time he'd made the effort to check Tayla. Maybe he had let everything slide too much in his obsession to land this job.

'Look at your suit!' Tayla was slow to see the dangerous glint in Max's eye. 'And why did you have to be the one to go with her? There were half a dozen obstetricians there but, no, you had to leave me at the altar like a fool.'

Max glanced across at Georgia and the sleeping baby. 'I'm sorry about your wedding, Tayla,' he said. 'But perhaps in private and later.'

Tayla faltered and stretched her face into a smile, finally connecting Max's displeasure. 'It was your wedding, too.' The plaintive note sounded clearly. 'And the magazine was there taking photos. No wonder we couldn't find you when the ambulance turned up. When it was called off my father searched everywhere for you.'

'Your father would have done better to spend his time checking on his new great-niece.' Max raised his eyebrows. 'I'm sure you, too, were concerned that Georgia's baby almost lost her life.'

Tayla glanced at the baby in Georgia's arms with barely concealed disinterest. 'Of course.' She dragged her arm across her face. 'It's been such a horrible morning. I think they will still print the photos from the church but as a disaster now. I've been quite distraught.' And quietly she began to sob.

Max dropped his jaw in amazement and Georgia shifted her baby up to her shoulder and slid to the edge of the bed.

In sudden clarity Max realised if he didn't step in Georgia would rise from her bed to comfort her cousin and take all the blame for something that no one could have prevented.

'Stay there, Georgia. Rest. You've had a big morning, too. I'll take Tayla away and calm her down.'

Tayla lifted her head and he admitted she cried very prettily but some of the sterling reasons he'd had for marrying her had strangely seeped away.

'Come on, Tayla,' he said more gently. She really had been excited about the magazine shoot and he needed to be more patient. 'I'll make you a coffee in the consultants' tearoom and we can talk.' He turned her towards the door and glanced over his shoulder at the woman in the bed.

'Look after Thor.'

The sweetness of his smile made the lump of tears in Georgia's chest swell even more and she nodded stupidly and watched him leave.

She'd have to name her daughter or she'd begun to think of her as Thor. The problem was she'd only chosen boys names. More reason to dislike the inaccuracy of ultrasounds.

Actually, she would like to call her Maxine but no doubt the affinity she felt towards a certain obstetrician would pass. She was never falling for that again.

She wouldn't be calling her daughter after her father because the memories of Sol's dangerous possessiveness left her quivering in her bed. She shuddered and forced her mind back to the present.

Her daughter was like a little lioness with her roar and her power and her aggressive hold on life. No man would try to run her life. She should call her Elsa after the lioness in *Born Free*. Actually, she liked that. She liked it a lot.

'Hello, Elsa.' Elsa opened one dark blue eye and glared at her mother before thick black lashes fluttered down again and she drifted back to sleep.

Well, that was settled. She looked up as a knock sounded at the door and her uncle poked his head around it.

'You available for visitors?'

'Come in, Harry.' She gestured to the seat beside the bed and her nearest living relative sank onto the hard plastic with relief. He peered at the baby in her arms.

'So she's well? No ill effects from her dramatic entry into the world?' He lifted one finger and stroked the baby's soft hair.

'The paediatrician said she'll be fine. Because Elsa was so vigorous at birth, we're sure she coped with whatever fall in oxygen she suffered.'

Harry raised his bushy white eyebrows. 'Elsa. Strong name. Still, you must have been terrified. I'm glad you're both well. I gather Max did a great job.'

'He was very calm and caught her beautifully.' She leaned towards her uncle. 'I'm so sorry about Tayla's wedding.'

'Water under the bridge.' He looked at her and they both smiled at the poor pun. 'Tayla threw hysterics in the church when the limo drove off. I was glad to get out of there.'

Georgia bit her lip. She felt too guilty to smile at her uncle's dry amusement. 'She's with Max now. I'm sure he'll calm her down.'

'She'd better show a more attractive side than I saw this morning or it won't matter how much he needs a wife.' Her uncle looked at Georgia quickly and then away.

'I did not say that.' Distressed, he rubbed his gnarled hands together. He was a self-made success and proud of his hands, but he wasn't proud of that slip. 'I'm an old man and get mixed up sometimes.'

He looked around the room—anywhere but at Georgia. 'You look after young Elsa here and I'll see you soon.' Harry bent down and kissed her cheek before he lumbered out of the room as fast as he could.

Georgia stared after him. 'Good grief,' she said out loud. 'What do you make of that, Elsa?'

'So you've named her?' Max spoke from the door. Georgia looked serene and competent with the baby nestled in her arms, and he stifled the pang of pain he'd thought he'd got over about not having children.

Imagine someone like her to come home to after work. During his engagement Max had eventually realised that at best Tayla would fly to visit him every few weeks and he'd accepted she would continue with her life as charity social queen.

At the time it had seemed enough because he could never offer a maternal woman a family and Tayla made no secret of the fact that she didn't want children. A realistic Tayla was better than the beauties who had chorused that IVF would do the trick.

Imagine if it had been possible to marry someone like Georgia? They could have even worked together and he'd have a real insight into the care the women were receiving.

Enough. He wouldn't be searching for another wife. One close shave was enough. Maybe he could run his disastrous day past the board and they'd consider his circumstances against the fact he wasn't married. He'd sort something out.

He frowned at the strange expression on

Georgia's face and he wondered what new complication had arisen.

For Georgia, after the first quick glance, she didn't know where to look. Perhaps she'd caught her uncle's affliction of avoiding eye contact, but this was a bit awkward after hearing Max needed a wife.

She flicked another peek at him and away again. 'Harry just left.'

'Yes, I know.' Max frowned. 'I saw him but he seemed in a bit of a hurry. I'm not sure he's speaking to me after I failed so dismally as a son-in-law.'

Georgia winced and looked down as Elsa slept contentedly in her arms. That was definitely her fault. She wished her daughter would wake up and yell. At least she could avoid conversation then. Her brain was spinning from Harry's bombshell. Max just didn't seem the type to need a wife.

The guy had everything. Looks, money, fabulous career. A sliver of ice slid down her back. Maybe he wanted to own a trophy wife, like Sol had.

'How is Tayla?' It was all she could think of to say.

'Unengaged. She doesn't want to marry me any more.' Max dropped the words into the room like an afterthought. 'But she'll be fine. I've sent her home with my brother. I think they will do very well together. We don't normally get on but Paul's been a godsend this week.'

Georgia frowned and played back his comment

in her mind. Unengaged. Needed a wife. 'Did you say the wedding is off?'

'Definitely. I couldn't guarantee to her I would never rush off like that again and she said it wasn't good enough.'

'She's a fool.' Georgia had thought the words and somehow they slipped quietly into the room for Max to hear.

'I think so—but there you have it.' He was irrepressible and she couldn't help smiling. They both grinned at each other and the camaraderie was back.

Georgia decided she must have misunderstood Uncle Harry. Max didn't seem too upset for someone who needed to have a wife. She would go with her instincts and her instincts said Max Beresford could be trusted.

'So why were you marrying Tayla if you didn't love her?'

He sighed and sat down. She realised he was dressed in theatre garb so he must have changed out of his soiled suit at some time. He pulled his hand over his strong chin as she watched him gather his thoughts.

'The board of directors for the new job were adamant. They wanted me but no wife, no job. Tayla seemed like a good idea at the time.'

Georgia felt disappointment lodge in her throat. She was a damn poor judge of character. The man was shallow. 'Not a good reason to tie yourself to one person for the rest of your life.'

'It was only for a year if it didn't work out.' He

looked up at her and smiled sympathetically. 'I gather your foray into married life wasn't a roaring success either.'

She wasn't the one who needed the sympathy. 'I believed in commitment when I took my vows.'

'And how was your marriage?' The gentle tone in which he asked the question made her eyes sting with sudden tears.

She did not want to go there. 'None of your business.'

'That bad, eh?' He pressed his lips together as if holding back further comment, and suddenly she could at least admit how bad it had been to herself.

It was her turn to sigh. 'Worse. How did you know?'

He shrugged his shoulders slightly. 'From something you said when you were in labour about not missing Elsa's father.'

The limo ride came back to her in Technicolor and she shuddered. 'Labour. Could you call that labour? That horrific few minutes when I thought I would lose my baby?'

She shook her head. 'That was like being hit by a truck.' She couldn't begin to imagine the desolation she would be going through now if Elsa hadn't survived. 'I haven't thanked you for being there when I needed someone.'

Max smiled. 'And I haven't thanked you for saving me from Tayla. So now we have that out of the way, let's forget the others. What are you going to do now?'

Georgia tilted her head. 'My situation is fine. I'm free. I have a healthy baby, a home and a nanny arranged for the future when I go back to work.'

He looked a little taken aback at her well-laid plans. What had he expected?

'I can see you are organised.' He stood up. 'And you must be tired. I'll go. Congratulations on your beautiful daughter. My best wishes to both of you. Good bye.' He smiled and left.

She watched him go, watched him walk out after all they had been through, and now she really was alone. Well, what had she expected? He wasn't even her cousin-in-law now so she probably wouldn't ever see him again.

Of course, she couldn't sleep after that.

Elsa woke and gratefully Georgia fed her and stroked her hair and began to feel the peace she'd dreamt of when her child was safely born.

She tried to imagine how she would have felt if Max hadn't been there and she'd been alone when Elsa had been born. If Elsa hadn't been fine. It didn't bear thinking about.

Then the cold ice of fear in the base of her stomach reminded her there were other things to be afraid of. What if Sol came back and tried to take Elsa, as he'd threatened? Could she keep her baby safe? Could Max help her keep her baby safe? It was a dangerous thought.

The next morning Dr Sol Winton stepped out of the lifts on the maternity floor and no one tried to stop him. The quality of his suit and the half-exposed stethoscope poking out of his pocket ensured that nobody questioned he belonged there.

He inclined his head at two nurses and his slow smile brought the colour to both their cheeks. The gilt-ribboned chocolate boxes screamed money and he placed one box on the nurse's desk and kept one in his hand.

'I'm looking for my wife. Georgia Winton?'

'Certainly, Doctor. She's in room four, down the corridor on the left.'

'Thank you. Enjoy the chocolates.'

He set off as if sure of his welcome. A tall, well-dressed, charming man, who drew the eyes of women and exuded authority.

When he entered the room only the baby was there wrapped up in a bunny rug in the Perspex cot. A name card tucked into the end read, 'Elsa, baby of Georgia, five pounds two ounces.'

He reached across and stroked the baby's cheek and her downy skin was silky soft beneath his finger.

CHAPTER THREE

MAX FROWNED and strode quickly down the corridor as he saw the man enter Georgia's room.

He knew most of the consultants across the hospital but not this one. Some latent protective instinct raised the hairs on the back of his neck and all he could think about was that Georgia might need him.

His suspicions firmed at the sight of the man bent over Elsa's cot.

Max loomed in the doorway. His voice came out low and hard. 'Can I help you?'

Sol straightened slowly and he lifted his chin. 'No. I don't think so. Thank you.'

The man smiled but something about his phoney amusement increased Max's own wariness and disquiet.

Max moved to one side of the doorway to allow a free exit from the room—though only if the man left Elsa in her cot.

'Are you a friend of Georgia's?' Max enquired

politely, yet the hint of steel suggested it wasn't a frivolous question and he required an answer.

'I'm more than that.' Sol smiled gently. 'Are you her doctor?'

'You could say that.' Max looked up as Georgia opened the bathroom door and his instincts firmed as her eyes widened and then closed for a second as if her worst nightmare had come true.

Her hand hovered over her mouth. 'Sol?' She shook her head but no further words came.

'My dear wife.' Sol smiled.

Georgia shook her head again and the words burst out in a vehement whisper. 'I'm not your wife.'

Sol smiled again, and from the outside he looked quite pleasant yet something made Max take a step closer to Georgia in support.

Sol ignored him. 'You'll always be my wife. But I do see this is not a good time so I'll leave you. Our daughter is beautiful.' He placed the chocolates squarely on the bedside table.

'Good day.' He turned nonchalantly and sauntered away.

Georgia belted the robe as she rushed to Elsa to check she was fine. 'Thank God you were here.'

Fighting back tears, she looked at Max. 'Did he try to take her?' She lifted and hugged Elsa to her as she sank onto the bed as if unable to support the weight on her legs. Her hands shook violently.

Max didn't know what to do to comfort her.

'No. He didn't pick Elsa up. He just looked at

her.' What the hell was all that about? Max thought, and he glanced at the door through which Sol had disappeared. He'd love to ask the sleaze but he'd gone and Georgia needed him.

Max sat down beside Georgia on the bed and slid his arm around her shoulders. She quivered under his arm like a new lamb.

'I'll put safeguards in place. Your ex-husband won't be able to get to you if that's what you want.'

She shook her head and shuddered as she wrapped her arms around her baby. 'I don't want to stay here.'

Max squeezed her shoulders. 'Where do you want to go?' Her distress affected him in a way he hadn't expected and he'd like to have shaken the truth out of the other man.

Georgia's free hand was at her throat. She could barely speak because of the panic she was trying to control. 'I was afraid this would happen. There is something I need to explain. Something I haven't told anybody.'

She hesitated with reluctance to dwell on the whole distressing nightmare but it had to be spoken of. Her reluctance had almost cost the ultimate price. Elsa.

Sol would take her baby if he possibly could. He'd threatened her in those silky tones of his and the thought terrified her, made her sick to her stomach, and now it grew to epic proportions, like a phobia about spiders—except her phobia was all about Sol.

Even what he had done to her before was nothing to this fear that he might take her baby, and even though a tiny spark deep in her brain whispered she was being irrational, she had no control over the dread that was rising in her throat.

Georgia drew a deep breath and her voice sounded weak and strained even to her own ears.

No wonder Sol could smile.

And no doubt Max would hear the paranoia too but there was nothing she could do about that except try and master it at a later time when she had time to regroup. At this moment she just needed Max to understand.

She hadn't progressed to why that seemed so important at this moment.

'Before I met Sol I was happy in my work, a senior midwife in my unit and studying for my master's in midwifery.'

Max nodded. 'Harry said you were well respected and then you became sick—is that right?'

'In the end I began to think I was sick. I need to start the story before then.'

She closed her eyes for a second to gather her thoughts. 'I met my husband, the new senior consultant at our hospital, Sol Winton, and he swept me off my feet. He promised nothing would change, and marriage would only enhance my full life, and that he couldn't live without me.'

She laughed without amusement. 'I was flattered. I'd passed thirty waiting for Mr Right. I'm no raving beauty and he was distinguished, handsome, and I'd begun to think I'd missed out on love and marriage and children. He caught me at a vulnerable time and I thought I loved him.

'In truth I was married for two years to a man who wanted to own me, body and soul, and rule my life down to the smallest degree.

'In the beginning I believed his excessive protectiveness was because he treasured me but I soon realised it was because he felt I was his prized possession and he was training me to jump.'

Georgia drew a shuddering breath and her shoulders shook until Max edged back closer and leant against her. 'You OK?'

The tremor stopped and she nodded. 'I don't like to go over it but I have to so that you'll understand.'

Max shook his head. 'Not if you don't want to.'

'I have to,' she said with resolve.

'OK.' Max pressed harder against her as if he knew she needed that support.

She felt strangely safer with Max's hip and shoulders touching hers, which was ridiculous but it helped her to go on. 'I tried to make Sol see that marriage wasn't a power game and I needed to be my own person, but my charming ex-husband, the highly esteemed obstetrician, informed everyone I was a paranoid depressive. That's not an easy thing to dispute if you have reason to be unhappy.'

'That would explain what Harry said about your marriage getting you down.'

'Harry mentioned it, did he?'

She saw the look on Max's face and sighed. 'This

is what I meant about disputing people's opinions. Sol made it seem I protested too much.'

Max frowned. 'It's OK. I believe you. Go on.'

'I was a professional woman with a career and friends before Sol. But he became more and more demanding. He isolated me from my friends and began to dictate my daily routine. He would change it at a whim.' She clutched Elsa to her as she remembered.

'He cancelled my appointments with my uni, pulled my shifts so that when I turned up, cases had been replaced by another midwife, and that was when I realised people had begun to talk. He'd arranged a visit to a psychiatrist and circulated that I suffered from an anxiety-driven mental illness. The saddest thing was that I almost began to believe him, but I kept telling myself it was his problem, not mine, and refused to take medication. Finally I left him.'

'Leaving was a good thing.' Max nodded.

'I left him for a year but I had to stay at the hospital because they were paying for my master's. The day the divorce papers hit Sol's desk he upped his campaign to win me back but I knew I would never go back to him. That was when he finally realised it wasn't just another extended game.'

She laughed without humour. 'Sol wanted me back, and had everyone at work on his side, and then he threatened my best friend's credibility over a drug order that he'd tampered with. He'd moved on to blackmail.'

'So prove it.'

'It was her word and mine against Sol's, and he said he'd drop his case if I went back to him.'

'You went back?' Max leaned forward incredulously.

'I thought I had it all worked out. I prepared safeguards against any problems. I was going to stay with him until she was safe. Stay only until she couldn't be charged.'

She looked away so he couldn't read her face.

She didn't mention the horror of what Sol had forced her to endure and that she doubted she'd ever want to make love with a man again.

She didn't mention the fact that she woke up at night in a lather of sweat and a pounding heart. Or that now she had an even bigger fear. 'Well, in the end, she wasn't charged. I left again. Later I found out I was pregnant.'

Max raised his eyebrows. 'Why didn't you discredit him?'

'Sol is a powerful man. People believe him.' Georgia could feel palpitations in her chest and unconsciously she rested her hand there. He'd said he would take her baby at birth. He'd said he would if she didn't come back.

All the old fears and uncertainties and even unreasonable guilt that she'd heaped on herself began to surface and she fought to keep them away. She needed to conquer this. Elsa needed her to conquer this. 'It seemed easier just to leave and never go back.'

Max muttered an oath under his breath.

She went on because the sooner she did so, the sooner she could stop thinking about those horrible few weeks.

'Sol had been here to tell Harry I was depressed and paranoid. He covered himself in case I told them what he was really like. He is very plausible and dangerous.

'When Harry suggested I move in with them, I decided it would be good for my baby to know family because she would never know her father if I could help it.' She kissed the top of her daughter's head.

She could see Max was trying to understand and at least he was trying. It was more than a lot of other people did.

Max squeezed her shoulder. 'We'll all help you feel safe again.'

She looked at him and he read the disbelief in her face. 'A month ago I received a repeated threat on my mobile phone against my unborn child. He would find a way to take her if I didn't come back to him,' she whispered.

That wiped the smile off Max's face and he felt his hand tighten protectively over her shoulder. 'Mongrel.'

She sighed under his arm. 'The police said nothing could be proved because Sol had used a public phone to make the call. All I could do was change my number.'

Max shook his head. 'He's put you through hell. I wish I'd known when I had him here.'

She shuddered. 'He's seen her now. I'm losing control of my life again. I left Sol because I needed to get control back.' She looked at him with determination in her eyes. 'And I will. I am. Just.

'I decided to move here and start again because I need family for my baby and I can make a good life for myself and my daughter. But now I'm scared again.'

He could help her. He felt the shift. She needed help and his gut tightened. He barely knew the woman but suddenly it all felt ordained. No doubt there would be flak along the way and the ex-husband sounded like a loony, but suddenly all that was unimportant if he could protect her. There was something about Georgia that he truly admired and was irresistibly drawn to.

Now their closeness during Elsa's dramatic birth and today's near abduction made him realise that she probably needed him more than he needed her.

Win-win situation.

It was a strangely satisfying feeling for Max that had nothing to do with suddenly being eligible for the job again if she agreed. That he could protect Georgia was paramount. 'We could help each other.'

Georgia looked up at him. 'How?'

'Your divorce was finalized, wasn't it?' He tilted his head hopefully.

'Yes. I made sure that happened.' She frowned.

'Why?' The guy bounced all over the place and she couldn't keep up. 'I'm beginning to think Tayla had a lucky escape.'

He shrugged. 'Tayla was getting exactly what she wanted. An indulgent life with me to parade every now and then at her charity functions, and I had a wife I needed for my job. Neither of us planned on having children.'

No children, no living together, all for the sake of a job. What was wrong with these people? 'Wrong era,' she said, with barely concealed distaste. 'Employers can't make you marry any more.'

Max shrugged. 'The directors wanted a married man because they've had so many problems with people leaving the role. The last one ran off and eloped when he was most needed. The powers that choose knew of my impending marriage and that gave me the edge.'

He shrugged. 'Unfortunately, the idea of living with Tayla just won't gel any more for me either.' He said the words as if he he'd decided to change his brand of deodorant.

'And you're telling me this because…?' She couldn't keep the disappointment out of her voice. She'd liked him and he wasn't worthy of that. Despite everything, she still believed true love was out there for most people, and Max cheapened it when he talked like that.

He lifted his head and captured her gaze with his own as if he sensed her disapproval and it mattered to him. His golden eyes warmed. 'I'd been having second thoughts about marrying Tayla earlier. Even before your water broke.'

Georgia winced at the memory of that time in the church. That certainly wouldn't go down as a high-light of her life!

He grinned. 'Don't be squeamish. You're a midwife. As an obstetrician I think labour is great, as long as your baby is due.'

She watched him pull himself back to the topic, and she had to smile as he went on.

'You've made me realise how close I'd been to disaster with Tayla. I can see now I want more in a wife than convenient paperwork.'

How had they started this conversation? Now she was confused at a time when she most needed clarity. 'You want to tell me what you want in a wife?' Suddenly she felt like crying. She knew what she didn't need in a husband.

He went on and she tried to blink away her tears before he could see them.

Max was getting to the point. He just hoped she saw it the way he did. 'Ah. Yes. The big question. Now I want a partner. Someone who understands what I do and even has a passion for it. I can't fight Tayla every time someone has a baby out of hours or obstetrics have an emergency.'

He noticed the way her hand tightened over her baby and he couldn't begin to imagine how she must feel to have been so close to losing her daughter a second time.

Maybe he had stumbled on someone he could come home to or meet at work and bounce problems off. Someone who had a social conscience and a warm heart. Someone like Georgia.

He couldn't help the glimmer of hope that maybe the last twenty-four hours had all worked out the way they had for a reason—or with divine intervention, as requested.

No doubt he was mad, but the idea he'd just had wouldn't leave. He could even salvage the job from something Georgia had said if he played up the business aspect, but suddenly that wasn't as important as protecting Georgia from the creep. He paused and looked at her again. 'You could marry me.'

She held up her hand. 'You don't know me.'

He sat forward. 'I know enough. I'm sure you are a sensible woman and wouldn't normally entertain the idea. That's why I'm pursuing you now when your guard is down.'

She huffed humourlessly. 'My guard isn't down that much. I've just seen my ex-husband and my protective instinct hormones are surging. I don't need to waste another couple of years of my life finding out if the next guy I marry is a jerk, or worse.'

She had a point, but Max didn't believe he was a jerk. 'What about a temporary marriage with, say, a year's contract? You save me and I'll protect you.' He frowned with concentration as he marshalled his best arguments.

'I'm serious, Georgia. I need to be married and after today I only have one week left. I've a friend I can get a dispensation form to get a licence in forty-eight hours, and you would be out of your ex's reach until you are stronger.'

He sat back a little in case he was crowding her. 'It doesn't look like I will fall madly in love at my age and I like you. I like you a lot. I need a temporary wife and Harry said you were looking for a job after the baby. You could work with me when you're ready.'

'It all sounds so coldly clinical.'

'We could warm it up.' He saw her face close and he backed off quickly. 'I'm sorry. Joking. We won't go there.' He paused and risked a lighter comment. 'Especially as you've just given birth.'

She had to smile and he knew it. But he was intrigued.

'Would it help if I told you I think we would deal very well together? Much better than expected?'

'Much better than whom?' She shook her head. 'You and Tayla? Two selfish, immature, rich people who think marriage is a sham or an excuse to wear feathers?'

He held up his hands. 'The feathers were not my idea. In fact, a condition of marrying me is that you are not allowed to wear feathers.'

'I'm not marrying you, Max.' She turned her shoulder on him. 'I'm not even sure I like you after this conversation. And I can't believe that Harry was a part of this whole sell-my-daughter-to-a-loveless-marriage thing.'

'Harry wanted to have Tayla safely married before he was much older.'

He saw the moment she understood, and the sudden sadness in her eyes as she sat back against him, all else forgotten. 'Why the urgency?'

'That's for Harry to tell, not me.' It was Harry's secret, not his.

'Poor Uncle Harry.'

He squeezed her shoulder. 'Leave it. He is dealing with this in his own way.'

She stared and shook her head. 'So that's why Harry agreed?'

'One of the reasons.' He smiled sympathetically and then went off at a tangent again. 'I do have one burning question that's puzzled me.'

She raised her eyebrows and his arm slid away from her shoulder so he could look at her fully.

'Did you want a place in the wedding party or did Harry lean on you?'

She grimaced. 'Who wants to be a pregnant matron of honour? Harry was so pleased that Tayla was settling down, and he wanted to see that, as cousins, his daughter and I were friends. Knowing he's unwell explains why he was so insistent. I wanted to please Harry and the idea that I did have a family was comforting.'

Max admired her warmth for Harry. 'Harry thought I would make a good husband.'

'I understand that.' She looked worriedly at him.

'I've already made one mistake in marriage, though, and I'm frightened I'd make a bigger one with you.'

Max could feel the swing his way and he vowed she wouldn't regret it. 'That's the beauty of it, Georgia. This is a business arrangement.'

Her voice was quiet but determined. She spoke slowly. 'I'm thinking. I can't believe I'm doing it but I am considering your proposal on the basis of a one-year contract.'

She shivered under his arm. 'My biggest problem is that I'm still frightened. Especially now Elsa has been born. Sol has seen her, and will want her. And me. I'm too vulnerable.'

She looked up at him to read his face and make sure he understood what she was offering. To make clear all she wasn't offering and the risks.

She spelt it out. 'In a business relationship I could build up my strength in a safe environment and you need a wife in name only. To be honest, that's all I've got to offer anyway. And I need to ease back to work and get on with my life.'

He squeezed her shoulders and she felt so frail under his hand. He would guard them both. 'Fine. Come home with me and I swear I will keep you both safe.'

He smiled crookedly because he didn't want to say it but in all honesty it needed to be said. 'I don't wish to take advantage of your shock unfairly. Your uncle would probably also be able to offer you protection from your ex-husband.'

She shook her head. 'That won't work. You say

Harry is unwell and I'm not up to Tayla's recriminations.'

'Not a relaxing thought.' He smiled at her and the tension lightened a little in the room. That was it, then. He had what he wanted. Hopefully so did she. He stood up. 'Let's go, then.'

She tilted her head and looked up at him. 'It's that easy?'

'It will be. You pack and I'll sort out the rest.'

She shifted Elsa onto one arm and pulled the toothbrush from her pocket. 'I'm packed.'

When Georgia walked out of the hospital and into the sunlight it felt as if Tayla's disastrous wedding had been a year ago not just one day.

Max's hand hovered near the small of her back and she carried Elsa tightly against her, as if to defend her from an unknown assailant.

Incredibly, with Max, she did feel safe, even after the shock of knowing Sol had found her.

'Why do I feel so protected with you when I barely know you?' She'd met him such a short time ago and she'd made a disastrous marriage before. Was she making another mistake?

'Because I'm a mature and respected consultant,' he said. 'I've known Harry for years and your uncle trusted me enough to marry his only daughter off to me.'

That part sounded acceptable.

Then she saw Max's big square, ostentatious, boy's toy shiny black Hummer parked outside the door and she shook her head. 'You're just a kid with your ego.'

Max patted the bonnet of the huge all-terrain vehicle. 'Cool, isn't it? At least I get my baby dirty when I go offroad.'

'Where's your chauffeur?'

'He has other jobs. I don't use that car often. It belongs to my mother.'

She sniffed and looked again at the vehicle. 'Does your baby have an infant capsule?'

He smirked. 'Now she does.'

She looked at him. 'When did you get the time to organise that?'

'The capsule belongs to Maternity and I promised I'd have it back tomorrow.'

'You have connections.'

'I'm one big connection, but to answer your question…' He paused and looked her full in the face. 'You trust me with Elsa, don't you?'

'Of course.'

'Then you can trust me with you as well.'

She had no answer for that.

CHAPTER FOUR

MAX and Georgia's wedding was simple, at the registry office, and the only guests were Max's housekeeper and Harry.

It was done two days later, as soon as the licence came through, and Georgia didn't wear feathers.

As she stood beside her new husband and watched him sign the marriage certificate, she realised how little she knew about this man. And yet even in the last forty-eight hours he had shown a kindness and sensitivity that brought tears to her eyes. Hormones again, of course, but nonetheless Max was a darling and even Elsa liked him.

Goodness knew what he had told Harry, but her uncle had nothing good to say about Sol and kept patting her on the shoulder. What could have been horribly awkward as they arranged their hurried wedding and transfer north proved an amusing and relaxed time, thanks to Max.

They moved north to Coffs Harbour straight after the ceremony.

* * *

Living with Max was an experience. Where Sol had been obsessive about cleanliness and order, Max was oblivious and gloriously extravagant.

He thought nothing of dropping towels by the pool, having his St Bernard in the house, and arriving with an enormous bunch of bananas to hang on the veranda.

Thankfully he had an eccentric housekeeper, Mrs White, who adored him and didn't mind.

For the first six weeks of Elsa's life, Max ensured that Georgia had little to do except be there for her baby, eat well-cooked meals provided by the amazing Mrs White, and sleep in between attending to Elsa's needs.

Thank goodness, because Elsa roared and screamed and barely slept with colic for most of that time, and Georgia shuddered when she thought of how it would have been if she'd had to manage a household as well.

The first night Elsa had screamed, Max had just come in from an emergency Caesarean at two a.m. and Georgia had been down in the kitchen to try Elsa with some boiled water in a bottle.

Max had found Georgia nightie-clad and barefoot, her thick hair pushed distractedly behind her ears, and every time Elsa had emitted a tiny broken sob he'd seen it had torn at her mother's heart.

'Give her to me.' He held out his hands and he saw the way she hesitated. It was amazing how much that hurt. 'I do know about babies, you know.'

'Of course you do.' She passed Elsa over and he hated her hesitation to trust him.

Distraught and exhausted, Georgia looked at her wits' end and Max just wanted to hug her.

Georgia ran her fingers through her hair. 'But so do I! I know more about babies than you,' she said, and there was a break in her voice. 'But it's not working!'

Baby Elsa felt tense and coiled with pain in his arms, and he saw why being unable to comfort her daughter would upset Georgia so badly.

She watched him like a hawk as he cupped her baby's head in his hands and rested her body on his forearms. Then he propped her bottom against his stomach so that she was folded with her legs up his chest. He'd seen the midwives carry babies this way at night when they had pain. When Elsa stopped crying, Georgia rolled her eyes.

'Typical,' she said, and he couldn't help the smirk.

'See.'

'Hmmm.' She crossed to the sink and filled a glass with water. 'You can hold her while I have two headache tablets for the damage caused by the last two hours.'

'Have a hot chocolate. I'll join you. Little missy here looks like she wants to sleep.'

Georgia sniffed. 'She inherited it from her mother, who also wants to sleep.' Georgia literally drooped in front of him and his need to comfort her returned. Normally she was so efficient, he actually admired her more for being human.

'Forget the chocolate. Why don't you grab a couple of hours' rest? I imagine you've not long fed her so she'll probably sleep until morning if the pain leaves her alone. I can bring her back to you when she wakes up.'

'You've been up all night and you have to work tomorrow.' He saw the struggle with the concept of leaving her baby with him.

'Tomorrow is Saturday and I'm only on call.' He watched her rub her forehead as she tried to concentrate.

'Saturday. So it is.' She smiled wearily and he felt his gut contract at her vulnerability.

The more he saw of her the more he just wanted to pull her into his arms and protect her from her own stubborn, independent self. And a few other things crossed his mind like freight trains, but he wasn't going there.

The last things she needed from him were pressure and lust, and he'd promised himself he would leave her to heal the deep wounds left by her former husband for at least the year.

He didn't know if he'd last that long but he was going to damn well try, if it killed him.

By the time Elsa was smiling and cooing at two months Georgia felt as if she'd lived in Max's wonderful house for ever—but it wasn't the real world.

She saw very little of Max, though, except when

he appeared in the early hours to give her a break if Elsa was having a bad night. Even at those times she was usually so exhausted she just handed Elsa over and crashed into her bed so she felt that she knew less about him than she had when they'd first met.

He was unfailingly polite, wonderful with Elsa considering he had no real experience of babies apart from helping them into the world, and provided the safest haven a woman in need could wish for.

The disconcerting thing about Max for Georgia was the speed with which he seemed to disappear. She knew he was busy at work but she wondered if that, in fact, accounted for his hurry to get away. She really would have liked to have seen more of him.

In the tenth week Georgia had had enough of being the lady of leisure and Max's avoidance techniques had begun to irk her.

On the day it all changed, she wandered into the kitchen in search of Mrs White while Max was away at work. She found another potato peeler to help with the vegetables and prepared her assault. 'What time will Max be home tonight, Mrs White?'

Mrs White, who would not be diverted from calling Georgia Mrs Beresford, or allow Georgia to call her Miriam, was a little round woman who, despite her name, dyed her short hair jet-black and wore heavy eyeliner.

She looked up from her own peeler and smiled at Georgia like a jolly panda. 'It's Monday so they have a regional discussion at five. Probably seven-thirty or maybe eight tonight.'

'He works long hours, doesn't he?'

'Always has, but he used to try to get away off-roading on weekends.' She pointed her peeler at Georgia. 'Though he hasn't had the Hummer out in the bush since we moved up here.'

Georgia knew Mrs White didn't understand their relationship. Obviously the housekeeper was aware they slept in separate rooms and usually ate meals at different times because of Elsa's regime. They weren't even housemates as such because their paths rarely crossed.

But Mrs White had seen they were happy enough and that was good as far as she was concerned, especially compared to the close shave of Tayla—an opinion she'd shared with Georgia very early on.

For Georgia, the initial space Max had given her had been perfect, but now the distance he'd created frustrated the life out of her.

It was like living in the snow with a big, roaring fire on the other side of the window she wasn't even allowed to warm her hands at. His company was becoming more desirable all the time.

If she didn't want to fall into the trap of building her life around the flashes of company Max gave her then it was time to begin to think of a few hours of work or she would never regain her independence.

'I'd like to share my evening meal with Max from now on, if that's OK. Elsa is starting to go to sleep by seven. Perhaps I could set the table in the dining room tonight.'

Mrs White didn't quite clap her hands but she did beam approvingly. 'Of course. I'm sure he'd enjoy the company.' She smiled across at her. 'And if Elsa wakes up, I could mind her so you won't be interrupted during your dinner.'

Georgia opened her mouth to demur when she realised that if she was interrupted then Max would be also, and she could see Mrs White was keen on the idea.

'Thank you. That would be lovely.'

When Max arrived home that evening, the table was set for two. Georgia had taken the trouble to dress for dinner and put make-up on for the first time in over two months.

She felt like a schoolgirl on her first date, which was ridiculous when she considered how up close and personal she and Max had been at Elsa's birth.

When he first came in, Georgia felt a fluttery tingle of excitement reverberate through her, just by looking at the way he smiled at seeing her. He looked tall and handsome and his white shirt sat snugly across his shoulders and chest in a disconcertingly sexy way.

His smile held a hint of surprise when he saw the table, but the expression was there so fleetingly she couldn't be sure, and she hoped it was a pleasant change for him and not one of those save-me-from-the-nuisance moments.

'I thought I might join you for dinner in the evenings if work permits, Max. Is that all right with you?' Georgia heard the uncertainty in her voice and she winced. It wasn't like she was asking to sleep with the guy.

'I'd like that. We don't seem to have seen much of each other.' His eyes crinkled and his golden eyes warmed as his gaze drifted over her. 'You look beautiful.'

'Thank you.' She didn't know what else to say but some of the nervousness in her stomach subsided.

The conversation faltered and they both looked out the window.

Max broke into the silence. 'Elsa seems to be settling with her colic.'

Georgia winced. She'd felt so guilty about that. 'It must have been very distracting for you, and I am sorry.'

Max smiled that particularly sweet smile that always brought a lump to Georgia's throat. 'It has been very distracting to have a gorgeous ghost wandering around my house in the early hours of the morning. I'd grown used to her, though, and actually quite miss bumping into her in the wee small hours.'

Georgia began to relax. 'I'd think myself more of a gargoyle than gorgeous, but I did feel like a ghost in those early days. You were pretty wonderful with Elsa.'

'Nonsense,' Max said. 'She liked me.'

Georgia pretended to glare at him. 'Excuse me.

She liked me, too, but she would not stop crying sometimes.'

He tilted his head. 'Ah, no. There is a difference. She adores you and knows you feel her pain.' He smiled again. 'I'm just the shallow bloke she can go to sleep with when she's too tired to cry. But I think she's grown out of me now.'

Georgia couldn't imagine anyone growing out of Max. He was such a sweetie.

She'd been going to edge slowly towards discussing her plans but it seemed too complicated. Suddenly she just needed to get it all out into the open.

'I want to go back to work, Max. One or two days a week. Or even half-days, if I could. That way, I can come home to Elsa for feeds.'

Max nodded but he felt like shaking his head. Violently. He looked at her and thought Georgia had grown even more stunning over the last two months. He was having a hard time keeping her out of his thoughts at work, and the idea of her on the hospital ward would complicate things enormously.

'Are you sure it's not too soon?' he said quietly, and he passed her the lemon squash with ice she always seemed to ask for on the rare occasions they shared a drink in the evenings.

It was hot up here, he'd noticed that, and now they wanted him to do three months past Murwillumbah near the Queensland border. They'd actually asked if his wife would be interested in a little part-time work. That would be an even smaller hospital to run into her in.

'I'm bored, Max. I'm sick of living off you. I want to regain my independence. Elsa doesn't need me twenty-four hours a day now. Mrs White would love to have her to herself for a couple of hours in the daytime.'

Georgia paused and then said, 'Thanks to you, I feel safe, Max. And ready to do more.'

Max nodded. 'You're the one who has to decide. If you think you're ready then I'm sure you are. I'll ask around tomorrow.'

He poured himself a glass of beer. 'I've had an offer for three months up past Murwillumbah where the one obstetric GP has retired. The idea would be to take over his practice for a few weeks but really they'd want me to see if it is still viable as a maternity unit. It's pretty much a midwifery-run unit and almost in Queensland. If I go, would you want to come or stay here with Mrs White?'

'Is she staying here?' Georgia looked startled and he wondered why.

'She will do if you do!' Georgia had more need of Mrs White with Elsa than he did.

'I'm a big girl. You have to stop looking after me, Max.'

'You're my wife,' he said. In truth, he did very little and would love to do more, but she valued her independence and the other thing, the one he tried not to think about but kept him awake at night, needed time.

'In name only,' she said.

Bingo. That was the crux, Max thought, and the devil answered. 'We could change that.'

She laughed. 'I'm two years older than you. That would be taking advantage of you.'

'Yes, please, madam.' They both smiled but Max didn't feel amused. She really didn't get it. Probably never would, But now wasn't the time to push it, even though it would be so easy to lean over and kiss those laughing lips of hers.

Down, boy, he warned himself. 'Seriously, Georgia. You may be older by year or two, but not in the ways of the world.' That was what he said. What he thought was, Can't you see I want all of you and I'm trying to stay away?

'Anyway,' he said, 'my aunt left me an old house overlooking Byron Bay, which she bought when she went through her arty phase. I thought I'd stay there and commute to Meeandah.

'The house is run down but if you're bored you might be interested in organising to have some work done on it. A gardener comes once a fortnight and the house itself gets springcleaned every couple of months so it will be perfectly habitable.'

She frowned. 'I appreciate your confidence in my interior decorating skills but I don't need amusement, Max, I need to rebuild my life so I can regain my independence.'

He knew she expected them to part after the twelve months, she'd told him so several times, and he'd deliberately put no pressure at all on her about his own growing feelings.

Perhaps if he spent more time with her she'd decide he was the catch of the season. What a joke. She'd confirm what he had always known that he didn't have much to offer her.

He couldn't have children and she was a great mother and should have lots of children.

He wasn't used to such negative thoughts and lack of self-confidence and if this was what falling in love did, he wasn't impressed.

He'd just have to put up with the agony in the slim chance that she'd realise they would deal very well together in the long term.

'Why don't we go for a drive on Sunday in the Hummer?' he said to change the subject. 'My poor baby hasn't had a rough-up for a few months now and Mrs White has offered to mind Elsa for a few hours.'

She glanced at him quickly and then away. 'Fine,' she replied, though she sounded surprised.

It wasn't roaring enthusiasm. She'd said fine, so he'd work on it from there.

He hadn't been out for a while and it would be interesting to see whether Georgia was a bush-bashing girl or not. Tayla certainly hadn't been.

'What are you smiling at?'

He looked up at her. 'I was thinking about the one time I took Tayla out in the Hummer and she had hysterics as soon as I turned off the main highway. She liked sitting up above all the other cars with people watching on the main road.'

'That would be the part I'd hate most.'

'Wait until you see what she can do.'

'Should I regret agreeing?'

He raised his eyebrows suggestively. 'We'll see.'

Max loved having Georgia beside him in the Hummer. They took a short drive into the hills that first day and the rough fire trail he'd chosen carried them deeper into the forest in a slow incline towards the trig point at the top of the hill.

The overhanging branches slapped the side of the vehicle and Georgia laughed with delight as they bumped and crashed their way through the bush.

'I'm impressed, Max,' she said, laughing at him as another huge frond of prickly lantana swished down the side of the paintwork. 'You really do take your baby offroad and rough her up. You're not just a show pony.'

'I'll give you show pony,' he threatened, and turned down another trail that seemed even more overgrown than the last but then cleared and opened out to a rocky outcrop overlooking the valley floor.

When Max turned off the engine, bellbirds pinged their songs in the scrub and the rustle of lizards could be heard, scuttling away from the now invaded open ground.

'You were lucky this wasn't a dead end.' Georgia gazed around in delight.

'Technically it is. But call me lucky,' he said,

and then pulled the map from the door. 'Actually, I cheated.'

'Pretty cool navigating anyway,' she said and, undid her seat belt. 'Can I get out?'

'Absolutely. Do you want a hand to climb down?'

'No.' She pretended to frown at him. 'Thank you. I'm a big girl.' Max watched her jump from the cab and he climbed out himself with a grin.

This was another side he hadn't seen of Georgia. She glowed with vitality and enthusiasm as she crunched her way across short grass and small boulders to lean, a little recklessly, he thought, over the edge.

On the other side of the canyon a waterfall fell hundreds of metres to the valley floor and the twisting sliver of a silver river at the bottom.

Max came up next to her, ostensibly to share the view but really to grab her if she overbalanced, and when she looked across at him her eyes sparkled as she took in the magnificent views.

Max smiled back indulgently at her. He was falling deeper and deeper in love with this woman every minute and he was beginning to think she wasn't as immune to him as he'd thought.

'There's nobody within miles and miles of us, is there, Max?'

'Nope,' he said. 'All this within an hour from home.'

'Elsa would love it.'

'We'll bring her next time.' Max looked forward

to more days like this. His family—if only it were really so. 'No doubt she has her mother's adventurous heart.'

'I love it. I love the Hummer. I love the bush.' She looked around eagerly. 'Thank you for bringing me today, Max. I needed a total change and this is wonderful.' She spread her arms and in doing so shifted a collection of rocks from under her foot that threw her off balance for a moment.

Max pulled her back against him before she could really grasp that she had been in danger and then she didn't know whether the thumping in her heart was from the near fall or…from being in Max's arms against his delicious chest.

Thankfully he made light of it as he righted her and shifted her to a safer position. 'Falling for me, are you, Georgia?' he said.

She could do that—despite all the reasons she shouldn't. Why wouldn't she? She felt so connected to him at this moment. Two consenting adults in the wild with no one to see what they did. Deep inside a little voice cried plaintively. Why hadn't he kissed her?

'You're a safer place to fall than over the edge,' she said lightly, hoping he'd put the breathlessness in her voice down to her near miss when, in fact, it had come from her own unexpected erotic thoughts that wouldn't go away.

'Glad you think of me as safe,' Max said dryly, but Georgia was busy with her own thoughts.

Fairly explicit, unexpected thoughts. Nymphs and satires. Naked in the bush. Max's chest.

Ants and rocks in your back... Her sensible side brought her back to earth, and Georgia turned away to hide her flaming cheeks.

What on earth had those fantasies come from? She pushed the graphic pictures from the front of her mind and searched for diversion in other appetites. 'Let's picnic here.'

'Fine.' Max's answer was short and she glanced at him. He was watching her and she could feel the blush steal up her cheeks just from looking at him so she turned away again to find Mrs White's picnic basket.

'I'll get it.' Max had the other door open. 'You find a spot to put the rug. I don't want ants in my pants.'

She laughed. They both had ants on the brain. Max came across with the basket and suddenly she was ravenous.

After the first Sunday trip when Max discovered Georgia enjoyed an adventure as much as he did, a whole new facet of their relationship opened up.

They began to take Elsa with them for excursions in the Hummer as well. They travelled along old fire trails and explored deserted gullies lined with lush tropical greenery and soaring gumtrees.

Elsa had her feet dangled in tiny tumbling streams and Max taught Georgia how to winch logs that had fallen during storms and the best way to chainsaw the heavier timber that often blocked the trails.

Max promised more trips when they moved north and the tenure at Murwillumbah grew closer.

The Byron Bay house overlooked the ocean across rolling green hills, and Georgia felt at peace there immediately.

The house was a white-painted Queenslander design with decorated gables and wrought-iron rails that marched out of sight. Two-storied, it had more wrought-iron fans that embraced the veranda posts, like the wedding cake they hadn't had.

Two of the front wide bay windows faced the not-too-distant ocean and to sit and dream over the shifting sea always made Georgia sigh with pleasure. There was even a telescope trained on the horizon to idle away time.

Her temporary posting had come through for part-time work at Meeandah Hospital and last night she'd decided that no matter how beautiful it was on the swing seat here with Elsa on her lap, she'd spent almost ten years of her life gaining experience and qualifications for a job she loved—and it was a good thing she would finally use those skills.

It was time to go back to work and the day had arrived. She just needed to get her act together.

Georgia weighed the keys to Mrs White's car in her hand and suddenly wished she didn't have to go. She'd feel differently once she was there but it was hard to leave Elsa for the first time for eight full hours.

The last four months had been necessary to rebuild her shattered confidence and learn the art of motherhood. She knew she couldn't stay in this bubble. The real world was out there and she needed to prepare herself for when this hiatus was gone.

When the year was up she and Max would part ways and that thought brought greyness into the bright sunshine of the morning. It had become harder to imagine no Max in her life, which in itself was dangerous.

Apart from when he worked, since that night she'd began sharing meals with Max, they'd rarely been apart.

They been to the beach at Byron Bay and the lighthouse and shopped at the cosmopolitan markets that sold everything from home-grown coffee-beans to the finest silk and jewellery. They'd picked herbs from Max's aunt's herb garden and lain on the lawn in the evening to see the first stars.

Yet always at the back of her mind Georgia had known it had to end.

She had to end it, because even though they'd managed to keep out of Sol's orbit for the last few months, she knew there was more trouble to come.

She would never forgive herself if anything happened to Max. Max had no idea how obsessed her ex-husband was, and when Sol actually found out she'd married Max she had no idea what he would do.

Now that she wasn't the gibbering mess she'd been after Elsa's birth, it had come home to her how unfair it was to drag Max into her troubles, and she could feel the stormclouds gathering on the horizon.

With their locum move to Meeandah, she had the opportunity to sink her teeth into obstetrics again even if it was only for a couple of weeks, and that meant she would be one step closer to independence.

Max had been wonderfully supportive about her starting work and her daughter would be settled with Mrs White in the new house for the hours she'd be away.

Her first shift since she'd become a mother herself had arrived.

She slipped back into Elsa's room one last time to check her baby was still asleep. Elsa's tiny fist was jammed against her mouth and every few seconds she'd suck gently in her sleep. Georgia knew she had to go.

When Georgia walked into Meeandah Maternity Ward she could hear the cry of a hungry baby and it brought a tiny smile to her face. She really did love being around birthing women and their babies.

Her biggest problems in her work had not been the clients or the midwives, it had been old-school, entrenched-idea doctors. Those medical officers

who interfered with the natural process of birth
because of their own impatience or lack of confidence in the birthing woman. Those who called a
woman's labour a 'failure to progress' when often
it had been a doctor's 'failure to wait'!

The nurse manager of the hospital had seemed
impressed with Georgia's qualifications and experience and Georgia had felt the warmth and quality
of the care and facilities from the moment she'd
stepped through the doors. This hospital met the
needs of their clients first and she couldn't wait to
be a part of it.

For her first morning Georgia's handover report
was given by another senior midwife who greeted
her with delight. 'You came. I thought it was too
good to be true.'

Georgia smiled and held out her hand, but the
woman hugged her instead.

'I'm Karissa, and I've been trying to secure at
least a week's break for a couple of months now, but
staffing hadn't made that possible. With you here I
can leave without feeling like I've abandoned the
ship.'

Georgia looked around her and it felt so darned
good to be back in a maternity unit. 'I'm just as keen
to get back to work. My baby is four months old and
I've left milk with our housekeeper. I hope she'll be
fine.'

'I fed my son, Hamish, like that for a year when
I went back to work. He managed well. We're glad
to have some help here.'

'So you have someone in labour?' Georgia felt the exhilaration build.

'Yep. I'll take you in and introduce you. The rest of the ward can wait. We've only two other maternities in. The general ward staff will watch them while we have someone in labour. Most of the alternate lifestyle women here go home four hours after birth and the two mums we have staying are Caesareans births back from the base hospital.'

Georgia followed her new friend down the ward to the end of the corridor and was given a chart from the bench outside the birthing-room door.

'So let's do it.' Karissa tapped the notes. 'Mel and Tim are having their second baby. The first labour was quick and with no problems two years ago.

'Mel is due tomorrow. She began regular painful contractions at five this morning and the pains are now gradually increasing in intensity.' Karissa pointed out the graph she'd charted.

'Her waters broke at six.'

That's how it's supposed to be, Georgia thought as Elsa's wild birth came to mind. And then she thought of Max, but he was too distracting a thought when she was at work. 'It sounds great.'

'They're excited. She seems to be well established in this labour and, except for some baseline observations, I've left them pretty much to themselves to get settled in.'

Karissa knocked and pushed open the door. Mel was leaning over a bench and Tim was massaging her lower back with a rolling dolphin massager.

They both looked up briefly and smiled but withdrew their attention until after the contraction finished.

Georgia liked that. The mother needed to stay focussed. She glanced around the homey room. Floral home-made curtains, comfortable recliner rocker, beanbag and gym mat in the corner. It all made for a relaxing atmosphere.

Karissa quietly reminded her where all the emergency medical equipment was hidden behind flip-down cupboards and Georgia had been orientated to the rest of the ward a few days previously by the nurse manager.

While they waited for Mel's contraction to end, haunting instrumental music strummed from somewhere unseen, and it added to the mood in the room which was intense but focussed.

Mel sighed long and loudly and Georgia saw her shoulders drop with the release of air and the prompt of Tim's soothing stroke on her shoulder.

She stepped forward to introduce herself quietly before the next contraction hit. 'Hi. I'm Georgia. I'm taking over from Karissa. You're both very good at this, aren't you?' She smiled.

'So far it's better than little Andy's labour,' Mel said.

'Great.' Georgia picked up the foetal heart monitor. 'That's a great tummy you have there, Mel. Will it disturb your rhythm if I listen to your baby's heart rate through the next contraction, please?'

'Go ahead. We love to hear the baby.' Mel patted

her stomach. 'It is a pretty cool watermelon but I'll be glad to swap a heavy bulge for a baby.'

Georgia leaned in next to Mel and placed the finger-shaped ultrasound doppler a few inches below Mel's belly button and the clip-clop sound of Mel and Tim's baby filled the room. Everyone smiled until the next contraction started and Mel and Tim went back to work.

The baby's heart rate continued strongly and even picked up pace for most of the contraction before evening out again. Mel sighed as the contraction finished and the baby's heart rate clopped along merrily. Satisfied, Georgia stepped back and wiped the conducting jelly off Mel's abdomen.

'That's great. Baby is cruising in there. I'll leave you for a few minutes to complete the handover with Karissa and then I'll be back to do a few observations on you. Then we'll talk about your preferences for the birth.'

Georgia followed Karissa out the door and closed it behind them. They could hear the murmur of the next contraction starting.

'They're wonderful.'

'Yeah. Lucky you for a nice shift and you get to catch a baby. Come on, I'll show you the rest.' Karissa breezed into an open ward where two women sat up in bed, eating their breakfast.

'This is Leanne and Tanya, our two postnatal ladies. And this is Georgia, who is your midwife on today.'

'Good morning.' Georgia waved. 'I'll see more

of you when we've had our baby, but for the moment do you need anything in case I get tied up in the birthing room?'

'I'm fine.' Leanne waved them away with her piece of toast and Tanya smiled and shook her head.

'I'll see you later, then. You can buzz if you need someone, but otherwise just have a lazy morning and we'll catch up later.'

'Sounds good,' Leanne said around her next bite.

'Leanne likes her food,' Karissa whispered with a grin as they walked back towards the desk. 'I just wish I could put it away like she does and still stay that thin. And if you can't find Tanya, she pops out for a cigarette. She's trying to give up.'

She glanced at the clock and grimaced. 'That's about all. When Mel's ready to birth, push the red call button and one of the girls will come down from the ward to help you.'

'The on-call doctor…' Karissa grinned cheekily '…in this case your husband, can be contacted on the pager number if you need him.'

Georgia nodded and fought down the warmth that spread through her just thinking of Max. It was happening more often when she thought of him. What was wrong with her? 'What about pain relief orders if Mel wants something?'

'There is a doctor's standing order book there which spells out the options, and it is countersigned by the locums when they come the first day. I usually let the doctor know if I give any analgesia or do an internal examination so they know where the woman is in her labour in case we need them. Otherwise they will drop in before and after work.'

'Thanks,' said Georgia. 'That all seems pretty standard to any of the small hospitals I've worked at.'

Karissa picked up her bag. 'I have a feeling Max would like to be here but if you ring him don't let him push you out of the way for the birth. We can't have him begin bad habits and we catch our own babies here. But he'll let you know when he does his morning round.'

Georgia savoured the thought of having Max there for their first professional birth together. It would be lovely to share such a moment with him and until she knew what sort of back-up the general ward nurses wanted to be, the idea seemed sensible.

Karissa went on. 'It works for us. On paper, it's sad our only OB GP has retired, but in fact he rarely came for deliveries and high-risk women were shipped out anyway. If we stick to low-risk labours, I can't see why we couldn't do what we've always done and keep training midwives to be autonomous and the unit open. Fifty miles away from her family to the base hospital is a long way to send a woman to have a normal delivery.'

'I agree. It's crazy that it all depends on some number-cruncher in a distant city.'

'Don't start me on that. That way is madness, girl.' Karissa had obviously been there. 'We're just dots on the big picture.' She shrugged and yawned. 'But I've been up all night and what I vote for at the moment is going home to bed. Good luck and happy birthing.'

She pulled the drug keys from her pocket with a wry smile and handed them over. 'I'm so glad I didn't accidentally go home with the keys and have to come back.' She yawned again. 'Bye.'

CHAPTER FIVE

ALONE and in charge of a labour, Georgia thought wryly. It had been a while.

She had a quick look through the two inpatient records to check there were no medications due and why the women had chosen to have Caesarean births. Both had had babies in the breech position and their doctor had suggested they not attempt vaginal deliveries.

She reminded herself to ask Max what his stance on that question was.

She picked up Mel's chart and quickly scanned her previous labour and antenatal history, before tucking the chart under her arm and heading back to the labouring woman.

'Hi, guys. How are you going in here?'

Tim looked a little more stressed and Mel's smile had slipped. 'It's getting tough now,' Mel said through clenched teeth, and the next contraction cut off her sentence as she began to rock and moan with the force of the pains.

When the contraction had eased, Georgia quickly checked Mel's blood pressure, temperature and pulse, and then listened to the baby's heart rate through the next contraction. All observations were normal and she documented the progress in the nurse's notes.

When she'd finished she crossed to the cupboard where the large blue exercise ball was kept. Georgia rolled it across the floor to show Mel and Tim. 'Would you like to try sitting on the ball in the shower for a change, Mel?'

'I might fall off.' Mel gave it a quick glance and shook her head. 'The ball wasn't here last time.'

Georgia rolled it around in front of herself and sat down on it to show Mel. She tried to move it with her hands while sitting on it and the ball didn't budge. 'It sticks to the floor and won't roll away when you are on it, Mel. Balls are very safe.'

Mel frowned and then nodded that she understood.

Georgia went on. 'Your legs must be tired. Sitting here will straighten your back and encourage the contractions to work straight down with gravity and onto the cervical opening to make the contractions achieve as much as they can, just like the position you are in now.'

Georgia studied Mel's strained face and her instincts told her Mel would get some relief sitting for a while. 'The position you're in now has been great but you may benefit from a change of position, even if for a few minutes. It's getting tough.'

'Too right it's getting tough.' Mel glared at her husband and Georgia restrained her smile. When a woman began to express irritation towards her partner, it often meant good progress in labour.

'You could take the ball into the shower and while you sit you could direct the heat of the water onto the area giving the most pain. You can sway from side to side too—all those things will give good relief from the pain.'

Tim grinned. 'What a salesperson. Do you have shares in the company that sells birth balls?'

'Absolutely. Have a go, Tim, and tell Mel if it feels safe.'

Tim lowered himself gingerly onto the ball and never looked in danger of rolling away. 'I see what you mean about it sticking to the floor. If you don't want the ball, Mel, I might sit here to rub your back. Mine feels better already.'

That was too much for Mel. 'Get off. My turn.'

She sat, sighed into it as her back straightened, and smiled. 'Ok. Let's try the shower with this thing, then.'

Georgia wished that Max had been here to see that. Pain relief wasn't always something you had to prescribe. She went ahead and turned on the water to warm and placed the ball in the corner of the shower room.

Two rails on the wall gave Mel safe purchase as she lowered herself onto the ball and when the handheld shower was directed onto her lower

abdomen where the contractions hurt most, she
sighed blissfully. 'Oh, my. That is good.'

The next pain began and she pushed the nozzle
close to her stomach, streaming the hot water across
her abdomen. Georgia could see she'd gained relief
from the change.

Georgia pulled the shower chair up behind Mel
and gestured to Tim. 'If you sit behind her like this
you won't get too wet and can rub her back firmly
with your massager when she gets pain. Your back
will get a rest, too.'

Tim settled himself and soon they were back into
a rhythm.

Georgia could see they were getting close to the
end of the first stage of labour and she quietly went
back into the main room to ensure what she needed
was ready. She toyed with the idea of phoning Max
but held off until she had everything ready because
sometimes the arrival of the doctor put pressure on
the woman.

The baby resuscitation trolley was in the corner
and she checked the oxygen and suction were both
functioning, even though she didn't expect to need
either.

A green-draped trolley held a kidney dish,
clamps, scissors and some sponges, and she turned
back the bed for Mel and her baby to lie on afterwards.

A tray rested on the bench in case Mel bled too
much after the birth. It contained the IV line and
infusion and drugs they might need. She glanced

around and couldn't think of anything else she should prepare.

She went back into the bathroom. 'So where do you want to have your baby, Mel?'

'Don't I have to have it on the bed?'

'Not if you don't want to.' It amazed Georgia when women did not realise they had choices in birth position. 'You can use the birth stool or stand up or kneel down. It doesn't matter. Whichever you find the most comfortable.'

Mel glanced at Tim. 'How about I use the stool for the pushing and maybe move to the bed if I want to at the last minute? I remember last time and it would be good if I could just lie back with our baby after the birth.'

She looked at Tim again and remembered something. 'And I don't want the needle afterwards because I want Tim to cut the cord when it stops pulsating.'

Georgia nodded. 'That's fine. If your placenta doesn't come on its own after half an hour or you bleed heavily, you might need the needle, though.'

Mel checked with Tim and he nodded. 'That sounds OK,' he said to Mel encouragingly.

'Fine,' Mel said.

Georgia handed her a bottle of water and a straw to sip with. 'I'll have the stool ready when you want to get out of the shower.'

'Do I have to get out?'

Georgia laughed. 'Not if you don't want to.

When you get to the pushing stage, you can swap the ball for the stool in the shower.'

'Won't the doctor mind?'

'No, the doctor won't mind.' Max's voice came from behind the bathroom door and they all looked up. Georgia felt that warm pleasure she was beginning to associate with Max's presence.

His voice came again. 'Hi, Mel. I'm Max Beresford, the doctor on call. Sister can come out when she's ready and fill me in. You keep doing what you're doing.'

Georgia and Mel exchanged smiles and Georgia slipped out of the door.

Max watched her shut it behind her. 'Hello, Sister,' he said. In his mind he said, hello you gorgeous thing. His stomach dropped as she smiled up at him. She looked incredible.

Her eyes were shining with anticipation and yet her movements were calm and unhurried and she exuded an aura of confidence in the natural progression of events.

He fancied her badly. The tension on his side was building every minute that he was with her. Over the last few, amazingly wonderful weeks in Byron they had become closer than ever.

He knew she still needed recovery time, and he needed to give her that to have any chance for her to trust herself fully to a man again—and he wanted that more than anything.

She was way too vulnerable to make any physical demands on, he could tell by her body language if he even brushed against her, and no matter how much he ached to hold her and make her his, she had to be the one to initiate any change in that.

He had to protect himself too because all he could see on her side was appreciation of the safe harbour he provided and he was becoming more fascinated every day.

Even knowing she would be at work today was distracting but worth the opportunity to see her during the day. He hadn't been able to stay away once he'd known that it was Georgia's first morning back at work.

She was looking at him with that tiny frown he wanted to smooth away with his fingers, and he pulled himself back into the present. She expected him to say something, not stand there like a goose. 'So here I am. Were you going to call me at all?'

She looked at him quizzically. 'Yes, Doctor.'

Maybe she wasn't sure if he was serious so he smiled to reassure her.

'Mel sounds fine. I'm here before I go into the rooms for my day patients. I've read your notes and you're obviously happy with her progress and condition. Do you want me to say hello to her or just leave it until later?'

'Would you mind popping your head in to say hi now? I don't think she'll be long anyway, and it's better than meeting when the baby is here.'

Before Max could even open the door they heard Mel's voice. 'Georgia-a-a.'

Georgia stepped back into the bathroom and rested her hand on Mel's shoulder. 'It's OK. What's happening?'

'In the middle of that pain I wanted to push, but the feeling has gone now.'

'That's fine. Each pain will probably give you that feeling for a longer time and then it will come to the stage when you won't be able to do anything but push.'

Mel nodded.

Georgia went on. 'It's all good.'

Mel chewed her lip. 'I remember I hated this part last time.'

'That's OK. You might have been scared because your body is taking over. Don't hate it. Work with it and listen to your body.'

'I'm trying.'

'You're doing amazingly well.' Max's quiet voice came from the door.

'You can come in,' Mel said with half a smile in the pause between contractions. 'I really don't care if the world's in here and at least you can help me if I need it.'

They could hear the smile in Max's voice. 'Which you won't as Georgia is there and you're all doing so well. I won't come in unless you or Sister call me.'

The pains increased their intensity and soon Mel was pushing gently with each urge. The next minute she looked up at Tim and glared at him. 'I want to move. Get me out of the bathroom.'

That was a good sign. Georgia smiled as Tim almost fell over in his hurry to do what Mel asked. They stood and she moved between pains towards the bed. Mel looked up once as she passed Max and nodded to him.

'Hi, Doctor,' she said briefly.

By the time she'd eased herself back on the bed her baby was almost ready to be born, and Tim had paled to an interesting shade of alabaster.

'That's the way to do it, nice and slow.' Georgia helped Mel lean back onto the beanbag and slipped her gloves on.

Max stood back and watched Georgia. She had it all under control, brilliantly. He'd suspected she would be a great midwife and the last few minutes had proved that.

Mel's next pain came and with her steady breathing, the baby's head crowned and then extended, until only the shoulders remained to be born.

When the first shoulder came through, Georgia guided Tim's hands down and encouraged him to lift his own baby up onto Mel's chest as he was born.

Max stared at the sight of a loving father's hands lifting his son onto his wife's breasts, and the pain seared him unexpectedly, like a blow torch in his chest.

He would never do that for his own child. He would probably never share such a look as Mel and Tim shared at that moment.

'Oh my goodness,' Tim said, as he stared down

at his baby. 'It's a boy. I've got another son! My Billy.' He swooped down to kiss Mel. She laughed up at him and they both had their hands on their new son.

'There you go. Eight thirty-one a.m.' Georgia checked the clock and then she looked at Max.

He smiled back at her but there was such a wealth of sadness behind his eyes that her breath caught and she wanted to comfort him for something she didn't understand.

Then the look was gone as if it had never been. Maybe she had been mistaken and he was just tired.

Max moved to the baby and placed his stethoscope on the baby's back to listen to his chest as he lay against his mother. He stepped back and nodded.

'Baby sounds great. Congratulations, Mel and Tim.'

Georgia watched his gentle handling of baby and realised she knew so little of this man who was legally her husband and here they were together at such a special event and yet she still didn't know what he was thinking.

Georgia glanced down at the thick shiny umbilical cord and suddenly a tiny gush of blood indicated probable separation from the uterus. They were ready to complete the final stage of labour.

If the placenta had sheared off from the uterine wall then it certainly wouldn't have a pulse and Tim could cut the cord.

Georgia curved her fingers around the cord and gently squeezed the thick rope. 'The cord has stopped pulsating, Mel. Is it OK for Tim to cut the cord now?'

Mel looked up. 'Yes, that's fine.' She smiled at Georgia. 'Isn't our son beautiful?'

'You are a very handsome man, Master Billy,' she said to the baby, and then returned her attention to the job at hand.

'I'm just sealing his umbilical cord with this little clamp and pinching another section a few inches down so Tim can cut between the two clamps.' She looked up as she held out the scissors. 'You ready, Tim?'

Tim nodded and took the scissors to saw away at the cord until it was severed. 'Either the scissors are blunt or it's pretty tough.'

They all laughed when the job was done and a few seconds later the third stage was complete.

'No damage,' Georgia said after a quick check down below, and she lifted out the disposable sheet from beneath Mel and tucked the warm blanket over her chest and the baby.

Max wandered over to the bench to start writing in the patient notes and Georgia checked Mel's abdomen for a contracted uterus once more before pulling the blanket down and joining him.

Georgia frowned and checked again. Mel's uterus was soft and spongy and not the hard ball she had expected. She lifted back the sheets and a sudden column of blood spread into a widening pool that seeped away underneath Mel onto the bed.

The blood didn't just trickle, it flowed heavily in

a serious postpartum haemorrhage that needed immediate treatment.

'Max,' Georgia said, and his head flicked up immediately at the tone of her voice. He crossed over to the bed and Georgia leant over and pressed the red button for help. Max already being there was a godsend, but they might need extra hands.

Georgia's palm had gone straight to Mel's abdomen again to rub the top of her uterus externally and make it clamp down on the bleeding. Max's hand came in over hers.

'I've got it.' He rubbed Mel more firmly.

'The uterus has no tone at all. Get me cannulas for IV access and I'll slip them in.'

Georgia grabbed the tray from the bench and slid it onto the shelf beside the labour bed.

Max took one of Mel's hands and slid the tourniquet Georgia handed him over her wrist. 'Have to pop in a couple of needles so we can get a drip up. Sorry, sweetheart.'

Georgia picked up the injection tray she'd had prepared with the declined injection in it. 'You get the needle now, Mel.'

Mel nodded. 'I feel a little woozy.'

Georgia glanced at Max before speaking to Tim. 'Gently pull two of her pillows out, Tim, so Mel can have her head lower.' Tim moved the pillows and grew paler by the second as he watched the puddle of blood that filled the space on the bed below Mel's waist.

'Then can you rub Mel's tummy here.' Georgia

took one of his hands and guided him to where the top of Mel's uterus lay just above her umbilicus after the birth.

'This feels like a squashy grapefruit and it should feel like a big hard lemon.'

She looked at Mel, who was clutching her baby with one hand as she tried to breathe calmly through her nose. 'You won't like Tim much for it but it is very important he rubs your tummy fairly firmly until the uterus contracts and stops the bleeding.'

She turned to Max. 'OK if I give the first Syntocinon intramuscularly? I had it ready in case.'

'Sure. Then check the placenta. Maybe there is a bit left behind that's stopping her uterus from contracting properly.' Max concentrated on finding Mel's veins before she lost too much blood. Soon the lack of blood volume would make her veins collapse and it would be more difficult to find the blood vessel he needed.

Georgia explained to Tim, 'I need to check the placenta to see there is none missing. Sometimes a small piece of placenta can stay behind and stop the uterus from fully clamping down on the rich blood vessel bed that it's detached from.'

The nurses from the ward appeared and froze at the door, as if they didn't want to come in. 'I'm Flo,' said one, and the other just stared worriedly at the blood.

Georgia smiled at them. 'Come in, Flo. It's OK. Maybe you could take over from Tim so he can help Mel hold the baby.'

Flo nodded and hurried to do as she'd been asked.

Georgia pointed at the tray and said to the second nurse, 'Could you draw up four ampoules of the Syntocinon and put it into that flask for Doctor, please? That will help stop the bleeding. Then put another saline flask up to run as fast as it can through the other cannula to replace at least the volume of fluid Mel has lost.'

The nurse nodded and hastened to her tasks, obviously relieved that it was something she understood how to do.

Tim cradled his son and Georgia checked the placenta and then stripped off her gloves to check Mel's observations. Max had the drip up as soon as it was loaded.

Still the haemorrhage continued and Max frowned as he looked across at Georgia. 'Vital signs?'

Georgia didn't like the persistence of this bleed and she was very glad Max had come when he had. 'Her BP has fallen to eighty on forty and pulse rate is up to one thirty. I've some ergot here.'

'Thanks. I'll push it IV and see what we get.'

'Mel?' Tim's voice startled them as he leaned over his wife. Mel's face was ashen and her eyelids flickered but didn't open when Tim called out.

Max had injected the drug and now he frowned as no immediate response was noted. 'I'll have to manually compress the uterus,' Max said. Thankfully, when he did bunch Mel's uterus between his hands the bleeding slowed, though as soon as he removed his hand it started again.

'Oxygen,' Max said at the same time as Georgia passed him to reach the flip-down cupboards with the resuscitation equipment. She slipped the mask over Mel's face and tilted the whole bed so that Mel's feet were higher than her head.

'I may need the Prostin F2 alpha,' Max said quietly, and Georgia nodded and moved to prepare the syringe.

Not often used, the last drug was injected straight into the muscle of the uterus, which meant Max compressed Mel's uterus against one hand and injected the medication with the other.

Within less than a minute the gushing blood slowed to a trickle and Georgia and Max looked at each other with ill-concealed relief.

'Tricky,' Max said.

'Very, but that's done it.' Georgia breathed out with the reprieve and after checking Mel's blood pressure even allowed herself a small smile.

Mel moaned and her eyes flickered open as Tim sagged with relief.

Max checked Mel's abdomen again and her uterus finally remained well contracted. Max nodded and looked at Georgia. 'Better.'

'Thank you,' he said to Flo, and he smiled to include the other nurse, who blushed and backed away. Then Max looked at his wife. 'Well done, Georgia.'

He leant down and spoke to Mel's abdomen. 'Now, why did you do that?'

The tension lightened in the room and Mel roused enough to say in a weak voice, 'What happened?'

Tim sighed with relief and then suddenly paled further, sighed and sagged sideways.

'Grab the baby,' Max called to Flo, who scooped Tim's son from his arms as Tim fell back in a dead faint. Max caught the new dad easily under the arms before he hit the floor, and dragged him into a chair.

Max looked down at the ashen Tim. 'Just to top it off, poor guy.'

'Never a dull moment,' Georgia said, as she carried a damp facecloth across to Tim, who stirred groggily as the blood returned to his brain.

By the time a sheepish Tim was sitting upright, Mel had recovered some of the colour in her face as well.

Max jotted down the sequence of events with times and then crossed the room to speak to Tim and Mel. 'Unfortunately we probably will never know why your uterus decided not to contract after birth.'

'Mel's BP is back to ninety on fifty and her pulse is one twenty,' Georgia said.

Max nodded and spoke to Tim. 'Mel's compensating for the lower volume of blood she has circulating now, but childbearing women have extra safeguards for the risk of bleeding after birth. We'll check what her actual red cell levels are and think about blood transfusion or not and discuss it later.'

He smiled that smile Georgia really did love. 'Everyone in the room has a pulse of one twenty at the moment but it's all settling now. Mel's uterus is firm and behaving itself and the bleeding has stopped.'

He spoke to Georgia. 'We'll run the drip over four hours to make sure it stays that way and keep her in this room for a while so we can keep an eye on her to ensure it doesn't start again. But it shouldn't.'

Mel spoke faintly from the bed. 'So much for not having a needle. That was a bad choice.'

Max shook his head. 'Not so. Don't lay blame on anything in particular. Lots of people decline the needle after birth and though it statistically increases risk, it didn't cause what happened.'

Max paused to let the words sink in. 'Unless you have a history of bleeding! Now you have that history…' he shrugged ruefully '…I think your choice is limited for the future.'

Bravo, Max. Georgia wished she could clap because she knew a lot of medical officers who would have ground Mel down for her choice. She would tell him so tonight. In fact, she couldn't wait until dinner tonight and the chance for their first real discussion about a specialty of medicine they both obviously loved.

Baby Billy nudged at his mother and Georgia smiled. 'Would you like a hand to put your son to the breast? During breastfeeding more hormones are released, which will help prevent further bleeding as well.'

When Billy was settled at the breast, Georgia and Max left the new parents to enjoy their son in peace after the traumatic events following the birth.

Max slipped his arm briefly around Georgia's shoulders and hugged her before he dropped his arm to his side again. 'We're a good team. That could have been much worse if the F2 alpha hadn't worked or you hadn't been prepared.' Max smiled down at Georgia and she nodded.

'I was glad you'd dropped in when the floodgates opened. It's always tricky to do everything at once when things go only slightly unplanned, let alone a full-blown PPH. I wouldn't have enjoyed the stress while I waited for you.'

Max's eyes softened. 'Is it still good to be back at work when you have occasions like that?'

Georgia looked at him and nodded without any doubt. 'When it all turns out as well as that did then, yes, of course. And the birth was lovely.'

His face clouded again and she put her hand on his arm. 'What's wrong?'

He smiled and she wondered if it was forced. 'Nothing. I was very proud of you, my wife, in there. But now I'll have to go to work and crunch some numbers around until you call me again.'

He patted her shoulder and just before he moved off he said, 'Do ring me. Any excuse to get out of the office is gratefully accepted.'

'Perhaps you could come back at lunchtime and check on Mel and share my sandwiches.'

'Sounds like a plan.' He smiled and waved and she watched him go.

He'd been a pleasure to work with and as cool as ice in an emergency. But, then, she'd known that since Elsa's birth.

She was trying to ignore the fact that her heart had given a jump when she'd first heard his voice, and just watching him talk to Mel had made her so proud to think that for the moment, at least, he was her man.

She gave herself a little mental shake. She needed to think more about her work and less about Max.

That night at dinner it seemed the floodgates of work discussion opened. They'd never really discussed much about Max's work but it was as if he'd finally decided he could talk to Georgia and she would not only understand but be deeply interested and have much to offer him in response.

'I had no idea how much I missed the face-to-face obstetrics that I grew away from in administration.'

'How could you not notice you'd left a clinical role?' Georgia listened with her chin on her hands and watched the play of emotions cross Max's handsome face. How had she come to be with this man? His kindness to her seemed to have no limits.

'I started teaching.' He shrugged. 'And that always moves you back a pace as you encourage students to gain skills and be safe. The only way to impart that knowledge is to let them do it—which meant I didn't.

'That access to students meant people were always asking about change and why things were done in a certain way. Soon I was the person advocating change and fighting against the old school of habit.'

She smiled. He would be a good teacher. 'That must have been satisfying.'

'In its way it was,' he said with a twitch of his lips, 'but that pushed me further away from the births and into the boardrooms and medical committee meetings. Before I knew it, funding had become the big issue.'

She wouldn't like that herself. 'You must have been good at creating change?'

'Maybe, but it is paradoxical that the more I see of grass-roots obstetrics the more I want to be part of it again.'

She could listen to him all night. She'd never had this. As an only child she'd never had a sister or brother she'd been able to really relate to and she'd never been close to Tayla.

Her loving parents had died together when she had just left her teens—too young to have really understood her mother yet old enough to see that true love was a worthwhile goal.

Her marriage, after the initial honeymoon period, had never included an equal partnership so any conversations had been dominated and directed by Sol.

With Max she felt she could dispute, digress or

downright disagree, and her contribution would be appreciated. He must have felt the same because he stood up and held out his hand.

'Come and sit with me for a while on the veranda. We'll look over the ocean and check out the stars. It is a beautiful night.'

She took his hand and the feel of his fingers around hers as he helped her up made her realise she had never felt so relaxed and cared for by a man who had no expectations of her.

CHAPTER SIX

THEY rose and crossed the room and strolled out through the French doors to the veranda. A soft breeze blew tendrils of hair across Georgia's cheek and she felt Max's gaze on her as she sat down on the swing seat. He sat next to her and his strong thigh brushed hers as they swung.

Georgia took a sip from her glass and tried to retrieve the light mood they'd shared in the dining room.

The focus had shifted suddenly so that she was aware of Max's weight against her and the subtle scent of his aftershave even with the breeze carrying scents from the garden her way.

She remembered those crazy fantasies she'd had on the mountaintop and shifted a little on the seat.

She cleared her throat. 'Meeandah Hospital is certainly grass roots. You might change your mind when you've had ten nights' broken sleep in a row from callouts.'

Max spread one arm to encompass the vista and

the other he dropped around her shoulders. 'A hospital like we have here has fewer than one hundred and fifty births a year. That leaves me two hundred nights with sleep at least—not counting the quick births in the night that I'm told about in the morning.'

What a dream life as far as she was concerned. Imagine living here, Elsa growing up in this wonderful environment, Max as a true companion and lover, plus the best of doctors to work with. They were damned attractive thoughts but Max could never settle here.

'Somewhere like this is a big step down,' Georgia said as she thought of the high-powered position he'd held in the city, and even the subtle state-wide ramifications of what he achieved now, along with his visits to the hospital. His position was important to the whole scheme of obstetrics in New South Wales.

Max looked across at her. 'Could you be happy working in a facility like this?'

'Of course.' Couldn't he tell? She glanced around them at the idyllic lushness of the garden and the endless sky, and thought of the birth she had already been privileged to share. 'If the health system will sustain it, I'd stay here for ever.'

Georgia exhaled a long blissful sigh and looked across at him. 'This is what I love to do. Before I worked at Lower Mountains Base, I had my own home-birth practice, but nowadays I couldn't make that kind of availability commitment with Elsa.'

'Why is that?'

She loved it that Max seemed so interested. 'I need the framework of other midwives around me and this sort of situation is the nearest I can get to the ideal world.'

Max sat back. 'I would never have imagined this sleepy town could be an ideal world.'

She sighed. 'For you it wouldn't be. You'd miss not having the city to call on for amusement.' As she said the words, disappointment washed over her. Of course she was being unrealistic.

That was sad but true. Max would move on and she might even think about staying here when the time came for them to part, if she could be safe. Suddenly she didn't want to think about the time when Max had moved on.

Max closed his eyes and felt her words slice into him. They hurt. When had he been bored in the last four months? When had he wanted to be anywhere but coming home to Georgia?

'Do you know so little of me that you imagine that? Do you think me so needy of the bright lights?' Sometimes he despaired he'd ever have a hope with this woman. She didn't even try to understand him.

He sighed and watched her reflect back over what she'd said, but judging by her expression she still didn't get it.

'How could I know more about you?' she said. 'You don't exactly talk about yourself. Apart from the last few weeks, I'd barely seen you except for night relief from Elsa.'

He supposed it was true, though to his mind she seemed to be everywhere. When they had rare time to talk his choice would be to hear about her, not himself.

If that was the price for her to really see him then maybe it was time he began to pay. 'What do you want to know?'

She laughed and he wanted to kiss her—not talk about himself. Her infectious chuckle had been there since Elsa's birth and he treasured these moments more each day.

She poked him gently with her elbow. 'Do you realise how dangerous it is for a man to offer to tell all?'

He tilted his head. 'I asked what you wanted to know—I didn't promise I would tell you.'

'Now you are being mysterious.'

And you are delicious. He swung the seat gently and she was carried with him back and forth. She wasn't in his arms but it was better than nothing. 'I'm not intentionally mysterious.'

'So start with Tayla.' Georgia folded her hands. 'How did you meet her and what made you think you would be happy together?'

Max shook his head. 'Why do women always start with another woman?'

'Fine.' She shrugged. 'What do you want to tell me, then?'

His gaze locked with hers. 'I'd rather tell you that

I have enjoyed the last four months with you more than any I can remember.'

Georgia's eyebrows rose in disbelief. 'Sure,' she said. 'It must have been a hoot for you. You enjoyed being woken up by a colicky baby ten times a night and having a grumpy, sleep-deprived housemate to live with.' Why on earth would he?

'Absolutely.' The tilt of his lips confirmed that he had only pleasant memories and though he spoke quietly, his tone of voice indicated it was the truth. 'I became acquainted with Elsa and she's gorgeous, like her mother.'

Georgia tilted her head. 'Same temperament, you mean?'

Max nodded. 'She's determined and independent, yes.'

'Ah.' She had him. 'So living with me is like living with a baby with colic. I can see why you'd be attracted.'

They were teasing each other and she was beginning to enjoy it too much. This was far too dangerous for her peace of mind and she tried to steer the topic away into more general waters. Maybe he did have an agenda with her after all or he'd managed to beam in on one of her fantasies.

'It is a glorious night,' she said.

Max wouldn't be diverted. 'I appreciated each and every vision of you at night since Elsa was born.'

Georgia thought back over the range of short cotton nighties and men's T-shirts and boxer shorts she'd worn, with her hair a mess. Not much to admire there.

He hadn't finished and his voice brushed her skin with his breath as he turned to face her. 'And I was privileged to see your hair wild and loose and the real you without the public face of composure that keeps me at arm's length so very efficiently.'

This was serious stuff and she wasn't sure where it had come from. The mood on the veranda had deepened to one of charged closeness and she couldn't help softening against him. Georgia forced her arms to cross to block out the intimacy. To block it out because suddenly she wanted to reach across the seat and hug him for seeing a real person and not an object to own, like Sol had.

Obviously Max recognised the moment too and she must have given away more than she'd intended because she saw his surprise and the next thing he'd acted on the impulse she'd denied herself.

Very slowly but with intent his hand slid up her spine to the back of her head to hold her in place and then he leaned across and kissed her gently.

His lips savoured hers in a long slow exploration and his breath was warm as it mingled with hers.

Suddenly boneless, she sighed into him because it felt so damn wonderful and right and what she desperately wanted, and just for a moment she followed Max's lead as she felt her fingers tighten on his shirt and she pushed her hand against him back and forth just to feel the hard heat of his chest.

But this wasn't right. She forced her fingers open

and then his shirt slipped away, just like the moment had to. The last thing Max needed was a clinging vine, he'd said himself he admired her independence, and she pushed the feelings away along with his chest because she already owed this man too much.

She could not get involved with Max. Not while Sol's presence in her life hung over her.

She sat back and, Max being Max, he let her go. Which was a shame but the right thing to do.

For her to offer something that wasn't really there wouldn't be fair to Max and she was beginning to think if she let down the barriers and allowed him into her own rapidly beating heart, she would never find herself when she left.

'Thank you, kind sir,' was all she said, and she leaned forward to stand up. 'I think I'll check on Elsa.'

Max's hand caught her wrist and the strength in his fingers halted her rising.

'I'm sorry if I embarrassed you.'

She looked at him, at his strong jawline and then his warm golden eyes, and she said quietly, 'You didn't embarrass me, Max.'

'Then why are you running away?' His voice, too, was barely audible.

She breathed in and the faintest tinge of his after-shave remained on her skin. 'You had a nice life before I came along.'

He laughed cynically. 'I nearly married the wrong woman before you came along. You saved me from a fate worse than death. I've been very happy with you, Georgia.'

'Tayla offered what you wanted, Max. A free life without the dramas of a family. Elsa and I have plenty of dramas. You haven't married the right woman yet. I'm only the stopgap.'

Just when he thought they might have made progress, he'd lost her. He could see it. 'What if it doesn't feel that way to me?'

'Then you would be thinking with another part of your body, not your brain.'

Ouch. She definitely wasn't ready to change their relationship. He'd like to get his hands on that ex-husband of hers and throttle him. He was beginning to think there was more to his nastiness than she'd said. He let go of her wrist and she stood up.

She nodded and left almost at a run, and Max gazed out over the veranda. He'd scared her—but for a moment there he'd thought she was on the same wavelength as he.

Max watched a tiny meteorite arc down towards the ocean and disappear before it reached the water, a bit like the opportunity that had just passed him.

He could wait. He would have to. He would wait until she was secure in herself.

He guessed that wasn't going to happen until she knew Elsa was safe from her father, but he hoped he, Max, wasn't too old to enjoy it by then. It was so damn hard to keep his hands off her.

He wondered what he could do differently to dissipate the awkwardness he'd created between them.

For someone who had never had a problem with come-hither lines, he'd botched it badly. No doubt the difference being this time he was emotionally involved and becoming more so every second.

The feel of her lips against his had been as poignant as he'd anticipated. The need to feel the rest of her against him rose like Mount Warning in the distance and just as appropriately named. He would have to be patient.

Georgia gently pushed open the door to Elsa's room and moved to stand beside the cot. Her tiny daughter lay in a shaft of moonlight and her rosy cheeks glowed with health as she sucked her lip gently in her sleep.

Why couldn't she and Elsa have the wonderful life she had begun to suspect Max could offer her?

Because even now Max might be hurt when the time came that she had to leave with Elsa because from what he'd said tonight, he could certainly become attached to her daughter.

Max had told her he'd planned not to have children with Tayla so the same reasons were still there. Yet here she was with a baby that was anything but easy at times. The upheaval in Max's life had been caused by a child he wasn't even the father of.

Apart from recently, the poor man hadn't even

left the house except for work because of her and Elsa. Even Mrs White saw that.

But she, Georgia, was a mess and Max didn't deserve that or the danger she would bring in the future.

Max had no idea how much trouble Sol could be and although she really needed to leave now, before she did any more damage, she couldn't. It wouldn't be safe to leave while she was still vulnerable to Sol with Elsa so young.

She glanced down at her defenceless daughter again and reality slapped her with the obvious she had begun to forget. What was she doing even contemplating her own happiness before the safety of Elsa?

As a mother she should be concentrating on her baby and setting up her future life, not fantasising about a man she could bring to ruin by association.

Her problems were not Max's, though he obviously was beginning to think they were. They needed to avoid the type of comments and moves he'd made tonight or it was all going to become much harder. She would never be free to take on emotional issues with any man and Max didn't deserve that.

On Tuesday morning Georgia stayed out of the kitchen until Max had gone to work.

Cowardly, but she hadn't been able to face him, because some time in the night she had discovered that with all the reasons for not staying with Max the one that loomed largest was the fact that she'd fallen irresponsibly in love with him.

She was a fool. Though this time, at least, she had fallen for a worthy man. Which was all the more reason not to drag him into the danger she knew was ahead.

What was becoming obvious was that Max wanted more, wanted to move their relationship onto a whole new plane, and she had too much baggage to drag him down with her.

She'd just have to be careful to keep him safe by maintaining her distance. And she'd make sure Max did, too.

That night at dinner, sitting across from Max, she tried really hard not to glance out to the swing seat on the veranda and think of Max's kiss at this time last night.

From the way he kept glancing at her, she had the feeling Max was remembering too.

'How's your sawdust?' Max said conversationally.

'Fine,' Georgia said, as she tried to rationalise with herself about how she was doing the right thing to block Max out. Then his words sank in.

'What did you say?'

'We're both chewing away diligently but I had to look again to see what I was actually eating. I think we should both accept that while it is very nice to kiss it causes problems in our day-to-day world for the moment.'

Georgia could feel the heat in her cheeks but she

was glad Max had had the courage to clear the air before she'd had to.

'I agree,' she said, which was pretty lame but that was the best she could do at the moment. She forced herself to meet his eyes. 'Thank you, Max, for understanding.'

'You're welcome. Now let's talk of something else. You didn't miss any obstetrics at the hospital today so I hope you have someone to play midwife with tomorrow when you go in for your next shift.'

She followed his lead gratefully. 'You did say your statistics pointed to one birth every two days.'

'I'm infallible. I know you enjoyed your first day.'

Georgia thought back to her first shift and smiled. 'They even paid me to have fun and brush up on my emergency obsterics. And it worked well because I was home by three in the afternoon and still had a few hours to feed and bath Elsa before you came home. Mrs White is looking forward to tomorrow with her.'

'So you are happy to be back at work?'

'As long as Elsa is fine, I love it. I should at least be able to do next week and if possible a short stint full time to allow Karissa her holidays, which would give me a good basis to refresh my skills for the future.'

He raised on eyebrow in disbelief. 'I don't think your skills need much refreshing, Georgia. I'm extremely comfortable that you would cope with anything.'

Max's approval meant a lot. She had been surprised how at ease she'd felt at Meeandah, but
Max's presence had been that extra insurance she'd
needed to make it easier. 'Thank you, Max.'

She avoided looking at the swing again and
decided she did feel a little easier already.

'So tell me about your day at home,' Max said.
'What exciting things did I miss?'

He even looked interested. 'Big news. Elsa opens
and shuts her hands now.' Georgia smiled reminis-
cently. 'You wouldn't think something so small
would captivate both of us but she lay there for
ages, watching her fingers open and shut, and I had
to watch, too.'

Max smiled. 'I'll have to ask her to show me in
the morning. When you go to work she shares her
breakfast with me and I read the paper to her.'

'She'd like that.' Not many men would do that for
a child that wasn't even his own. Georgia fell more
in love with him than ever and went back to eating
her sawdust to avoid his eyes.

At Meeandah hospital Georgia had agreed to three
staggered morning shifts in the first week.

The idea had been to see how Elsa and Mrs
White got along and how Georgia coped with being
away from her daughter for the first time since
Elsa's birth.

Her second shift was uneventful.

Max came in and discharged Mel to go home.
He'd issued a prescription for double-strength iron

tablets to increase Mel's red blood cell count because she hadn't wanted the blood transfusion Max had offered after her haemorrhage.

'Don't expect to do much except breastfeed Billy for the first two weeks to keep building up your milk supply,' Georgia said.

Max stood beside her to wave them off with a few cautionary words for Mel. 'Your low blood count will slow your lactation so Billy will be extra-demanding and you will be tired.'

Mel shrugged. 'I'm too excited to be going home to worry about that. Tim's going to do everything except feed. He's got three weeks off work.'

'Good man,' Georgia said, and she slanted a sideways glance at Max. 'Max is excellent with Elsa, too.' The two women smiled at each other as Tim looked proudly down at his son tucked under his arm.

Max shook his hand. 'Good luck, mate. At least the men outnumber the women in your house.'

Tim grinned and carried Billy carefully to the car and strapped him into his new baby seat next to his brother, Andy.

Both Caesarean patients, Leanne and Tanya, had decided to go home too, and after Max left the ward Georgia worked in the medical end of the hospital.

She enjoyed the challenge to brush up on the medications and treatments she didn't deal with in obstetrics. It also gave her a chance to get to know the other nurses she might have to call on in the future.

She gathered that Flo and her colleague didn't feel as comfortable as they'd like at the obstetric end and Georgia could see why if they only went there for the last minutes of labour or in emergencies.

'When it's quiet, would you be interested in prac-tising some obstetric emergency procedures, just so you would have more of an idea what we might want you to do?'

'That sounds great.' Flo was in her sixties, round and energetic with a host of grandchildren she loved to talk about. Georgia loved the way she and Gerry, the other nurse, were keen to update their skills and be as helpful as they could.

Gerry was tall and thin with a mournful face, but her wicked sense of humour appeared at the strang-est times. Both women's interest in learning about obstetric emergencies encouraged Georgia to go on. 'If you find it helpful, we could do a different emergency each shift that I'm on.'

Later that day, when all the patients were resting, Georgia went through the postpartum haemorrhage tray with Flo and Gerry.

'I thought we'd start with the emergency we've already had.' She couldn't help thinking of the way Max had so competently directed the emergency. No doubt it was still very fresh in the minds of Gerry and Flo as well. So she was pretty sure she'd have their attention.

'With a postpartum haemorrhage the excessive blood loss can happen for different reasons. You can have a sudden heavy bleed, like we had with

Mel the other day, where the woman bleeds quickly and things need to happen fast before she goes into shock from blood loss.'

Flo nodded. 'Shock is when the body makes changes to ensure enough blood goes to the brain isn't it?'

'Yep. Like Mel's pulse rate going up because her heart has to circulate fewer blood cells faster to get enough oxygen to her brain. That's why the patient feels faint. If a person faints, they automatically lower their head and make gravity at least push blood to their brain. That's why I raised the foot of the bed for Mel's feet to be higher than her head.'

Georgia saw that they had the concept and moved on. 'Or you can have a woman go back to her room and bleed quietly in a steady trickle until she is in just as much trouble. They're usually the ones who buzz because they feel faint when they get up to go to the toilet.'

'We had a lady do that…' Gerry nodded soulfully '…at my training hospital back in the bad old days. When we went to make her bed she'd trickled steadily under the covers over a couple of hours and we nearly had a fit when we went to help her get up. She nearly died.'

Flo's mouth formed an 'O' of surprise. 'So that's why we check postnatal women for the first four hours, just like a post-operative patient gets checked in Recovery.'

Georgia nodded. 'But remember it's not normal for

a healthy woman to do that. The body has mecha-
nisms to prevent it, but some women don't know they
are in trouble. Basic observation is very important.
Rapid emergency treatment can save lives, and that's
where having everything ready to go is so important.'

Georgia removed the haemorrhage tray from the
cupboard. 'Let's have a look at the tray we have
here. You obviously need your IV fluids, a tourniquet, your cannulas to insert into the vein for access,
and connection tubing for administering the fluids.
You both remember Doctor connecting these to
Mel. Then there are the drugs that can help with
contracting the uterus.'

Georgia held up a sheet of paper in a plastic
sleeve. 'This is the order and dose of the drugs you
would need, and that can be very helpful if no one
has time to repeat what they asked for.'

Gerry snorted. 'Typical. I wish I'd known that
was there, even though I did manage to get them all
in order.'

Gerry acknowledged she'd worried the previous
day and Georgia was glad they were talking about
it again. She realised Gerry had probably been re-
hashing the events and needed this discussion to
debrief after Monday's excitement.

'An emergency is a stressful time. Extra reminders are always helpful. These trays save everyone
from running to find different things, too.'

Flo nodded enthusiastically. 'Boy, do I know
what you mean. Every emergency I've ever been in
I seem to be hunting for things other people want.'

Georgia smiled. 'The most important thing to get is help. Even the kitchen lady to write down what you gave and when and what steps you've taken can be good if you are short-staffed. That's why the pad and pen are here.'

She held up a pen with a long cord attaching it to the pad. 'We all find it difficult to get the time drugs were given exactly right even if we record an event immediately afterwards.

'The beauty of recording events at the time is that we can make fine adjustments when we go over our treatment and actions and review later.'

Gerry snapped her fingers in enlightenment. 'Is that what a critical review is? I thought it was when you were critical of what people did or when they'd done something wrong.'

'No. It's feedback to make the next situation run even more smoothly. Max is going to sit down with us later today and we'll go over it together and see if we missed anything.'

'I don't think there was anything anyone could have done better,' Gerry said dryly. 'I thought you guys were amazing.'

'We were a team and you and Flo were an important part of that. I think you both were pretty wonderful, too.'

On Thursday Max was called into Maternity just as he was about to go home for the evening meal and he didn't return until after Georgia had gone to bed. They'd had a sick baby with congenital heart

problems and Max had waited for MIRA to arrive
to stabilise and take the baby to Newcastle Hospital
with her mother.

He'd rung and let Georgia know he'd be very late
and she'd sat in the dining room by herself and had
then gone to bed early. She couldn't believe how
much she'd missed his company for that one
evening.

She had geared her day off to when Max came
home. Things she'd planned to tell him. An article
she'd thought he might be interested in. And the
extra time she'd taken with her appearance.

These were all warning signs that Max was
assuming a larger part of her life than she'd
promised herself she'd let him be.

CHAPTER SEVEN

ON GEORGIA'S third morning shift the day dawned cold and damp, with thick fog that engulfed the mountain and the road on the way to work. Georgia had left fifteen minutes early to be on the safe side and still only arrived as the clock hit seven.

Minutes after the night staff had departed a young woman hobbled miserably into the ward with her friend. She stood at the nurses' desk with her hand cupped protectively around her small belly and her lips pressed tightly together.

Georgia came back from the medical end of the hospital at the sound of the buzzer and something about the young woman's stance sent alarm bells ringing.

'Can I help you?' The young woman nodded but didn't speak.

'She's having contractions,' Her friend said, 'and you need to stop them.'

Georgia blinked. OK. This was different. 'I'm Georgia, the midwife. Would you both like to come through to the observation room and we'll see what's going on? Then I can ring the doctor.'

The spokeswoman nodded. 'I'm Shannon and this is my friend, Del. She's got eight weeks to go.'

Georgia glanced at the silent Del and her heart rate picked up. They'd have to fly her out if she was in labour—they couldn't handle a baby that size here. Even the base hospital wouldn't take her at that gestation.

Shannon went on. 'She's having twins.'

Georgia's eyebrows rose. They'd have to fly her out urgently, which would be interesting with the fog. A twin pregnancy was even more likely to progress to a premature delivery.

Del froze as she went to sit on the bed and she grabbed Georgia's hand and squeezed it as her contraction mounted. Georgia slid her other hand down to gently feel Del's belly through her shirt, and it felt rock hard against her fingers.

Georgia reached for the buzzer and pressed for assistance. She glanced at Shannon and although Shannon looked scared, at least she could talk. Del certainly wouldn't be talking for a minute. 'How long has Del been having contractions?'

'It took us an hour to get here and an hour before that.'

Two hours shouldn't be too advanced in labour for a first baby, Georgia thought hopefully. 'Is this your first pregnancy, Del?'

Shannon came to the rescue when all Del did was

shake her head. 'Her third. The last one took two hours.'

Georgia smiled at Shannon. 'I'm glad you came with her.' She looked at Del. 'You're not much of a talker, then, Del?'

Before Del could answer, if she was going to, a slightly breathless Flo arrived.

Georgia smiled at her. 'Today we're going to study the premature labour tray.'

Flo grinned and headed for the cupboard. She reached in and put the tray on the bench. 'I hope it comes with instructions.'

'You'd better ring Doctor, first, on his mobile. Tell him thirty-two-week twins in labour. He'll come straight in.'

Flo's mouth formed her favourite 'O' and she pulled the phone book across.

Georgia helped Del to lie on the bed and connected the monitors to her stomach. 'These belts hold on the listeners that hear your babies' heart rates and record your contractions at the same time. In your case we have two listeners for two babies' hearts.'

Del nodded and winced as the next contraction started. Georgia could hear Flo's brief conversation with Max.

She looked up. 'Ask him if I can give the first dose of nifedipine as her contractions are three minutes apart.'

Flo nodded back. 'He heard you and said give the first dose. He'll be here before the next one is due.'

She hung up and came back across to Georgia. 'You want some observations done?'

'Please. I need to check Del's antenatal records as well.'

Shannon was the only one with a shoulder-bag and Georgia directed her next enquiry to her.

'Have you got Del's antenatal card?'

'She doesn't have one. She's only been the once because the doctor said she'd have to go to Brisbane to have her babies. She didn't want to do that so she never went back to him.'

Georgia's heart sank at the lack of antenatal care and information now available. 'Where were you going to have your babies, Del?'

Del looked at Shannon. Shannon answered. 'Here.'

Thirty-two-week twins here and no antenatal care. Meeandah was good but not that good.

Georgia rummaged through the tray and removed a strip of tablets and two spoons. 'We want to stop your labour Del. I'll crush this tablet between two teaspoons and you have to put it under your tongue until it dissolves. It's actually a blood-pressure tablet that works on the muscles of the blood vessels but it relaxes uterine muscles as well.

'The plan is that you have fewer contractions the more tablets you have.' And the doctor arrives soon after, Georgia thought hopefully. 'Do you understand?'

Del nodded. Georgia looked at Shannon and lowered her voice. 'Does Del talk at all?'

'Sometimes if she has to, but she finds it hard.'

'That's OK, Del. As long as you understand and let me know if you need to know more—OK? And as long as Shannon stays.' She grinned at Del's friend.

Del nodded and opened her mouth and Georgia thought she was going to speak. She held her breath but Del only waited for the crushed tablet before closing her mouth again.

'When the doctor comes, he'll want to examine you to see if your cervix is opening. That makes a difference to what we do next. OK?'

Del nodded.

'We'll probably give you an injection to help your babies' lungs mature in case they are born too soon.'

Del nodded and Georgia found herself nodding too. It all began to feel like a farce with all the head-bobbing.

Georgia selected the cortisone injection from the tray and set it aside for Max to decide on. They'd need to liaise with whatever referral hospital had beds for premature twins but MIRA would set up the conference call between the parties as soon as Max rang them.

MIRA, standing for Mobile Infant Retrieval Australia, would fly mum and babies wherever they needed to go with expert personnel—as long as the mist lifted and they could land.

'Can you give Del's doctor's name to Flo and she'll get him to fax what info he has to us here?'

she asked Shannon. Shannon nodded and followed Flo out.

Max arrived sooner than was prudent, considering the road conditions, and Georgia was glad to see him safe as well as have access to his assistance.

'This is Del.'

'Hi, Del. I'm Max. I'm the doctor. Georgia says you're in premature labour. You must be pretty scared at what's going on.'

Del looked around for Shannon and Georgia held off answering for her to see if Del would speak.

She nodded.

Georgia did Shannon's job. 'Del's not much of a talker. She's having contractions three minutes apart, third pregnancy, quick labours. One antenatal visit, one ultrasound at eighteen weeks. They're faxing it through as soon as they open the surgery, I guess.'

'Good stuff.' He held his hands up. 'May I feel your tummy, please, Del?'

Georgia nodded along with Del and then realised what she'd done. She was going mad.

She left Max to jot down what she'd found so far and by the time she'd finished Max was ready to examine the patient.

Afterwards he pulled the chair up beside the bed to talk to Del. Georgia leaned out the door and called Shannon to come back in.

'Shannon is spokesperson and she does a great job. It might be worthwhile waiting for her.'

Max raised his eyebrows and looked at Del. 'Is that what you want, Del?'

Del nodded vehemently but she didn't say anything.

Max sat back and Shannon hurried back in with Flo at her heels.

Georgia took Flo aside. 'Can you switch both humidcribs on in the storeroom? Probably won't need them but if it looks like we will then we'll move them to the power points outside the door. Just leave them where they are for now as long as they are warming.'

Flo nodded and left.

Max had introduced himself to Shannon and then spoke to Del. 'You're four centimetres dilated and your babies need to be looked after by paediatricians when they are born.' He paused to let his words sink in.

'That means they're too little to be looked after here at Meeandah. In fact, they're too little to be looked after at the base hospital so they'll have to go to Newcastle, if they have the neonatal beds free, or Sydney.'

Del's eyes filled with tears and Max rubbed her wrist in sympathy. 'I know it's scary to think of going a long way away but you have to for your babies' safety. When your babies are bigger, you will be able to come back here for them to finish growing up.'

Del nodded and looked at Shannon, who asked

the question. 'How long before she would come back?'

'That depends how Del's babies grow and the treatment they have when they are born.'

Max went on, 'It is much better for babies to be transferred while they are still inside your tummy. It takes a lot of very sophisticated equipment to make an environment close to as good as your uterus is for your babies. We need to get you to a big hospital before your labour gets any further along. Do you understand?'

Shannon, Georgia and Del all nodded.

Max smiled at the three noddies. 'I'll be speaking to a doctor who will find where and when you'll be going and when I know I'll come back and tell you.

'In the meantime, Georgia is going to give you two more tablets twenty minutes apart. Maybe later also an injection that will help the babies lungs mature for when they are born. Let Georgia know if you think your labour is getting stronger, OK?'

'Than' 'ou.' Del's quiet voice stopped Georgia as she turned away. So Del could speak. Trust Max to have elicited a response when she couldn't. Were any women immune to the man?

'You're welcome, Del.' He gave the young girl one of his special smiles and Del smiled mistily back.

Max stood up and examined the CTG tracing. 'Your contractions have slowed a little to five-minutely so the first dose of drug is working. Georgia will give you another tablet now.'

He looked up at Georgia. 'I'll be in the office on the phone if you need me.'

In the next twenty minutes Del's contractions slowed to ten-minutely but they didn't stop. Flo had been outside to see if the fog had lifted but the mountain still lay shrouded.

Georgia sought Max out as he finished the admission letter for whichever hospital would finally take her.

'Del's contractions are strong and very regular, sitting at ten minutes apart.'

He spread his hands. 'There's a chance one of the outlying Sydney hospitals may take her, otherwise she may have to go on to Canberra.'

'If they don't decide soon, she'll get her wish and deliver here.' Max seemed very calm considering they might have premature twins on their hands. 'We'll send her out by road ambulance to the base hospital until the fixed-wing aircraft can land.'

Georgia frowned. She'd tried that. 'They refused her.'

'With the airfields shut, they've OK'd it now. They said they'd even send the escort. But if she's in strong labour they won't take her on the plane either so she'll have to go somewhere.'

Georgia smiled. Max had really done some ringing around. 'You wanted the joys of rural obstetrics.'

He grinned at her. 'Aren't you having fun?'

'The more the merrier.'

Max looked at her. 'You may have spoken too

soon.' The screech of tyres could be heard coming hard round the bend into the hospital and they looked at each other as another screech heralded the arrival of someone in a great hurry.

A tall, bearded man rushed in, his eyes panicky with emotion. 'Help us. My wife, Susie, is in the car, and she's having the baby right now.'

Georgia tapped Max's arm. 'You go. I'll get the emergency kit and a warm blanket and meet you there.' Max nodded and jogged after the man.

Georgia hurried to collect the small tray, a warm blanket and infant rug from the hot box and a wheel-chair in case they could move the woman to a more comfortable place for delivery.

By the time Georgia arrived they needed the warm blanket for the baby and the cord clamp and scissors.

The husband was calmer now that he wasn't alone to cope and it was a very relieved family that moved into the ward to ensure all was well.

Susie clutched her baby to her as if she didn't know where he'd come from.

'It's all a shock but you did beautifully,' Max said with a smile. 'Your son didn't mind in the least being born in the car. He'll probably grow up to be a rally driver.'

Flo stuck her head into the room. 'There's a phone call for you, Doctor.' Max nodded to indicate he was returning to the other room, and Georgia had to smile at his mode of communication. Very appropriate for Del.

Susie shuddered. 'Not if he drives like his father did on the way here. The fog made it a nightmare.'

'Susie's blood pressure is up,' Gerry said mournfully.

'Mine would be, too,' Georgia said with a smile. 'Perhaps you could just check it again in fifteen minutes, please. I'll go back to Del if you settle everyone and maybe offer a cup of tea in here.'

'Sure.' Gerry was happy to have something to do with all the excitement. 'Flo's had all the fun this morning,' she said.

Fifteen minutes later the ambulance arrived to take Del to the base hospital until the fog lifted, and Georgia only just finished all the transfer papers in time.

Max put the phone down. 'They don't want the steroids given or any more nifedipine.'

'Do they want us to check her cervical dilatation before she leaves?' Usually patients were assessed to ensure delivery wasn't imminent or likely to occur during the transport period.

'None of those things,' Max said with a frown. 'I queried it but the consultant was adamant.'

'Things change all the time. Must be a new study out that I haven't heard of,' Georgia said, but it did seem strange to her as well.

Georgia signed and printed her name and packaged her letter and Max's letter to the consultant stating what they'd done to go with Del.

A midwife from the base hospital had arrived as

escort, which meant Georgia didn't have to call anyone in to cover for her.

Suddenly the ward was quiet. All they had to do was clean up and prepare for the next person to come in.

After all the excitement it was a bit of an anticlimax and she wished Max could stay and have a coffee with her but she didn't ask because it felt needy.

He waved and left and instead Flo and Gerry helped Georgia restock the trays.

'This tray thing works pretty well.' Flo repacked with satisfaction.

'I wonder which one we get to use next,' Gerry said gloomily, and Georgia laughed.

When Max walked in after work that night, Georgia had Elsa on a rug on the floor in the lounge. Elsa was stretched out on her tummy, kicking her legs with her nappy off as if trying to swim.

For Max, seeing mother and daughter so relaxed in his home, squeezed his heart so hard it was almost chest pain.

He despaired of ever being a part of their closeness. He should just enjoy this now because since the other night Georgia had created a distance between them he could feel growing every day.

At this moment she was laughing at the fierce expression on Elsa's face as she tried to propel herself forward.

Georgia glanced up at him with her face alight

as if to say, Will you look at her? This was what he wanted. She looked pleased to see him. It shouldn't be this hard—they were legally married. It had to be a start.

He threw his briefcase on the lounge and gave in to the impulse to casually drop a kiss on the top of Georgia's head as he passed.

'What was that for?' Georgia laughed up at him and he swore then he would fight for the right to be a part of their lives.

'That is the new order of things. I'm home and I want to play, too.' Then he knelt down in front of Elsa and tickled her. 'Hey, young lady. Who said you could learn to crawl?'

He may have spoken to Elsa, who grimaced at him ferociously, but he listened for a response from Georgia to see how she had taken his welcome salute.

'Right, then,' she said. 'You get to stay with the naked-bottomed one and I will change, because time has slipped away, and then you can shower after me.'

Georgia rose gracefully to her feet. She grinned at him and passed the disposable nappy she'd tucked under her arm before she sailed from the room.

Not too bad. At least she hadn't banned him from head kisses. 'Mummy thinks she can boss me around. What do you think of that?' He bounced Elsa on his hip. 'Though it is no hardship being left with you, young lady.'

That morning Max had shared his breakfast again with Elsa after her mother had gone to work. They'd had a fine old time and if Georgia worked the next few weeks, he planned on sharing his breakfast with his stepdaughter every day. 'Let's get this nappy on and we'll have a walk out in the garden with the puppy.'

He carried a glaring Elsa out onto the veranda and the big dog moaned with pleasure when Max bounced the baby's toes on his back for a moment. Elsa's frown fell away and she chortled at the feel of rough doggy hair on her feet and then Max swooped her away to walk around the garden.

'See the birdies? Birdies.' On cue, the rainbow lorikeets screamed between themselves as they fought over the flowering bottlebrush bush, ripping the fine needles of flowers as they sought the nectar.

'Noisy birdies,' Max said, and Elsa crowed and opened and shut her hands in delight. The sun was heading behind the hills and the shadows were lengthening in the garden by the time Max took her back inside. The mosquitoes would be out soon and Elsa was tiring.

Dinner and bed for the baby. If only it was dinner and bed for Max, he mocked himself.

He knew who he wanted to bed, though even just holding Georgia through the long nights would be heaven. Nothing new there.

Georgia looked beautiful again tonight, Max thought soberly two hours later when they both sat down at the table. Her hair was loose and she had some flowing shirt with a deeper neckline than usual that highlighted the smoothness of her long throat.

They'd skipped pre-dinner drinks on the veranda because of Elsa's late settling and now he was separated by the width of the table. He just wanted to touch her.

The sky grew inky outside, with clouds obscuring the stars, and Mrs White had retired for the night, leaving dinner in the kitchen.

Before he'd come home Max had rung through to see which receiving hospital Del had ended up in and how the babies were. Mother and the newborn twins were stable and settled. The one bad piece of news had been the consultant who had received them—Sol Winton.

Max still debated if Georgia should be told because he suspected the news would upset her. He knew her ex-husband had given Georgia an emotionally hard time as well as making her severely depressed.

During the last four months Max had seen no signs of paranoia or depression—and anyone with a colicky baby could easily plead depression—so Winton had obviously had some hidden agenda.

Still, she was away from him now and, theoretically, hearing about his hospital shouldn't upset her too much.

He dragged his thoughts away from his quandary and caught Georgia in the middle of a half-hidden yawn. She even looked cute when she yawned.

'You must be tired,' he said. 'It takes a while to get used to shifts again.'

She tucked her hand away from her mouth ruefully. 'Not really. Do I look it?' In fact, she looked a little crestfallen at his observation, and Max grinned.

'You look positively haggard, darling,' he drawled, and Georgia blinked before she realised he was joking.

'Teaser.' She shook her head at him and changed the subject. 'How was the rest of your day?'

Max tilted his head. 'Actually, you look stunning.' He watched her frown at him but he was darned if he shouldn't say it when he meant it.

He moved on when she grimaced at him. 'Now, what was your question? My day? After our exciting morning?'

He ticked off his fingers. 'Del's twin girls were born at midday and all are well. They weighed over twelve hundred grams each so I don't know where she was hiding that weight. The girls are breathing for themselves and may start tube feeds tomorrow.'

'That's wonderful.'

Before Georgia could ask more he went on hoping to change to another topic. 'Even bigger news is that Tayla and my brother, Paul, have decided to get married. We're invited to the wedding but guess who is not invited to be bridesmaid?'

'Me?' Georgia tried to look sad.

He shook his head sadly. 'I know you must be dreadfully disappointed.'

Georgia put down her spoonful of pumpkin soup and looked up with a grin. 'That's wonderful. On both counts.' Her eyes sparkled with laughter.

She stirred her soup with a smile. 'You know, I think they will do very well together.'

She tilted her head. 'Which hospital did you say had the neonatal beds? Del didn't have to go to Canberra, did she?'

CHAPTER EIGHT

MAX should have known her empathy with her patients wouldn't wane. She'd need to know Del was happy where she was.

'No. I didn't say.'

Max hesitated and then answered. 'Lower Mountains Base Hospital.' He wondered if they were both going to pretend the connection to her ex-husband's hospital didn't exist.

Georgia's spoon stilled and then she took another mouthful. The colour had left her face and he cursed himself for not withholding the information.

She swallowed slowly and then spoke to her spoon. 'I'm glad all went well. I wonder how she'll manage without Shannon to talk for her.'

She went on without pausing but at least she looked up at him. 'I hear Susie has recovered from having her baby in the car and wants to go home tomorrow morning.' Her voice was extra-bright and his chest tightened in sympathy for her.

'I'm sure that will be fine.' Max was in a different dilemma now. He didn't want to upset Georgia by bringing the subject up again but she needed to know he was happy to talk about how she felt if she wished.

If she gave him the option. The silence lengthened and he guessed they were both going to pretend nothing was wrong.

Georgia felt gutted. She wasn't even sure Max knew it was Sol's hospital.

She tried to quell the pictures that rose unbidden into her mind. It's OK, she told herself. The connection with Del wasn't so bad. Was it?

Sol would have to be the receiving consultant on duty to have had any contact with Del. Even then the registrar would probably have been the one to read the nurse's notes.

There really wasn't much chance Sol would track them down, and she doubted Del would speak much about Meeandah except to nod.

Georgia just wished she hadn't been the one to sign and print her name on the nurse's transfer letter—along with Max's. She still signed her maiden name because of the rigmarole of changing names through the nurse's registration board so Sol would recognise it.

'We have the weekend before us. What can we do to put a smile on your face?'

Georgia looked up at him blankly.

'Would you like to go somewhere? For the weekend?' This time it had been Max to change the subject and she was glad because her own brain still felt sluggish with shock.

The idea of hiding away from the world appealed to Georgia greatly. 'Let's go away. Drive bush roads for the weekend. Follow where the tracks take us.'

Nobody would find them and she would be able to push the thoughts of Sol far into the back of her mind again. She'd just begun to feel settled and happy but now the secure rock Max had built for her had crumbled away with only one obstetric transfer to Sol's hospital. Her response in itself was disheartening.

'Go camping, you mean?' Max was looking at her as if to judge how serious she was.

The idea promised sanctuary, Georgia thought, clutching at anything to divert her mind away from the past. 'No phones, no people—just the bush and us.'

'I think it's a great idea to take some picnic supplies and get offroad,' Max said cautiously, and she looked up in surprise. She'd thought he would have jumped at the chance to camp out.

He went on. 'How about we run back into the coast at night to sleep with civilised showers and comfortable beds? Away from the mosquitoes, for Elsa's sake.'

The urgency to hide loomed larger than comfort for Georgia. 'Elsa will be fine. I thought you enjoyed roughing it.'

'Logistically it's a little easier for me to camp than you and Elsa. If you don't fancy the coast there are fabulous mountain retreats in the Lamington National Park. We could slip across into Queensland and go up into the mountains and make log fires in the retreats at night when Elsa goes to bed.'

She sighed with relief. They could still go. 'That would be wonderful, Max. Could we?'

'Sure.' He stood to collect their plates. 'We can decide where we'll go after dinner. I'll go online later and check it all out. I do have friends up that way who own a lodge.'

She watched him head for the kitchen. She normally would have jumped up to help him. He was solicitous and she guessed he must have connected the hospitals, too.

She felt like someone had dropped a boulder on her smooth life when she wasn't looking. To get away this weekend would at least give her time to get her thoughts together without jumping at every sound.

She hugged herself and the feel of her arms reminded her how it had felt when Max had first agreed to look after her. That first day that Sol had seen Elsa.

She stood up, walked to the window and gazed out into the inky blackness. Far away on the ocean a container ship rode the horizon. Alone and undefended it could still look after itself.

She wasn't ready to do the same and she didn't know what to do for the best.

What if Max was in danger, too?

Max entered the room and placed the dishes on the table, not trying to be quiet. He expected her to turn from the window but she didn't seem to hear him return.

When he touched her on the shoulder she flinched so violently that his hand pulled back and his own pulse rate soared.

'Hey.' He stepped closer now that she knew he was there and slid his arm around her shoulder. When she didn't pull away he turned her into his chest and encircled her. She was shaking and his chest tightened. He would protect them both with his last breath.

'You only need to tell me how you feel and I'll share it with you,' he said and teased her gently. 'You're not alone and I'm deeply offended you think you are.'

'I'm sorry, Max.' She sniffed into his shirt and his hand slid up and brushed the hair out of her eyes. Her expression of deep foreboding twisted his stomach.

He wanted to snatch up Georgia and her daughter and carry them away from any chance of Sol finding them and that was when he began to realise she would never be free until the Sol issue was resolved.

'Even if it is only for a year, I am your husband. Who better to protect you? I may seem a flipperty sort of fellow but I do have hidden strengths.'

'You don't seem flipperty at all. You're wonderful.' She glanced at his muscled arms and gave a twisted smile. 'Your strength isn't hidden and I don't deserve your patience with my bogeyman.'

'Cut it out, Georgia. If we are anything, we are friends.' He lifted her chin. 'Isn't that right?'

'Yes.' She nodded and buried her face back into his shirt.

'So friends trust each other and your worries are my worries. But we do need to communicate. It is very hard to help you when you shut me out.'

'I know.' She straightened and he hugged her one last time before he forced himself to let her go.

'Come and eat. Then we'll talk. Unless we feed all this food to the dog, Mrs White will find out we didn't enjoy her hard labour.'

'I couldn't eat a thing.'

Max stared down at her and she looked so forlorn and lost that his heart ached to ease her pain.

He leant forward again and kissed her gently on the lips with all the tenderness she inspired in him. She sighed against him and didn't pull away, and when he drew back she turned her face towards him and leaned up to kiss him back. He forced back the desire to pull her into his arms and really kiss her so she could forget the man that stood between them.

'I'm scared, Max.' Georgia leant her head on his chest again.

'I know, darling.' He had felt her tremble beneath his lips when their lips had met. He couldn't see how one man could inspire such dread but Georgia obviously could.

'Hold me,' she whispered.

He'd imagined holding her in his arms many times, but not for this reason. Poor baby. 'Any time you want, Georgia. You only have to give me a sign.' He gathered her in and she rested her cheek against him. Then she turned to look up at him.

When she closed her eyes and invited another kiss, he could no more stem his response than stop the waves on the beach he could hear in the distance.

He cupped her chin and traced the pure lines of her face with his mouth as he'd longed to do since Monday night. Her skin felt like velvet and glowed like cream, and he wanted to taste both. He brushed her eyebrows with his lips and then the tip of her nose before settling on her lips in homecoming.

She tasted divine, as he'd known she would, and he searched deeper, always waiting in case she pulled away, but she responded with a hunger that smouldered like his own. Her response tore at him so strongly it was difficult to remember he had to hold back.

When he raised his lips from hers to stand back, she murmured in denial, still with her eyes closed, so he leaned forward and took her mouth again in a kiss that left them both breathless and stunned by the connection between them.

They stood, wrapped in each other's arms, breathing as one, and for Max it was as if he were standing under the full brunt of a waterfall, and he could no more hold back the water than he could hold back the urge to carry Georgia to his bed and make her his.

'I need you to take me, Max.' Her words echoed his own desire, but the need in her voice inflamed him as nothing else could have. When he lifted her into his arms her head lay back to expose the soft column of her throat, and he brushed his face against the tender skin there to inhale the perfume of her skin before straightening.

She sighed into him with such softness and warmth he pulled her against his body and whisked her up the stairs before either of them came to their senses.

When he placed her gently on his bed she reached up for him without hesitation, but a brief moment of sanity stilled his hand before she tugged at him and he lowered himself down beside her.

'Are you sure?'

'Kiss me, Max.'

He'd dreamed many times that he would hold her in his arms and protect her from the world. Yet though he wanted to make her his, he needed to ensure her own feelings of self-belief were restored. That was more important than anything. For him this was right, but what of her?

For Georgia, all intrusion from Sol had vanished with the safety of Max around her. Somewhere in the distance her brain disagreed, but the last time Max had lowered his mouth she'd felt the leashed force of his need and that had made her forget. She wanted that again. She pulled him closer and

answered the call without permission from any
inner voice.

She slaked his hunger with her own and when,
peripherally, she felt her clothing move and then his
bare skin against hers, she could no more stop her
response than she could stop her own heart beating.

His chest was rock hard against her and flattened
her breasts gloriously against him. Her fingers
skimmed the V of hair on his belly and she exulted
in his caressing hands as she caressed him.

It wasn't enough.

Suddenly there was no time for niceties, neither
did she want them. She wanted Max.

She wanted Max over her, in her, joined to her,
and she wanted him now. She'd never felt a need as
strong and overpowering as this before, but the need
was ancient and she demanded his response to wipe
out all that had come before.

She could feel Max try to slow the pace but deep
inside her a dark fear despaired that something
would prevent their union, that some sinister force
would tear them apart, and the very least she wanted
was this consummation to make her whole again.

Max rose above her and she stared up at him. His
strong throat soared above her and his chiselled
features were outlined in the darkened room. His
golden eyes stared down at her with all the fierce
need for possession she'd stoked in him with her
own need.

Their eyes locked and she reached up to savour
the bulge of taut muscles in his arms as he lowered

himself gently against her. Her eyes widened as he entered her, slowly, intimately questing, deeper and deeper, until his whispered name escaped her.

He stared down and the adoration in his face made the tears slip beneath her lids and then he withdrew until she protested. He smiled and entered her again. Slow and steady and deep until again she moaned his name and only then did he quicken the pace.

Georgia clutched at his back to stay with him and they rose and fell together in a long slow erotic dance that drove everything out of their minds except the feel of each other in union.

When it was over they lay together, her head on his chest and his arm encircling her as if he'd never let her go.

She knew the moment he slept and she turned her head and kissed his chest. 'I don't want to hurt you,' she whispered. 'Maybe there is hope. We'll see.'

Through the night they joined again, but this time in a slow dance of discovery that scaled the heights again in a different way until much later they slept, entwined.

This time Max lay awake until the morning when he watched her wake up to see if he had been a fool.

He'd promised he would keep her safe and what had he done at the first temptation but taken her like a caveman bearing his prize? He hadn't been able to resist and now he scanned her precious face for any sign of regret.

At least he couldn't make her pregnant. He

winced with the pain that reflection brought, but the pain was nothing to the thought of losing Georgia.

She'd been mind-blowing and incredible but even in the midst of their magical storm he'd feared she'd only wanted to escape from her memories and that he'd taken advantage of her when he should have waited for the right time.

Now he was afraid he had created more dilemmas for her, which was the last thing he had intended.

He knew he loved this woman above all things but he also accepted he had to create an out for her if that was what she needed. No matter that it would rip out his heart to put distance between them again—a greater risk was destroying any chance of their future.

Not when he'd found the one woman he'd never known had been out there. He could not taint that again with her regret.

'Good morning?' He couldn't help the question mark at the end of his greeting and inside his head a devil mocked him.

'Good morning, Max.' Georgia chewed her lip.

Max's stomach plummeted and he forced himself to smile. He'd known she would regret it.

'There is something I need to tell you,' she said and his gut twisted.

At least she hadn't said she regretted the night, yet. Max brushed her cheek with his hand and then reached for her fingers to hold in his. 'So tell me.'

She searched his face and what she saw there encouraged her to go on. 'When I moved back in with Sol to protect my friend…' She paused and closed her eyes for a second as if compelling the words to come, 'He overpowered me and forced himself on me in a horrific night I thought would never end… And that is how Elsa was conceived.' She shook her head at her own stupidity. 'I hadn't foreseen him doing that.'

Max's voice was low with shock and how he would have done things differently if he'd known. He didn't know what to say. 'Did you go to the police?'

'Who would believe me when he was my husband? He's respected and I was supposed to have paranoia. They'd say that I went back to him and cried rape. I was shattered and the whole situation was a nightmare.'

Max felt the words hammer into his brain and unconsciously he squeezed her hand. He could tell there was more. 'Go on.'

'I ensured my friend was safe from him and I left. I vowed no man would ever do that to me again. I never wanted to think about sex again. Last night all that changed. I needed you and you answered my need.' She smiled crookedly. 'Handsomely. You've taught me to trust my instincts again.

'I'm sorry if you think I used you but suddenly I needed you to wipe the slate clean and show me that making love is just that. And you showed me how it should be and I can never thank you enough for restoring my faith and my self-esteem. But last night was not the beginning for us.'

Max felt as if his heart was breaking for her courage. 'My poor darling.'

He didn't know how she'd stayed as sane and strong as she had with such a man. Max ached to come across Sol in some dark alley some time and make amends for Georgia.

He had trouble getting the words out past his regret that he hadn't known her then. 'Not all men are like that.'

She shook her head as if to say that wasn't her concern. 'I'm scared for you, Max.'

How could she worry about him at a time like this? 'Don't be, because I swear to you now, that man will never hurt you again. If he tries, he will have me to deal with.'

He wanted to tell her that he truly loved her with all his heart and soul, but to pressure her now with that would be selfish. He needed to step back and lay more groundwork before he went there.

Instead he said, 'Let's still go away for the weekend. Forget all this and just relax together with Elsa.'

'Could we?' He saw the way she looked up eagerly.

He nodded. 'We could pack and be out of here by ten, if you still want to.'

Her eyes met his. 'I'd like that.'

Down the hallway the baby cried and the chance of more discussion was lost as she slipped from his bed. She pulled on his robe and he knew she would go to her room with Elsa and not return. He knew from the way she didn't even look back as she left.

He knew what he was fighting for and he was even more determined. He would woo her as she deserved.

CHAPTER NINE

THEY drove to the mountains and the spectacular scenery lifted Georgia's spirits in a way she couldn't believe, especially now that there was even more to think about.

It seemed Max was going to make it easy for her by not discussing last night. Her body glowed every time she thought of those stolen hours—but that's what they had been. Stolen and not to be repeated.

Max had no idea what they were up against. Their time together had been an amazing escape from the reality and despair that just hearing Sol's name had again left her with.

Thankfully, it seemed that Max would bide his time and perhaps, if a miracle occurred, maybe some time in the future they could travel that road.

At least Max had helped her understand that when someone cared for you, making love was just that—making love. Love in a way both parties felt more together—not less!

But though their intimate time had strengthened

her acceptance of how much she loved Max, it had also given her more reason to leave.

Max desired her, there was no doubt about that, but this morning's relaxed dismissal of their night together had made her wonder if he had the capacity to love or just make love.

Maybe it was better if Max didn't love her. Safer for everyone.

They stopped many times along the way north to Queensland. The all-terrain vehicle crawled along hardly used bush trails, showed them great vistas over rainforests and let them enjoy escarpments decked with eagles and graced with tumbling waterfalls that smashed down onto boulders far below.

Lunch was another picnic packed by Mrs White, which they had beside a cold mountain stream, and afternoon tea saw them back on the coast and an hour and a half east of their destination.

They drove through the Lamington National Park three thousand feet up to the rainforest retreat and Max was greeted like a long-lost friend.

The owners, Paddy and Morgan, had even arranged for their daughter, Trish, to sit with Elsa in the room later that evening while Max and Georgia enjoyed their dinner.

The suite Max had secured, instead of the two single rooms she'd expected, made her pause at the door, and Max's hand rested on the small of her back as he waited for her to say something.

They could see over the canopy of trees from the

window but it was the two big canopied beds that dominated her vision.

'The suite is lovely, but it seems strange they didn't have two single rooms.'

'I didn't ask for singles, Georgia. We're a family, even though you and I may not sleep together tonight.' Max met her eyes unswervingly. 'I thought you'd be more secure if I was right here with you and Elsa.'

When she didn't answer he went on. 'Despite last night, you can trust me. As you can see, we have two doubles and there's a cot for Elsa.'

He shrugged and changed tack. 'Actually, I did it for myself. The nightmares have been a problem and tonight I'll have you to protect me.'

Georgia glared at him. She wouldn't make a fuss. It would be ridiculous after what had passed between them, but she'd thought he'd understood. 'I hope Elsa keeps you awake all night.'

He shrugged. 'She's done that before.'

This wasn't happening. Last night had been a mistake that she couldn't regret but had no plans to repeat. 'Any designs you have on me will not come to fruition, Max.'

'I'll have you know that I am saving myself.' Max averted his face primly.

As if. 'You're not a virgin any more, Max.' Georgia couldn't help the reluctant grin he'd dragged from her, despite her best efforts to remain cross.

'That was only my body,' he said solemnly.

'You…are…mad.'

'I'm crazy with it all right,' he said, and this time no humour lit his face. She was a fool. He really had only thought of her, but before she could apologise for doubting him, Elsa stirred.

'I'll see you down in the lobby where the maps are displayed,' he said, and she filled the silence with movement as Max slipped out the door.

He'd told her to trust him and she'd never had cause to disbelieve him. That was the baggage Sol had left her with, and she wasn't going to start not trusting Max.

Elsa settled quickly after her feed, and Trish arrived with her own dinner on a plate.

After a brief discussion over what to do if Elsa woke up, Georgia completed her make-up and brushed her hair again. Strangely nervous, she went to meet Max downstairs.

As she came down the stairs the way his gaze travelled over her made her glad that she had spent the extra few minutes on her appearance and her nerves dissipated like smoke from the chimney.

This was Max. Tall, gorgeous Max, with his incredible body and amazing hands and amazing mouth that just thinking about sent waves of colour to her cheeks. Max, her refuge, her husband, even if it was only for a year, and the man who was looking at her as if she were the one person he'd ever wait for.

Max smiled that wonderful smile of his and held

out his hand, and when she put her fingers in his she realised how right it had been to get away.

'Welcome to our first real date,' he said as the waiter showed them through the doors to a private table in a bay-windowed alcove.

She smiled. After all they'd been through. 'For first-timers we've had our moments of interest together,' she said, and the thought of last night tingled her skin in a pink glow.

'That's no excuse not to catch up on the stuff we missed out on,' Max said, and she saw the flutes of champagne and laughed.

A long-stemmed red rose lay across her setting and she glanced up at the waiter with a smile. 'Does everyone get a rose when they come here?'

'Only those on their first date,' the waiter said, and smiled. The man pulled out her chair and Georgia sat and looked around at the restaurant as Max chose the wine for the meal.

The room was long, with several bay windows overlooking the valley below that disappeared in the darkening twilight.

A log fire crackled in a central fireplace and added pleasant warmth without overheating the room. Her throat felt warm but she knew the heat was from something else.

Exposed wooden beams crossed the ceiling with relics from the roaring days of the pioneers, but there was nothing rough about the service or the fine china.

The waiter left after ensuring they were happy,

and Max raised his glass to hers in a toast. 'To a tranquil weekend.'

She'd drink to that. 'Utopia.' They clinked the delicate crystal and she sighed blissfully. 'What a gorgeous place. You've obviously been here before.'

Max glanced around and his face softened. 'My aunt loved this restaurant. I used to come here at least once during my holidays with her.'

There was a note in his voice she'd never heard before. 'Tell me about your childhood and parents.'

He put his glass down and grimaced. 'Now, that's a boring story.'

She frowned at him and he held up his hand. 'But I did say I'd answer questions.'

He smiled whimsically. 'My father was a worthy man, an excellent surgeon with very little sense of humour, who retired one month before he died of a heart attack.'

Georgia stretched her hand across the table and touched his in sympathy where his fingers lay against the tablecloth. He looked at her briefly and then looked away.

'My mother now lives in America with her new husband and apparently is reasonably happy.'

It sounded emotionless and she couldn't help being disappointed by his distance.

'Try a little harder, Max,' she said. Though what did she expect when she was the one creating distance all the time?

He sighed laboriously and then went on. 'My parents had very little in common with each other, or me, but led a very civilised life together. My brother and I spent a lot of years at boarding school.

'Fortunately, I spent a lot of my holidays with my mother's sister, who owned the house in Byron, while Paul stayed home and became even more worthy.'

His face softened and his beautiful mouth curved. 'My Aunt Beatrice I could talk about for hours.'

'Please, do,' she said softly, aching for the boy who had obviously been lost in boarding school and at a family that hadn't known how to love.

Maybe that was why he had chosen Tayla and had such low expectations of marriage.

'Beatrice was a widow. Her husband died early in their marriage, which was very considerate of him. I'm sure she was happier doing as she liked. She was an Amazon of a woman who adored bright colours with the black she said she wore for mourning.'

He grinned at the memories. 'She could put colours together. Black and gold stripes, black and emerald spots, black and hot pink, sometimes all of them at once, and always adorned with lots of beads.'

He shook his head. 'She'd have sunflowers growing in her garden and they were all over the house in vases. She'd sing the blues in this gravelly voice that would raise gooseflesh on my arms.'

He glanced around the room as if seeing memories from the past. 'She loved to sculpt and paint and you've seen all the luminous stars she glued onto the ceilings in the house at Byron. She loved the stars.'

'Beatrice sounds wonderful.' But best of all was the affection she could see for his aunt on Max's face. He'd loved his aunt. There was hope yet.

'I adored her. She could be incredibly selfish but that appealed to me too—so much more interesting than worthy. She listened to me and told me she loved my company, when my parents couldn't wait to send me back to school.'

His face became expressionless. 'She nursed me when I was sick in my late teens and made me see how much I had to live for.'

She didn't like the sound of that illness. 'In what way were you sick, Max?'

'Hodgkin's disease. I had it for two years and stayed in Byron with her. She drove me to Brisbane for treatment.'

Georgia knew Hodgkin's could kill and that it struck down adolescents and young adults, more often young men. 'You were one of the lucky ones, then?'

'They say I'm cured.' He nodded but there was the sadness behind his eyes she'd seen before. Suddenly she realised why he'd never seemed to want children—the radiotherapy would make that unlikely. She didn't comment because he didn't, though her heart ached for him. But it all began to make sense.

'How did your aunt die?'

'Beatrice? In her sleep. Peacefully. After a big dinner party one night five years ago. She loved company and food—the higher in cholesterol the better.'

He glanced down at the béchamel sauce on his steak and smiled wryly. 'Enough about me. Try to enjoy your meal without my sob story to put you off.'

Conversation turned desultory and time passed.

With dessert Max had questions of his own. She could tell he was happy to not talk about himself any more. 'So, did you have a perfect childhood?'

She shrugged, reluctant to lose the mood of warm companionship. 'My parents were very much in love, and instilled in me that love is worth waiting for. But they died when I was young and an only child.'

'Who brought you up?'

'Harry. Tayla's mother was very like Tayla. She wasn't a warm woman and Tayla resented my presence in her family.

'Harry tried to make up for it because he is a kind and decent man, but that only made Tayla worse. Harry's always been able to see Tayla's faults and he protected me to some extent. I tried not to be too much of a problem.

'Tayla's mother died when I was eighteen and Harry and Tayla are my only relatives, except for my darling Elsa.'

His hand came across the table and squeezed

hers for a moment where she held the glass. 'And your darling husband, Max.'

'That's true.' She smiled at him and then glanced at the grandfather clock against the wall. 'That was a wonderful dinner. Thank you, Max.'

Max looked at the clock, too. 'It's still early. Let's take a stroll before we go up. There's a night walk to the glow-worm forest that only takes about half an hour each way. You could check on Elsa first and then join me.'

'Glow-worms?'

'Yes,' he said, and his voice dropped low and portentous, like a 1950s horror film. 'The larvae of the fungus gnat.'

She burst out laughing. 'Imagine having that pearl of information at your fingertips.'

'You have no idea what information I have.' Max steepled his hands. 'Hurry and you will learn more.'

'Yes, sir.' She saluted and turned for the stairs.

She chuckled all the way up to the room. If it was fine with Morgan's daughter, seeking glow-worms sounded like a lovely way to end the evening.

Max watched her walk away. The curve of her hips, the column of her neck under her swinging hair. So close and yet so far.

He wasn't going to make the same mistake twice. He'd just have to make sure he didn't touch her because there was no doubt they had ignition problems he couldn't be sure he could control.

She was back within minutes, pulling her woollen wrap around her shoulders. 'Elsa hasn't stirred and Trish is halfway through a movie she wants to see the end. So we are free for an hour. Show me the worms.'

'I love it when you talk dirty to me,' he said with a deadpan face.

'I'm a very earthy woman.' she quipped back, and they smiled at each other.

It was blissful to feel so relaxed and carefree. She couldn't remember the last time she'd felt this way and it was all due to a fabulous dinner, a place no one could find them, and Max and his care.

She followed him out past the tennis courts and the light of the moon reflected off the beaten dirt path in patches to illuminate their way.

Lush foliage closed in on the path but the moon made the leaves silvery and unthreatening. Somewhere she could hear water as it tinkled over rocks, and nocturnal animals scurried away from the intruders who had interrupted their night's business.

'So where are we going?' Georgia stumbled over a tree root that had bulged into the path and Max caught her wrist to steady her. His fingers sent warm trails up her arm and she felt cocooned in an aura of protection she didn't want to push away.

'Glow-Worm Gully is along this path called the Wishing Tree Track.' He squeezed her hand. 'You'll just have to hang onto me.'

'How fortunate you know where you're going.' She glanced up at him.

'Isn't it? This was my favourite treat when

Beatrice stayed here, although she complained all the way down and all the way back. I can remember much trivia from those times so watch out or I may inflict it on you.'

Georgia stumbled again. 'Don't normal people carry a torch?'

'Sorry.' Max slowed his pace. 'Yes, and I have one, but if I shine it on a glow-worm, it won't turn its light back on for fifteen minutes.'

'So we stumble along in the pitch black.'

He sighed loudly. 'It is not pitch black. It's called becoming accustomed to the dark.'

'Sheesh. It's like school again.' She could feel his smile even though she couldn't see it, which made the smile widen on her own face. 'So tell me about glow-worms. What is a fungus gnat?'

'A fungus gnat is a bit like a mosquito—hence the gnat part—and the larvae it lays are encased in bioluminescent cases that attract insects onto the sticky threads hanging below.'

'And if I was to ask the definition of bioluminescent?'

'It means luminous from chemical byproducts produced by the larvae. The blue-green glow from the larvae's taillight attracts the larvae's food.'

'So excretion? Poo light?'

'You are such a downer.'

'Realism, sunny boy. I'm a realist.'

'If you want realism, that's not all the glow-worms attract. They attract tourists—about six million dollars' worth for tour operators a year.'

The conversation stopped because they'd rounded a bend in the path and ahead and to the side, in the cracks and crevices under a deep overhang of rock, tiny tendrils of blue-green luminescence shone in hundreds of strands.

The more she looked, the more she saw. Georgia was silenced. Her hand tightened on Max's and she sighed with delight.

'Wow. Now, that's one spectacular show.'

She could tell Max was pleased with himself and her response.

'You should appreciate the world of the glow-worm,' he said. 'Every time a midge or similar insect runs into a hanging line it sticks and is hauled up by the worm, using its mouth, and stored for later.'

'So much for my fantasy of pretty glowing worms swinging in a friendly fashion in the dark.'

She frowned. 'In that case, they have a remarkable similarity to my ex-husband.'

She felt Max's scrutiny and he didn't say anything for a moment. Then he squeezed her hand again. 'Let's not spoil the night. Would you like to know about the mating habits of the parents?'

She appreciated his effort but she was upset with herself for destroying the mood.

Georgia slipped her hand out of his and rubbed her arms. It had been fun but now she just wanted to get back to Elsa. 'I don't think so. It was lovely, Max, but let's go back.'

Max got it. She could see that even in the semi-dark. 'Of course. Tomorrow we might come back and see the path by daylight. It is magnificent along here.'

'Sure.'

They returned to the guesthouse and Morgan's daughter was happy to see them. Elsa had woken up and in her less than discreet way had decided she wanted her mother.

By the time Georgia had calmed her daughter, Max had showered and reappeared in boxers and white T-shirt for bed.

Georgia tried not to look but the fabric stretched across his chest and biceps lovingly and activated somnolent nerves deep in her stomach. He looked far too masculine to easily ignore and she wasn't sure she was safer sharing a room with him at all.

'I'll take her if you want to change.' He held out his hands towards the baby and Elsa went happily to him.

For Georgia it felt as if she'd just handed over her only form of protection and she stepped back quickly.

Max frowned but didn't say anything as he turned away with Elsa and walked to the window. 'See the stars, Elsa? They're like glow-worms in the sky. Mummy saw the glow-worms tonight.'

Georgia could hear him talking away to Elsa as she closed the bathroom door. Now, why had she behaved like that? It wasn't as if Max was going to jump on her.

More likely she'd had the urge to run her hands

over him—though he did have a partiality to follow her lead when she made an offer—so it would be very easy to start something.

All through her shower, every touch of her own hand made her think of last night and of Max.

When she dried herself, even the towel seemed to sensitise her skin.

She was not going there. No matter what Max said or did she would not sleep with him. Absolutely. She chewed her lip as she opened the door.

When she came out of the bathroom Max had settled Elsa back in the cot, climbed into his own bed, and turned his bedside light out.

She guessed it was his way of saying she didn't have to worry. It was unfortunate that she felt lonely and frustrated when she climbed into her own generous bed and pulled up the thick duvet.

'Goodnight, Max,' she said, and she blushed in the dark at the forlorn note in her voice.

'Goodnight, Georgia.'

The next morning was fun.

After breakfast served in front of the fire Max carried Elsa in a pouch on his chest and they tramped along winding bush tracks and picnicked beside a mountain stream above a waterfall.

Elsa loved being with Max and Georgia wouldn't have minded it herself to be that close to Max's gorgeous chest. She was definitely becoming more fixated. Luckily the other scenery was spectacular as well.

When they arrived back at the retreat for afternoon tea, they were all exhausted but exhilarated from the mountain air. It was sad to have to pack to leave.

Max promised they would come again in the not-too-distant future, and Georgia added the day to her increasing store of wonderful memories with Max.

The phone call came just as Max carried Elsa to the car.

Georgia had gone back to the room for one last check that they hadn't left anything behind when the room phone rang.

She frowned and picked it up. 'Had a nice weekend, Mrs Winton?'

Sol! Nausea rose like a wave in her throat and she sucked the air in through her nostrils and swallowed before she could open her mouth.

Her voice when it came out was husky with distress. 'I'm not Mrs Winton!'

'No,' Sol said. 'You're Mrs Beresford—so I hear—but not for long! I'm coming for you and our daughter. But something needs to be done first.'

Then he rang off.

CHAPTER TEN

THE handset dropped from her fingers and spun giddily at the end of its cord beside the table. Georgia backed unsteadily across the room until she bumped into the bed behind her just as her legs collapsed from under her and she sat back limply. She hugged her knees.

How had Sol tracked her up here? She straightened slowly and looked around the room for inspiration. She had to tell Max he was in danger.

Then the next thought crashed into her. If she told Max, what would he do? She knew what he would do. He'd search out Sol—if Sol could find them then Max could find Sol—and Max had sworn he would not let Sol upset her again.

She needed to think this through before she talked to Max. He had to be safe. She heard his footsteps before he arrived and she tried to school her face.

'What are you doing?' Max stopped at the door and looked in. 'Elsa's in the car and Morgan is watching her. Are you ready to go?'

She didn't meet his eyes and something made him cross the room to sit beside her. 'Hello? You OK, sweetheart?'

Her eyes met his briefly but skidded away as if searching for something. 'I'm sorry, Max. I just had a really rotten pain in my head and it made me feel quite sick.'

Max frowned. He didn't like the sound of that. 'You're not going to have a cerebral aneurysm on me, are you?'

She forced a laugh. 'Typical doctor. Always assume the worst case scenario. Not anything as dramatic. I've a headache. Maybe even the beginnings of a migraine.'

She stood up and he saw that she was quite unsteady on her feet. He took her wrist and measured her pulse. Her heart rate was flying.

'Maybe we should stay here until you feel better. We can do that if you like.'

'No!' She'd answered too sharply and Max watched her try to play down her agitation and his gut tightened. 'Elsa's already in the car, you said. I'll be fine. It will be good to be home.'

Max studied her face. 'Are you all right, Georgia?'

'I'll be fine.' She turned towards the door and he could see she forced herself to take steps that she could barely manage. 'I'd really rather go home.'

At least she thought of it as home. 'All right.' Max put his hand under her elbow. 'Lean on me if you have to.'

Max tucked Georgia into the car and shut her door. He didn't like the way she looked and he would be happier when he had her home and settled.

He kissed Morgan's cheek. 'Thank you for making us so welcome.'

'You come back soon, Max. Your wife is a lovely woman.'

'Thanks, Morgan. I think so.'

Paddy came out from inside and wiped his hands on his trousers. 'Safe trip, friend.' He peered into the car and waved at Georgia. 'Your wife get the phone call from the other doctor, did she?'

Max stared at him and then nodded. He plastered a smile on his face when it was the last thing he felt like doing. 'Yes. Thanks.' They shook hands and Paddy and Morgan stood arm in arm to watch Max climb into the car.

Max kept smiling until they left the driveway. He didn't know what else to do. He glanced across at Georgia but she had her head back and her eyes closed.

Obviously Georgia had been in contact with Sol and she wasn't going to tell him.

That knowledge hit him like a hammer. It certainly explained the sudden headache and also his sudden urge to squeeze the life out of the defenceless steering-wheel beneath his fingers. He concentrated on loosening his grip without taking his eyes from the road.

If she didn't trust him then there wasn't much he could do except watch and wait.

But it was galling to think she wouldn't share her troubles with him. He'd thought them closer than that.

When they got home Georgia went straight to bed after feeding Elsa and Max watched her go. She'd said thanks for the weekend and nothing else and Max took his disappointment through to the library.

He'd do some background checks on Dr Winton, and he had a friend at Lower Mountains who owed him a favour.

Georgia knew that the sooner she distanced herself from Max the safer he would be. She needed to prepare a reason for her sudden disappearance and do as much as she could to safeguard Max's reputation. She needed to go to work one more day.

On Monday morning Karissa handed over the ward keys to Georgia. She turned back on her way out. 'By the way, I faxed a copy of the notes from your premature twins lady the other day. Some doctor wanted a copy of drugs given and not given. So if they ring, I've already done it.'

Georgia felt her stomach plummet. 'Did they say who wanted it?'

Karissa thought for a moment and then reached into the waste-paper basket and pulled out a screwed-up scrap of paper. She straightened it out. 'Yep. Didn't say why they wanted it but it was addressed to this guy. Dr S. Winton.'

It had started again. She'd known it would and yesterday's call had at least slightly prepared her.

The specialist's desire for Del to not have the treatment they'd expected became ominously clear. Sol had risked Del's twins' welfare to trap Max into not giving optimal care.

This was it, then. It was as if a blinding light flashed on in her head. The time for feeling sick and frightened had long passed and he was not going to win.

Now was time to put an end to this. She would not allow Sol to do this to Max. She, and anyone close to her, would not be a victim ever again.

She would leave this afternoon. Her mind was incredibly clear as she planned ahead.

'Before you go, Karissa. I need to let you know I can't do this week or next week after all. I'll be seeing the nurse manager today. My uncle is sick and I have to go back to Sydney. Max is staying here for the moment.'

Karissa sighed and then shrugged. 'I'm sorry about your uncle. Hope he's OK.'

Georgia could answer that honestly. 'He's been like a father to me since my parents died. I won't know how sick he is until I get there.

'In a few months I might even be looking at coming back up this way so I will try to get a few weeks together to help you get away.'

'Bummer you're leaving.' Then Karissa smiled philosophically. 'I hadn't booked anything yet in case it didn't work out. No worries. I can wait or something will come along.'

'I'm so sorry to have to let you down.'

Karissa shrugged. 'Maybe we'll catch you again.' She gave Georgia a hug. 'Never mind. Hope your uncle improves. It's been nice meeting you.'

Georgia watched her go and told herself she hadn't lied. Harry was sick. And if she didn't do something about Sol for once and for all, her life would continue to be a series of abrupt departures.

The time had come and she wasn't even afraid any more. Just incredibly, volcanically angry. How dared he?

For the moment all she knew was that she would never go back to Sol but she just as surely couldn't stay with Max. When she left Max, Sol had better leave him alone—or else.

Tayla's wedding plans would keep Tayla out of her way and Uncle Harry would have no problem with Elsa and herself moving into his house while she planned Sol's downfall.

If she told Max why she was going, he would want to take Sol on and save the world for her. But this was something she had to do for herself and for Elsa.

She would not allow Max to be dragged though the type of mud-slinging investigation Sol would have in mind. It was all her fault and it was time that she stopped being a victim.

The last thing she wanted was for Max to go

after Sol so she'd have to leave without telling
him. Georgia looked down at her mobile phone.
She'd have to turn it off or Max would phone her
and she knew she would cry.

CHAPTER ELEVEN

GEORGIA was gone.

She'd hired a car and left with Elsa as if there had been nothing between them.

Mrs White was devastated and the house had felt like a morgue without Georgia and Elsa when he'd come home from work. Now her phone was switched off.

Max knew Georgia had left because of Winton but how could she respect *him* so little that she hadn't even told him her ex-husband had contacted her. Or even that she was going?

What did she want him to think and why? Why not tell the truth?

Max stared out over the ocean and thought about all the possible reasons she had felt unable to talk to him. The most obvious one fell into place with a dull, ominous thud.

How had Winton got her back last time? Max slapped the veranda rail. With a threat to her friend! What if this time he'd threatened not Georgia or Elsa, but *him*?

Max glared out to sea and his hand tightened on the veranda rail. He wasn't worried about any threat Sol Winton could make to him but he was livid that Georgia had felt so powerless that she'd left to protect him.

Her lack of faith in his ability to protect himself, or her, hurt the most.

She had no idea of the cut-throat world of hospital administration, then, he thought, and smiled without humour.

It was his job to sort out troublemakers and those with plans for self-gain. He dealt with mini-gods like Winton all the time.

That would explain why Georgia hadn't told him about the phone call if she was concerned he would take matters into his own hands.

He had to find Winton, disarm him once and for all, with a cast-iron insurance against any further threats. Then he, Georgia and Elsa could get on with their lives together.

After that he would find Georgia and tell her he loved her.

Enough of this pussyfooting around. He wanted his family. She'd be with Harry. It was the logical place for her to go.

He rang the retired doctor from Meeandah who agreed to come back on call for the next two days while Max was away.

Then he offered Mrs White leave if she wanted it but she said she'd prefer to stay in case Georgia came back.

He threw some overnight clothes in his case and after one last phone call to his friend at Lower Mountains he climbed into his vehicle. Sol's plan had been quashed and an investigation started. The paper trail would catch Winton in the end and Max had made sure he would be drummed out of the medical fraternity.

When Max pulled out into the highway traffic the headlights of a truck coming straight for him made him swerve violently towards the side of the mountain.

Normally it would have been easy to correct the swerve. This time when he applied the brakes the pedal sank uselessly to the floor.

His last thought as the Hummer crashed through the guide rail was that he'd underestimated Sol, but at least he was in a decent vehicle for the hurtle down the mountainside.

Georgia's hand shook as she dialled Sol's home number. Elsa was finally asleep and cars whizzed past the motor inn she'd stopped at for the night.

She hadn't wanted to land on Harry's doorstep at midnight but she needed to let Sol know she had left Max and hopefully forestall any plans Sol had to cause trouble.

The phone rang six times and with each ring Georgia could feel her heart rate increase. Her mouth dried and suddenly she realised how emotionally fragile she was—and playing into Sol's hands. She put the phone down and stared at her fingers on the handset.

What was she doing? Hadn't she learned that weakness and not being prepared for confrontation with Sol caused more problems? She needed to be much smarter this time. It wasn't just herself at stake.

She needed proof that Sol was unbalanced and that he intended to threaten and blackmail her into submission again. She needed to ensure Sol could never take Elsa.

She would buy herself a tiny tape recorder to wear on her person. Then she would take the proof to the police and formally charge him. She should have done that a long time ago and she owed it to Max and herself to do it now.

Max's faith in her stood clear and firm and she knew she would do it this time. She would do this and then she would find Max and tell him she loved him.

The next morning, she and Elsa set things in motion. This time she would ensure she was safe.

She tucked the tiny voice-activated tape recorder inside her shirt and patted the small cylinder in her jacket pocket. The final purchase had been a last-minute decision and one that provided reassuring support.

She glanced in the rear-view mirror at her sleeping daughter. It was time to set up a meeting with Sol somewhere safe, like a public park.

She watched Elsa in the car outside the phone booth. Her daughter slept on as she dialled Sol's office.

'Dr Winton has gone away on urgent family business.' Sol's secretary's comment sounded as though it had been repeated many times. 'He won't be back until Wednesday.'

'Thank you.' Georgia put down the phone and returned to the car. She looked at Elsa. 'Now, that's an anticlimax, Elsa. I wonder where he went?'

Suddenly Georgia's heart rate picked up. Georgia snatched the mobile phone from her bag and checked the missed calls.

They'd flooded in. One from Max, one from Sol, four from Max's house at Byron Bay.

She stared at the calls and shuddered. Then the phone vibrated in her hand and she checked the number. Private.

She looked back at Elsa, drew a deep breath and pressed the button.

'Hello?'

'Georgia Beresford?' She didn't recognise the voice and her shoulders dropped in relief that it wasn't Sol.

'Yes?'

'Constable Ethan Moss, Byron Police Station.'

Georgia's heart thumped so loudly in her ears she could barely hear the man. She forced words out. 'Is something wrong?'

'We've been trying to contact you. Do you have a husband by the name of Max Beresford?'

Oh, no, please, God, she thought. 'Yes I do.'

'I'm sorry to have to tell you your husband was involved in a vehicle accident on the Pacific Highway last night and was airlifted in a critical condition to Newcastle Hospital.'

In slow motion she took the phone from her ear and looked at it. This couldn't be happening. She put the phone back to her ear and her hand was shaking. 'Is Max going to be all right?'

The voice was sympathetic but pragmatic. 'I suggest you ask his doctors that question, Mrs Beresford.'

'I will. Newcastle, you said.'

'That is correct, madam. His vehicle was destroyed in the descent but managed to protect him enough for the rescue crews to be able to transfer him to hospital alive.'

'Thank you.'

'Good morning, Mrs Beresford.'

Georgia dropped the phone on the seat beside her and lowered her head onto the steering-wheel.

Max. In an accident and critical. For a moment she couldn't think of the direction she needed to take to head north. She didn't know where to start.

Sol's whereabouts were the last thing she had to worry about now. She needed to get to Max.

Her phone rang again and she snatched it off the seat. 'Yes?'

'Mrs Beresford?'

'Mrs White?'

There was a pause then, 'Thank God I've been

able to contact you.' Georgia could hear the tears in Mrs White's voice and her own throat closed. 'The doctor is dangerously ill.'

Georgia tried to keep her own voice steady. 'I know. The police just rang me. I'm in Sydney but will drive to Newcastle as soon as I hang up.'

'I'm at the hospital but he's still in Theatre. Has been all night. They won't give me any information because I'm not the next of kin.'

Poor Mrs White. She loved Max like a son. 'I'll be there in an hour. We'll wait together with Elsa. Did you drive down last night?'

'They rang for you at eight and I left soon after that when I couldn't get you on the phone. I thought you would go to the hospital as soon as you heard and would need me there.'

'Thank you, Mrs White. It's good to know I have someone to share the waiting with. I'll see you soon.' Georgia ended the call and put the phone down.

She looked at Elsa strapped in the back and started the car. She concentrated resolutely on her driving. She couldn't allow negative thoughts to take her concentration. Max needed them to get there safely.

Deep down, inside her, along with the ball of fear in case she was too late, she knew that Max needed her.

When Georgia arrived at Newcastle Hospital she was directed to a waiting room outside the intensive care unit. Mrs White was there with mascara-stained tissues spread around her.

'I'd been trying to ring you all night since they rang me.' Mrs White's big panda eyes were smeared from crying.

'I know. I'm sorry.' Georgia gave her a hug and Mrs White hugged her back.

'How is he?'

'He came out of Theatre about half an hour ago and they took him straight into Intensive Care. I said you would be here soon and they said to ring the bell as soon as you arrived.'

Georgia took a deep breath and stepped across to the door to push the bell. 'I'll take the baby.' Mrs White held out her hands and Elsa glared at her mother as she was handed over.

'Mummy will be back soon,' Mrs White said to Elsa. 'She needs to make sure Daddy is all right.'

Georgia heard the housekeeper's words as she opened the door and tears stung her eyes. Mrs White was right. Max was Elsa's daddy in all the important ways and she vowed that if Max made it they would be the family she had come to realise they had both always wanted.

Stepping into Intensive Care was like stepping into a nightmare.

Georgia knew what the equipment did, she knew the sounds and smells, but she'd never had someone she loved totally dependent on the machines and personnel in this unit.

'I'm Mrs Beresford. I'd like to see my husband,

Max, please. I understand he has just come out of Theatre.'

The intensive care nurse nodded sympathetically. 'I'll just get the registrar to see you before you go in, Mrs Beresford.'

The registrar was tall and gangly and he looked far too young to be in charge of Max's survival.

'I'm Dr Blaxland, Mrs Beresford. This all must be a horrible shock for you. It is for us, too. Max is well liked and respected in this hospital and we will do everything we can.'

He may have looked young but intelligence shone from his eyes, along with warm empathy, and Georgia revised her opinion.

'How is he?' Georgia didn't like the sound of 'everything we can'. 'I understand he is lucky to be alive.'

'He's been in Theatre most of the night. The surgeons had problems with severe internal bleeding as well as a blow to the head. Luckily there doesn't seem to be any spinal involvement.'

'He will live?'

'Dr Beresford has a tenacious hold on life and is breathing for himself, yes. He's critical but stable at the moment. Our main concern is his lack of consciousness since his return from Theatre but cerebral oedema would account for that and hopefully will resolve over the next few hours or days. Thankfully the CAT scan doesn't show any cerebral bleeding.'

Georgia couldn't take it all in because she needed to see for herself that Max was alive. 'Can I see him?'

'Of course. This way.'

Dr Blaxland showed Georgia into a single room. When Georgia first saw Max it was hard to see the man she loved beneath all the equipment. The blinds were drawn so it was dim but the beeping of the cardiac monitor proved that Max was alive. Thank God.

A young nurse stood up from the chair beside the bed and Dr Blaxland introduced her. 'This is Ellie. She's one of our brightest stars in ICU. Your husband is in good hands.'

'Mrs Beresford.' Ellie smiled and indicated for Georgia to take the chair she had vacated. 'He's not responding at the moment but that doesn't mean he can't hear your voice. I'll just step outside for a moment to give you privacy but I'll be watching the monitors at the desk.'

'Thank you, Ellie. And for your care of Max.'

'Dr Beresford was very good to me when I did my obstetric rotation in my training. It's a privilege.'

The young woman left and Georgia sat down.

She picked up Max's hand and pressed it to her cheek, careful not to entangle any of the intravenous lines. He felt warm and that in itself was reassuring.

'Oh, Max. Why didn't I tell you I loved you when I had the chance?'

The heart-rate monitor continued its steady beat and she could see the gentle rise and fall of his chest. He was alive and there was hope.

Lots of hope.

Max was going to make it and they would start again.

In the face of this Sol was nothing, and somehow she knew he would never be a problem again.

Georgia stayed with Max for an hour and then she left to allow Mrs White to go in.

Sitting in the waiting room with a sleeping Elsa beside her on the lounge, Georgia could do nothing but stare at the walls.

She remembered the tape recorder in her shirt and pulled it out. She'd left it on by mistake. Voice activated, it had recorded what she had to say to Max. She sat and listened to the doctor's words again.

When she came to the part where she told Max that she loved him the tears flowed down her cheeks and she turned the playback off and slid it back into her pocket to put it away.

The man at the door paused as he saw her. Slowly he smiled. 'Don't cry. I'm still here for you.'

Georgia turned her head slowly and her eyes narrowed. Sol. Here. The last place he was wanted.

How had he known?

Her fingers curled into fists and she felt for the recorder and activated record.

'What are you doing here, Sol?'

'I've come to claim what is rightfully mine. To bring you and my daughter home.'

Suddenly it all became clear that she had been the one who had allowed Sol's control over her to continue. From this moment and this place it would never happen again. Not in a million years.

'Go away, Sol.'

'I'm not leaving.' He was so confident. She could see it in his conceited face. He was a despicable bully and a fool and finally she was immune.

She stood up and faced him and all the love she held for Max rose inside her like the walls of a fortress.

'I'm not afraid of you any more, Sol.' She raised her chin and cold contempt dripped from her voice.

'The man I love is in a critical condition through those doors and if I find out that you have done anything to harm him I will take you and your high-profile job apart piece by piece.'

Sol raised his eyebrows and shrugged. 'I don't know what you mean.'

Georgia's eyes narrowed. 'I remember when you threatened to discredit Denise at Lower Mountains. I know you have acquired papers to attempt something similar to Max at Meeandah.'

He smiled down at her and then at the sleeping Elsa and Georgia's skin crawled with contempt. She felt like snatching Elsa up and walking away but she wanted him properly hung and this was her chance.

Sol went on conversationally. 'If you and our daughter come with me, he'll be safe.'

'What are you saying and what are you planning, Sol?'

He smirked. 'Just a little medication review. But

if he doesn't wake up, that won't be necessary.' It was as she'd thought. Then his last words sank in.

'What do you know about Max's accident?'

He shook his head but he couldn't help his smile. 'Had a little brake problem with his fabulous Hummer, did he?'

Georgia felt the nausea rise in her throat and her hand tightened over the can of mace in her pocket.

Her voice hardened to steel and she felt as though she were ten times his size.

Small, insignificant, despicable little man that he was. 'Leave now, Sol, and be very, very frightened. Because I am going to drum you out of this country, if not into gaol, and you will never work again. I should have done it a year ago but I will do it now. I have the proof and I will use it.'

She smiled at him through her teeth. 'Don't ever come near myself or my daughter or anyone in my family again.'

He took a step back from the implacability in her face and she stared him down.

'Get out.' She said it with finality and he went.

When he left there was no jaunty spring in his step and she forgot him as soon as he was out of her sight because Mrs White had returned.

She didn't see the policeman step up to him and take his arm and march him away. She had other more important things to worry about.

'They said for you to come back in.' Mrs White looked down at Elsa who woke up as the door shut with a clang. She bent to lift Elsa but Georgia stayed her arm.

'I'll take Elsa in to her daddy this time.'

Mrs White bit her lip and nodded.

'I'll be back soon,' Georgia said, and pushed open the doors with her daughter in her arms.

'You're not supposed to bring children in here,' Ellie said quietly, but she didn't try to stop Georgia.

Georgia smiled. 'I know. But I want Elsa to see her father for a few minutes and then I'll take her out.'

'That's fine. I'll be just outside.'

Georgia sat down in the chair with Elsa on her lap and Elsa crowed when she saw Max.

'Yes, darling. Here's your daddy and when he is well, we will all go home together.'

Tears stung her eyes. Max had to get better. Elsa needed her dad and she needed her man.

'My past is over, Max. Sol can't frighten me any more. He will never intrude on us again and I need you to wake up so we can start our lives together.

'Elsa needs her daddy and I need the man I love to come back to me. I want to deliver babies with you. I want to be a grandparent with you when Elsa grows up. Please, Max. I love you so much.'

Max's eyelids flickered and Georgia held her breath.

His tongue moved to moisten his lips and she lifted his hand again and kissed it. 'I'm here, Max, darling. Elsa and I are both here. We love you, Max, and you need to get better to be with us.'

Max opened his eyes and stared at the woman he loved. She was here and she'd said she loved him. His gaze travelled to the baby girl frowning fiercely at him and his lips twitched in a smile.

'Hello, family,' he said croakily, and went back to sleep.

CHAPTER TWELVE

THREE months later the chapel floated like a snow-flake against the backdrop of the lush Hunter Valley Gardens and an old-fashioned organ, not a string quartet, delivered soaring notes out over the waiting guests.

Max Beresford stood tall and straight at the front of the church and knew without doubt he was doing the right thing.

Winton had been charged with attempted murder and Georgia's recording made at the hospital had helped convict her ex-husband, along with the testimony of more people than they'd realised he'd affected, and the results of Max's own investigations.

Winton had signed adoption papers and Georgia and Elsa were safe—just as Max had promised in the beginning—but now it was a new beginning.

When Georgia, the woman who had been his wife but never his bride, paused at the door of the church, Max's heart swelled with the music and everything else left his mind except the fact that this woman would share his destiny for ever.

Georgia looked radiant in a long simple cream dress with the tiniest cream veil holding back her glorious hair. This time was for real and he smiled at the tiny feather she'd tucked into her veil to tease him.

Georgia walked slowly but confidently towards him on her uncle's arm and her eyes shone with the love he'd been humbled to realise was truly his.

When he took Georgia's hand he cradled her fingers against his cheek for a moment and she smiled shyly up at him.

'Hello my bride.'

'Hello, Max.'

They both looked across the congregation to Elsa, who glared at them both from Mrs White's arms. Georgia shook her head at Elsa's quivering lip.

Max glanced at the minister and said something quietly to the man then held out his arms. Mrs White brought the little girl across and Max tucked her onto his hip before they proceeded.

He smiled down at Georgia. 'She should be here with us,' Max said. 'After all, she introduced us.'

SPANISH DOCTOR, PREGNANT MIDWIFE

BY
ANNE FRASER

Anne Fraser was born in Scotland, but brought up in South Africa. After she left school she returned to the birthplace of her parents, the remote Western Islands of Scotland. She left there to train as a nurse, before going on to university to study English Literature. After the birth of her first child she and her doctor husband travelled the world, working in rural Africa, Australia and Northern Canada. Anne still works in the health sector. To relax, she enjoys spending time with her family, reading, walking and travelling.

CHAPTER ONE

ANNIE slid into a pew of the cool, cavernous Spanish church and let the peace wash over her bruised and battered soul.

In two days' time, her holiday would be over and she would be returning to England and Penhally Bay. Which meant work and reality.

Despite her parents' entreaties that she join them on at least part of their Christmas and New Year worldwide cruise, Annie had insisted that she wanted to take this break on her own. Once and for all, she had told them gently, she needed to put her heartache behind her, including the break-up with her fiancé Robert and especially the horribly cruel reason behind it. The last thing she needed was to be on a luxury liner filled with happy families or, even worse, spend Christmas in Scotland with her sister Fiona and her young family. Even staying in Penhally Bay for the holiday season would be more than she could bear.

But her holiday to the small whitewashed village in Andalucia *had* helped. She had spent the days tramping the narrow streets and walking the hills, tiring herself out until she had fallen into bed too exhausted even to dream. Although nothing would ever take away the terrible void in her life, she was beginning to feel she could face the future. Whatever it might bring.

A group of excited children accompanied by a heavily pregnant woman disturbed the silence. As Annie looked at the brown-faced children with their heads of shiny dark hair, she felt her heart tighten. One little girl in particular caught her attention. Unlike the others, she was subdued, her thumb stuck in her mouth as she looked about her with wide-eyed solemnity. She hung back from the rest of the group, resisting the pregnant woman's attempts to pull her into the circle.

Annie followed the youngsters with her eyes, wondering once more what it would have been like if she had been able to have children of her own. She eyed the expectant mother's bump enviously. She must be nearly at term and Annie would have given anything to be in her position.

She would even have been prepared to adopt. God knew, there were enough children out there who needed the pent-up love Annie had to give and she knew she would have made a good mum, if only she had been given the chance. She sighed. But men didn't seem to think that way. Was it so very different for them? After she had accepted that she'd never be able to conceive naturally, she had suggested to Robert that they consider adoption. But he had been horrified at the idea, and over the following months he had withdrawn from her bit by bit until she had finally forced the truth out of him. He couldn't face a future without children. His *own* children. It had been a double blow to her when he had left. She had thought he had loved her. Well, no more. From now on it was just her, by herself. And she would manage. More than manage, she told herself firmly. She would throw herself into her work at Penhally Bay. She would make a good life on her own. It was the start of a new year and a new beginning. Of that she was determined.

Squaring her shoulders, Annie slung her bag over her shoulder and stood up. She had only taken a few steps when she heard a cry of pain ringing out and she swung round to see the heavily pregnant woman bent over, clutching at her stomach.

Instantly, Annie was by her side.

'What is it?' she asked. 'Are you okay?'

The woman stared at Annie with enormous brown eyes stretched with pain and fear.

'Bebé,' she gasped. And then doubled over again.

'When is your baby due?' Annie asked, keeping her voice calm, but the woman just frowned at her and shook her head. It was obvious she spoke no English. Annie bit back a sigh of frustration. Although she had learned a few words of Spanish, it wasn't up to the demands of the occasion. She needed someone to translate. And soon.

'She say the baby is coming. Now.'

Annie placed a hand on the woman's abdomen and felt the contractions. She counted slowly. They were coming one after the other, at two-minute intervals. She was absolutely right. The baby was on its way.

Annie lowered herself to the level of the little girl. 'What's your name, sweetheart?'

'Maria.' She gestured to the woman. 'This is my cousin, Señora Lopez.' She removed her thumb for only as long as it took to impart the information.

'Okay, Maria, I need you to be my helper. Can you do that?' When the little girl nodded her head, Annie continued, raising her voice above the babble of excited voices.

'Has your cousin other children?'

Maria nodded again. 'Three.'

'Ask her if they were normal deliveries. Then find out if anyone has a phone. We need to call an ambulance.'

An older woman with a nut-brown face pulled a mobile out of the pocket of her cavernous overall and, muttering something frustratingly incomprehensible to Annie, punched numbers into the phone. Hopefully she was calling an ambulance.

In the meantime, Maria had spoken to the labouring woman and listened to her reply.

'She say her other children all come quickly. This baby not supposed to be here for another few weeks.'

'Okay Maria, Well done. I need to find somewhere private for Mrs Lopez to lie down. Could you ask if there is such a place?'

As Maria spoke to the watching, chattering audience, Annie felt her hand being squeezed tightly as another contraction racked Señora Lopez's body. It was clear that the baby was going to be born right here. Annie guessed it would take time they didn't have for the ambulance to get here from the nearest town. The narrow, winding roads weren't built for speed.

Suddenly the crowd of chattering women parted and a dark-haired man pushed his way through. Annie only had time to note deep brown eyes and high cheekbones. The man spoke in rapid Spanish to the distraught woman holding Annie's hand and Annie saw her visibly relax.

'*Mi hijo,*' the older woman with the mobile said, nodding down at him. '*Médico.*'

My son. Doctor. Annie felt a wash of relief. At least she wasn't on her own any more. She prayed he could speak English. It would take the responsibility of translating from Maria. Although the little girl was doing her best, waiting for her questions and commands to be translated was frustratingly slow.

The man bent over and scooped the woman into his arms as if she weighed nothing. His mother gestured him to follow her while the other women took control of the children. Annie noticed that little Maria followed behind, obviously feeling as if she had a stake in the drama.

'I'm a midwife,' Annie said as she followed the dark-haired man with his burden to the rear of the church. 'Do you speak English?'

For a second, he stopped and looked at Annie. His mouth quirked. '*Sí*. Yes, I speak English. I am Dr Raphael Castillo, obstetrician. My mother has called an ambulance, but it will be some time before it gets here. It has to come from the city and the roads aren't very good. Have you made an assessment?'

'I haven't had a chance to examine her properly, but the contractions are coming one after the other. She could deliver at any time.'

He nodded. 'I think you are correct.' He smiled, flashing even white teeth. 'Looks like it is going to be you and me delivering this baby—right here.'

As he spoke, Señora Lopez cried out again, followed by a string of Spanish words. Dr Castillo responded in the same language as he laid her down on a couch in the priest's room.

'She says the baby is coming,' he said, stripping off the jacket of his suit and rolling up the sleeves of his white shirt. 'There is no more time.'

Noticing a sink at one end of the room, Annie crossed to it and began to scrub her hands. Dr Castillo, speaking to Señora Lopez over his shoulder, joined her. It was obvious from the look on Señora Lopez's face that she knew that the baby was going to be delivered in this tiny room. At least it wasn't a stable, Annie thought wryly. Then while the dark-haired doctor finished rinsing the soap from his hands, Annie examined the woman.

'The head is crowning, Dr Castillo,' she called over. 'I'll deliver the baby if you tell her what to do.' She turned to Maria, who had slipped in beside them. 'Go and see if you can find some towels, sheets anything. Something to wrap the baby in.'

As Maria ran off, Annie turned to him. 'How many weeks is she?'

'Thirty-nine,' he said. Although heavily accented, his English was perfect.

'How sure of her dates is she?'

'She is certain. By the way, her name is Sophia.' Then he turned back and said something to Sophia. Annie didn't need to understand the words to know that he would be telling her to push.

Just as Maria and the doctor's mother appeared at the door with a bundle of shawls and scarves, the baby's shoulder appeared. But then, to Annie's horror, the baby's progress down the birth canal halted. It was stuck. She felt her own heart rate rise. Where was that ambulance? But in the same moment Annie realised that even if it turned up in the next few minutes, it wouldn't help. Sophia was in no position to be moved right now.

She looked up and found Raphael Castillo's calm brown eyes on hers.

'What is it?' he asked quietly.

'The baby's stuck,' she said. 'I think we have a shoulder dystocia.' Seeing the answering look of concern in Raphael's eyes, Annie knew he grasped the gravity of the situation. If they were in a hospital, it would be serious enough, but here, without instruments, not even a pair of forceps, there was every chance they could lose the baby. She stood aside to let him examine Sophia while Maria and the older woman watched silently from the doorway. Sensing something was wrong, the labouring woman called out in panic. Raphael's mother rushed to her side and spoke softly to her. What ever she said seemed to reassure the woman and she flopped back down.

After another couple of minutes of Sophia pushing and the baby not making any progress, Annie was certain they were in serious trouble. It seemed as if Raphael had arrived at the same conclusion.

'I'm going to ask my mother to help me pull Sophia's legs above her shoulders. Then I want you to press down just above the pubic bone as hard as you can.' His expression was grim, but his voice was calm. Somehow Annie felt confident that if anyone could save mother and child, he could.

As soon as Sophia's legs had been manoeuvred into position, Annie followed his instructions. With a cry of pain, Sophia gave a final push and the baby slithered into the Annie's arms, giving a gusty cry a few seconds later. Annie and Raphael's eyes locked over the exhausted mother. He grinned widely, his eyes crinkling at the corners, and Annie's world tilted.

'A healthy baby girl,' he said, repeating the words in Spanish to the new mother.

Quickly Annie checked that the baby's breathing was unrestricted before wrapping the tiny infant in a shawl and passing Sophia her daughter to hold.

'*Gracias, gracias,* Raphael,' Sophia whispered, nuzzling her newborn. She looked up at Annie. '*Gracias, Señora.*' In the distance Annie could hear the sound of a siren approaching. They just had time to deliver the placenta before the ambulance crew hurried in.

Raphael spoke to the paramedics as they prepared to transfer Sophia to the hospital, and Annie studied him surreptitiously. He really was the most gorgeous-looking man she had ever seen in her life! His black wavy hair was worn slightly too long and a lock fell across his eyes. He swept it away impatiently with long, tapered fingers. He had high cheekbones, an aquiline nose and his olive complexion showed off even white teeth. He wasn't overly tall, but every muscle was clearly defined under his white shirt. Tailored trousers clung to thighs that looked as if they had been honed by hours in the gym. All in all he exuded sex appeal. Annie had never met anyone like him before. Quite simply, he took her breath away.

'Well done,' he said to Annie over the cries of the infant. 'I am sorry, I don't even know your name.'

'It's Annie,' she said. 'Annie Thomas. And there's no need to thank me. I was glad to help. Although I'm relieved you appeared when you did. I'm not sure I would have coped—even with my two helpers here.' She nodded at the older woman and the young girl, who were now fussing over the baby.

'My mother—' he indicated the older woman with a nod of his head '—called me. Fortunately, I was waiting for her in a café nearby. She wanted to say a prayer before we went home for lunch.'

His mother glanced up from Sophia and the baby and Raphael introduced them. Señora Castillo nodded vigorously and said something to her son in rapid Spanish.

'She says you must come for lunch too.' By this time Sophia and her baby were being loaded onto a stretcher, with Raphael helping.

'Shouldn't we go with them to the hospital?' Annie asked.

He looked at her and grinned. 'I will go with them. There is no room for you. Anyway, you are on holiday, no? I am sure you have other things you would like to do. Even if you don't care to join my family for lunch.'

Annie felt unreasonably disappointed. But whether it was because she wouldn't be able to follow up her patient as she was used to doing, or whether it was because Raphael was about to disappear from her life for good, she didn't know. Not that she was in any mood for romance. Not when she had just decided to get her life back on track. The last thing she needed was more complications in her life.

'What about this little one?' Annie asked, indicating Maria, who remained watching with enormous brown eyes.

Raphael laughed and chucked the little girl under her chin. 'Maria is staying with my mother. She will go home with her. Everyone will be there. It is our New Year family gathering. Maybe you will think about coming and I will see you there later?' He quirked an eyebrow in enquiry and Annie felt a shiver dance down her spine. How on earth was this man having this effect on her? She had only just met him, for goodness' sake! Maybe it was something to do with those intense brown eyes and that body, an inner voice whispered. Maybe it's because she'd never met anyone who looked like him before. Everything about him sent warning signals flashing in Annie's head and she knew the wisest thing she could do was put as much distance as possible between her and this man—and the sooner the better.

As she opened her mouth to protest that she couldn't possibly intrude, Raphael smiled again. 'Actually, you can't say no. Mama will not let you, so you might as well give in now. My mother is—how do you say? Formidable. But, look, I must go. The ambulance is about to leave.' He stared down at her for a long second, holding her gaze with the intensity of his own. 'I hope you will decide to come.' And then he was walking away, leaving Annie reeling.

Sure enough, Mama Castillo was tugging at Annie's arm, making it clear that she expected her to follow. Silently Maria slipped her hand into Annie's and it seemed that she was going for lunch whether she wanted to or not. Well, it wasn't as if she had anything else planned for the rest of the day, and, if she was honest with herself, she'd had enough of her own company. Moreover, hadn't it been one of her New Year resolutions to try and experience more of life? She refused to let herself think too long about the real reason she wanted to go. The thought of seeing Raphael again was irresistible, no matter what the sensible part of her brain was telling her. What could it hurt? She was leaving soon and she would never see any of them again. And what was the point of being wise anyway? Right now, she had nothing left to lose.

'Okay. I'd love to,' she said, finally throwing her hands up in surrender. When Maria translated for her an enormous grin lit up the tiny woman's weatherbeaten face.

They stepped outside just as the ambulance sped away. Although it was winter, the sun was high in the sky and Annie could feel it warming her skin. She felt a shiver of anticipation. This holiday was turning out to be not at all what she had expected!

Unsure of where they were going or how they were going to get there, Annie was dismayed when Mama Castillo lifted her voluminous skirts and climbed onto a small moped, indicating that Annie should jump on behind her.

Annie looked to Maria for confirmation.

'She says she will take you. I will walk. It is not far. Just up there.' Maria pointed up a narrow road towards a cluster of whitewashed houses. 'In the hills,' she added.

'Could I not walk with you?' Annie said doubtfully. But Maria shook her head decisively. 'No, you must go with Grandma. She says it is too far for an English woman to walk in this sun. I am used to it. It is better if you go on the bike.'

It seemed to Annie as if she had little choice in the matter. Mama Castillo looked in no mood to debate the matter. Reluctantly Annie climbed on the moped and hoped for the best.

In the event Annie kept her eyes closed as they raced up the hill, scattering chickens and goats in all directions. For the whole of the ten-minute journey, Mama Castillo didn't slow down once, not even for a group of men trudging up the hill in front of them. It was obvious to Annie that she only had one speed, and nothing and no one was going to slow her down.

When they eventually stopped outside a farmhouse perched on the side of the hill, Annie felt a huge wave of relief. There had been moments when she'd been sure that she wasn't going to survive the journey.

As soon as they climbed off the moped they were surrounded by what seemed to Annie to be most of the village. There were a number of young men, at least two of whom bore a striking resemblance to Raphael, as well as half a dozen women. There were also children, almost too many to count, running around the large courtyard, squealing and laughing.

Overwhelmed by the noise, Annie stood back, feeling suddenly shy. Why on earth had she agreed to come here? she wondered. After a few minutes a stunning woman with thick wavy hair and hazel eyes detached herself from the crowd and came across to Annie holding out her hand.

'Welcome to our home,' she said. 'Mama told me you helped Sophia and her baby today. Sophia is a cousin of my father's so we all are in your debt.' So this dark-haired beauty must be Raphael's sister. Annie could see the resemblance in the high cheekbones and sensuous mouth.

'It was nothing,' Annie replied. 'I was glad to help.'

'My name is Catalina.' The woman continued. 'I heard Raphael was there too.' She stood on tiptoe, looking over Annie's shoulder. 'So where is my brother now? He promised to be here.'

'He went with Sophia and the baby to the hospital. To make sure there were no complications. He said he would come as soon as he was finished there.'

Catalina pouted. 'That's Raphael for you, always working. We don't see him very often. He is supposed to be on holiday with us, just for these few days, but we've hardly seen him. Pah! But seeing as it is our cousin he is attending to, I won't tell him off when he comes.'

And then, before Annie had a chance to say anything, she was being led into an enormous farmhouse kitchen where a large table had been laid out as if to feed the five thousand. It was covered with bowls of fruit and olives and large platters of paella as well as other Spanish dishes that Annie couldn't identify, but which smelled delicious. Soon she was part of the chattering group, absorbed into their friendly warmth that needed little translation. Catalina made some introductions, but there were too many for Annie to possibly remember all their names. It seemed that she had guessed right and the two men she had thought were Raphael's brothers turned out to be just that. Apart from Catalina, there were another two women who were his sisters. Annie had just been guided into a seat at the table when Maria, smiling shyly appeared silently at her side where, after squeezing in beside her, she remained for the rest of the meal. Gazing around the crowded table, Annie couldn't be sure who Maria belonged to. As far as she could tell, all the children appeared to be shared.

During a spell when no one's attention was on her, Annie wondered wistfully what it would be like to be part of a family just like this one, and in an instant the sadness came flooding back. She squeezed her eyes closed, forcing back the never-far-away tears. She would never know.

When she opened her eyes again, it was to find Raphael looking down at her, his dark-winged brows knotted in puzzlement. His eyes had an intensity that made her feel as if he could see into her soul, and as he held her gaze Annie thought she recognised an answering sadness in their depths, but knew she had to be mistaken. What could this vibrant, gorgeous man have to feel unhappy about? As far as Annie could see, he had everything. Her eyes swept the happy chattering family again; at least, everything that mattered.

He leaned over her. 'Don't be so sad,' he murmured in her ear.

She could smell his aftershave and his breath on her cheek was like a caress. Her heart gave an involuntary leap. What *was* it about him that made her feel like a schoolgirl with her first crush? She couldn't remember the last time she'd had such an instant and powerful response to a man. In fact, she couldn't remember responding like this to a man ever—and that included Robert. Maybe it was the Spanish sunshine and the couple of glasses of sangria that had been served with lunch. Whatever it was, she couldn't deny she was pleased that he was back before she had made her excuses and left.

'I'm not sad,' she retorted. There was a sudden lull in the conversation and her words rang out around the table. To her acute embarrassment, all eyes swivelled her way. There was a moment of deathly silence before everyone resumed their conversations. Annie felt herself blush to the tips of her ears.

'How is Sophia?' she asked, determined to change the subject.

'Mother and baby are doing fine,' he said. 'She told me to thank you again.' Then he turned towards the others and said something in Spanish to which they all raised their glasses. 'To Sophia! To Annie!' If it were possible, Annie felt more self-conscious than ever, and it seemed by the broad grin on his face that Raphael was enjoying her discomfort.

All of a sudden she wanted nothing more than to put as much distance between herself and this man as possible. She stood, almost knocking over her wineglass in her haste to get away. 'Thank you for the meal, but I really think I should be going,' she said breathlessly. 'I've taken enough of your family's kind hospitality.' She stumbled as her head spun with the sudden movement.

His hand shot out and grasped her wrist, steadying her. The touch of his fingertips seemed to burn her skin.

'I will take you. Where are you staying?'

'Oh, no, it's quite all right. I'm sure I can find my own way. My apartment is opposite the church. It won't take me more than half an hour to walk back. And after that meal, I could do with the exercise.' She was miserably aware that she was babbling on, but she seemed powerless to halt the words erupting from her mouth. The longer she was in his company, the more she felt like a star-struck schoolgirl.

'Anyway, you haven't had a chance to eat yet.' She checked her watch. 'It's almost 5.30! You must be starving by now. Please don't worry about taking me.'

'It is no trouble. My mother would never forgive me my poor manners if I didn't see you home. I told you how formidable she can be. I wouldn't put it past her to—how do you say?—box my ears!'

Annie laughed, suddenly relaxing. 'Okay, then. I wouldn't want to be responsible for that,' she said. 'But I insist you have something to eat before we leave.'

'Only if you promise me you will stay a little longer.' Then he frowned. 'But forgive me, I am stupid. You are sure to have someone waiting for you? Back at your apartment?'

'No,' Annie said heavily. 'I'm on my own, so there isn't really a need for me to rush away.' If she were honest with herself, the last thing she felt like doing was returning to the little flat she had rented. After two weeks of her own company, she was heartily sick of it. Besides, there was something about this family group that made her feel warm and wanted. Perhaps just for tonight she could pretend she belonged and forget about her life back home?

Raphael looked puzzled. 'You are here in Spain on your own? Over Christmas? And New Year! How can that be?'

Annie had no intention of telling him the truth. The last thing she wanted was his sympathy. 'I thought a little bit of winter sun would be nice,' she said.

If anything, Raphael looked even more perplexed. 'It is winter here, too,' he said.

"At home, right now it's snowing.' Annie had to laugh. 'I can assure you there is no comparison.'

'Whatever,' he said, grinning back at her. 'I for one am glad you came to Spain.' There was something in the force of his gaze that sent shivers of anticipation up Annie's spine. 'And I know Sophia is, too,' he added.

The last comment was a reality check. Of course, Annie thought. Why would a man like Raphael Castillo be interested in someone as ordinary as her?

It was growing dark by the time they left and Annie felt a pang as she was subjected to dozens of warm embraces and repeated pleas to return and see them again. All in all, it had been a magical afternoon, and she wished she could stay for ever. But, of course, that wasn't possible. She had her own life to return to even if it was a lonely and barren one—in more ways than one. Just as Raphael opened the wrought-iron gate to the road, Maria came running over and flung herself into Annie's arms, burying her face in Annie's shoulder. Annie felt her heart contract as she cuddled the little girl, breathing in the scent of oranges on her skin. What she would give to be able to hold her own child in her arms.

She released the little girl as Mama Castillo called to her with softly spoken words and Annie watched Maria cuddle up, the inevitable thumb back in her mouth, in the older woman's lap. Regretfully Annie gave a final wave, before following Raphael down the dirt road away from the house.

'Who does Maria belong to?' she asked. 'She is such a sweetheart, but she seems so…I don't know…lost.'

'Ah, little Maria,' Raphael said slowly. 'Her mother, my cousin, died suddenly a few months ago. Her father…' he sucked in his breath, his mouth tightening with disapproval. 'He is weak. He left Maria behind. What kind of man is that? If Maria were my child, I would do everything I could to keep her with me.'

Suddenly the warmth drained from his eyes and Annie

shivered. Instinctively she knew that Raphael was not the kind of man to give up anything he thought he had a right to. He was not the kind of man she would ever want to cross swords with.

'He must have been in some state to abandon his child. People do all sorts of things that are out of character when they are hurting,' Annie said. But she couldn't really understand how any father could abandon his child—especially when that child had just lost her mother. It was too cruel.

'There is no excuse,' Raphael said curtly. 'A father has his duty. How he feels is of no importance when it comes to the child.' He looked away, but not before Annie read the bleakness in his eyes. 'So now she lives with my family. She loves my mother but she still grieves for her own,' Raphael went on. 'She is sad—like you—but every day she is getting stronger.'

There it was again. The reference to her sadness. Was she so transparent? Or did this man just seem to be able to see into her soul?

They walked along the narrow road, the scent of the heavily laden orange trees that edged the pavement drifting in the still air, the velvet sky punctuated with stars. He asked her about her job, and she told him about Penhally Bay, how much she loved living there and how much she enjoyed her job at the hospital. He listened closely, then he told her about his job in Barcelona. That he missed the countryside and regretted that he wasn't able to see his family more often. He grinned down at her.

'As you can tell, we Spaniards are big on family. What about you?'

'I have my parents and a brother as well as a sister. They both have small children. My brother lives in Australia and my parents are going to stay with him there for a few months after their cruise. My sister is in Scotland with her family.' She slid a glance at him. 'I envy you, having your family all so close,' she admitted.

Once again, she thought she saw a shadow pass across his face. But when he smiled she knew she must have been mistaken.

'It's not all good. I have to put up with my sisters and my mother wanting to know everything about my life. *Dios*, they never give me peace.'

Before Annie knew it, they were outside her apartment. The nearby houses were draped in Christmas lights, lighting the cobbled street.

She didn't want the evening to end and it seemed as if Raphael didn't either. He hesitated then said, 'If you are not too tired, there is this little restaurant a few minutes' walk away. It has the most excellent tapas. And I am suddenly hungry again. Will you come with me?'

She let her gaze sweep his muscular frame. There wasn't an ounce of fat on it as far as she could see. Where did he put all that food?

'Okay,' she said softly. 'It's my last night. I might as well make the most of it.'

He steered her towards a small restaurant behind the church. It was packed inside, but there was no one sitting at the outside tables in the plaza.

'Do you mind if we sit here?' Annie asked.

'Of course. If that is what you want.' He took off the thin sweater he had been wearing, revealing a short-sleeved shirt. 'But I insist you put this on.'

Sensing that it would be useless to argue, Annie slipped the sweater on over her shoulders. It smelled faintly of a mix of citrus aftershave and the warm tang of his scent. It was much too large, falling almost to her knees and slipping off her shoulder. Her breath caught in her throat as he leant forward and turned up the cuffs. The gesture was both tender and erotic and as his fingers lightly brushed against her bare skin, Annie felt darts of electricity tingle up her arms.

Raphael studied her slowly, his smile turning up the corners of his mouth and creasing the corner of his eyes. Annie thought yet again that she had never seen a man so gorgeous yet so sure of his masculinity. A part of her, sensing danger, wanted to run from him as fast as she could, but at the same time she knew that she couldn't bear to see him walk out of her life. At least, not yet.

When their order of seafood arrived, it felt like the most natural thing in the world for Raphael to feed her small morsels of lobster and shrimp with his fingers. The touch of his hands on her lips sent small explosions of desire racing through her body.

Then, without saying anything, they stood and Raphael took her hand again. She led him back up the path to the front door of her apartment. Knowing that what was about to happen was beyond her control, she opened the door and, keeping her hand in his, went inside.

'Are you sure?' he said. He looked into her eyes and it was as if he knew her most hidden thoughts. Despite the ready smile, she saw something in the depths of his ebony eyes that mirrored her own pain. All she wanted was to give comfort and to be comforted in return. The rest of her life could take care of itself.

'It's not too late to change your mind.' His voice was soft, yet there was an undercurrent that caused her pulse to leap.

'No,' she said, stunned by her brazenness. 'It's what I

want.' She knew she was risking danger. Not that she didn't trust him—she instinctively knew he would never harm her. But she could no more resist her need for him than she could walk back to Penhally Bay.

He picked up her hand and pressed it to his lips. She shivered as shock waves of desire coursed through her body. She had never experienced lust like it before, but she wasn't naive. She knew what those dark brown eyes were asking her. She didn't want to play games. All she felt was an overriding need to be held in his arms—to have her femininity reaffirmed. It had taken such a beating in the last few months. Surely just this once she could throw caution to the wind and take a chance?

He dropped her hand and pulled her hard against him, one hand on her hip, the other cupping her bottom. She could feel every muscle of his hard chest through his T-shirt and the pressure of his thighs on hers. Flames of desire flooded her body and she turned her face up to his, seeking his mouth. He brought it down on hers, gently at first and then harder as he seemed to draw her very soul. She snaked her hands around his neck, pulling him closer. She was drowning, her legs weak with her need for him.

He pulled away. She could see that he too was shaken by the strength of their mutual desire.

'Are you sure?' he asked gently. It was all she could do to nod, then with a triumphant smile he picked her up and, holding her close in his arms, he carried her up the stairs and into their own private world.

Later, when the sun was beginning to lighten the sky, she lay on one elbow, looking down on him. Asleep he looked softer, more vulnerable somehow. He had been a passionate but considerate lover, taking his time with her, waiting until she cried out with her need to have him inside her before he took her. She smiled. Several times he had taught her things about her own body that she hadn't known. Time and time again he had brought her to a climax that had left her shuddering and almost tearful with release. She traced a finger over his lips, memorising the contours of his face, knowing she would never see him again. But it was almost all right. In one wonderful night he had managed to heal something inside her that she'd thought was beyond repair. And for that, she would never forget him.

CHAPTER TWO

ANNIE read through the case notes again to refresh her memory. Not that she needed to. She had seen Claire and Roy several times already and knew their history well. Satisfied that she was completely up to date, she sat back and waited for them to arrive.

The rain pattered depressingly against the window and Annie felt her mind drifting back to the magical last night of her Spanish holiday. Almost four months had passed and yet her memories of Raphael and the time they had spent together hadn't diminished. She could still remember his every touch, their every kiss. It was as if she had found the missing part of herself. The man she had been waiting for all her life. Her soulmate. She hadn't believed that such a person existed— but now she knew differently.

Her heart lurched. Sometimes she wished she had never met him. Because it had made being alone all the more painful, as if she'd left half of herself back in Spain. Annie sighed wistfully, remembering his last words to her.

'Cariño,' he had said huskily the morning she had left. 'If only you had come into my life before. But now it's too... complicated.' She hadn't pressed him to explain. What would

have been the point? Still, she couldn't help trying to fathom
out what he had meant. Was he married? No—she was sure
if he was, his family would have made some reference to it.
In love with someone else, committed in a relationship?
Perhaps. But it didn't matter. Even if he had begged her to
stay with him, she wouldn't have said yes. Not so soon after
Robert and all their problems. No, much better to lock the
memory of him in her heart. Much safer.

Annie pulled her gaze away from the window and swung
her chair back round to her desk. There was no point in
thinking of Raphael. She had to get on with her life. Hadn't
she vowed to do just that? Besides, the irony of not being able
to conceive made her a better midwife. At least she could
console herself with that realisation. And her work in
Penhally was more than satisfying and enjoyable. It was what
got her up each morning, determined to put her own heartache behind her and help the couples who streamed through
her door hoping to realise the dream that she would never
have.

Like her next two patients—Roy and Claire Dickson, who
were being ushered in. Annie greeted them warmly, knowing
they were nervous. The couple had been trying for years to
have a baby, and finally with the help of IVF had succeeded.
Their initial scan had shown not one but two healthy heartbeats and now Annie, who had a special responsibility for
mothers with high-risk pregnancies, was following them up
regularly.

'How have you been feeling?' she asked Claire, while
checking her blood pressure.

'As if I'm on cloud nine!' Claire smiled with delight.
'Apart from that, nauseous and tired and more than a little bit
scared.'

'The nausea will pass. Take it as a good sign in the meantime,' Annie said.

Although she shared the couple's joy, Annie couldn't help a pang of envy. How she would love to be in Claire's shoes, looking forward to her first babies with a loving supportive husband by her side. But she wasn't even a candidate for IVF, she thought sadly. And it wasn't as if there was a rush of people wanting to marry her either, but at least she could help this couple experience what she never could. And she found comfort in that.

'Your blood pressure is absolutely fine, but I want to keep an eye on you and these little ones. I'm sure you both know that the first twelve weeks are the riskiest.' Catching Claire's look of alarm, she hastened to reassure her. 'But you're well past that now. It's just that twin pregnancies are riskier over the whole of the pregnancy. But we are going to do everything possible to deliver two healthy babies and right now everything appears to be going fine.'

'They gave us a choice at the IVF clinic,' Roy said, as if Annie didn't already know, 'about whether we wanted one or two embryos put back. They explained the pros and cons, that there was a greater risk with twins, but we decided to take a chance and have two embryos replaced. This way we'll have a complete family in one go, and Claire doesn't have to put herself through it all again.' His grin almost split his face in two. 'I still can't believe it,' he said, patting his wife's tummy with a proprietary air. 'Two babies. Isn't she clever?'

Annie saw the happy couple to the front door of the maternity wing, and watched Claire struggling to open the umbrella over her head as she battled against the slanting rain, She was delighted for them, but it was early days yet. Twin pregnancies had a greater risk of problems developing and although that had been explained to the couple, she wondered if they really understood.

Annie felt a wave of fatigue wash over her. She always felt so caught up with her patients, sharing their see-saw emotions as she followed them through their pregnancies. Although she loved being part of the team that looked after high-risk pregnancies at St Piran Hospital, sometimes it was hard to remember that most women sailed through their pregnancies and gave birth to healthy babies without medical intervention.

But today was different and Annie knew it wasn't just concern for her patients that was bothering her. She couldn't continue to ignore what was staring her in the face, no matter how much she wanted to. She hadn't had a period for months now and she had begun to put weight on around her middle. All the symptoms of an early menopause.

Unreasonably, even though she knew she couldn't conceive naturally, there had always been a faint glimmer of hope that one day she might have a child. No matter how much she had tried to convince herself otherwise. But with the menopause, any hope would be completely extinguished. Annie was painfully aware that she had to see someone about it, but there was only one person she really trusted and who would understand exactly how she was feeling. She would pop in to see Kate Althorp, the senior midwife at Penhally Bay Surgery, on her way home.

Annie enjoyed working with Kate and her colleague Chloe, who were both midwives based at the surgery. To begin with, they had discussed patients they shared over the phone, but over time they had become friends and Annie would often drop in at the surgery on her way home from hospital for a chat. Occasionally the three women would meet up for coffee or supper too.

Making up her mind, Annie picked up her coat. Kate would know what her next step should be. It was time for Annie to face up to whatever the future had in store. Hadn't she made that promise to herself just months before?

Annie found Kate in her office, catching up with paperwork. The older midwife looked up and smiled when she noticed Annie standing in the doorway.

'Grief, is it that time already?' She looked at her watch. 'Six o'clock! I'm due to pick Jem up from football practice in forty minutes.' She glanced back at Annie and something in Annie's expression must have alerted the experienced nurse. 'But time for some coffee before then. You look a bit peaky, methinks.'

As Kate fished out a couple of mugs, Annie wondered whether there was any point in confiding her fears. But if she was right, she would need to consider whether to start hormone replacement therapy and wanted to discuss the option with Kate before she saw Dr Nick Tremayne, her GP and also the senior partner at the practice.

'Hey.' Kate turned and looked at her closely, her brown eyes warm with concern. 'So, what's up? Is Claire's pregnancy going okay? I know she and Roy were seeing you today.'

'Oh. No, that's fine. I intend to keep a close eye on them, but so far—touch wood—everything seems to be going as expected.'

'It's good to see them so happy. They've been waiting for this for so long. I'll call round and see Claire tomorrow,' Kate said handing a mug to Annie. 'But back to you. Something's bothering you. You didn't come here just to tell me about Claire and Roy, did you? C'mon, whatever it is, out with it.'

Annie hesitated. Once she told Kate, it would be the same as having it confirmed. Was she really ready for that?

Kate came over to Annie and dragged a chair across so she was sitting beside her. 'You don't have to tell me, but perhaps I can help?' she said gently. The older woman was always the one everyone went to with their problems. Annie wasn't sure why—perhaps because she always made time to listen and never seemed to judge. Annie felt tears sting her eyes and she blinked furiously. She wouldn't cry. She had shed enough tears to last her a lifetime.

'I never told you this, but I can't have children,' Annie blurted. 'I'm infertile.'

'Oh, Annie, I'm so sorry. Are you sure?'

'Positive,' Annie said, trying to keep her voice steady. 'You know I told you that I was seeing someone before I came back to Penhally Bay?'

Kate nodded and waited for Annie to continue.

'Robert and I were together for five years. We were in love—or so I thought. We planned to marry and started trying for a family. But after six months, when nothing had happened, I went to one of the doctors I worked with who specialised in infertility and he suggested we get tested. There was nothing wrong with Robert but they have a new blood test that they use to check a woman's fertility. Well, the result came back. My ovarian reserve, you know the number of eggs I have left, was so low as to be immeasurable.' Annie's voice broke. She remembered the day she had been given the news as if it were yesterday.

Kate put her arm around Annie's shoulder. Her silent sympathy gave Annie the strength to continue. 'The test is very reliable. A pregnancy, even with IVF, would be almost impossible for me. They also warned me that it was likely that I would have an early menopause.' She steadied her voice. 'Well, I think it's happening,' she said, trying not to show how much it hurt her to say the words. 'I haven't had a period since...' She thought back. 'Well, before New Year. And,' she continued, 'I don't know how else to describe this, but I kind of feel all hormonal, as if my emotions are all over the place. You know it took me all my willpower not to cry when I saw how relieved and happy Claire and Roy are, and that's not like me. Not that I don't care about them, of course I do, but I don't usually let it get to me like this.'

'But it's understandable, isn't it?' Kate said softly. 'It's bound to remind you of your own loss. And losing the ability to have a family is a loss. Just as much as a death.'

'I know all that,' Annie said, 'but I've been feeling so much happier since I came back from Spain. When I was over there, I knew I had to stop looking back and try and think positively about the future. Accept that children weren't on the cards for me and make something of my life. Be happy with what I have, instead of hankering for what can never be. But if I'm right and I'm experiencing the onset of the menopause, it's like having to deal with it all over again.'

'And you are certain that that's what's happening?' Kate said thoughtfully.

'There can't be another explanation. Missed periods. Emotions all over the place, and I swear I'm starting a middle-age spread. I could hardly get into my jeans the other day.' Annie tried a smile.

Kate looked at her sharply. 'All this since your holiday? Hmm. I don't suppose you had a holiday romance while you were away?'

Annie felt a blush creep up her cheeks. Seeing it, Kate

grinned. 'You did, didn't you? Well, good for you. It's about time you let yourself have some fun.' Then she frowned. 'If it was fun. Oh, dear, I didn't mean for it to come out that way. You know what I mean.'

Annie felt her blush deepen as she thought back to that night. Fun? Yes, but now one of her most precious memories.

'And, if you had sex, did you use contraception?' That was typical Kate. Straight to the point.

'Yes, I mean…no.' Annie blushed again. 'I mean, I told him it wasn't necessary and he just assumed I was on the Pill.' Oh, dear, this was so embarrassing. Although she felt comfortable discussing most things with Kate, there really was a limit.

'What I'm getting at,' Kate said gently, still looking thoughtful. 'I don't suppose you've taken a pregnancy test?'

Annie was stunned. A pregnancy test! The thought simply hadn't occurred to her. She had accepted that it was impossible, so hadn't even considered it. Not even for a second.

'Well, no. It's hardly likely is it? Not with my history.' Suddenly she felt dizzy. 'You don't think? It couldn't be? Could it?' Although she knew it was impossible, the sudden leap of hope was almost too much to bear.

Kate stood up, all business. 'It wouldn't hurt to make sure, would it? Come on.' She rooted around in a cupboard. 'Off you go to the Ladies and produce a specimen and we'll do a quick test. At the very least we'll be able to rule it out.'

Ten minutes later, Annie was sitting stunned in front of Kate. 'You're sure?' she said. 'There couldn't be some mistake?'

'I'm sure,' Kate replied smiling widely. 'We'll arrange a scan just to be absolutely certain, but there is no doubt in my mind. You are pregnant. Apart from the test, I could feel something when I palpated your tummy. I've seen it happen before. Just when a woman thinks a baby is out of the question. Then bam.'

Annie felt a wave of pure joy suffuse her soul. A baby! She was going to have a baby. She had longed for this moment for so long, and now it was here, she could hardly bring herself to believe it. Now the tiredness, the roller-coaster emotions, the hormonal mood swings all made perfect sense. She hugged herself, barely able to contain her delight.

'I assume you're not still in touch with the father? I mean, you've never mentioned him,' Kate was saying.

Raphael! Of course it must be his. He was the only man she had slept with since Robert.

'No. I haven't spoken to him since, well, you know.' How *would* Raphael feel about it? Was there any point in telling him? She neither expected nor wanted anything from him and his silence had made it perfectly clear that he wanted nothing from her, either. Her head reeled. She would have to take time off work, of course, at least for the first few months after the birth, but she had a small inheritance from her grandfather that would supplement her maternity pay. One way or another she would cope. One thing was for sure—her baby wouldn't be short of love.

'God, should I tell him? I don't know. I'm still trying to take it all in. I can hardly believe it myself. But I suppose he has the right to know.'

Annie thought she saw something move behind Kate's eyes, but almost as quickly it was gone. She knew Kate had brought up her child, Jem, on her own since the death of her husband, James. Although it must have been a struggle, Kate had had no choice. James had died before he had even known she was pregnant. All this must be bringing back painful memories for the older woman.

'Only you can make that decision,' Kate replied gently. 'Whatever is right for you.'

'I don't know if I want him in my life, Kate. It's a complication I could do without. Besides, he lives in Spain. Even if he wants to get to know his child, it won't be easy.'

Once again, Annie thought she saw a shadow cross Kate's face, but Annie knew her friend well enough not to ask. Although always willing to offer guidance and support, Kate rarely discussed her own personal life.

'As I said, it's up to you,' Kate said. 'But if you don't tell him, what will you say to your child when he asks about his father?'

Instinctively, Annie knew Kate was right. Whatever the consequences, telling Raphael was the right thing to do, even if he then wanted nothing to do with the baby. One day her child might want to seek out his father. How could she tell the child that its father didn't even know they existed? And if Raphael wanted contact, it wouldn't be right to deny her child the opportunity to know his father. But she had so much to think about right now, the decision could wait. The important thing was that she, Annie Thomas, ordinary woman with an ordinary life, had had this extra-ordinary thing happen to her. And for that alone she would always be grateful to Dr Raphael Castillo.

After Kate had seen a deliriously happy Annie out, she sat deep in thought. She remembered the day she had found out she was pregnant with Jem. A day infused with happiness but also regret and profound sadness. Her son had been conceived the night she had lost her husband to the first big storm almost eleven years ago. But Jem hadn't been her husband's child. While James had been out there fighting for

his life, she had been in the arms of senior partner Nick
Tremayne, and the guilt had haunted her every day since. She
hadn't been able to tell Nick that Jem was his when she'd
found out she was pregnant. It wouldn't have been fair. He
had still been married to Annabel with children of his own,
but he had found out the truth anyway and in the worst
possible way when he had overheard her telling pathologist
Eloise Haydon.

Kate rose and went across to the window. It was dark
outside and the glass pane reflected back her blurred image,
softening the faint lines that had started to appear around her
eyes. Although she was no longer in her first bloom of youth,
she still remembered in minute detail the passion her younger
self had felt all these years ago, and, if she was honest with
herself, the feelings had never truly faded.

What if she had told Nick that Jem was his as soon as she
had found out? Would he have accepted Jem as his child
then? But it was no use thinking like that. Rightly or wrongly
she had made her decision and had lived with the consequences. Now Annie had to make up her own mind whether
to tell the father of *her* child. Kate just hoped that her story
would have a different outcome from hers.

After leaving Kate, Annie had spent the rest of the night tele-
phoning her parents and siblings with her exciting news.

'Oh, darling, that's wonderful news!' her mother had said.
'I can only imagine how delighted you must be. I can't wait
to tell Dad and David. They're all down at the beach at the
moment with the children.'

Annie had felt a pang. She would have loved to share her
news face to face with her family. Instead, they were thousands of miles away.

'Do you want us to come back?' her mother had added anxiously.

'Of course not, Mum. I know how long you and Dad have been looking forward to this trip. Anyway, you'll be back in August. In plenty of time for the actual birth.'

There had been silence for a few moments.

'Does that mean you and Robert are back together?' her mother asked. Annie could hear the caution in her voice. She had never really taken to Robert and when he had left Annie after hearing she couldn't have children, she had admitted as much to her daughter. 'Any man who behaves the way he did isn't worthy of you, darling,' she had said. 'You are better off without him.'

Annie knew she'd be thinking back to her words.

'It's not Robert's baby,' Annie said quietly. Once again the silence stretched down the phone line. Annie knew her mother was dying to know who the father was, but wouldn't ask.

'The father is someone I met in Spain—a doctor,' Annie said uncomfortably. 'Not someone I'll ever see again.' She felt her toes curl with embarrassment. How could she possibly explain to anyone, even her mother, about Raphael? How he had made her feel as if they were meant to be together? And how hopelessly wrong she had been?

'As long as you're happy, darling,' her mother had said finally, gently and without judgement. 'And you won't be alone. Dad and I will be back to help you with the baby.' After a few more minutes of conversation Annie had rung off and phoned her sister Fiona. The conversation had followed a similar pattern except Fi, while thrilled for her, had in typical fashion come straight to the point.

'Does your Dr Castillo know?'

It was a timely reminder to Annie that there was more than her involved in the life growing joyously inside her.

'Not yet,' Annie admitted. 'I'm planning to tell him, but…' She let the words tail off. It wasn't a conversation she was looking forward to, especially over the phone. There was no way of knowing what his reaction would be. He would be shocked, but would he be pleased? Angry? Disinterested?

'But you will tell him,' Fi prompted. 'You know it's the right thing to do.'

'Yes,' Annie replied heavily. 'And we both know I always do the right thing.'

But she had kept putting the telephone call off. She hadn't spoken to Raphael since the morning she had left Spain, although she thought of him often, hugging the memory of the night they had spent together. If she was honest, she had hoped he would get in touch with her. There had been such a connection between them, she just couldn't believe he hadn't felt it too. But if he had, he would have found a way to contact her, wouldn't he? But he hadn't and Annie had resigned herself to never hearing from him, concentrating instead on making a life for herself that was rich and varied and relied on no one.

After a couple of days of prevaricating, she made up her mind. She looked up the number of the hospital in Barcelona and, after taking a few deep breaths to calm her nerves, dialled and asked to be put through to Dr Castillo.

As she waited for the switchboard to page him, her heart thumped painfully. How would he take the news? It was bound to be a shock, however he felt about it. When they had made love, she had told him that there was no need for contraception, although she hadn't told him why.

She chewed on her nail until suddenly she heard his unmistakable voice on the other end of the phone.

'*Hola!* Raphael Castillo.'

Immediately memories came flooding back. She could see his face in her mind, almost feel the touch of his fingers on her skin.

Her hands were shaking so hard she thought she might drop the phone. 'Raphael, it's Annie.' There was a long pause on the other end of the line. Whether it was because he couldn't remember who she was or because he was shocked to hear from her, she couldn't tell.

'How are you? Is something wrong? ' His voice sounded cautious.

'No, nothing's wrong. At least…' She let the words hang in the air. Nothing was wrong as far as she was concerned, but how would he feel? 'I'm sorry to call you at the hospital, Raphael, but I didn't know how else to contact you.'

'*De nada,*' he said. 'Please, go on.' He sounded brusque, almost distracted, as if speaking to Annie had been the last thing on his mind. She couldn't help the way her spirits dipped. How could she expect anything else? If he had wanted to get in touch with her before now, well, he knew where she worked. That night obviously hadn't meant as much to him as it had to her, but it didn't matter, she told herself firmly. She didn't need him. She had all she ever wanted growing inside her.

All of a sudden she couldn't remember the words she had rehearsed, but she knew she had to say something as he was waiting for her to speak.

'I'm pregnant,' she blurted finally, not at all how she had planned to tell him.

There was another pause, longer this time.

'Pregnant? I thought you said…'

'That I couldn't get pregnant,' she finished for him. She had told him it was safe for them to have sex. He had assumed she was on the Pill and there had been no point in disabusing him.

'I didn't think it could happen, but it did!' She couldn't keep the joy out of her voice. Every time she said the words she felt a fresh burst of happiness.

When he spoke again his voice was cold. 'Is it mine?'

Annie reeled. What was he suggesting? That she was passing off some other man's child as his? Or that she slept with so many men she couldn't possibly know which one was the father? She felt the first stirring of anger.

'Yes, it's yours. It couldn't be anyone else's. You were the only man…' She hesitated, feeling a blush steal up her cheeks. It was so difficult to talk about this over the phone. At least he couldn't see how mortified she was. 'You are the only man I've slept with since…' Once more she stumbled over the words. 'It can only be yours.'

Another long silence. Why hadn't she just written to him? It would have been so much easier. But she had never been one to take the easy way out.

'You must be over three months by now in that case,' he said slowly. The pause must have been while he had worked the timing out in his head. 'Why didn't you let me know sooner? I'm assuming you're going to keep it.' His voice was cool. He seemed so utterly different from the man she had met in Spain.

'Of course I'm going to keep it! I would hardly be telling you now if I wasn't. I've only recently found out myself.' She stumbled over the words. 'Just a few days ago, but…' She took a deep breath. How could she explain the conflicting thoughts she had had about telling him? 'I just didn't realise I was pregnant. It didn't occur to me that I could be before then.' She could only imagine what he was thinking. How could a midwife not know she was pregnant? But she didn't really want to get into her medical history over the phone. As far as she was concerned, she had done her duty in telling him.

'And?' His voice was heavy, almost suspicious. 'Why exactly are you telling me now? What do you want from me?'

Annie felt a wave of anger wash over her. She hadn't expected him to be pleased, but this reaction, as if he didn't believe or trust her, as if she had ulterior motives for contacting him, wasn't what she had expected either.

'I'm just phoning to let you know. I thought you had a right.' She laughed but the sound was mirthless even to her own ears. 'But don't worry, I don't want anything from you. Not a thing. In fact, I want to be clear that this baby is my responsibility and mine alone,' she continued. 'I don't intend to keep secrets from my child. I plan to be honest about everything from as soon as they can understand. It might be that one day, when they are older, he or she may want to find you. That's why I'm telling you. No other reason.'

'*If* it is my baby—' he emphasised the first word '—then, of course, you were right to tell me. But how can I be sure?'

Annie felt as if she'd been slapped. But to be fair he wasn't to know she didn't make a habit of sleeping with strangers, especially not men she met on holiday. She took another breath to calm herself.

'It's yours. There is absolutely no doubt. But if you don't want to accept that, it's entirely up to you. I have done my bit. I'll say goodbye now.'

She thought she heard him say, 'Wait, Annie,' as she replaced the receiver, but she was in no mood to continue the discussion. As far as she was concerned, Raphael would play no part in her or her baby's life. And that was fine by her.

Raphael replaced the phone thoughtfully. It had been a shock hearing Annie's voice after all these months. He remembered every cadence of her soft accent and as soon as he had heard her speak, it had been as if she had been back in his arms.

It wasn't as if he hadn't thought about her every day since the night they had met. He hadn't been able to get her striking pale green eyes out of his mind, her wounded mouth, her pale skin a striking contrast to her luxurious dark brown hair and that deep but unmistakable air of sadness. How could he forget the curve of her hips, the sweep of her thighs, her tiny waist? He groaned aloud at the memory. He had done his best to put her out of his mind, and now, when he least expected it, she was back in his life. Because she was pregnant. With his baby. Or so she said.

He started pacing. There was no reason for Annie to lie about such a thing and she had made it perfectly clear that she wanted nothing from him. But he had been lied to before and he knew he couldn't trust his heart. It was why he had stayed away from her in the first place, even when every part of him had longed to be with her again. He swore under his breath. If she was lying, he would find out. But if there was any chance she was carrying his child, any chance at all…

He clenched his jaw against the painful memory of Sebastian. *Dios!* This time no one was going to take his child from him. He had to know the truth and there was only one way to find out.

CHAPTER THREE

OVER the next week, Annie mulled over her conversation with Raphael. She wondered if there had been any point in telling him she was pregnant. It might have been the right thing to do, but it had obviously made no difference. She hadn't heard a peep from him since the call and that was fine by her. What he chose to do with the information was up to him.

Nevertheless, she couldn't help acknowledge that she felt sad about his response. Not for herself, but for the child growing inside her. One day, he—or she—might want to know about their father and she would have to find a way of telling her child that his father had shown no interest.

Everyone at work knew about her pregnancy and it was all Annie could do to stop herself accosting strangers in the street and telling them that she was expecting a baby. She was so happy she wanted to shout it from the rooftops. But as far as who the father was, that would be her secret. Somehow explaining about Raphael would make it sound like a casual fling—when it had been anything but. Besides, as he had shown no interest, there was no reason for anyone, apart from her immediate family, to know his identity. She would be raising this child on her own and that was fine by her.

Annie chewed her lip. She looked around her tiny home with its double bedroom, minute single bedroom, kitchen and lounge. She loved it. It was so cosy, especially in the winter when she would light a fire and cuddle up on the sofa with a good book, but it wasn't really big enough for her and a baby. The second bedroom would only just be large enough for a cot and a changing table. However, it would have to do. Despite the small inheritance from her grandfather, money was bound to be tight after her maternity pay came to an end. But what did money or any material possessions matter when balanced against having a baby? It didn't. She would have happily given up everything she owned if she'd had to just to be in this position.

A knock on the door interrupted her thoughts. Annie wasn't expecting anyone. Sunday was a day that everyone she knew spent with their families. Puzzled, she opened the door to find the last person she expected standing there, a half-smile on his face.

Raphael! It couldn't be! What on earth was he doing here, in Penhally Bay? And why did her heart feel as if it had stopped beating?

Speechless, Annie stood aside to let him enter, and as he passed her she felt her skin prickle. Her breath caught in her throat as instantly she was transported back to the night she had spent in his arms.

She waved at a chair, still unable to speak, but he shook his head. Instead, he paced her small house with nervous energy.

'I had to come,' he said simply.

'Why?' she said, dry-mouthed. 'I told you there was no need.'

'Because if there is a chance you are having my baby,' he

said, sounding incredulous, 'I want to be here for him. He will need a father. I don't even know if you can look after a child.'

Annie felt her temper rise. Just who did he think he was, coming here to check up on her, questioning not only her morals but her ability to look after *her* child?

'Believe me, I am having *your* baby, and I'm perfectly able to look after it by myself. I certainly didn't expect you to come charging over here like a knight on a white horse.'

'But now I am here to find out if it is really mine.'

Annie swallowed, forcing herself to stay calm. 'You have to make up your own mind whether you believe me or not—although I can't think why you imagine I'm lying to you. As far as I'm concerned, I've told you. What you do with the information is up to you.'

He looked at her with flat eyes.

'You told me it was safe for us to have sex. Why did you tell me that if it wasn't true?'

'I thought it was safe. I never dreamt I could fall pregnant,' Annie replied, trying to keep her voice even. 'Look, I don't care whether you believe me or not. I'm not asking anything from you, so you are hardly in a position to demand proof from me!'

Suddenly the tension left Raphael's face. He grinned, the lopsided smile reminding Annie once again of the man she had met back in Spain.

'Please forgive me. I didn't come to make you angry with me. I want to believe it is mine and as long as there is that chance, I'm staying. Right here. In Penhally Bay.'

'You're staying here?' Annie said incredulously. 'But what about your job back in Spain?'

Raphael shrugged. 'I managed to persuade them to give me a six-month sabbatical. And I have a post for that time in the hospital at St Piran.' He nodded in the vague direction of the hospital a good thirty minutes up the road.

'You have a job? At St. Piran's?' Annie was only too aware that she was repeating his words parrot fashion. But it was all such a shock. At the very most, she'd imagined her staying in touch with him by phone, at least until the baby was born. Then the odd visit. But it seemed she had totally underestimated the man.

'How on earth did you manage to get a job at the hospital so soon? I only phoned you last week.'

'I know many people,' he said. 'I have many connections through my work. In the end it was not too difficult.' He smiled, a flash of white against his bronzed skin. 'And I specialise in high-risk pregnancies. So they were happy to have me on their team.'

Annie sat down in the chair. He could stand if he liked, but she needed something more solid to support her legs, which seemed to have turned to rubber again. He specialised in high-risk pregnancies. That meant they'd be working together. Every day.

'I need to know everything is all right with the baby,' he continued. 'You must be in your second trimester by now. Have you had a scan? Is everything normal? Have you been taking folic acid?' He fired the questions at Annie as if he were an interrogating officer of a hostile army.

'Perhaps you'd like to know what size feet I have while you're at it,' Annie muttered under her breath. Whatever he said, these weren't the questions of a man who doubted that he was the father. Suddenly she relented. He was here now and he was entitled to know how her pregnancy was progressing.

'Please, Raphael, sit down,' Annie said quietly. She

couldn't think straight while he was prowling around her like a lion circling its prey. For once he did as she asked and sat down in her armchair, still eyeing her warily.

'Everything is normal, and, yes, I have had a scan.' She stood up, relieved to find that her legs could support her, crossed over to her bookshelf and pulled out the photograph of her scan. Silently she passed it over to him.

She watched as Raphael studied the photograph carefully. A kaleidoscope of emotions crossed his face ranging from awe to intense interest. Then he looked at her and it was if the shutters came down.

'Good,' he said flatly. 'Everything looks as it should. Is it a boy or a girl?'

Annie hid a smile. He seemed determined not to show her how affected he was, but pride—or was it possessiveness?—was written all over his face. Suddenly she felt uneasy.

'I don't know the sex,' she said. 'I want it to be a surprise. Look, Raphael, if you wanted to check up on how the pregnancy was going, you could have phoned me, come for a visit even, but from what you've told me, you're planning to stick around. For the next six months at least.'

'If it is my child,' he said, 'then it needs a father as well as a mother. I don't have to stay here, you can come back with me to Spain. It will be better. You can stop work, stay with my family.'

Annie shook her head, dismayed. 'You can't be serious.' She gave a small laugh. 'Why on earth would I want to do that? My life is here. My job, my friends, my family. My baby will be born here and live here. We don't need you to support us. Is that the reason you think I called? So you would come running with financial support?'

Annie was trying hard to keep her tone even. Just who did

he think he was to come barging back into her life? Hadn't she made her position perfectly clear?

Suddenly Raphael looked contrite. 'I am sorry,' he said. 'I came in here like a bull in a…how do you say? Field? Shop?'

'China shop,' Annie answered automatically.

'Whatever. Forgive me?' he said, the boyish grin back on his face. 'It is just that I too want this child very much. I have to be part of his life. Can you understand?'

'Yes. Of course. It's just that I wasn't expecting you to come rushing over here, taking a job. Speaking of which, what happens after your job comes to an end?'

'Oh, I will not go back to Spain—not until I can take my child with me. Until then, I will stay here. It is settled.'

'You plan to live here? Permanently?' Annie said shocked. Whatever she had been expecting, it wasn't this.

Raphael crossed his arms across his chest and nodded emphatically. 'If I have to.'

'I suppose I can't stop you,' Annie said slowly. 'But I want to make one thing clear—this baby is my responsibility.'

'And mine.' His mouth was set in a determined line.

'I am happy to be on my own. I don't want any thing from you—least of all a relationship. Although I guess the fact that you never tried to contact me means that it was never an option as far as you were concerned, either.'

Raphael narrowed his eyes at her. 'We never made any promises, either of us. There were things…' He paused, shaking his head. 'It just couldn't be.'

He was right, of course. There hadn't been any promises on either side, but that hadn't stopped her hoping he would get in touch, even while she knew she had nothing to offer him.

'Where will you live?' Annie asked, dragging her thoughts back to the present.

'I have taken a room in a hotel near the hospital for the time being, but I will look for a place here in Penhally Bay. I want to keep an eye on you and the pregnancy.'

Annie's thoughts were all over the place. He was here and if that wasn't a big enough shock, he was planning to stay.

'I should tell you that I have consulted a lawyer, in Spain as well as in the UK. I'm going to ask for shared access. No one is going to stop me seeing my child.'

Annie looked at him, aghast. Her growing feeling of unease was spot on. He was here and determined to interfere with her life. It was one thing letting him know he was going to be a father, quite another him demanding legal access. Too late, the memory of the words he had spoken in Spain came rushing back. 'If she were my child,' he had said referring to Maria, 'nothing and no one would stop me claiming what belongs to me.' At the time his words had meant little but now they burnt into her brain, sending a frisson of fear down her spine. What on earth had she done? And what could she do about it now?

CHAPTER FOUR

ANNIE studied the CTG of the pregnant woman whose labour she was monitoring for the umpteenth time. Although the contractions were still several minutes apart, the baby's heartbeat kept slowing down. Over the last couple of hours it had returned to normal within a few seconds, but this time the baby's heart rate stayed slow. The baby was clearly in distress and Annie knew that the mother should be delivered right now. Making up her mind, she asked one of the staff midwives to page the on-call consultant and let them know they were needed straight away.

While she waited, Annie explained to her patient that it was likely she would need to have a C-section.

Audrey looked at her with frightened eyes. 'I really wanted a natural birth,' she said.

'I know you did,' Annie said softly. She had been involved with Audrey's pregnancy all the way through and had helped her put a birth plan together.

'But sometimes things don't turn out the way we'd hoped. This is the best for your baby. And that's what's important in the end, isn't it? We should be able to give you a spinal, so at least you'll be awake to welcome your child into the world.'

ANNE FRASER   53

Audrey sought her husband's hand. 'Of course you're
right. All that matters is that my baby is okay.' She grimaced
as another contraction hit her. 'I trust you to decide what's
right for us,' she told Annie once the wave of pain had passed.

During the contraction, Annie had been watching the
baby's heartbeat on the monitor. As before, it slowed down,
but this time it was almost three minutes before the heart rate
returned to normal. Where was the obstetrician? She tried to
remember who was on call for labour ward, but couldn't.
There had been so many changes recently with people going
on leave, it was hard to keep up

Just as she was about to ask Julie, her fellow midwife, to
call the consultant again, Raphael strode into the room.

'Someone paged me,' he said, seemingly oblivious to the
fact that Annie was in the room. Although she had known
she'd bump into him sooner rather than later, she was unpre-
pared for the way her heart started pounding in her chest.

'It was me, Dr Castillo,' Annie said, thankful her voice
didn't betray the unsteady beating of her heart. 'Audrey's
baby is having repeated prolonged decelerations. She's only
5 cms. I think we need to get her delivered straight away.' She
handed the CTG printout to Raphael, who studied it for a few
moments before nodding.

'You're absolutely right,' he said. 'We need to get Audrey
to theatre straight away. Could someone let the anaesthetist
know we need him to do a spinal? Come on, let's get going.'
As everyone reacted to his words, he bent over Audrey. 'Try
not to worry. We'll have your baby out and in your arms
shortly.'

There wasn't time in the next few minutes for Annie to
think about anything except her patient. Quickly she and
Julie, with a few words of reassurance to Audrey and her

husband, started wheeling the bed down to theatre. Minutes later, Annie was washing her hands next to Raphael while he scrubbed up.

'Excellent call,' he said approvingly. 'It's good that you didn't wait any longer before calling me.'

'I have been a midwife for several years, Dr Castillo.'

Raphael arched an eyebrow but said nothing. Annie followed him into theatre.

Annie stood back ready to receive Audrey's baby while Raphael, after checking with the anaesthetist that Audrey's lower body was suitably numb, cut into the abdomen and then into the uterus. They all waited with bated breath as he pulled out the baby. There was a second of complete stillness before a lusty cry of rage broke the silence. Everyone smiled. Raphael passed the baby across to Annie who promptly wrapped it in a blanket before checking that the airway was clear.

'You have a beautiful baby boy,' she said to Audrey, passing her the newborn to hold. 'And he's absolutely perfect.'

While Raphael was suturing the wound in Audrey's abdomen, Annie, a lump in her throat, watched as Audrey and her husband cooed over their son. No matter how many times she delivered a baby, it always got to her, but for the first time in as long as she could remember there was no stab of envy as she watched a mother with her baby. In a few months' time, she would be holding a child of her own.

Glancing up from the happy trio, she found Raphael's speculative eyes on hers and wondered if he was thinking the same thing.

'We'll get you up to recovery as soon as Dr Castillo has finished closing,' she told Audrey. 'I'm just going to weigh your son and then I'll give him right back to you. Then you can try giving him a feed.' As soon as she finished checking the baby over, she passed him back to Audrey, and helped her settle her son onto the breast. Happily the tiny infant got the hang of it straight away and was soon sucking contentedly. Annie felt her throat constrict. Damn the tears that were never far away these days. At least these were the right kind of tears.

As soon as she had settled mother and baby in the postnatal ward, she headed off to the staff room. She needed to find a place where she could be alone with her thoughts. How on earth was she going to cope over the next few months, seeing Raphael every day? Yesterday she had asked him to leave, promising that they would talk again, but what could she say to him? That she had never stopped thinking about him and the night they had shared together? That it had taken all her willpower not to call him and that seeing him again had made her greedy for more? That suddenly she wanted it all—a child, yes, but also someone who loved them…both. But she knew that wasn't going to happen. If that night had meant anything at all he would have found her before now, despite what they had told each other.

As she tried to concentrate on her paperwork she became aware of someone watching her. She looked up to find Raphael studying her with an odd expression in his eyes.

'*Hola,*' he said softly. 'Can I come in?'

'It's not really a good time. I have to finish this paperwork before my afternoon clinic.'

He ignored her and, frowning, stepped into the room. 'When, then?' he demanded. 'When would be a good time? Because you and I need to talk about this baby,' he said. A muscle twitched in his cheek. He wasn't quite as casual as he had first seemed.

'I'm not sure that there's anything left to talk about,' Annie said. Then she relented. It had been a shock seeing him again, but now he was here, and she would be working closely with him over the coming months, she could hardly ignore him.

'Look,' she said. 'Why don't you come over this evening? Around seven? We can talk then, okay?'

He crossed the room and leaned over the table, his brown eyes drilling into hers. Annie felt like a moth trapped in a light and it was all she could do to stop herself from leaping up and moving away. Somehow she found the resolve to return his look steadily. He searched her face for a moment.

'Okay,' he said. 'Until tonight.' And, turning on his heel, he was gone.

As soon as Annie got home, she rushed around tidying up before jumping in the shower. As she soaped her body, she felt the small burgeoning lump of her pregnancy under her fingers and smiled. Then, as she let the hot water ease away the tiredness, her thoughts focused on Raphael. How would she cope, seeing him every day? Especially when the rapid beating of her heart every time she looked at him told her that the connection she had felt with him in Spain was still there. It hadn't just been the Mediterranean sun after all, though she had always known it had been much more than that.

Finishing her shower, she went to slip on a pair of jeans, but to her dismay, and secret delight, she couldn't do up the button. It was time to go shopping for some maternity clothes. She hadn't allowed herself to think that far ahead until now. A little suspicious side of her was afraid of tempting fate. She discarded the too-tight jeans in favour of a simple dress. Then she brushed her long dark hair until it shone, before adding a touch of eye shadow and lipstick. She refused to ask herself why she was taking so much time with her appearance.

The late spring evening was unseasonably warm, so she opened the window and the smell of her climbing roses floated in on the breeze. Should she offer him a meal? she wondered. What was the polite way to behave when meeting the father of your child after a one-night stand? Once again, she felt her face grow warm at the memory. She thought about phoning Fiona to tell her Raphael had turned up, and asking her for advice, but before she had the chance, there was a knock on her door. She felt a tingle of apprehension dance up her spine as she opened the door.

Raphael stood in the doorway, holding a bunch of tulips. She couldn't read the expression on his face, and before she could say anything, he handed her the flowers.

'Thank you,' she said simply, burying her nose in their fragrance. 'They're lovely.' She stood aside to let him enter. Once again she was dismayed at the way her heart was thumping.

'I thought we could go for a walk,' Annie said, feeling the need for neutral territory. 'I could show you Penhally Bay.'

'I would like that.'

Annie draped a sweater over her shoulders and soon they were following the road down to the harbour.

'How are your family?' she asked. 'And little Maria? I have thought of her often.'

'They are all well. Maria asks after the British woman with the sad green eyes often.' He stopped and turned towards her. 'But you don't look so sad to me any more.' He traced a finger down the line of her jaw. 'You look happy.'

'I am. Very happy.'

They continued following the road until they came to the lighthouse. They stood looking across the harbour to the sea beyond.

'It's hard to believe right now, when everything is so calm, but there was a bad storm here,' Annie said. 'It caused a lot of damage and there are still a lot of repairs being carried out to some of the buildings. A couple of people lost their lives. It's a small community and everybody feels it when something so awful happens.'

'It must have been hard on everyone. It is like this where my mother lives in Spain. Everybody knows and helps each other. It is a good way to live.'

'It's quiet now,' Annie continued. 'But you wouldn't believe how busy it gets in the summer months. I love it here.'

'In my country, we are always outdoors.' Raphael stopped and looked at her intently. 'It is a good country for a child to live. They can be outside playing instead of inside playing computer games, like so many of the children in this country.'

It seemed their walk was just another opportunity for Raphael to try and convince her to come and live in Spain, she thought, unable to prevent a stab of disappointment. Couldn't he see it was out of the question?

'Children here in Penhally Bay have a good life too,' she said. 'Many of them surf or sail, and there's always the beach for the younger ones. I loved it here when I was a child. It is a good place, a safe place for children. The community looks out for each other. Admittedly it attracts thousands of tourists in the summer, but that is a good thing too. It means that there is plenty going on for teenagers as well as adults. We have a very low crime rate here.'

'It is beautiful,' Raphael admitted, his eyes sweeping the bay. 'Almost as beautiful as where I live. But the weather.' He spread his hands. 'It is cold. And the rain. In Spain, there is always family around. The children spend time with their grandparents and aunts and uncles as well as cousins. Like you say, there are always people to watch out.'

They carried on walking, falling into step alongside each other. 'What about your family?' he asked. 'Don't you mind being far away from them?'

'I go to see my parents and my sister often and sometimes they come here. I'd always planned go to Australia to see my brother and his family, but I guess I'll have to shelve that plan for a while.' She smiled, thinking of the reason a visit to Australia would be out of the question for some time. 'We lived in Penhally Bay until I was about seven, when we moved to Edinburgh, so it always felt like a second home.'

'Why did you come back? Did you not like Edinburgh?'

'I'm not really a city girl. I love being able to open my front door and let the sea air in. I love the way everyone knows everyone else here—even if it does mean people know more about your business than you'd like.'

She slid a glance at him, wondering if he realised that the pair of them were bound to become a source of gossip. Not that it would be malicious, but people were bound to speculate eventually about the pregnant midwife and the Spanish doctor.

'So, they will talk about us,' Raphael said, shrugging his shoulders. 'It is of no importance. I am not ashamed.'

'Look, Raphael, can we talk about why you're here?' Annie was panting slightly as she spoke. Raphael placed a hand on her arm, indicating a bench with a tip of his dark head and leading her towards it.

They sat in silence for a few minutes, watching the surfers out at sea. The waves were a decent size and a number of people were making the most of it.

'You told me you've spoken to the lawyers about access. You didn't need to do that. I wouldn't stop you from seeing your child, not as long as you came to see him when you were supposed to. The only thing I don't want is a father who flits in and out of my child's life. A father who can't be depended on. I would much rather you have no involvement than that. But it scares me that you are consulting lawyers. I don't really understand why you seem to feel the need. I would have done anything to have a child. The last thing I would do is to take it away from you.'

Raphael brought his eyebrows together. 'Is that what happened, Annie? You wanted a child and you used me to have one?'

'It wasn't like that!' Annie insisted. 'You don't understand…'

He turned cool brown eyes on her. 'What is there to understand? You have what you want,' he said. 'Now I will have what is mine.'

Annie shivered. There was no mistaking the determination in the set of his mouth.

'In which case,' she replied, 'if that is what you think of me, I don't think there is anything left to say.'

She stood, leaving him sitting there staring out to sea.

CHAPTER FIVE

OVER the next week Annie kept bumping into Raphael but apart from his pointed enquiries into how she was feeling, their contact was limited to clinical discussions. When she saw him with his patients she was struck by his easygoing manner and they all seemed to love the way he managed to achieve the right balance between casual joking and interested concern. However, when he looked at her, his expression turned cool.

And it wasn't just the patients. He was causing quite a stir among the other female members of staff too. Annie was constantly overhearing conversations speculating about whether Dr Castillo was involved with anyone. Thankfully no one guessed that Annie and Raphael had met before, let alone that she was carrying his baby.

Annie was looking forward to a couple of days off over the weekend. She loved her job, but she hadn't been sleeping well the last few nights. Not since Raphael had turned up, in fact, and she was longing for an early night in bed with a good book.

She only had one more patient to see before she called it a day. Morgan was an anxious-looking woman who had come for her first antenatal appointment. She had taken a home pregnancy test and estimated she was about eight weeks pregnant.

'We'll just do another one here,' Annie said. 'If that's okay with you?'

'Is that necessary? I mean, there's no doubt I'm pregnant. The test was positive and my breasts are tender and I've even developed a bump already.' She dropped her hand to her stomach, a dreamy smile on her face. But there was something that was sending alarm bells ringing for Annie. She couldn't quite put her finger on it, but she knew she'd be happier when she repeated the test herself.

When she looked at the stick, she knew that her instincts had been correct. The test was negative. Not even the faintest blue line. Her heart sank. She hated days like these when she had to be the bearer of bad news. If Morgan had been pregnant, she wasn't any longer. Just to make absolutely sure, Annie decided to ask Raphael to come and see her.

Morgan must have seen the look on her face when she came back into the room. Her face puckered.

'I am so sorry,' Annie said gently. 'But the test is negative.' She could feel every word pierce the woman like an arrow.

'But I have to be! I've wanted this for so long. And I have all the symptoms. Your test must be wrong.'

'I don't think it is, but just in case, I'm going to ask Dr Castillo to scan you. He has the most experience of scanning women in early pregnancy.'

Morgan started to cry and Annie's heart went out to her. She paged Raphael, hoping that he hadn't left for the day. She was relieved when he answered, and when she told him about her concerns he said that he would come immediately.

Annie had only enough time to prepare her patient for the scan when Raphael arrived. As usual he looked breathtakingly handsome, but Annie, still reeling from his revelation about consulting a lawyer, told herself that she couldn't care less how he looked. Any man who suggested that she had used him to get pregnant and in the same breath threatened to take her child from her wasn't a man she wanted anything to do with. How she could have fooled herself into thinking that they were some kind of kindred spirits was beyond her. And if he made her heart tumble every time she saw him, that was just physical attraction and she would get over it.

Annie brought him up to speed and Raphael took Morgan by the hand and looked into her eyes.

'I am just going to have a look at your uterus,' he said softly. 'If there is a baby in there, I will find it. Have you had any bleeding?' Morgan shook her head silently.

Raphael waited while Annie squirted some ultrasound gel on Morgan's belly. Then he glided the probe over her tummy while watching the monitor intently. Finally he shook his head.

'I'm sorry, but there is no baby there. In fact, there is no evidence you have been pregnant recently.'

'But I am,' Morgan wailed. 'Please look again. It must be there. I swear I even felt it move yesterday.'

Raphael and Annie shared a look across the top of Morgan's head. Annie was bewildered. What was going on here?

Raphael took Annie outside while their patient got dressed again.

'I think she has a ghost pregnancy,' he said.

'You mean a phantom pregnancy?' Annie was astonished. She had never come across one of those before, although she had read about them. Apparently it could happen when women so desperately wanted to be pregnant they managed to convince themselves that they were.

Raphael nodded. 'She must want a child very much.'

Annie could understand Morgan's feelings and her heart ached for her. She knew what it was like to yearn for a baby, to feel that something was missing from life. Although she had never imagined herself to be pregnant, she would have done anything to have a child.

Annie almost smiled at the irony of it. Robert hadn't loved her enough to want to adopt a child with her and now here was a man who was determined to be a father to her child, and she wasn't sure she wanted him around.

'I need to talk to Morgan,' she said.

'Would you prefer me to?' Raphael asked.

'No, she's my patient. It's my job,' Annie said heavily. 'But I wish I were about to tell her something different.'

Annie saw a distraught but resigned Morgan out a little later, and after finishing her paperwork for the day left for home herself. She was surprised to find Raphael waiting by the hospital exit. She nodded a goodnight in his direction, but he caught up with her and walked beside her.

'Are you okay?' he asked, searching her face. 'That must have been difficult for you.'

'I'm fine. It's all part of the job after all, isn't it? Most of the time our work has a happy outcome, but sometimes…' She shrugged. 'Things don't work out the way we want.'

'But it upset you. You tried not to show it, but I could see it on your face.'

There it was again. This man's uncanny ability to perceive every emotion she felt. Even when she did her best to hide her feelings. Everyone thought nothing ruffled her, that she was able to keep herself emotionally detached, and she let them think that. Not least because it was the opposite of the truth. Her colleagues would be dismayed if they knew just how keenly she felt her patients' pain.

Perhaps it was because she understood their longing for a child only too well.

'Yes, it did upset me. But I'll put it behind me. And move on.'

'Can you? Can you really put your feelings aside? Just like that?' He placed his hands on her shoulders, stopping her in her tracks before turning her around and looking into her eyes. She felt a dizzying sense of being caught up in his aura like a leaf in the wind. The rest of the world seemed to recede until it was just the two of them, in a bubble of their own. 'I need to know that you are okay,' he said roughly, breaking the spell and bringing her back to reality.

For a second Annie thought he was talking about her, but as his eyes dropped to her stomach she realised he was talking about her baby. Of course. Well, he had never pretended he was interested in her. As far as he was concerned, she was just a walking incubator for his child. She felt a flash of temper.

She sighed. 'Don't worry, Raphael. *I'm* still pregnant. And I will let you know if there is a problem.' However, seeing the look on his face, she took pity on him. It must be difficult to be a man sometimes. To feel excluded. But that wasn't her concern. He would just have to deal with it.

'The baby's fine, honestly,' she said. Then she couldn't help herself. 'I think I might have felt it move yesterday for the first time.'

His eyes glowed and he dropped a hand to her stomach. He left it there for a second. Once again Annie felt electrifying shocks shoot through her body and her knees turned to jelly.

She stepped away from him as if she'd been stung. 'Hey, you'd have to stand there for a long time if you're waiting to feel it move.' She looked around the car park. Although it was almost empty, there was always a chance somebody would see them and what they'd make of Dr Castillo with his hand on her belly was anyone's guess. One thing was for sure, though, she wasn't ready for anyone to know that he was the father of her child. Not yet, at any rate.

'You haven't told anyone, have you?' she said, suddenly horrified at the possibility that the identity of the father of her child was no longer a secret.

'No, just my mother. She is delighted that she is going to be a grandmother again. She remembers you well, the way you were with Maria, and thinks you will make a very good mother. She is looking forward to meeting her grandchild in a few months' time.'

Annie decided to let that pass. At least for the time being. She had no intention of letting her baby out of her sight and certainly not to Spain. Not without her at any rate. She had heard too many scary stories about kidnapped children and the way Raphael was about this baby, she'd put nothing past him.

She started back to her car. She didn't want to be rude but all she wanted to do was get home and gather her thoughts.

'Do you need a lift?' Annie asked. 'Or have you sorted yourself out with a car as well as a job?' She hadn't meant it to come out quite so waspishly, but the way this man was organising his life around her baby was unsettling her.

'Yes.' He waved in the direction of a sleek silver sports car. 'I drove it from Spain. And I have found a house in the village to live in, just ten minutes from your home.' He quirked an eyebrow at her, as if gauging her reaction to his news.

'So you're definitely staying, then?'

He looked surprised. 'Sí. I told you I was. I accepted this job at the hospital. I cannot leave now, even if I wanted to.'

He took a step towards Annie. 'You have to accept it. I am not going anywhere without my child.'

The next day was Saturday and Annie had been invited to a barbecue at Lucy and Ben's home. She didn't know Lucy, who was one of the doctors at the surgery and Nick's daughter, and who had gone on maternity leave before Annie had started at St Piran's, but she knew Ben, who was an A and E consultant at the hospital. She hadn't wanted to go, not sure she was ready to field questions about her own pregnancy, but Kate had pressed her.

'You should get to know more people in Penhally, Annie. I know your friends and family are far away, and once you have the baby, you'll appreciate knowing more of the mothers. It's helpful to have someone to compare notes with.'

Annie waited until she knew the barbecue would be almost over. Sure enough, by the time she arrived, the guests with young children were already beginning to leave, although there was still loads of food. Tables had been laid out on the lawn, which overlooked the sea, and the scent of grilling sausages filled the air.

There were a few familiar faces as well as some that she didn't recognize, but there was one in particular that made her heart thump. She hadn't expected to see Raphael there.

As she greeted the other guests she watched Raphael from the corner of her eye. He looked completely at ease, as if he'd known everyone for years. It seemed as if he felt her eyes on him, because he turned and stared directly at her. Annie felt her breath catch in her throat. He really was the most beautiful man she had ever met, with his Latin colouring emphasised by his crisp white T-shirt and the faded jeans that clung to the contours of his thighs. Once again the memory of the night they had shared came rushing back. She remembered only too well the touch of his hands and mouth on her body, the way he had made her feel as if she were the only woman in the world, and the most beautiful woman he had ever held in his arms. And the intensity in his deep brown eyes told her he was remembering too. She felt a heat low in her body and she almost groaned aloud. Why did he have to come back into her life right now, when she thought she had everything all planned out?

Kate must have noticed her hovering on the fringe of the party. The older midwife came over and touched her briefly on the arm. 'Are you okay, Annie? You look as if you've seen a ghost. Do you want a drink of water or something?'

'No, I'm fine,' Annie said, summoning a smile, rubbing her lower back. A niggling ache had started that morning. She had put it down to the added weight of the baby putting a strain on her lower muscles, but an underlying anxiety that something was wrong wouldn't go away. For a split second she wondered whether to ask Kate's advice, but immediately dismissed the idea. She was probably just being over-anxious. Besides, she didn't want to draw attention to herself or ruin her friend's day off.

'I just feel a bit tired. You know how we are always telling our pregnant patients that it's normal to feel exhausted? It's quite different to experience it yourself.'

'You don't have to stay long,' Kate said. 'Lucy and Ben will understand.'

'Thanks, Kate. I'll probably just say hello to everyone, then make my excuses. But I'm dying to see little Josh again.'

She picked up an orange juice from a table and sipped the drink, happy to have something to distract her from Raphael. She glanced around.

Ben and Lucy were showing off their latest arrival, baby Josh, to a group of admirers. Apart from Chloe and her husband Oliver, a GP at Penhally Bay Surgery, there was Nick Tremayne with a blonde woman Annie hadn't seen before. Dragan Lovak, another of the partners, was there too, with his stunning wife, the village vet. Their young son sat at their feet, playing.

Annie went over to join them. It was the first time that she had been able to see a baby without feeling a wash of regret and she was happy to join in the crowd fussing over the cheerful, plump baby. Nevertheless, as she watched Oliver stand with his wife wrapped in the circle of his arms, she felt a sharp stab that she and her baby would never be part of a loving unit. She moved away, wanting to be alone with her thoughts.

How would it be to have Raphael around—a permanent part of her child's life, if not hers?

As if he could read her mind, Raphael excused himself from whatever conversation he'd been having with Ben and came towards her. For a moment she wanted to run away. Her heart was pattering away inside her chest and she was finding it difficult to breathe. Her symptoms only increased as he came to stand beside her.

'Dr Castillo,' Annie greeted him formally, aware of Kate's speculative gaze. 'I didn't expect to see you here.'

'Dr Carter—Ben—asked me. We met at the hospital. He thought it would be good for me to meet some of the locals. He knows I am far from home.'

'Everyone is very welcoming here. It's a small community.' Annie let her eyes sweep the garden. Usually she avoided gatherings such as this one. Everyone always brought their children, and until now she had avoided occasions where she would see loving couples proudly showing off their offspring. But now everything was different. For the first time she could admire the babies without the tiniest bit of envy.

'Are you all right? You look pale,' Raphael asked, his eyes dropping to her belly. Once again Annie was reminded that, as far as he was concerned, she was little more than a human incubator for his unborn child. She felt a crippling stab of disappointment. But what else did she expect?

He was watching her, his brown eyes glinting, and she shivered. She wondered if he knew how much he affected her. He wasn't to know that the night they had spent together had been the most exhilarating night of her life, one she knew she would treasure for ever. He wasn't to know that she had been unable to get him out of her mind ever since. Thank God.

'I'm okay,' she said. 'If a little tired. I don't plan on staying long.'

Again there was a sharp look from eyes the colour of the mountains in the evening. His eyes raked her body.

He bent over and whispered in her ear. She could smell the tang of his aftershave and feel the heat of his breath on her neck. It took all her willpower not to shiver with delight. 'Pregnancy suits you,' he said softly. 'You are all curves and your face…' He hesitated as if searching for the right words. 'Your face is glowing. You don't look tired. You look beautiful.'

This time Annie couldn't prevent the blood staining her cheeks. There was something intimate in the way he spoke to her that made her feel as if they were the only two people in the world. 'If you want to leave,' he said, 'I will walk you home.'

'We don't want people to talk,' Annie managed through a dust-dry mouth. He had walked her home that night in Spain and look where that had led! Was he suggesting that they pick

up where they had left off? Was he *flirting* with her? No, the
idea was ridiculous.

Raphael looked around in surprise at the people gathered
in the room. 'But they will have to know some time. Do you
think you can keep us a secret for ever?'

'There is no "us",' she reminded him coolly.

'But there is. You, me and our child. I will be proud to
be known as the father. And I am certain you are proud to
be pregnant.'

'Of course I am, and everyone at the hospital knows about
the baby already—I'm booked in at St Piran's after all. Kate,
Chloe and Nick all know obviously, Kate's my midwife as
well as my friend and Nick is my GP. But as for them
knowing who the father is? Can't we keep that under wraps
for the time being? Please?'

Raphael frowned. Then he smiled gently. 'If you wish. For
the *time being*.' He echoed her words. 'It will give us a chance
to get to know each other properly. Now, would you let me
walk you home? It will give us the chance to talk.'

Suddenly Annie wanted nothing more than the comfort of
her own house. Her mind was whirling, whether from
Raphael's proximity or the promise in his words she couldn't
be sure. As he had pointed out they did need to get to know
each other—so that they could reach some sort of arrangement for their child. And she was curious to know more about
this enigmatic man. For her baby's sake, of course.

'I just need to visit the bathroom first,' she said, trying to
sound casual.

Since they'd been talking the dull ache she'd been experiencing earlier had grown in intensity. Her heart thudding, she
told Raphael that she wouldn't be a minute, and hurried away.

When she made it to the toilet she was distraught to

discover that she had begun to bleed. Not huge amounts admittedly, but enough to scare her witless. Was she having a miscarriage? She slid down onto the bathroom floor and hugged her knees to her chest, gasping as a wave of terror and shock raked her body. She *couldn't* lose this baby. Not now. Not when the dream she had longed for, had thought was out of her reach, had finally come true. But hadn't she, deep in her soul, known that it was too good to be true? That somehow it wasn't in her destiny to be a mother?

She didn't know how long she had sat there when she heard a soft tap at the door.

'Annie, are you all right?' Raphael's deep tones penetrated the fog of grief and fear. She scrambled to her feet. He would know what to do. He would help her.

She opened the door and Raphael took one look at her face before gathering her into his arms.

'What is it? What is wrong?' he demanded. He held her at arm's length, forcing her to look at him. 'Is it the baby?'

Annie nodded, unable to speak. His face paled and she saw her anguish reflected in his eyes.

'What is happening?' he coaxed gently. 'Tell me exactly.'

Annie drew strength from him. 'I'm bleeding,' she said simply, and then in a rush the tears came and she was crying in his arms. 'My baby,' she gulped between the sobs that racked her body. 'I can't lose my baby.'

Raphael scooped her into his arms and carried her, still sobbing into his chest, past the startled glances of the other guests. Everyone stopped speaking for a moment and then Annie and Raphael were surrounded. But it was Kate who spoke first.

'What's wrong?' she asked quietly.

'She's bleeding. I am going to take her to St Piran's.' Even in her distress, Annie could hear he was having difficulty keeping his voice even.

'I'll come with you,' Kate said. 'I'll drive while you take care of Annie.'

'I'll come too.' Annie recognized Chloe's anxious voice.

'We can manage, Chloe,' Kate said gently. 'Hopefully it's nothing serious. I'll call you later.'

And then Annie felt herself being lifted into the back of the car. Raphael covered her with his jacket before getting in beside her. He pulled her into his arms and stroked her head while her sobs turned to hiccups. Kate started the car and with a squeal of tyres headed towards St Piran's. They were the most dreadful minutes of Annie's life, but she was glad that Raphael was with her. He, more than anyone, would know what she was going through.

At the hospital, Raphael insisted on carrying her up to the maternity wing, Kate having to run alongside to keep up with him. Annie knew that come tomorrow, when all this was over, she would be mortified at all the attention. But right now she didn't care. If anyone could help her it was Raphael, and she trusted his medical skills absolutely.

He set her down on a couch in one of the examination rooms, calling for the ultrasound scanner in a voice that suggested that, if it wasn't brought to him this instant, there would be hell to pay. Fear closed Annie's throat and numbed her lips, but she answered Kate's questions as best she could. No, she hadn't bled before. She'd only had mild cramps tonight. Nothing until tonight. She had even felt the baby move earlier, but couldn't feel anything now.

Raphael, his eyes tight with concentration, was spreading cool gel on Annie's tummy. In any other circumstances she might have felt awkward as his hands lifted her dress, revealing her lacy underwear, but right now all she could think about was her baby.

Kate held her hand as Raphael scanned her abdomen, his attention fixed on the monitor. Suddenly his face creased into a smile and Annie felt the first small tug of hope since she had been to the bathroom.

'I can see the heartbeat,' Raphael said, relief in his voice. 'Look, Annie, there.' He turned the screen towards her and even through her swollen eyelids she could see the fluttering of a heartbeat. Her heart soared. She was still pregnant. For the time being, at any rate. She shook the thought away. She had to stay positive, for the baby's sake. There was no way she was going to give up on this baby, not until all hope was gone. And right now the baby was still there, inside her, needing her to be strong. She counted four limbs on the 3D image. Tiny legs folded and was it…? Yes, it was sucking its thumb. She felt a fresh wave of tears prick her eyes. But this time it was with relief and a wash of love. That was her baby, safe inside her womb.

It seemed as if Raphael was experiencing the same sea of emotions as he too stared at the tiny image. He muttered something in Spanish in a voice filled with awe. Kate was also smiling.

Through her relief, Annie was aware of Dr Gibson, her obstetrician, coming in to the room.

'The midwives told me our miracle mum was in,' she said. 'So I thought I'd pop in to see how you were.' She looked at Raphael, curiosity evident in her bright blue eyes. 'Although I can see Dr Castillo is already here.' She squinted at the monitor and nodded, looking satisfied.

'Baby looks fine, although I'm sure Dr Castillo has already told you that.'

'We should keep you in under observation, Annie. Just to be on the safe side,' Kate said.

'Will it make any difference if I stay?'

She saw Kate and Raphael exchange a look.

'No,' Raphael said gently. 'If you are going to miscarry, it will happen anyway.'

'Then I want to go home,' Annie said softly but firmly.

'I think you should stay,' Raphael responded. 'I will stay with you.'

Once again, Annie was aware of Dr Gibson's puzzled eyes on Raphael, before the older doctor looked at her.

'I know how much this pregnancy means to you, Annie. Particularly when you thought it could never happen. I don't think a night in hospital would do you any harm.' Dr Gibson turned to Raphael. 'I'm sure you'll be aware that Annie was thought to have ovarian failure.'

Raphael drew his brows together and Annie watched as realisation dawned that she had been telling him the truth. Emotions chased across his face. Delight followed by—could it be shame? Despite herself, she enjoyed watching him squirm.

Annie struggled into a sitting position and Kate came forward to help her.

'Look,' she said. 'We all know that it will make no difference whatsoever to the outcome if I stay in hospital. This pregnancy will either continue or…' Her voice broke. 'It won't. Staying here isn't going to change anything as you have just admitted. Am I right, Dr Gibson?'

'Yes. Bed rest won't make a difference. But you know that your medical history means you have to be extra-careful. So no vigorous exercise—and that includes penetrative sex. Just to be on the safe side.'

This time it was Annie's turn to squirm and she felt her face burn. Before she could help herself she slid a glance in Raphael's direction. Out of sight of Dr Gibson and Kate, he raised an eyebrow in her direction, a small smile tugging at the corner of his mouth. Her embarrassment deepened. Had the man no shame?

'I can't stay in hospital for the rest of my pregnancy,' Annie said, swinging her legs over the side of the bed. 'If I thought it would make the slightest difference, I would be happy to remain flat on my back and not move a muscle for the next few weeks or so. But it won't. So I'm going home where I feel more comfortable.'

'Okay, Annie,' Dr Gibson said, as her pager bleeped. 'You can go home if you wish, but remember what I said about taking it easy. I need to answer this, but come and see me at my clinic in about a week.'

'I'll stay at your house with you,' Kate offered after Dr Gibson had left the room. 'That way, you won't be alone if anything happens. We hope it won't, but we can't be sure. I can ask Rob if Jem could stay over at his house.'

But Raphael interrupted. 'No, I will. It is my responsibility.'

Kate narrowed her eyes and looked from Annie to Raphael. Annie could tell from the slow realisation dawning in her eyes that she was putting two and two together. What she made of Raphael being here in Penhally Bay was anyone's guess. But Annie knew that whatever her thoughts she would keep them to herself, and she was grateful for the older midwife's well-known discretion.

'I can stay on my own,' Annie protested. 'I have my phone. Kate only lives a short distance away. If I need her she can be with me in minutes.'

Irrationally Annie felt that if she stayed in the hospital, it would only make matters worse. At home she could pretend that everything was as it had been when she'd left the house earlier in the day.

'Either I stay with you at home, or you will stay here.' From the tone of Raphael's voice, Annie realised she wasn't going to win the battle. She didn't really have the strength for it. All she wanted now was to go home and climb into her own bed and sleep, comforted with the knowledge that her baby was okay.

'All right,' she agreed reluctantly. She would agree to anything as long as it got her out of the hospital. But she couldn't prevent a flicker of relief and happiness that Raphael would be coming home with her. If only for a night she could pretend it was for all the right reasons.

Kate dropped Annie and Raphael off at Annie's place with a final entreaty to Annie to call her any time, no matter what the hour, if she needed to. Once again, Raphael insisted on carrying her as if she was too fragile to stand on her own two feet, but for once she let him take care of her. She had looked after herself for so long, it felt strange but not unpleasant giving herself, even temporarily, into the care of someone else. In his arms she could believe that everything would turn out all right.

He laid her gently on her bed and insisted on removing her tights and her dress as if she were helpless. She felt every touch of his fingers burn into her skin. Then when she was left wearing only her bra and panties he looked down at her and she could hear his breath catch in his throat. But he shook his head and, muttering something in Spanish that sounded like a curse, he held the duvet up so she could crawl into bed. He surprised her even more by lying next to her, on top of the quilt, and pulling her into his arms so that her back rested against his chest. His hands were on her hair, soothing her, and she let herself drift away, secure in the knowledge that he was there if she needed him.

Raphael stroked Annie's dark brown hair, feeling the weight of it under his fingertips. He inhaled her perfume as her breathing deepened and became regular. He stole a glance at her sleeping face, the pale skin and tiny creases of worry at the corners of her eyes. He wondered if she had any idea how vulnerable she appeared despite that tough independent exterior. He was surprised by a rush of protectiveness she aroused in him. When he had come across her in the bathroom, one look at her had told him that she was almost destroyed at the thought of losing her baby. And he had been surprised at his own feelings, too. He wanted this baby, but the gut-wrenching sorrow he had felt when he had thought she had lost it had shaken him.

And then the realisation, back at the hospital, that she had been honest with him all along. He had misjudged her and felt acutely ashamed. Just because Ruth had lied to him, it didn't mean Annie was the same. He should have known she was telling the truth when she had been so adamant that she didn't want or need him in her life. He could only imagine what his reaction must have done to her. It would have taken courage to phone him, and then for him to doubt that the baby she was carrying was his. After everything she had gone through. Any other woman would have lashed out, but not Annie. She had done what she thought was right—for the baby.

There was no longer the slightest shred of doubt in his mind. She was carrying his baby. His child. And he hadn't been mistaken about Annie. She was the woman he had thought she was back in Spain. She had told him about the baby because she thought he had a right to know—not because she wanted anything from him. But was she as strong as she liked to make out? Somehow he doubted it. And as long as she was carrying his baby, he would stay and watch over them both—whatever she said.

CHAPTER SIX

WHEN Annie opened her eyes the next morning it was to the delicious aroma of fresh coffee. She stretched luxuriously beneath the sheets, unable to think at first who could be moving around in her cottage. But then the previous night's events came flooding back. She dropped her hands tentatively to her tummy, feeling the reassuring swell of her pregnancy, and then a tiny movement made her gasp. Her baby was still there, alive and kicking. She smiled to herself, feeling a bubble of happiness. One day at a time. She'd take one day at a time, just as she'd told so many of her patients.

Raphael appeared at the doorway, a tray balanced in his hands. Despite his rumpled appearance, Annie felt her breath catch in her throat. How could any man be so damned handsome? It just wasn't fair. As he walked towards her, she pulled the bedclothes up to her chin, suddenly self-conscious under his searching eyes. It was a bit late in the day, she thought ruefully, to be trying to hang onto her modesty. After all, this man had explored every inch of her already with his lips as well as his hands. She bit back a moan as a delicious heat flooded her body. She had to stop thinking about him in that way. No good could come of it. He was here because of his child. No other reason. And she'd do well to remember that.

'*Buenas días,*' he said evenly, but he couldn't quite hide the anxiety that darkened his eyes. If Annie had ever wondered how much he wanted this baby, any remaining doubts had disappeared when she'd sensed his anguish when he'd shared her fear that she might lose it. He propped the tray on her lap as she sat up.

'Morning,' she responded awkwardly. Then she added, 'I felt the baby kick just now.'

Knowing he would want to feel the reassuring movement as much as she did, she set the tray aside and took his hand, guiding it to her belly. As she felt his warm hand on her bare skin she felt goose-bumps prick her skin. Just then the baby moved and Annie was touched to see a look of relief and joy in his eyes. They smiled at each other and it was as if the air between them was alive. As if a cord bound them together. Or was it just their shared hope?

'My baby,' he said softly, before lowering his head and kissing her ever so gently on her small bump. Once more jolts of pleasure shot through her body. How was she going to cope having him around for the duration of her pregnancy if her body reacted like some wanton harpy every time he touched her?

As soon as he raised his head, she scrambled for the duvet again, snuggling under the protective folds. Not knowing what else to do to break the atmosphere that fizzled and sparked between them, she picked up her tray and almost laughed out loud. The coffee was fine, he had managed that, and the single rose clearly picked from outside her front door was a sweet touch, but the toast looked as if it had been dropped in water then wrung out and placed on her plate. What was he trying to do? Poison her?

He must have seen her look of incredulity as he looked hurt for a moment. '*Lo siento*—I am sorry about the toast,' he said. 'I didn't know what to do with it. I never eat my bread like that.'

'It's fine,' Annie said. 'I'm not particularly hungry, anyway. You needn't have bothered. I'm sure you'd rather be at home.'

'I am staying with you,' he said. 'I will go and change my clothes and then go to the shop and get us some proper breakfast. You stay where you are until I get back. Kate phoned to say she is coming to check on you, so she will be here with you while I am away.'

For a moment Annie was tempted to tell him to stop treating her as if she was a child, in fact, would everyone stop treating her like a child, but bit back the words. Right now she didn't have the energy nor the willpower to argue. As soon as he was gone she'd shower and dress. He would soon see that she wasn't the type of woman who he could order about. He might be used to getting his own way in Spain and at the hospital, but this was her house and she would do as she pleased.

'I didn't hear the phone,' she said.

'It has been ringing constantly, but I unplugged the extension in here so it wouldn't disturb you. So many people want to know that you are okay. So many people care about you.'

Annie sank back in the pillows. He was right, she knew that. But what about him? Did he care for her at all? And as for all these people who had phoned. What on earth had they thought when Raphael had answered? Hopefully, no more than one colleague looking out for another. Nevertheless,

Annie knew that the jungle drums of Penhally Bay would be beating furiously. It was really only a matter of time before everyone guessed that Raphael was the father of her child. But she no longer cared who knew. The only thing that really mattered was the health of her baby.

Before she could ask him who exactly had phoned, there was a knock at the front door and she heard Kate's voice calling out. Raphael looked down at her, his eyes darkening. For a moment she imagined he looked reluctant to leave her. He leaned over towards her, and her breath caught in her throat. Was he going to kiss her? Her lips parted involuntarily but instead he brushed his fingertips against her cheek.

'I will see you soon,' he said, and headed for the door.

She could hear him and Kate talking in low voices, followed by the bang of the door. Moments later her friend popped her head around the door.

'Okay if I come in?' she asked.

'I don't seem to be able to stop anyone,' Annie grumbled before immediately feeling contrite. 'I'm sorry, Kate, please ignore me. I'm just feeling a little rattled, that's all. I can't help but feel that if everyone fusses around me, there must be something wrong.'

'Raphael said he felt the baby move. That's a good sign.'

'I know.' Annie sighed. 'But I can't help but worry.'

Kate's eyes were warm with sympathy. 'We're all going to do everything we can to get you through this,' she said gently. 'Everyone's rooting for you. I had to forbid them all from coming down here to see you in person. Although I suspect you'll want to see Chloe later?'

'Does she know? About Raphael?' Annie asked, easing herself out of bed and slipping her dressing gown on.

'I think most people, Chloe included, will have guessed

who the father is,' Kate said. 'None of them are so stupid that they can't put your holiday in Spain together with the sudden arrival of Dr Castillo. According to Ben, Raphael used all his connections to get the job at St Piran's so he could be near you.' Kate smiled at Annie. 'Besides, people would have had to have been blind not to see how torn up he was last night. Most obstetricians don't go carrying patients around in their arms, even if they are the most caring of doctors.'

'He certainly cares about the baby,' Annie said softly. 'I've got the feeling he's going to be my personal physician for the rest of my pregnancy.'

'Would that be so bad?' Kate said. 'God knows, we can all do with support sometimes, no matter how strong we like to think we are inside.'

Annie thought Kate looked sad for a moment, but before she could say anything the smile was back.

'By the way, he said that your sister had phoned. Fiona, isn't it? He told her you'd call her back. I'll just make us some tea if you want to phone her now.'

Annie searched her house, eventually finding her phone in the kitchen, which incidentally looked as if a bomb had hit it. Whatever talents Raphael had, domesticity wasn't one of them. Leaving Kate in the kitchen, she wandered into her sitting room and dialled her sister's number.

After reassuring Fiona that, yes, she really was fine and, no, there was no need for her to leave her family and come to Penhally Bay and, yes, of course she would call if she changed her mind, Fiona asked about Raphael, agog to find he had come to work at St Piran's.

'I couldn't believe it when he answered the phone,' she said. 'Then he told me what had happened, but that you and the baby were fine. So, Annie, what's the deal? Why didn't you tell me he had followed you? Are you two going to be together? I'm so excited for you.'

'I can't talk now,' Annie told her sister. 'I've visitors. I'll call later. But don't get too excited about Raphael being here. It's not what you think. And, Fi, don't tell Mum and Dad about last night. They'll only worry and insist on coming home early. And there's really nothing anyone can do.'

Annie hung up when she heard Chloe talking to Kate. She went into her kitchen and the young midwife handed her a cup of tea.

'How are you doing?' she asked. 'Kate says everything has settled down. She was good enough to phone me after she dropped you off, otherwise I wouldn't have slept a wink, worrying.'

Annie was grateful for the genuine concern in Chloe's eyes, but hurried to reassure her.

'And I understand our new doctor refused to leave your side.'

Annie didn't miss the teasing look she sent her way. She felt herself blush furiously.

'Does everyone know?' she asked.

'What about?' Chloe asked innocently.

Annie could feel her face get warmer. 'Do people know who the father is?'

'There is gossip. You must know there was bound to be, but most of it is just kindly interest. However, I'm afraid the way that our Dr Castillo carried you off and refused to budge from your side was a bit of a give-away.'

'I suppose it was inevitable that people put two and two together,' Annie said.

'Especially those who knew about your holiday in Spain. No one knew there was a vacancy at the hospital when, lo and behold, Dr Castillo turns up. Rumour has it that he called in every favour he was owed, to get the job. So, yes, I'm afraid the cat is well and truly out the bag. Do you mind very much?'

'No, I guess not,' Annie said quietly. 'People were bound to find out sooner or later. He's an experienced doctor, too. Anyway, St Piran's is lucky to have someone with his experience.'

'And what about you, Annie? How do you feel about him being here?' Chloe asked quietly.

How could she answer Chloe's question when she didn't know the answer herself? Annie knew she felt the same way about him as she had from the moment they had met. And that wasn't good. He would never feel the same way about her. And what if he carried out his threat to claim his rights as a father and demanded shared access? She didn't want her child to spend half its life away from her in Spain.

'I'm not sure. I don't really know that much about him,' Annie said evasively. 'I know he comes from a big extended Spanish family but that's about it.' She felt herself grow warm under their scrutiny. She wished she could at least say that they had been together the whole two weeks while she'd been in Spain, that their child had been conceived after spending time together, instead of it being obvious that she had spent very little time in the man's company before jumping into bed with him. She just knew she couldn't explain the instant, overwhelming attraction she had felt for Raphael.

'But anyway,' she continued, 'that is neither here nor there. As far as he is concerned, the baby is his and he is determined to stick around. Or so he says.' Annie hesitated then decided to confide in Chloe and Kate, knowing that neither woman would ever break a confidence.

'He tells me he intends to apply for legal access. What if he takes my baby to Spain for a visit and never brings him back?'

Two pairs of eyes studied her sympathetically.

'I don't think he could do that,' Kate said reassuringly. 'Anyway, the mother usually wins—what do they call it now—rights of residence.'

'But these days fathers have equal rights, don't they?' Annie tried to keep the panic out of her voice.

'Why don't you speak to him about it, Annie?' Kate suggested. 'It could be that you're worried about nothing. Maybe he'll put your mind at rest.'

Kate was right, of course. Annie needed to face up to the situation like the grown woman she was. But she couldn't help wondering whether she had done the right thing in letting Raphael know he was the father of her child. How much less complicated it would have been had she said nothing at all.

Kate and Chloe left shortly after Raphael arrived back. He had showered, and dressed in a thin cashmere pullover with a pair of jeans, looking, Annie thought, sexy as hell. Every time Annie saw him she remembered how he had made her feel that first night. How the atmosphere between them had seemed charged with electricity. But so far he was still an enigma to her. One thing was for sure, though, if the baby inherited its father's dark good looks it would be beautiful.

'What are you doing out of bed?' he growled at her. 'I thought we agreed you were going to stay in bed for the weekend and let me look after you?'

Once again Annie felt exasperated. While she welcomed his support, there was no way he was going to tell her how to live her life. Didn't he know that she would do whatever she could to protect the life growing inside her?

'Actually, no,' Annie said firmly. 'I agreed to nothing. As I said before, you and I both know that me staying in bed won't change a thing.'

'I had no idea you were so stubborn,' he said, his mouth twitching. 'But you will find out I am stubborn, too.' Before she had a chance to protest he had crossed the room and scooped her up in his arms. Annie had no choice but to wrap her arms around his neck and cling on for dear life while he marched into the bedroom and laid her, as if she could break in two, gently on the bed.

As he looked down at her, his eyes glowing, Annie felt her breath catch in her throat. For a second the world stood still and her treacherous body yearned to feel his hands on her once more. He bent over her and brushed a stray curl away from her face with a gentle finger. *'Dios,'* he said hoarsely, 'why do you have to look at me like that?' And then, almost as if he couldn't bear the sight of her, he straightened and moved to the other side of the room, apparently determined to put as much space as possible between them.

'I have brought supplies from the shop as well as newspapers and magazines. I had no idea what you like, so I bought the lot. I will bring them to you.'

By this time Annie had had enough. Raphael had to understand that she didn't need him fussing over her like a mother hen. If he wanted to stick around she had to make him realise that she needed to do things her way. For all she knew, he could disappear back to Spain at any time, leaving her to get on with it on her own, and the last thing she wanted was to become reliant on somebody who might not stick around. She knew he was enamoured with the idea of becoming a father, any idiot could see that, but what about when the harsh realities of being a parent struck home? Would he be so keen then? She had fought so hard for her independence, she was damned if she was going to give it all up now. Just because it suited him.

'I'm going for a shower,' she said. 'Then I'm going to get dressed. You,' she said crossly, 'can do what you like.' She felt a moment of pleasure as she saw the look of surprise on his face. Then she hopped out of bed and, wrapping the sheet around her as well as much of her dignity as she could salvage, she stalked off to the bathroom without a backward glance.

By the time Annie came out of her deliberately long shower, Raphael was nowhere to be seen. She ignored the flash of disappointment and, selecting a dress that was loose around the waist, finished dressing. She dried her hair, taking her time over the ritual until her brown hair was tamed into a neat bob. Now she felt almost human again and ready to face the world. There was no more spotting and no cramping. Everything seemed to have settled down.

'Hey, you,' she said softly laying a hand on her belly, 'you just keep fighting in there. You have a mummy who wants you more than anything in the world and who already loves you more than she can say.' As if in response to her encouragement the baby moved and Annie felt a surge of relief. It was a fighter, this little one. It was a miracle it was here in the first place.

She padded through to her sitting room. As he'd promised, Raphael had left enough magazines and newspapers to keep her occupied for the rest of her pregnancy, never mind the weekend. She frowned in confusion as she leafed through the pile. He had even included a copy of *Biker's Weekly*! She smiled, imagining him in the newsagent's, grabbing the first magazines that came to hand, unsure what she liked to read and in too much of a hurry to get back to check up on her to think about it. Her smile faded as another thought hit her—or did it show how little they knew of about one another? And yet they were going to parent the same child. She picked up a well-known travel magazine with a four-page spread on the part of Spain he came from. Now, was that deliberate? she wondered. Was he determined to persuade her to bring their baby to Spain? She couldn't make up her mind whether to be amused or angry. In fact, everything about Raphael confused her. She had been content on her own, and as soon as she'd known she was going to have a baby, her life had been complete. But now that he was back in her life again, all testosterone, making her go weak at the knees every time she saw him, he had gone and upset everything all over again. In many ways it would have been better if he had stayed out of her life.

Looking out the window, she saw that the sun was shining. It was a perfect early summer day and Annie felt restless. Maybe she should practise some yoga? That always calmed her and no one could say it counted as vigorous exercise. She felt her cheeks grow warm as she remembered what else Dr Gibson had said. No penetrative sex. As if! There was no worry on that score! It was clear that any desire Raphael might have had for her had long since vanished. Although when he had raised an eyebrow at her, back there in the hospital room, she had seen from his eyes that he had been thinking of the night they'd conceived the baby. She crossed over to the window and opened it, letting the gentle breeze cool her cheeks. It was a lovely day. Perhaps she would go for the walk she had threatened, but she didn't feel confident enough to go on her own. Whatever she had told Raphael, she was still scared—no, terrified—that she could yet lose her baby.

CHAPTER SEVEN

ANNIE was beginning to feel hungry when there was a tap on the door. She opened it to find Raphael standing there, holding another bunch of flowers. For a moment she was taken aback. It was almost as if he was wooing her. Despite everything she had told herself, she couldn't help a tiny spurt of pleasure at the gesture. But she needed to remember that this man would do anything to make sure he was kept in her baby's life. She mustn't let his little-boy grin get to her.

In addition to the flowers, Raphael was laden with cardboard boxes that smelled delicious.

'I had a look in your fridge earlier,' he said, 'but there was nothing. Don't you know you have to eat? To stay strong?'

'I know. For the baby,' Annie retorted.

'Isn't that what we both want?' He looked puzzled.

'Yes. Of course.' Annie was suddenly aghast. What was she thinking? That she wanted him to see her as more than the mother of his child? That she wanted him to see her as a woman? But she didn't. She would never have a relationship with a man who threatened her with lawyers. But he still hadn't actually told her what he was planning to do when the baby arrived. She should take Kate's advice and talk to him about it.

'We need to talk,' he said, as if he'd read her mind. 'But

first we need to eat. I for one cannot think on an empty stomach. I was going to cook for us, but I don't know what you like—except seafood. But best not to chance that while you're pregnant. So I got a selection of other things I thought you might like from the restaurant on the main street.'

He emptied the contents of the boxes onto plates he had fetched from the kitchen.

'Remembering the way you cook,' Annie said, smiling, 'I think you did the right thing.'

Raphael pretended to look hurt for a moment. Then he grinned and Annie's heart somersaulted.

'I thought about going for a walk later,' Annie said. 'I hate being cooped up inside. Especially when the weather is so perfect.'

Raphael's smile was replaced by a frown. 'I thought we agreed you were going to rest—at least for a day or two.'

Annie replied, not even attempting to hide her frustration, 'Dr Gibson said no vigorous exercise. I hardly think a stroll falls into that category.' She blushed, remembering what else Dr Gibson had said. 'You can hardly stand guard over me for the rest of the pregnancy, Raphael!'

Raphael put his fork down and, reaching across the table, took Annie's hand.

'Cariño,' he said softly. 'If I thought standing guard over you would help, I wouldn't leave your side, but as you are determined to go for a walk, there is nothing for it except that I go too!'

Before Annie could protest, he dropped her hand and touched her lips with his finger. Annie swallowed a moan as her body thrilled to his touch.

'No more arguments,' he continued, tracing the line of her lips. 'You will find I can be as stubborn as you. Now—' he looked at her with mock severity, thankfully unaware of Annie's furiously beating heart '—let's finish eating. Or make no mistake—you won't be leaving this house.'

After they had eaten, they followed the road down towards the shore. The early evening was warm and the scent of flowers and sea filled the air. Annie loved this time of year in Penhally Bay. Soon she would need to make a start on converting the spare room into a nursery and had already decided she would paint it buttercup yellow.

They followed the road until they came to the lighthouse.

They stood in companionable silence for a moment, watching as the sun turned the sky to strips of red, gold and lilac. Eventually Raphael turned molten brown eyes on her.

'I owe you an apology and an explanation,' he said. 'I should never have doubted you and I cannot have you worrying about me taking the baby from you. You must understand I would never do that. It is not easy for me to tell you why I went to a lawyer, but I feel I must. Can I ask you not to tell anyone else—do I have your word?'

'I can keep a confidence,' Annie said.

Raphael took a deep breath before speaking. 'I was married. Until last year.'

Annie felt her heart thump. Was he going to tell her he was still in love with his wife?

'My wife and I had a child. Sebastian. He is three now.' Raphael smiled grimly before continuing, 'I love that little boy. He is my life.'

Annie drew in a breath. The pain in his voice was evident. She hadn't known he had a child. Where was he? And what was Raphael doing so far away from his him? If he loved him, and it was evident he did, how could he bear to be away from him?

She waited quietly for him to continue. It was obvious he was having difficulty keeping his emotions in check. His eyes were dark and Annie had to sit on her hands to prevent herself leaning towards him and brushing the stray lock of hair from his eyes.

'My wife left me,' he said baldly. 'And she took my son with her. Only it turned out that Sebastian wasn't my son after all. He belonged to the man she ran off with.'

Annie was appalled. But in that instant she knew more about Raphael than she had thought possible. His hurt was written all over his face.

'I'm sorry,' she said. 'That must have been hard.' She longed to reach out and comfort him, but something in the way he held himself, in his forbidding expression, warned her that he wouldn't welcome her touch.

'She wouldn't let me see him. So I went to the court and asked for access. But it was denied. They said that I wasn't the biological father, so I had no rights.'

The bitterness and pain in his voice shook Annie. No wonder he was so determined to have some legal rights to their child.

'It didn't matter that I was the only father he had ever known, that he loved me and I loved him. None of that counted when it came to access. She took him away to another part of Spain. I don't know how he is, if he is missing me. I know nothing about my child's life. And he *is* my child. Even if I am not the biological father.'

'I'm so sorry, Raphael. I can only imagine what that must be like for you. Not to be able to see him. Not to have any contact whatsoever.'

He stood up and turned away as if he couldn't bear to look at her. 'I don't want your sympathy,' he said roughly. 'I just need to be certain that the same thing won't happen again.'

Annie's blood chilled. But it must be difficult for this proud man to admit that he had been deceived.

'Did you love her very much?' she said quietly. 'Your ex-wife?'

'Ruth? I told myself I loved her. When she told me she was pregnant with my child, I asked her to marry me. I thought we could make it work. For the sake of the child. But we were never really happy, and eventually she met with the real father again.' His voice was bitter with the memory. 'She started seeing him again while she was still married to me. I was such a fool.'

This time Annie couldn't help herself. She got up and went to stand beside him, touching his arm. He flinched almost as if she had burnt him.

'And Sebastian? What about him?'

His voice was raw when he spoke. 'Whatever she says, he *is* my son. I was the one who looked after him in the night when he couldn't sleep. The one who kissed his knee when he scraped it. Whatever the court says, he is still my son.'

'Do you see him at all?'

'No. That is why I am speaking to the lawyers about this baby.' He smiled grimly, still looking into the distance. 'I can't lose this child too. You must see that.'

Annie *could* see it. Just by looking at him she could tell how badly he had been hurt. More than hurt, betrayed. It was the sadness she had seen inside him the night they had first met. And it was still there. But that didn't mean she could risk losing control over her child's future to appease a hurt Raphael had experienced at the hands of another woman. No matter how sympathetic she felt.

'I wouldn't stop you seeing your child. Not unless I thought it was harmful in some way. Can't you trust me to do the right thing? After all, I needn't have told you I was pregnant.'

'I know. I misjudged you. And for that I am sorry. Can we start over again? Please?' He smiled his killer smile which never failed to make Annie go weak at the knees.

She felt a shiver of excitement, and her heart beat faster. Did he mean start over from where they had left off in Spain? Did he still feel that same connection she did?

'Can we be friends for the sake of our child? Work something out between us?' Raphael continued.

Annie's heart plummeted. Of course, she should have known. All he was interested in was the child. But he had a point—no matter how disappointed she felt that he didn't want anything more than friendship from her, they needed to reach an agreement about what was going to happen once the baby was born.

'You can come and see him any time you like,' Annie said through stiff lips.

Raphael drew his brows together. 'But I would also want him to come to Spain. He must get to know his family, what it is to be Spanish. I would want him to visit often.'

Instinctively, Annie placed her hands protectively on her belly. Could she trust him? This man she barely knew, yet was the father of her child? How was she going to bring herself to let this precious little one out her sight for a second, never mind to another country.

'Don't you trust me?' he asked softly, as if he had guessed what she was thinking. 'What can I do to make you believe me that I only want to do what is right for my child?'

Raphael raised a finger to her cheek, tracing a line down

to her jaw. She couldn't have felt his touch more keenly if he was drawing a knife across her skin. 'What are you thinking? Please—tell me, *cariño*.'

This time it was Annie who drew away. She wrapped her arms around her body.

'A year ago, I was going to get married, to Robert. We had known each other almost all our lives and planned to have a large family,' Annie said slowly after a few moments. 'But my periods had been irregular for years and somebody at the clinic I worked in, back in Edinburgh, suggested I have a fertility test.' She looked into the distance, remembering. 'I took it more out of curiosity than anything else. It never really occurred to me that there could be a problem.'

'What was this test?' Raphael asked.

'It's called an AMH. It's fairly new but deemed to be very reliable.'

Raphael nodded. 'I have read about it in the medical journals.'

'Apparently my ovarian reserve was so low that even IVF would be out of the question.'

Raphael looked at her steadily.

'Go on,' he said.

'It hadn't even crossed my mind that there wasn't plenty of time to think about having a child. You don't think when you're twenty-seven that it's already too late do you? At least, I didn't.' She remembered only too well her feeling of shock and disbelief. 'When I told Robert he was dismayed. And once he realised that even IVF was out of the question, he began to change. I told him that we could always adopt, but he said that he could never bring up another man's child. After that we drifted apart. There was no more talk of weddings. I realised he couldn't love me the way I thought he did, so I called the whole thing off. I think he was relieved. That's when I decided to come to Penhally Bay. To start afresh. But the pain follows you, you know. It's ironic, being a midwife. Every day you're confronted with what you can't have. Don't get me wrong, I love my job and I love bringing happiness to all these couples, but it used to hurt.'

'He couldn't be much of a man, this Robert,' Raphael said, frowning.

'I can't blame him. He wanted something I couldn't give him. It was unfair to expect him to give up the chance of a family for me.'

'If you were my woman, I wouldn't have let you go. You should be with someone because you have to be. Not because you want children.' His eyes were warm with sympathy. 'But now I understand. Our baby will be very special for you. But for me, also.'

Annie nodded, relieved that he seemed to understand. 'Raphael, this baby is like a miracle to me. I can't believe how lucky I am. It's unlikely, though, that I will ever fall pregnant again. This is my one chance to have a child.' Annie struggled to keep her voice even. She knew there was no way that she could convey properly how devastated she had been when she had thought having a child of her own was an impossibility. And anyway, did she want to reveal anything more of herself to this man? She had already shown him too much of her soul. He was the father of her child, that was all, and she'd do well to remember that. Even if it almost broke her heart.

CHAPTER EIGHT

A FEW weeks later, Annie was back at work, feeling much more rested. She was surprised to find Claire and Roy waiting to see her. Claire wasn't due to come in for another couple of weeks and Annie was immediately concerned to see her back so soon. She was even more worried when she saw the look of anxiety on the couple's faces.

'What is it Claire?' Annie asked gently. 'What's bothering you? Is it the babies?'

'I've had a little spotting,' Claire said anxiously. 'I know it can happen sometimes, but—'

'We just wanted to make sure everything was all right,' Roy finished for her.

Annie's heart went out to the couple. She knew they'd be terrified. Claire had seemed so fragile the last time Annie had seen her that she was worried that if she lost the babies she would sink so far into depression that she might not come out the other side. Claire was already in her late thirties and the chance of another pregnancy was diminishing with every passing year.

'I'm going to page Dr Castillo. His special interest is high-risk pregnancies and I'm sure he'll want to scan you, Claire, to see what exactly is going on. I'll ask him to come as soon as he's free. In the meantime, could you try and drink as much as possible so your bladder is nice and full for the scan?'

Claire's eyes filled with tears and she reached for Roy's hand. 'I'm so scared, Annie,' she said shakily. 'I don't know if it's better not knowing, if you see what I mean? As long as I don't know I—we—still have hope.'

Annie stood up and went over to Claire and wrapped her in her arms. 'You're way ahead of yourself. I know how scary all this can be. Believe me. Let's just take one step at a time, okay?'

When Claire nodded, Annie picked up the phone and asked switchboard to page Dr Castillo. While she waited for him to answer she filled a glass of water from the jug on her desk and handed it to Claire.

'Dr Castillo.' Annie heard his deep voice on the other end of the phone. 'You were paging me?'

'Dr Castillo,' she said formally. 'It's Annie. I have someone I'd like you to scan. Could you come down to the antenatal clinic?'

'I'm due in theatre in fifteen minutes. Can it wait until later?'

Annie looked over at Claire, who was drinking the water as if her life depended on it. 'No,' she said, 'it can't.'

'Are you all right?' Immediately the concern was back in his voice.

'Of course,' Annie said. 'It's a couple with a twin IVF pregnancy. She's had some bleeding and is feeling anxious.'

'I'll be right there,' Raphael said, and disconnected.

Annie only had enough time to prepare Claire for the scan before Raphael arrived. He was wearing his theatre scrubs, which framed his muscular body perfectly. Once more, despite herself, Annie felt a thrill when he came into the room. Must be the pregnancy sending her hormones into overdrive, she told herself.

Raphael introduced himself to the worried couple and his easy and relaxed manner soon put them at ease.

While he set up the scanning machine Annie gave him an overview of Claire's history to date. 'This is their third attempt at IVF. Neither of the first two goes resulted in a pregnancy, but this time both the embryos put back implanted successfully. Claire had a scan around seven weeks and two heartbeats were clearly visible at that stage. She's been well up until now, but had some spotting last night. They thought it best to have it checked out.'

Raphael caught Annie's eye. It was obvious from the sympathetic look in his eyes that he knew how close to the bone seeing Claire was for her.

'How many weeks into the pregnancy are you?' he asked Claire, bringing her into the conversation.

'Twenty-four,' Claire replied.

Roy held his wife's hand as Annie covered her stomach in ultrasound gel. They all watched the screen as Raphael scanned. As the image came up on the monitor, Annie could immediately make out two heartbeats. She felt a surge of relief, but almost as quickly it was replaced with concern. While two babies were clearly visible, neither of the babies were the size they should be for the dates. To make matters worse, one was significantly bigger than the other. As Raphael turned to look at her, she could see he shared her concern.

'I have some good news for you and some not-so-good news,' he said gently. 'As you can see from the monitor—' he indicated the two beating hearts with his finger '—there are two heart beats—there and there.' Claire and Roy craned their heads to see what he was showing them. 'The problem, however, is that one baby—' he pointed to one of the tiny forms '—is significantly smaller than the other. This suggests that the bigger baby is taking more than its fair share of the nutrients from the placenta, meaning that the smaller baby is struggling to get enough to grow.'

'What does it mean?' Roy asked.

'It means,' Raphael said, 'that both your babies are still alive. That's the good news. However, we will have to monitor both of them carefully over the next couple of weeks. If it looks like the second baby isn't getting enough nutrients, we will have to think about what to do.'

'What might those options be?' Although Roy's voice was calm, Annie knew he was only keeping it together for Claire's sake.

Raphael looked at him sympathetically.

'It's too soon to know. As I said, we will monitor your babies very closely over the next couple of weeks. Keep an eye on their growth.'

'And if the second baby doesn't grow? What then?' Roy insisted. 'Look—' he turned to his wife and gripped her hand tightly '—we'd both prefer to know, so please tell us. What is the worst that can happen?'

'We might have to deliver the twins much earlier than we would like. I know this a lot for you to take in, and I believe it is important for patients to have all the facts so they can be fully involved in the decision making process, but I am not ready to make that decision yet. As I say, we should wait and see how they get on.'

Claire turned terrified eyes to Annie.

'I don't understand,' she said. 'Annie, is there a chance my babies could die?'

Annie put her arms around the distraught woman's shoulders. 'There's nothing to suggest that right now, Claire. I know all this is difficult for you to take in. But you are lucky to have Dr Castillo to look after you. He is one of the leading experts in his field. We have to trust him.'

Raphael looked at Annie, seeming surprised at her warm endorsement, but then he turned to the couple.

'I want you to go home and try not to worry, even though I know that will be difficult. I will scan you again in two weeks' time. We will have another look at your babies then, and think about what to do. In the meantime, all we can do is wait.'

And pray, Annie thought. Pray that this couple weren't going to have their dreams dashed. But Raphael was right, there was nothing more that could be done right now.

She made another appointment for Claire and Roy to come back to see her and Raphael before seeing them out of the department. When she returned to the room, Raphael was still there, writing in Claire's notes.

'What do you really think?' she asked him.

He looked up at her, surprised. 'Exactly what I told them. We'll know more in a couple of weeks. In the meantime, all we can do is wait.'

'Couldn't we have waited until the next scan? Now they'll have days of worry to live through when it might not be necessary.'

Raphael narrowed his eyes at her. 'I believe that parents have the right to know all the details. The days when doctors decided to hold back information from their patients for their own good are gone. No?'

'But if it means putting them through unnecessary worry? Can't you see how terrified they are?'

Raphael leaned back in his chair and looked at Annie thoughtfully. 'Tell me,' he said softly, 'if you were in her shoes, would you want to know the truth?'

Annie knew she was being unreasonable but she couldn't help herself. Having experienced the terror of thinking she was about to lose a desperately wanted child, she knew exactly what Claire was going through. Raphael leaned across the desk and touched her arm gently.

'They asked me for the truth, Annie. I couldn't do anything else but tell them. Can't you see that?' He dropped his hand. 'Maybe you are getting too close to your patients. We need to keep some professional distance, otherwise we can't help them.'

Suddenly all the anger went out of Annie. Raphael was right. Roy had asked and he had deserved an honest answer. And Raphael was right too about her letting her personal feelings get in the way. If she were to help the couple, she needed to keep her perspective.

Later that day Annie saw Mrs Duncan, a smiling mother of four young children.

'Nurse Kate sent me here for a scan,' she said, settling herself into the chair. 'I'm pregnant again. Number five! I know it's a bit unexpected—for me, too—but the more the merrier, I say.'

Annie looked at Mrs Duncan's notes. Her last pregnancies had been straightforward and Kate had looked after her at the surgery. The first two had been born at St Piran's and the last two at home, with Kate in attendance.

Instantly she was concerned. Mrs Duncan had been in her mid-thirties when her first child had been conceived and almost forty when her youngest, now four and a half, had been born. At almost forty-five Annie knew that the chances of the baby having some sort of abnormality were significantly raised. No doubt the same thought had occurred to Kate and that was why she had sent the woman to Annie's clinic for a nuchal scan. But it seemed as if the reason for the scan hadn't really sunk in with the happy woman in front of her.

'It's not the best timing,' Mrs Duncan continued. 'Not with the six of us still living in the caravan while our house is being rebuilt. Although we should be back in our own house by the time this one is ready to be born.'

Annie shivered as she remembered the storm that had devasted a large part of Penhally Bay months earlier. The buildings that had been damaged were almost repaired but two people had lost their lives and no amount of rebuilding would ever completely undo the trauma of that day in people's minds. She couldn't help but admire her patient's cheerfulness in the face of what must be very demanding circumstances.

'I'm sure Kate told you why she was sending you here for a scan, Mrs Duncan?' Annie asked. Of course, the senior midwife at Penhally Bay Surgery would have explained it all to her patient, but from Mrs Duncan's cheerful attitude, Annie sensed that she didn't seem to realise that she had a significantly higher chance of a chromosomal abnormality in this pregnancy.

'Oh, please call me Mary,' the older woman said. 'And, yes, Nurse Kate said that everyone was offered a scan when they were twelve weeks now. So that's why I'm here. I'll have my scan and then if you could give me the picture, I'll be on my way.'

Annie suppressed a smile, before inviting Mary up onto

the couch. News of the brand-new scanner they had at St Piran's had spread quickly. The 3D images were clear enough to see even minute details and patients loved taking home photographs of the images. But almost as soon as she started to scan Mary, she could see that her instincts had been right. The nuchal fold, indicating an increased chance of Down's syndrome, was obviously thicker than normal. Her heart sank.

Mary quickly sensed that something was wrong. She squinted at the screen and then turned to look at Annie.

'What is it?' she asked. 'There's something wrong, isn't there? I can tell from the look on your face.'

'I'll need to do a blood test to confirm it, but I have to tell you that there are signs that your baby has a higher risk of Down's syndrome. If the blood test comes back positive, you may wish to think about amniocentesis.'

'What's that when it's at home? Anyway, I thought that was why I was having this scan.'

'This scan and blood test only tells us whether you have an increased risk. We need to do another test to confirm the result.'

'I think Nurse Kate suggested I might want that test with my last one,' Mary said slowly, 'but I decided against it. And my baby was fine. All my babies have been fine. So surely I don't need to worry about that?'

'The older a mother gets, the greater the risk of a Down's syndrome baby. The test does carry a small risk of miscarriage with it. You'll need to weigh up the pros and cons. You don't have to have the test, but you should consider it.'

'If you think I should then I will.' Mrs Duncan replied cautiously. 'I'm not sure I could cope with a disabled child, not when I have four of them and we're all crammed into the tiny caravan up in the park.'

Annie could see how deflated she was. Mrs Duncan had come in full of hope and excitement and all Annie had done was burst her bubble. But, as Raphael had just pointed out, she wouldn't be doing her job if she didn't give her patients all the facts and let them make up their own minds.

'I think you should have a word with the doctor before you go. If you can wait a few minutes, I'll give him a shout.'

Mary nodded. Annie left the room and went in search of Raphael. Fortunately she caught him just as he was seeing a patient out.

'I have someone in with me I'd like you to see,' Annie said. 'When I did her booking scan I could see a larger than normal nuchal fold. I'm not sure whether to arrange for her to come back for amniocentesis in three weeks or whether we should be doing a CVS today. I suspect that depends on what you think and whether you have time.'

Raphael took Mary's notes and the picture of the scan Annie had taken. 'You're absolutely right about the nuchal fold,' he agreed. 'The hospital is lucky to have a midwife who can scan. It is much more efficient this way.' He held his hands up and grinned as Annie started to speak. 'I know you are highly trained. I recognise that. Shall we see Mrs Duncan?'

Mrs Duncan had finished dressing by the time Annie and Raphael returned. Although pale, she seemed composed.

'I gather Annie here has explained things to you?' Raphael said gently. 'I realise it's probably a bit of a shock, but we are going to do everything we can to help you make the right decision for you. Okay?'

Mary nodded.

'There are three options here. One—we do nothing. Two—we bring you back for an amniocentesis. That's where we take a sample of the fluid surrounding the baby in the

womb. We can only do that when you are a little further on.'
He glanced at the notes. 'In about three weeks' time. The third
option is that we can do a test today where we take a sample
of the placenta. I have to warn you that both the tests carry a
risk of miscarriage. So we have to weigh up whether the
risks outweigh the benefits. Do you understand all this?'

'I think so.' Mary turned frightened eyes on Annie. 'What
do you think?'

'I think you should go home and speak to your husband
about it before you decide anything.'

'But Bill's away fishing. He won't be back for another
three days—at least.'

'Another few days won't make much difference either
way, and it's something you should speak to him about. We
can, of course, do the CVS today, but I really feel you should
take some time to think about it. I can also ask Kate to pop
around and see you, if that helps. I know you saw her through
your last pregnancies and sometimes it helps to talk things
over with someone else before coming to a decision.'

'Doctor?' Mary turned to Raphael.

'I think it's good advice. Some women decide not to have
the test at all, but I'm afraid it has to be your decision.
Whatever you decide, whenever you decide, we will be here
to help.'

'I think I will wait, then. Can I let you know when I make
up my mind?'

'Of course, Mary. The important thing is not to leave it
beyond sixteen weeks. Having a termination after that can be
very hard, if that's what you eventually decide to do.'

'And I think it would be useful if I gave you some stuff
explaining about Down's syndrome to take away with you,'
Annie interrupted. 'Many women find that these children

can bring a lot of joy to the family. It may not be right for you, but think about it.'

As soon as Annie had seen Mary out, armed with all the literature she could find for her, as well as a few useful Internet sites that she might want to look at, Annie went in search of Raphael. She found him talking to one of the junior doctors at the reception desk. As soon as he noticed her he came towards her and, taking her by the arm, took her to one side out of the hearing of his colleague.

'What is it?' he said. 'You are pale. There's nothing wrong with the baby, is there?'

'No, everything's fine. It's just…' She tailed off, uncertain why she had sought Raphael out but knowing she needed to speak to him. Maybe it was the threatened miscarriage and the knowledge that she had an increased chance of going into early labour. She was so scared for her baby.

'Seeing these patients makes you worry about your own pregnancy. Is that it?' His warm brown eyes searched hers. He raised a hand to her face and brushed her cheek with a fingertip. 'It must be hard for you.'

'I'm just so frightened,' she admitted. 'I know the chances of me going into early labour are increased and, well, we both know what that could mean.'

Raphael put his hands on her shoulders, and ignoring the presence of his junior, pulled her close.

'I know you are frightened. Try not to be. I am here with you.'

Annie let herself relax against his chest. He was here with her. For now. But would he stay?

CHAPTER NINE

THREE weeks later, Raphael tapped the front door of Annie's house before walking in. They had slipped into a comfortable pattern and there had been no more scares with the pregnancy, much to Annie's delight. As the door led straight into the small sitting room, Raphael found himself confronted with the sight of an inverted Annie. *Dios.* What was she doing?

Her upside-down face peered at him from the gap between her legs. She had tied her hair in a ponytail and it hung almost to the floor. She was wearing tight-fitting trousers that emphasised the shape of her bottom and her crop top revealed the taut mound of her belly and just the merest glimpse of the mound of her breasts. He felt something primeval stir in his belly.

'Oh, hello,' she said. 'I'm just doing a few rounds of The Salute to the Sun. I'll be finished in a few moments.'

In a fluid movement she changed position, curving her sweet body through a series of movements. One minute he'd be staring at her delicious rear, the next he'd be watching as her toned arms took the weight of her body and she moved into a series of lunges. Eventually she stood upright and brought her hands together as if she were praying. He took in the tiny droplets of moisture on her skin, her face glowing with her exertions, the gentle rise and fall of her breasts. The swell of her pregnancy was outlined by her Lycra trousers. She had never looked so beautiful or so womanly to him before, and it took every ounce of his willpower not to pull her into his arms and run his tongue over her skin.

'Yoga,' she said, a small smile tugging at her lips. 'In case you are wondering. I've been doing it for years. And since it seems as if I am forbidden—' she looked at him with mock anger '—to do anything more strenuous, I've been practising every day.' She picked up a towel from her sofa and wiped the moisture from her skin. 'I find it helps me stay calm,' she added. 'And I'm hoping it will help me stay focused in labour.'

Raphael tore his eyes away. He loved the way her eyes sparkled with amusement. He hadn't seen Annie smile as often as he would have liked. More than anything, he wished he could be the one to bring the light to her face.

'I have come to ask you if you would like to come for a picnic. Catalina and Maria arrived last night and as it's a beautiful day, we thought Maria would like a trip to the beach. I know she would like it if you came too. Catalina also. She wants to meet the mother of her niece or nephew again.'

Dios, why had he said it in that way? Why couldn't he admit that he wanted to spend time with her, too? Because he couldn't, that was why. He had to remember that it didn't matter how much he wanted this woman back in his arms, an affair was out of the question. No woman was ever going to rip his heart out again. Not even this one. Especially not this one.

'Maria? Catalina?' She was frowning. A tiny pucker of her eyebrows. 'They are here? In Penhally Bay? To see me?'

Annie wrapped the towel around her shoulders, hiding the exquisite swell of her breast from him.

'To see you, yes, but also because my mother had to go to the north of Spain to see her sister and she didn't want to take Maria with her. So she asked Catalina to take her for the weekend. My sister thought it was a chance to come here for a couple of days and get to know you a little. And Maria still talks about you. It would be a good chance to kill a bird with a stone, as you say in English.'

'Kill two birds with one stone,' Annie corrected him automatically. She wasn't looking as pleased as he'd thought she'd be. 'I don't know, Raphael. I'd like to see them both again, especially little Maria, but…' She tailed off.

Raphael could guess what she was thinking. He wondered if she had any idea how easily he was able to read her. She'd be worrying whether this was another attempt to persuade her to come and live in Spain.

'Please,' he said. 'I know I have no right to ask you. Your time is your own, but Maria would be so happy to see you again.'

He knew it was unfair of him to play the Maria card. Annie might be able to resist a plea from him, but from the little girl? He doubted it. As soon as he saw the acceptance in her eyes he knew he had been right.

'Where are they?'

'I dropped them off at the beach. I told them I couldn't promise that you would come.'

'But you knew I would.' Annie quirked an eyebrow in his direction. She was right. He had been certain that she wouldn't be able to resist seeing Maria again.

'I'll just have a quick shower then change. You go on if you like. I'll walk down when I'm ready. It won't take long and I could do with the exercise.'

'I'll wait for you,' Raphael said, picking up one of the magazines he had brought over a few weeks ago, noting that they hadn't been read. What was wrong with Annie? Didn't she like motorbikes?

By the time they arrived at the beach, the sun was beating down and the beach was busy with locals making the most of the first really hot summer's day.

'In a couple of weeks the beach will be crowded with tourists,' Annie told Raphael. 'We'll feel the impact at the hospital, too.'

'It is like Spain. In the winter everywhere is peaceful. Then the summer arrives and suddenly it doesn't feel like home any more.'

'I don't mind, though,' Annie protested. 'We're all tourists somewhere at some time. And I quite like the buzz when the visitors arrive.'

'Buzz?' Raphael repeated, looking perplexed.

Annie laughed. 'It's an expression. It means, an energy—an atmosphere.'

Raphael pointed to a couple of figures sitting on a blanket near the shelter of a wall.

'There they are. You go on while I find somewhere to change.'

Annie tiptoed across the hot sand, her sandals in her hand. As soon as Catalina saw her she jumped to her feet and hugged Annie.

'It is good to see you again.' She smiled. 'And looking so well. I trust my brother has been looking after you? Is everything all right now? He told us…' She tailed off.

'Everything's okay,' Annie said softly. 'I got a fright, but I'm okay now.'

Annie looked past Catalina's shoulder. Maria, wearing

her swimming costume, was standing watching Annie carefully, her thumb in her mouth.

'Hello, little one,' Annie said in Spanish. She had been swotting up some basic Spanish. As her child would almost certainly be bilingual, it seemed sensible.

The little girl broke into a shy smile and, stepping forward, wrapped her arms around Annie. Annie's heart squeezed as she ruffled Maria's thick dark curls.

'Where is my brother?' Catalina asked glancing over Annie's shoulder. 'Don't tell me he decided that he was needed at the hospital?'

'No. He's just getting changed.'

Suddenly Catalina grinned. 'Here he comes!'

Annie swung round. Raphael was striding towards them, wearing a wetsuit and carrying a surfboard. His bronzed chest was bare, the top half of his suit gathered around his lean hips. Annie could see the muscles in his upper arms bunch with the effort of carrying the board and she let her eyes slide down his body, taking in the toned six pack of his abdomen. The skin-tight fabric of his wetsuit clung to his thighs and across his hips. Annie's skin tingled.

As Maria ran towards him, short legs sending puffs of sand in her wake, he dropped the board and opened his arms. Maria careered into him and he pretended to be knocked over.

Annie watched them, regret vying with the feeling of lust. She was glad about the baby—more than glad. Why, then, did she feel this aching sense of loss?

Annie paddled with Maria while Raphael took his board to an area a little further along, which was cordoned off from bathers. Out of the corner of her eye she watched him as he rode the waves, his body bending and curving as he balanced.

Every so often she would catch her breath as he disappeared from view, but seconds later he would reappear from under the wave still upright. He had surfed before, that much was obvious.

'I want to make a sandcastle,' Maria said after she had finished splashing about, so they left Raphael to make most of the waves and returned to where Catalina was setting out the picnic. Keeping a watchful eye on Maria as she played, the two women stretched out on the blanket.

'It is good to see my brother happy again,' Catalina said softly. 'It has been too long since I saw him laugh. I think being here, as well as you and the baby, has been good for him.'

'He told me about Sebastian, and Ruth,' Annie said softly. 'It must have been hard on him.'

'I have never seen him so…' Catalina paused. 'So distraught. He loved that little boy. You know, he left his room exactly how it was the day she took him. His toys on the bed, his football, everything, as if he expected him to come back. And he did expect him to come back, right up until the court case. When he knew he had lost Sebastian for ever, it was as though Raphael had lost part of himself.'

'What kind of woman was she, his ex-wife? I can't imagine anyone being so deceitful and then so cruel.'

'Ruth? I never liked her.' Catalina shrugged. 'She always seemed to me as if she thought herself above everyone. You know, before Raphael became a doctor he was a very good football player. He could have played professionally, but he decided to study medicine instead. I think she would have stayed if he had chosen a different profession. She wanted more money, a better lifestyle than a doctor could offer her. Raphael told her that he would never go back to football, that, apart from everything else, he was too old, but she never stopped trying to change his mind. Then she met Sebastian's father again. He is now a very important and rich man in Spain. She decided he could give her a better life. So she went, and took Sebastian with her.'

Maria had left her sandcastle and had come to sit next to Annie. She pressed her body into Annie's and Annie put her arm around the child, drawing her closer.

'He tried everything to get access, even just once a month, but he couldn't. I think it broke his heart. When he met you, he had just been at the lawyer to try one more appeal, but that failed, too.' Catalina looked at Annie thoughtfully. 'He was a good father. He will be a good father to your child. If you will let him.'

'I won't stop him seeing our child, Catalina. I wouldn't do that, not unless he gave me cause. But I worry sometimes that he will try and take our baby away from me. And I could never let that happen.'

Catalina looked Annie directly in the eyes. 'You are wrong to think like that. He would never do to you what has been done to him. Never. He knows a child needs a mother and a father. You have to believe me. Just be patient with him.'

Annie did believe her. She knew that she had been worried all along for nothing. Raphael wasn't the kind of man to remove a child from its mother. And if she hadn't been so scared she would have seen that before now.

Maria shifted in her arms and, putting a small hand up to Annie's face, turned it towards her.

'You are not sad any more?' she said

'No,' Annie replied, and included Catalina in her smile. 'I am not sad any more.'

The rest of the weekend sped past in a happy blur. Annie couldn't resist the entreaty in Maria's big brown eyes when

Catalina suggested that Annie go with them to explore some of the hidden coves along the coast. As the four of them tramped along the beach, searching rock pools and underneath rocks for crabs, Annie let herself imagine what it would be like if this were *her* family. She saw the way Raphael was with Maria, the way he rolled up his jeans to paddle in the sea with her, the way he made the sad little girl giggle, and Annie's heart ached. If only he felt about her the way she felt about him. If only *they* could be a family.

She could no longer pretend that the way her heart hammered every time she saw him was simple lust. She loved him. With all her heart and soul. She had loved him from the moment she had met him and she would love him to the day she died. But, she reminded herself, even though the realisation almost cracked her heart in two, friendship was all he had to offer, and for the sake of their child it would have to be enough.

The following Monday, Annie was down at the Penhally Bay Surgery for a check-up with Kate when Nick popped his head around the door.

'Oh, I'm sorry. I didn't realise Kate still had someone with her. I'll come back in a few minutes.'

'No, come in,' Annie said. 'We're finished here. I was just chatting to Kate before getting back to St Piran's for the clinic.'

'Actually, it's useful that you're here, Annie. The patient I wanted to talk to Kate about involves you too.'

He sat down opposite Kate and stretched his legs out in front of him. Annie didn't really know him that well. The older GP was always friendly and helpful, but there was a reticence about him that didn't really invite confidences. All

Annie knew about him was that he was a widower with grown-up children and that he and Kate had worked together for a long time.

'I gather you saw Tilly Treliving a while back at the family planning clinic?' Nick said to Kate without preamble.

'Yes,' Kate replied. 'Is there a problem?'

'You could say that,' Nick said grimly. 'She's come to see me this morning. She's around thirty weeks pregnant, I think. If her dates are right.'

Kate looked shocked. 'She came to see me, let me see, almost a year ago about wanting to start a family, but I thought I'd agreed with her that we were going to get her diabetes stabilised first and that she would continue to use contraception until it settled down. I think Gemma has been following her up,' Kate said, referring to the practice nurse.

'Obviously she decided to go ahead anyway. It was only when Gemma became concerned that she hadn't been attending the surgery and went to visit her that we discovered the reason she'd been staying away.'

'Oh, poor Tilly. She must have been scared we'd tell her off,' Kate said.

'She'll need to be followed up at the hospital, of course,' Nick continued. 'I'm referring her to Dr Castillo. I'm just waiting for him to call me back. I gather he's in surgery, but if he isn't free to see her could you fit her in to one of your clinics, Annie?'

'Of course I'll see her,' Annie said. 'I'm down to do the afternoon clinic with Raphael. It would be no problem to add her on. But if she's still here, I could have a chat with her now, if you like. Unless you'd prefer to see her, Kate?'

'It sounds as if you'll be following her up, so it's probably best for you to see her,' Kate said. 'Besides, I'm due to visit a couple of my new mothers this afternoon. But let me know if there is anything I can do.'

A few moments after Kate and Nick had left, there was a soft tap at the door and a frightened-looking Tilly came into the room.

'It's all right, Tilly,' Annie said gently. 'I just need to do a few tests so we can see what's going on. Where's John? Couldn't he get time off work to come with you?'

'He's really angry with me.' The young woman burst into tears. 'We're barely speaking. He didn't want me to get pregnant. Not after what Kate told us.'

Annie handed Tilly a tissue and waited until the sobs tailed off. It wasn't great that Tilly had gone ahead and fallen pregnant, but she couldn't find it in her heart to blame her. She knew only too well how much the desperate desire to have a child could take over everything. But Tilly was taking a risk. Her diabetes could bring all sorts of complications for the baby as well as the mother.

'I'm sure John will come round. He's probably frightened for you, but we're going to take good care of you,' Annie said. 'Dr Tremayne is going to speak to the obstetrician, Dr Castillo, at St Piran's. He specialises in pregnancies such as yours and will want to see you. He and I will follow you up at the hospital.'

'Won't Dr Castillo be angry with me too?' Tilly said. She had dried her eyes and was looking calmer. 'You promise you'll be with me when I see him?'

'Of course. But you mustn't worry about him being annoyed with you. He'll simply be concerned that we get you and the baby safely through the pregnancy. He's very kind, actually.'

Annie stood and went to fetch some more tissues. As she did, Tilly looked at her in surprise. 'Are you…?' she asked.

'Pregnant?' Annie finished for her. 'Yes, I am.'

'Oh, I didn't know you were married.'

'I'm not,' Annie said quietly.

Tilly looked embarrassed.

'Hey, it's okay,' Annie said.

'I don't care that I've put *my* health at risk,' the young woman said fiercely. 'I'm glad I'm going to have a baby. It's going to be loved.'

There was a tap on the door and Nick popped his head in. 'I've spoken to Dr Castillo,' he said. 'He's agreed to see Tilly at his clinic this afternoon, if she can manage that?'

'You can come with me in the car. I'm heading there myself. That way I can be with you when you see Dr Castillo. How does that sound?' There was no way Annie was going to give Tilly any opportunity to miss the appointment. Not when there was so much at risk.

Annie and Raphael saw Tilly together before the main clinic started. Raphael examined the young woman thoroughly before asking her to wait while he and Annie had a chat.

'I am not happy with her glucose levels, and the baby is already bigger than I would have expected for her dates. We are going to have to keep a close eye on her.'

Annie knew why he was concerned. Diabetic mothers often had problems in pregnancy and when the diabetes wasn't well controlled there was an increased risk of stillbirth. They would have to monitor her carefully and intervene just at the right time. It would be a tricky balancing act.

'Don't worry,' Annie said. 'I intend to. Luckily she stays in Penhally Bay, so I can pop in and see her from time to time.'

Raphael smiled broadly. 'Are you always so determined to get your patients safely through their pregnancies? Anyone would think you care about their babies almost as much as you do your own.'

Annie's heart flipped. Why did he have to be so gorgeous? Why did her hormonally loaded body react to him the way it did? But it wasn't her hormones. She had reacted this way to him from the moment she had met him, and she couldn't blame pregnancy hormones then. And the way he had been with Tilly. Kind, reassuring, not judgemental at all. It was a different, softer side to Raphael. And it just made her love him more.

'Speaking of your pregnancy, why don't we check your BP while we are waiting for the next patient to arrive?'

Before she could react he was wrapping a blood-pressure cuff around her arm.

'Hey, wait a minute,' Annie protested, alarmed to feel goose-bumps all along her arm where his fingers brushed her skin. 'Kate checked my blood pressure earlier. And it's fine. She's looking after me perfectly well. I wish you would stop treating me as if I were some walking incubator.'

Raphael narrowed his eyes at her. 'Is that what you think?' he said, amusement threading his voice.

'What else am I to think?' Annie said crossly. 'All you're interested in is the health and welfare of this baby.'

'Don't you think I'm interested in the health and welfare of the mother as well?' His eyes were unfathomable, but a smile tugged at the corner of his mouth. It was enough to make Annie's heart beat faster.

But before either of them could say more, the receptionist popped her head around the door to tell them that Claire and Roy had arrived to see them.

Annie watched as Raphael scanned Claire, who happily had no further bleeding. But as Raphael replaced the probe he had been using and Annie wiped away the lubricating gel from Claire's abdomen, Annie could tell that he was concerned.

He waited until Claire was dressed. As always Roy was there by her side. So far he hadn't missed a single appointment, even though Annie knew he had a demanding job that often took him away from home.

'The babies have grown since the last time I saw you,' Raphael said. 'But not as much as I would have liked.'

Claire's face paled and she clutched her husband's hand. The couple sat in silence, waiting for Raphael to continue.

'It's good that we have got the babies to over twenty-five weeks,' he continued. 'But now, I'm afraid, we have to make a decision.'

The couple nodded and waited for him to continue.

'We can continue to monitor the babies, and see how they progress, or we can deliver them now by Caesarean section. Both options carry a risk.' His voice was gentle. 'If we wait, it is possible that the smaller baby will die. If, on the other hand, we deliver them now, the smaller baby has an increased risk of not pulling through. The bigger baby also has greater risk of complications as all pre-term babies do.'

Claire and Roy absorbed the information silently, but Annie could see the fear etched on their faces.

'What would you do?' Roy asked Raphael. 'If it were your babies we were talking about?'

'I'm afraid this has to be your decision,' Raphael replied softly.

'Which option carries more risk for Claire? However much we want these babies, it is her that matters most.'

'Neither option is more or less risky for your wife,' Raphael said. 'Whatever you decide, it is more than likely that Claire will require a C-section. Any operation carries a small risk, but many, many women have this procedure every day without harm.'

Roy looked at Annie. She could see the tension in his face. The love he felt for his wife was written there plain for the world to see. 'What would you do, Annie?'

Annie shook her head. She didn't know what she would do if she were in their shoes. It wasn't a question she could answer.

'Both options carry a risk,' she replied. 'If we leave Claire, there is a chance the second, smaller twin could die suddenly in utero. The bigger twin would continue to grow and every day spent inside Claire's tummy increases its chances of being born healthy. If we chose to deliver both twins now, the bigger one will probably do okay, though there is still the chance of complications, but the second, smaller twin is more likely to struggle, because they are twins they are already smaller than they would be for their gestation. I'm guessing—' Annie turned to Raphael for confirmation '—from what we can see on the scan that the smaller baby is closer to twenty weeks' size.'

'So essentially you are saying that, whatever we do, we could lose either one or both of our children.' Although Roy's voice was calm, Annie could see that he was finding it difficult not to break down in front of his wife. Once again she marvelled at the very real love between this couple. Beside him, Claire was crying quietly. 'How are we supposed to decide what to do?' Roy continued.

'If I were you,' Raphael said, 'I would wait another week or two.' Annie looked at him, surprised. After everything he had said about not wanting to make a decision for the couple, here he was doing just that. But as she caught his eye, she knew what he was thinking. Waiting gave the couple a better chance of one healthy child.

'Essentially, what Dr Castillo is saying is that if you do nothing right now, you have a better chance of having one normal child. But there is a greater risk of the second twin dying in utero. If you go ahead and have a section today then the second twin could still die, and the bigger one still has a chance of complications. But there is a chance both could survive.'

'I don't want either of my babies to die,' Claire cried. 'I love them both. I can't sacrifice one for the other.'

'We will go along with whatever you decide, of course,' Raphael said. 'I just wanted to make sure you understand the options.'

'Thank you for your frankness, Dr Castillo,' Roy said quietly. 'I wonder if my wife and I could have a moment to discuss it?'

'You don't have to make up your minds right now,' Annie interjected. 'Go home. Have a think about it. Then let us know.'

'From what you tell us, every day we delay is a day that one of our babies could die. No, I think we need to decide now, today. We just need some time.' He looked up at Annie and she recoiled from the naked pain in his eyes. She had grown fond of the couple and she would have given anything in her power to make everything all right for them. But it wasn't in her power, she admitted sadly as she followed Raphael out of the room, leaving Claire in Roy's arms. They had done everything they could.

In the staff room Raphael turned to face Annie.

'Are you okay?' he asked gently.

Annie nodded glumly. 'I just wish we could wave a magic wand and make everything all right for them. They want this so much.' Her voice broke and before she knew it Raphael had pulled her into his arms. She leaned her head against his chest as he stroked her hair.

'You shouldn't take every case so much to heart, *cariño*.'

She let herself relax in his arms. Here it felt as if nothing bad could ever happen to her, or to anyone else. In his arms she felt as if she'd come home. Reluctantly, she eased herself away from him. She had to remember that all he was offering her was friendship. Even if her beating heart reminded her that she wanted so much more.

Raphael looked down at her, his dark eyes glowing, and Annie caught her breath. She knew she must be mistaken, but he was looking at her as if…as if he wanted to kiss her. The air fizzled and crackled between them, just as it had the night they'd met, and Annie felt her world tilt.

Before either of them could move, Roy appeared at the door, mercifully oblivious to the atmosphere in the room.

'We've made our decision,' he said.

Back inside the consulting room, Claire had dried her tears and was sitting pale-faced but composed.

'We are going to take Dr Castillo's advice and wait,' she said calmly, looking Annie directly in the eyes. 'I know we might lose one this way, but we have waited so long to have children we just can't take the chance of losing them both. It's not about whether they'll have problems, I will love my children regardless and with Roy and his family's support we would cope. No, it's the thought that if I have a section now, I could lose both my children. I cannot risk that.'

'For what it's worth,' Raphael said, 'I think it's the right decision. But I'm going to suggest you attend day-care clinic twice a week so we can monitor you. I know it will be diffi-cult for you, but it means if there is a sudden change we can act quickly.'

'I think you're being very brave,' Annie added. 'It's an impossible decision, but we are going to do everything we can to see you through it.' Glancing up, she caught the gleam of approval in Raphael's eyes. Almost imperceptibly he nodded at her. But it wasn't that she necessarily agreed with him, it was simply that the couple having made up their minds needed her full support. She just hoped for all their sakes that they had made the right choice.

CHAPTER TEN

ALMOST imperceptibly, Annie and Raphael developed a routine. Every evening, when he wasn't on call, Raphael would call at the cottage and after he had interrogated her about her health they would go for a walk down to the harbour. They would talk about Spain and Penhally Bay and places they had been on holiday. Everything, it seemed, except what was going to happen once the baby was born. But Annie didn't want to spoil the fragile peace between them. They discovered a shared love of opera and Annie admitted she loved country and western music and Raphael teased her about it. He told her that he played the guitar sometimes for the flamenco dancers for which his home town was famous.

'You must come back to Spain,' he said. 'There is so much I want to show you.'

Whenever he suggested it, which was often, Annie would smile. 'Of course I'll want to bring him or her to Spain. I want my child to grow up knowing about all their family.'

The evenings were getting lighter every day as her bump grew larger. Annie saw Kate at the surgery for her check-ups and the senior midwife declared herself happy with Annie's progress. Her baby was due at the end of September and towards the end of June, Annie decided that it was time to prepare the nursery. If she waited much longer she'd never be able to balance on the stepladder.

And that was where Raphael found her one evening when she was up the ladder, painting the wall of the soon-to-be nursery.

'Come down at once,' he said crossly. He had stopped waiting for Annie to open the door to him and would just come in after a brief warning knock.

'Whatever for? I've still a good half of the wall to do.' She carried on painting. 'If you want to help, grab a brush from over there.' As she indicated the brushes and paint for the wall, the ladder wobbled and Annie almost lost her balance. But in a flash Raphael was up the ladder, steadying her against him.

'Be careful, *cariño*,' he said. 'Please come down.'

'Hey, I'm okay. I just lost my balance for a moment. I wouldn't have fallen.' But Raphael clearly wasn't in the mood for an argument. He picked her up and lifted her down from the ladder. He held her tight against him and she could feel the thudding of his heart through the thin cotton of his T-shirt. Her body melted into his, at least as far as her abdomen would let her, and his arms moved down her body, pressing her closer. Annie felt dizzy with desire. Before she could help herself her arms snaked around his neck and she was lifting her face to his.

Gently he disentangled her arms from around his neck and stood back.

'I don't think it would be a good idea,' he said.

Annie was mortified. What on earth had got into her? Given the slightest bit of encouragement, she would have kissed him. It was what she longed to do. It was what she had been longing to do for weeks now, she realised with a thud of her heart. It didn't matter what she told herself, she found him as devastatingly gorgeous and sexy as the day she had first met him. She had tried to pretend that she didn't but she could no longer hide it from herself. Or from him, she thought ruefully. There was no mistaking her intent—at least not for a man as experienced as Raphael.

'No,' she said shortly. 'I can see that a heavily pregnant woman might not be everyone's cup of tea.'

'Mierda,' he groaned under his breath. 'You should see yourself. I doubt there is a woman in the world who looks more beautiful than you do right now. But it is not right. We have to be sensible. What is the point in having sex—no matter how much I would like to—when we are just becoming friends?'

Regardless of what he said, Annie felt rejected. Did he think she was trying to seduce him, to force him into a deeper relationship?

'I'm sorry,' she said stiffly. 'I don't know what I was thinking.' Then she tried a smile to ease some of the tension. 'They do say some women react like that to pregnancy hormones. I'm clearly one of them.'

Raphael looked at her quizzically then opened his mouth as if he were about to say something. But then he seemed to change his mind and picked up a paintbrush.

'I will finish this,' he said. 'You put your feet up and rest.'

'I'm not tired! In fact, I feel great. I'll make us something to eat,' she said.

By the time she returned from the kitchen to tell him the meal was ready, Raphael had finished the room. He stood back and surveyed his work, looking decidedly pleased with himself.

'I wonder what it will be. A boy or a girl.'

'We'll just have to wait to find out,' Annie teased.

Raphael wiped his hand across his forehead, leaving a yellow streak of paint behind. Impulsively, Annie stood on tiptoe to wipe away the smear.

Raphael reached up and trapped her hand in his. He brought her hand to his lips and kissed her fingers, sending a jolt of electricity all the way to her toes. Before she knew it, he was kissing her. Deep, searching kisses as if he wanted to possess her very soul. But even as she felt herself melt in his arms, Annie knew it was a mistake. Breathlessly she pulled away. They stood looking at each other. Before either of them could speak, Raphael's pager bleeped. He looked at the number and frowned. 'It's the hospital. Can I use your phone?'

As soon as he replaced the phone a little later, Annie knew something was up.

'It's Claire,' he said. 'She's gone into labour. I need to go to the hospital. I promised her I would do her section.'

'I'm coming with you,' Annie said, picking up her jacket.

'Of course. I know they both want you there.'

As they drove, they discussed Claire.

'At least she's made it to twenty-eight weeks,' Annie said as Raphael negotiated the narrow lanes to the hospital. Annie had been present when Raphael had scanned Claire the day before. Everyone had been relieved to see the second twin's heart was still beating strongly.

'Yes. It's better than I hoped or expected.'

'The twins will need to spend a few weeks in Special Care. But let's just hope the second twin survives.'

Too busy concentrating on the road, Raphael didn't reply.

As soon as they arrived at the hospital they rushed down

to theatre and were ready and waiting by the time Claire was wheeled in with an apprehensive Roy at her side.

Annie bent over the mother to be and smiled reassuringly. 'You'll be a mum soon,' she whispered.

Claire looked up at her with frightened eyes. 'I'm scared, Annie. So scared.'

'Everything will be okay,' Annie said. 'You've done really well to have managed this far. And both hearts are beating strongly. We'll need to take your babies up to Special Care as soon as they are delivered. But we'll let you see them as soon as we can. Okay?'

As soon as Claire's spinal block was working, Raphael made his first incision. It wasn't the first time Annie had seen him operate, but she never tired of the way his brow furrowed as he concentrated. He operated quickly, without wasting any time. Within minutes he was removing the bigger of the twins. As Annie stepped forward to take the girl from Raphael she was pleased to note that the first baby was a good size and, as it gave a loud cry, with a good set of lungs. The second twin was a little boy, and was more of a concern. He was very small and Annie knew that his parents were in for weeks of worry while his lungs developed fully. Very briefly, as promised, Annie showed Claire and Roy their babies before handing them over to the paediatrician.

'They're both so tiny,' Claire whispered.

'They both have a good chance, Claire,' Annie said. 'They'll look after them upstairs. I'll take you up to see them as soon as possible.'

Claire looked from Annie to Raphael, tears glistening in her eyes.

'Thank you,' she whispered.

Annie smiled back. She had a good feeling about the twins.

* * *

Later, after they had left Claire and Roy, Raphael drove them both back to Annie's house. Neither of them spoke, each too preoccupied with their thoughts. Annie thought back to the kiss they had shared. She had known that she loved him, had known from the day she had met him that she loved him, she just hadn't been able to admit it to herself. Whatever she had felt for Robert, it had come no where near the feelings she had for Raphael. Whenever he was near every atom in her body seemed to come alive, and when he wasn't there she missed him desperately.

She sneaked a glance at him from under her lashes. He was like the missing piece of the jigsaw that was her life. But it was no use. Although he was attracted to her, he didn't love her. And Annie would never again be with someone who didn't feel about her the way she felt about them. Whatever pain lay in store for her, she would have to deal with it. Even though it would be torture to see him, share her child with him, stand by while he married someone else, she had no choice. As long as he wanted to be part of their child's life, she would have to let him. She just had to make sure he never guessed how she felt about him.

The days passed and Annie felt well and continued to revel in feeling the life growing inside her. Although she still had a few weeks to go, she was happy that everything was ready for the baby. Raphael had finished painting the nursery and he had assembled the cot, with her passing him the tools, much in the same way as she passed him instruments in theatre. At the hospital they worked together often and had developed an easy understanding of how each other worked. Raphael's reputation was spreading and more and more patients, especially those with high-risk pregnancies, were asking to see him.

After her clinic one morning, Annie went in search of Raphael and she found him in the doctors' lounge, chatting with Ben Carter.

As soon as Raphael spotted her he stood and went across to her. He touched her hand. 'What is it, Annie? Are you okay?' His concern never ceased to touch her, although she knew it was mainly for his unborn child. They still hadn't spoken about what would happen after the birth. For the time being, Annie was content to let things ride.

'I've just seen Tilly down at the clinic. I wanted her to see you, but she wouldn't stay.'

'What's going on with her?' Raphael asked. 'Her blood-glucose control was terrible the last time we saw her. I had hoped she would have managed to bring it under control with changes to her diet and increasing her insulin.'

'That's just it. Her glucose profile was even worse today and the baby is much bigger than it should be for her dates.'

Raphael chewed his lip, looking thoughtful. 'Does her partner come with her?'

'He wasn't here today.'

'It would be useful to know what he thinks,' Raphael said. 'Tell you what, why don't I call in on them on my way home tonight? Would that help, do you think?'

Annie was relieved. She couldn't explain it but she felt really uneasy about Tilly. The young woman wasn't looking after herself and Annie knew she would be devastated if she lost her baby. Why wasn't she looking after herself better? Was it simply that Annie and Raphael hadn't managed to get across how crucial this was for the health of her baby?

'We should both go,' Annie said. 'I'll meet you there after work. Say about sixish. Would that be okay?'

'I have an elective section this afternoon after my main list is finished. But I should be able to make it, if everything goes according to plan. Which it will do.' He grinned down at her.

Her heart flipped. There was something so supremely confident about Raphael. In another man it might have come across as arrogance, but in him it was simple recognition of his own ability.

'But before theatre I have a postnatal ward round to do,' he continued. 'Are you joining me?'

Annie watched as Raphael went to see each of his patients. Each woman got the same attention, as if she were the most important person in the world to him right at that moment. If someone's baby was crying, Raphael would pick it up and rock it in his arms while he talked to the woman. He always managed to find some compliment for each baby that left the mother smiling with pride, believing her baby to have been singled out for particular praise. But it wasn't an act. Annie could see he was genuinely interested. It was a different side to Raphael, one she had seen countless times since he had come to work at St Piran's but it never ceased to surprise her. How much more tender he would be with his own child she could only guess at.

'I thought Spanish men were too macho to coo over babies,' she teased him as they made their way out of the ward.

'Coo?' He looked at her, puzzled. 'What is this coo? It doesn't sound very nice.'

'Fuss. That's what it means,' Annie replied.

'Spanish men love children,' he said. 'We don't see them as inconveniences to be hidden away, like some countries. I would like a whole brood of them one day. A football team—or at least a five-a-side.'

Annie felt her heart crack a little. It was another reason why she and Raphael would never be anything except co-parents. The baby she was carrying was enough of a miracle. There would never be any more for her.

Annie knocked on the door of Tilly's small cottage but there was no reply. It was strange. She had telephoned after speaking to Raphael to warn her that they would be calling in around six. Perhaps Tilly had popped out to the shops?

She knocked again and then tried the door, and was surprised to find it unlocked. She opened it and walked in. The residents sometimes left their doors unlocked in the winter, but with the influx of tourist at this time of year, people tended to be more careful. The house didn't feel empty. Music was playing on the radio and there was a bag of unpacked shopping at the door, as if it had been abandoned. Immediately Annie felt alarm bells ringing. She stepped further into the house, calling out Tilly's name. Perhaps she had gone for a bath? But then as soon as she entered the sitting room she saw her. Tilly was lying on the floor, unmoving, and Annie rushed to her side, dropping to her knees. The young woman was unconscious and Annie made sure Tilly was breathing before pushing her over on her side into the recovery position. She smelt for the distinctive odour of ketones, but it wasn't there. Tilly must be having a hypo. So she needed to get sugar in to her system. Quickly, she rummaged in her bag. Did she still have the glucose gel she kept for emergencies? Thankfully, she discovered it hidden under a glucose test kit—she'd need that too. Taking a generous dollop from the container she spread the gel inside Tilly's lips, hoping the sugar would be absorbed rapidly.

She wondered how long Tilly had been lying unconscious. Where was John? Shouldn't he be home by now? And where was Raphael? She could do with his help. She bent over Tilly, pricking her finger with the stylet from the testing kit. Her glucose was dangerously low, no wonder she was unconscious. She needed to get her to hospital. She was digging in her shoulder bag for her mobile when she heard Raphael's voice calling out her name.

He stood there, taking in the scene with a glance.

'I found her here like this just a couple of minutes ago. She's having a bad hypo. I've put some glucose gel on her lips, but so far it's having no effect and I haven't had a chance to check the baby yet. I was just about to call for an ambulance when you arrived.'

'What about glucagon?' he said, crouching beside Annie and checking Tilly's pulse. 'We teach all the diabetic mothers to use it an emergency. She must a keep a syringe of it somewhere handy.' He took the Sonicaid Annie held out to him. 'I'll check the foetal heart while you see if you can find it.'

'Shouldn't I phone for an ambulance first?'

'No, if we can get some glucagon into her that'll buy us the time we need. She could do with a drip, too.'

'Found it!' Annie exclaimed, taking the cover off the pre-filled syringe and plunging the needle into Tilly's leg. Thankfully she had left it in full view on the side table.

'She should come round quickly now,' Raphael said, and sure enough Tilly groaned. Over her stirring form Raphael and Annie smiled at each other. Their eyes locked and Annie felt her world spin on its axis. He was looking at her as if… Then his eyes seemed to lose their warmth—as if she was a professional he admired, she admonished herself. Nothing more.

'We still need to get her to hospital. The baby seems fine, but her diabetes is so badly controlled I'm not sure we should let the pregnancy continue much longer. She's thirty-five weeks. Maybe it's just as well to get her delivered.'

'I need to find out what's going on with her when we get her to hospital,' Annie said. 'I know how much she wants this baby so for her to be taking chances with her health like this seems out of character.'

'There will be time for that later. I agree it's important, but right now we have to make sure that the baby stays healthy long enough to be delivered. I suggest that once she comes round completely, we put her in the back of my car and take her there ourselves. If that's okay with you?'

Annie nodded. She'd feel happier once she knew that Tilly was in hospital where she could be properly looked after.

Tilly stirred and her eyes focused gradually on Annie. 'Where am I? What happened? Where's John?' She tried to sit up, her eyes frantically searching the room. As soon as she realised John wasn't there she sank back down and began to cry quietly. 'He didn't come back, did he? He's never coming back. What am I going to do?'

'Hush, Tilly,' Annie soothed. 'You slipped into a hypo, but you and your baby are all right now. Dr Castillo is here and we're going to take you to hospital. We can find John later. You can phone him from the ward.'

'You don't understand,' Tilly wailed. 'He's not coming back. He doesn't want me or the baby.' And then as Annie put her arms around the heaving shoulders of her distressed patient, Tilly sobbed as if her heart would break.

By the time they had Tilly settled in the ward it was almost eight. Annie was feeling tired and hungry. She and Raphael agreed that they would wait until the next day before making a decision whether or not to deliver Tilly's baby early.

'She's thirty-five weeks,' Raphael said as they made their way to his car. 'Obviously I'd prefer to wait another couple of weeks but I don't think we can afford to take the risk.'

'At least these days a thirty-five-weeker has an excellent chance of doing well. I agree with you, the longer we wait the riskier for Tilly's baby.'

Raphael opened the door of his car for Annie and helped her in. As she sat back in the leather seat Annie yawned. 'I think I'll go straight to bed,' she said. 'I'm too exhausted even to think about cooking.' Raphael looked at her sharply but slid the car into gear without saying anything.

'I wish Tilly had told me she and John were having problems,' Annie said. 'I would have kept a closer eye on her had I known.'

'What kind of man leaves his partner to cope with a pregnancy on her own?' Raphael said savagely. 'Especially when he knows there are difficulties.'

'From what she told us, they had been having problems for a while. That's why she got pregnant. She thought it would bring them back together. Poor girl.'

'Irresponsible, you mean,' Raphael said. 'Gambling with her own health as well as the health of her baby.'

'I don't think you can be too hard on her,' Annie said. 'She loves John and she really wants this baby. Sometimes we all do things that aren't completely rational. At least, I do. Can you say you've never done anything that wasn't logically thought out?'

He turned his head towards her and looked as if he were about to say something then thought better of it. 'I just wish people would realise that a baby isn't an accessory,' he said.

'That they are a commitment for life. Not just something you have on a whim.'

Annie heard the underlying bitterness to his words and knew he was thinking about Sebastian.

'It is not our job to be judgemental,' Annie insisted. 'Our job is to ensure a healthy baby at the end. Just that. And if that means getting involved with their lives to make sure of that outcome, it's all part of the job. At least, that's the way I see it.' Annie broke off, aware that she sounded heated. But to her, patients weren't just pregnant women, they were women with lives, women like Tilly with relationship problems, women like her who had to balance motherhood with a career, women who had financial worries, and all of that had to be taken into consideration.

Raphael pulled up outside her house and switched off the ignition. 'You really care about them all, don't you?' he said. 'They all matter.' He looked into the distance and Annie could see the lines of tiredness creasing his eyes—or was it sadness? 'But what about the fathers?' he continued softly. 'Don't they have rights too? Don't they play an important part?' He laughed mirthlessly. 'Or do we exist just to provide the sperm?'

Annie turned to Raphael. 'I know your wife hurt you badly,' she said, 'but not every woman is like her. Most of us just want…' She hesitated. 'Most of us want a loving relationship, someone to share the ups and downs of life. And if a baby is part of that…so much the better.' She had to force herself to look at him. 'I know we got it the wrong way round. In an ideal world, I would be having a baby with someone who loved me.' A muscle twitched in his jaw as he studied her intently. He looked as far away from Annie as she had ever seen him. 'But at least I know my baby will have a father who will cherish him. Who will, I know, be there for him. And when it comes down to it, that is the most important thing of all.'

Suddenly the clouds vanished from his eyes. 'What is important that you eat and then get some rest. Come on, let's see what you have in that fridge. I may not be any good at making toast but I can cook a great frittata.'

Annie thought about protesting. She didn't know whether she had the energy to deal with Raphael in her house. It was hard enough to hide the way she felt about him at work, but alone with him, with her guard down? The last thing she wanted was for him to guess, if, God forbid, he hadn't already done so. But Raphael was already out of the car and was holding her door open.

'I won't take no for an answer,' he said firmly. 'You're tired. Making you something to eat is the least I can do.'

He stretched out a hand and Annie had no choice but to take it. As she felt his hand wrap around hers she felt a warmth suffuse her body. It would be so good to have someone who cared about her. Someone who wanted this baby as much as she did, because they had deliberately made it out of love. But that wasn't going to happen. But just this once, just for tonight, even if it was only inside her head, couldn't she pretend that they were a normal couple looking forward to the birth of their baby, knowing they had the rest of their lives to look forward to?

'I want to do something for you.' He looked at her intently. 'Please?'

She couldn't refuse the look of entreaty in his deep brown eyes.

'Okay,' she said. 'I give in. Just as long as it is better than the breakfast you made me.'

Annie showered, leaving Raphael to rummage around in her kitchen for the ingredients for a meal. By the time she returned, delicious smells of bacon and garlic were wafting through the kitchen.

'What can I do?' she asked.

'Nothing. Just sit there and look beautiful,' Raphael replied, settling her into an armchair.

'I'm not ill, you know,' she protested, but she couldn't stop a smile from creeping across her face. He had called her beautiful. Did he really think so, or was it just part of the patter he gave every woman? The thought wiped the smile off her face. Don't think about that just now, she told herself. Just enjoy being here with him tonight.

After they had eaten—and Raphael was right, the frittata was delicious—Raphael made them some coffee. They sat in companionable silence for a while.

'What are you hoping for?' Raphael asked suddenly. 'A boy or a girl?'

'Oh, I don't mind. I'm just so happy to be having a baby at all. As long as it's healthy…' She laughed. 'You know, when mothers used to say that, I wasn't ever sure whether I believed them or not. Now I know that they meant it.' Suddenly she felt a kick just below her ribs. 'Oops,' she said. 'The way this one is kicking, I think we may have a footballer on our hands.'

In a flash, Raphael was off his chair and on his knees beside her. He looked up, searching her eyes. 'Can I feel?' he asked.

She nodded, suddenly breathless. He placed his hand gently on her stomach, just as the baby gave another vigorous kick. As she looked down on Raphael's bent head, she was tempted to place her hand on his thick curls and run her fingers through his hair. It took all her willpower to resist the impulse. Especially when he looked up at her and she saw the tenderness in his eyes.

'I would like a girl,' he said. 'One who looks just like you. A girl who is just like you.'

Her breath caught in her throat. He reached up and took her hand, kissing each finger in turn. The pressure of his lips was an exquisite pain and every bit of her cried out to be taken in his arms and kissed senseless.

Slowly he rose to her feet and pulled her upright. Then she was in his arms and he was kissing her. Unsure, she pulled away slightly but as he held her closer, dropping his hands to her hips, there was no mistaking his desire for her. She closed her eyes and gave in to the feelings shooting around her body. If he hadn't been holding her, she didn't think her legs could have kept her upright.

Suddenly he pulled away. He was breathing deeply, his eyes black with desire. She almost whimpered when she felt him release her.

'Mierda,' he said. 'It is not good to make love. Not now.'

But then she was back in his arms. His hands were on her breasts, his touch sending hot flashes of need to her groin. Slowly he pulled open her dressing gown, revealing her bra and panties and her swollen belly. She covered her belly with her hands, feeling shy.

'Let me see,' he demanded. 'Don't you know how beautiful you are to me, especially now, with my baby growing inside you?'

He eased the dressing gown off her shoulders and lowered her onto the rug beside the fire, the flickering light playing across his features. He dipped a hand under her bra and she felt her nipples tighten in response. Why was he doing this?

He had just said they couldn't make love. Then his hand reached behind her back and he undid the clip of her bra. Her breasts sprang free and he cupped them, his thumbs circling her nipples sending shock waves of pleasure through her.

'Ah,' he said, a smile on his lips 'But I didn't say there weren't other ways of making love that would be safe for the baby.' He trailed a hand down over her stomach. His hand rested there for a moment, then he lowered his head and took one of her nipples into his mouth. Annie was lost. She could no more have stopped him than she could have carried an elephant on her back. Every touch of his fingers made her want more. The sensations in her body were overpowering. She knew it wouldn't be long before she had to give in, but at the same time she never ever wanted him to stop doing what he was doing.

His hand resting on her belly slid lower until it was resting just at the top of her panties. He pulled his head away and looked into her eyes. 'Do you want me to stop?' he asked. She shook her head, unable to speak. She had just enough time to see the triumph in his eyes before he was slipping his hand under the silk and between her legs. Then she was moving against him, unable to prevent her body's response to his touch. Then slowly, as he touched her gently at first, then with increasing pressure and pace, she felt her body explode with pleasure and she cried his name.

Eventually the world steadied around them and Raphael held her in his arms as her breathing returned to normal. She wondered at his self-control, that he could have the restraint to love her without asking anything in return. All of a sudden she felt shy again. She reached over and undid his belt and he groaned as she touched him lightly with her fingers and pulled her closer.

'You don't have to,' he said, as if the words physically hurt him.

'But I want to,' Annie said quietly. She knelt over him and undid the buttons of his jeans, then they were off and he was lying naked beside her. Remembering from the night they had met, she touched him the way he liked it, teasing him, slowing down, sometimes stopping when she sensed he was near then starting again. Then when she knew he couldn't take much more she used both her hands until he, holding her in a vice-like grip, gave in to his own climax.

Later they lay in each other's arms. Annie laid her head on the smoothness of Raphael's chest where she could hear the steady thump, thump of his heart. His hands stroked her hair, smoothing it away from her eyes.

'Will you marry me, Annie?' he said.

Annie sat bolt upright. She felt a zing of happiness course through her veins. He wanted to marry her. He must feel the same way she did. The connection they had felt that first night was still there; it hadn't gone away.

'Pardon?' she said, wanting to make sure she had heard him right. 'What did you say.'

He sat up, grinning at her. The light bounced off his bronzed skin. She had never thought him so sexy as she did right them. She knew she loved every inch of him. His thoughtfulness, his humour, even his old-fashioned masculinity, and he loved her! It was almost too much to take in. She had resigned herself to never finding someone who loved her the way she needed to be loved. Wholeheartedly, without reservation, and now, just when she had thought she couldn't be happier…

'We could live in Spain. You, me and the baby. Be a family,' he said. 'A real family.'

An icy shiver ran up Annie's spine. She couldn't help but notice that he hadn't said he loved her.

'Live in Spain? But my job is here, my parents, my friends,' she said quietly. If he loved her, surely he'd be prepared to be wherever she was?

'You would be part of my family. My mother would welcome you like her own daughter. She will love you. I am sure of it.'

But still he hadn't said *he* loved her.

'And as for your job, you don't need to work. I have plenty of money and besides a woman should be at home with her child, no?' He continued, seemingly oblivious to her silence, 'Of course, then there will be no need to go to the lawyers for access.'

She was furious. She stood, picking up her discarded dressing gown and pulling it on over her shoulders.

'So that is what this is about,' she said through clenched teeth. 'My God, Raphael, is there nothing you wouldn't do to get your own way? Had you planned this all along? Did you really think that after you made love to me, I'd be so grateful that I would go along with your plans? Was this the only way left to get your child with you in Spain? And if the price you have to pay for that is marriage to a woman you don't really love, then so be it.'

She picked up his jeans and T-shirt and flung them at him. 'But what about what I want? Did that cross your mind? Please don't imagine for one minute that I would enter into a loveless marriage, no matter how convenient.'

If she hadn't been so angry she might have laughed at the bewilderment on Raphael's face as he slipped on his T-shirt and jeans. But she was in no mood for laughing. How could she have let her guard down? She knew how much Raphael

wanted this baby and she had completely underestimated the
lengths he would go to to get what he wanted.

'Let yourself out,' she said. 'I'm going to bed.'

CHAPTER ELEVEN

AFTER leaving Annie's, Raphael decided to go for a walk on the beach. He was far too restless to go to sleep and he needed time to think. He always thought better when he was doing something. He had thought about following her into the bedroom and trying to explain, but something told him that Annie was in no mood to listen to him, let alone believe him. *Dios*, he thought ruefully, she is like a tiger when she is angry. He had never seen her other than quiet and calm, but he didn't find the new side to Annie off-putting. He was delighted that there was still lots more to find out about her. And whatever she thought right now, he fully intended that they would have time to discover each other.

The night sky was shot with lilac. Until recently he had wondered if he had done the right thing coming here. He thought back to the day he had met Annie. He had been hurting then, and the pain he had seen reflected in her eyes had drawn him to her. It hadn't just been her beauty, although with her pale skin and light green eyes and that luscious body, there was no denying he had been powerfully attracted to her. So attracted he hadn't been able to stop himself taking her to bed, even though he had known in his soul that it was dangerous. And he had been right. But she had turned out to be dangerous in a way he couldn't have possibly imagined.

When he'd found out she was pregnant he hadn't been sure she was telling him the truth. After all, he had been deceived before. But the more he learned about her, the more he knew that she didn't have a deceitful bone in her body. She was too transparent for a start. He wondered if she realised how every emotion showed on her face—he always knew what she was thinking. But the worst thing of all was he knew he was falling in love with her. He couldn't stop thinking about her, he couldn't stop himself remembering how she had felt in his arms. Her soft, silky skin, the smell of her perfume, the way the pulse beat at the base of her throat, the way her thick hair fell across his face when they were making love covering him in her scent. And it wasn't just a physical attraction he felt any longer. If it had been he knew he would have been able to deal with that. It was her innate kindness, her laugh, the way she smiled, her mouth curving at the corners, and the way her eyes sparkled when she was happy.

He groaned aloud and, picking up a pebble, he threw it into the sea where it skipped over the waves. It was too late. He wasn't *falling* in love with her. He already loved her. With a passion. All he had to do now was persuade her that he meant it.

After Raphael left, Annie made herself a cup of tea, still fuming. How could she have been so naïve? She rubbed her back. She'd had a dull ache all day and now it was getting worse. A flicker of fear shot through her as her abdomen cramped. Dear God, no! She couldn't be going into labour. It was far too early. She was only twenty-eight weeks.

'Okay,' she told herself. 'Keep calm.' It could be Braxton-

Hicks contractions, couldn't it? Or a tummy bug. It was one thing being a trained midwife and being able to reassure her patients, but quite another being the patient herself. She looked at her watch. Ten o'clock. It was late, but Kate or Chloe would probably still be awake. She could phone one of them, just for reassurance. She could also phone Raphael, of course, but she quickly dismissed the thought. Right now he was the last person she wanted to speak to. She had told him she could cope perfectly well without him so she could hardly call him every time she felt a twinge.

Making up her mind, she phoned Kate. Happily she hadn't gone to bed, but straight away Kate picked up on Annie's anxiety.

'What is it, Annie?' she said. 'Is something wrong?'

'It's probably nothing,' Annie said. 'But I've been having some lower back pain and some cramping. I'm probably being over-anxious, but I just wondered...' As she said the words a sharp tight pain squeezed her abdomen and she gasped.

'I'm coming,' Kate said. 'But first I'm going to call an ambulance. Only as a precaution. Just hold on, Annie, I'll be there in ten minutes.'

Now Annie was seriously frightened. If Kate was calling for an ambulance, she must be worried too. But they had to be wrong. She couldn't be going into labour. She just couldn't. It was far too early. But Annie knew that it was entirely possible. The chances of premature labour had slightly increased after she'd had the miscarriage scare. Kate would know that, too. It was probably why she had called the ambulance. She sat down as another wave of pain washed through her body. She wrapped her arms around her body, almost as if by doing so she could keep her baby safe inside her. If she was going into labour she needed to get to hospital, perhaps there they could give her something to stop it. Every day the baby stayed safe in her womb was crucial at this point.

Unaware of how much time had passed since she had called Kate, she was relieved when she heard a knock on the door. Thank God, she thought. Kate had arrived. Maybe everything would still be okay.

Raphael had decided to go back and see Annie. Whatever she said, they needed to talk. He had to tell her how he felt.

But one look at her, curled up in the armchair, her eyes wild with terror, was enough to send his heart crashing against his ribs.

Before he could breathe he was by her side.

'What is it, Annie?' he said, taking in her pale face and pinched lips.

She moaned and clutched her stomach. 'The baby,' she gasped. 'I think it's coming.'

She reached out a hand and gripped his arm. 'Make it stop, Raphael. It's too early, please make it stop. I can't lose my baby. You have to help me.'

Raphael forced his own fear away. He needed to be strong for Annie right now.

'Tell me,' he said gently.

'I've been having backache all day, but it was different from before. I just thought I had strained a muscle doing yoga. But now I've started cramping.' Her eyes shimmered with tears as she looked up at him. 'I phoned Kate. She's phoning for an ambulance and then she's coming.'

Raphael's heart contracted. She had gone to someone else—not him—when she had needed help. She must really hate him. But he couldn't let himself think of that right now.

All that mattered was making sure that Annie was all right. Even the baby…his heart twisted…wasn't as important as Annie.

In the distance he could hear the wail of the ambulance and the door opened and Kate burst in, carrying her medical bag.

'Dr Castillo. I didn't realise you were here. What's going on?'

'I haven't had time to make an assessment,' he said. 'But I'm afraid it sounds as if Annie has gone into labour.'

Hearing his words, Annie moaned again and folded in on herself. Raphael had never seen such anguish before. But she mustn't give up hope. Not yet.

He crouched down beside her and lifted her chin, forcing her to look into his eyes.

'Listen to me, Annie,' he said. 'I am going to do everything we can to save our baby. You have to believe that. Okay?' It took every bit of strength to keep his voice steady, but he couldn't let Annie see how terrified he was.

Annie looked back at him, her eyes wide with pain and fear. But he saw resolve in her eyes. His Annie was stronger than she realised.

Kate passed him the Sonicaid from her bag so he could listen to the foetal heart. He felt almost weak with relief when he heard a steady beat.

'Baby's heartbeat is strong, Annie. We can do a better assessment when we get you to hospital.' He could hear the wail of the ambulance getting closer. 'Perhaps we'll be able to give you steroids. There may still be a chance we can stop labour.'

He looked over at Kate.

'Can you gather a couple of things, please? I will go with Annie in the ambulance.'

'I'm coming, too,' Kate said firmly. 'Annie is my patient

as well as my friend. As far as this baby is concerned, you are the father and not in the best position to make clear-headed judgements. Rob is over at mine, so Jem will be fine.' She took Annie's hand. 'I'll stay with you as long as you need me.' Then she looked at Raphael. 'As long as you both need me.'

Raphael took one look at the determined set of the senior midwife's mouth. He was glad she would be around. Annie needed all the help she could get. She was all that mattered.

Annie was barely aware of being lifted into the ambulance. All she knew was that the pains were stronger and becoming more frequent. She searched Raphael's and Kate's eyes as they bent over her, looking for any sign of optimism, but their expressions were guarded. However she felt about Raphael, she was glad he was there with her. Between him and Kate, Annie knew her baby had the best possible chance, but, if they didn't manage to stop her labour, then her baby would be born at twenty-eight weeks. Annie knew only too well that even if it survived, the chances of complications were hugely increased.

Raphael must have read her mind. He gathered her in his arms, pulling her head against his chest. She felt safe, as if he could protect her from her worst fears.

'We will give you a tocolytic when we get you to hospital,' he said. 'We may still be in time to stop your labour. If we aren't, the baby still has a good chance. Many babies of that gestation do well. You need to remember that.'

'And many don't,' Annie mumbled into his chest. She couldn't even cry now, the fear was too intense. All she wanted was for her baby to live.

Then she was being lifted out of the ambulance. Raphael was shouting orders and Kate was holding her hand. There were lights and people and fear and pain. Then she was in one of the side rooms in the labour ward. Kate was examining her and Annie heard her tell everyone that she was five centimetres dilated. And there was another obstetrician and Julie. Where had she come from? And her obstetrician, Dr Gibson, was talking to Raphael. She couldn't hear what they were saying, but she heard the word *paediatrician* and *too late* and she was more frightened than ever. But Raphael was by her side again.

'It's too late to stop labour,' he said gently. She looked up and she could see the concern and sympathy in Julie and Kate's eyes.

'Look at me,' Raphael commanded. So she forced herself to look at him, not wanting to, knowing that whatever she saw there would be the truth and she wasn't ready for the truth—she'd never be ready.

Her eyes found his and she read the anguish there. He couldn't hide it from her, no matter how much he wanted to.

'You're going to have our baby—soon.' Annie looked away, but he eased her head around. 'Everyone is ready to help. The paediatrician is here and as soon as the baby is delivered he will be taken up to the special care nursery. They will do everything they can up there to keep our baby alive. Right now, you have to listen to Julie and Kate. And I'll be right here.'

'Don't leave me,' she whispered through lips frozen with fear.

'I'll never leave you, *cariño*. I'm staying right here. Where I belong.'

Two hours later Annie gave a final push and felt her child slip into the world and into Kate's waiting arms. Desperately she listened, waiting for a sound to let her know her baby lived. She watched as Julie rushed the baby over to the waiting incubator as she and the paediatrician started working over the tiny form.

'You have a little girl,' Kate said. 'Well done.'

'Can I see her?' Annie asked. More than anything else she wanted to hold her baby in her arms. It could well be the last chance she had.

'We need to let Julie and the paediatrician do what they have to, Annie. Let them take care of our daughter,' Raphael said, but she could see his eyes were shining with unshed tears.

Tentatively she reached out her hand and brushed a lock of hair away from his eyes. 'Is she breathing? Please, Raphael, go to her.'

Raphael left her side, to be replaced by Kate.

'She is breathing, Annie,' she said. 'And although she's very small, she has a good chance. They'll be taking her away to Special Care as soon as they have her stabilised. They'll take you up to see her in a little while. Try and rest now. I promise you, one of us will let you know the second we have news.'

Annie looked past her to the incubator, but there were too many bodies in the way for her to see properly. She struggled to sit up. She needed to see her baby. Her daughter needed to feel her mother's presence. But Kate pressed her back down.

'Annie, we still need to deliver the placenta. And you'll only get in the way. I know it's horrible, but you need to let us do our job.'

Kate was right, of course. But it was so damned hard not being able to see her child. But just then a tiny cry filtered into the room. Her baby was crying. That was a good sign. There was a flurry of activity around the cot and Raphael came back to stand next to Annie.

'They are taking her upstairs just now,' he said. 'But she is breathing. She is beautiful. The most beautiful baby I have ever seen.' His voice cracked.

Hope flared as she saw the look of wonder in his eyes. He wouldn't look like that if her baby wasn't all right, would he? If she couldn't be with their daughter, at least Raphael could. Her baby wouldn't be alone.

'Go with them,' she whispered. 'Stay with her. She needs you.'

Suddenly the atmosphere in the room changed. 'She's haemorrhaging,' Dr Gibson called out. 'Get me some hemabate stat.' There was a flurry of activity and Annie felt panic clench her throat. Who was bleeding? What was happening?

Then Raphael's face swam into view. 'You have a bit of retained placenta,' he said quietly. 'They are giving you something to stop the bleeding.'

'We need to get her to theatre.' It was Dr Gibson. 'Julie, ring down and tell theatre to get ready for us. Then page the anaesthetist. C'mon, everyone, let's get moving.'

Raphael brushed a lock of hair from Annie's eyes. 'Don't be frightened, *cariño*. Everything's going to be okay. You'll be back on the ward before you know it.'

Annie clutched at his hand, amazed at her own strength. 'I need to see my baby before I go. Please. Just in case…' Her voice caught on a sob. She willed Raphael to understand. If anything went wrong, she might never see her baby.

'There isn't time,' he said. 'We can't afford to wait. We have to take you now.'

'Please, Raphael. Do this for me?'

She could see the hesitation in his eyes. But then he straightened.

'Let her see our baby,' he said urgently.

'There's no time,' Dr Gibson said. 'We have to operate on her *now*. She could bleed out.'

But Raphael moved towards the incubator. 'It will only take a second,' he said, and, picking up the tightly swaddled infant, he brought her over to Annie.

Annie gazed down at her child. She was barely the size of Raphael's hands and she could see every vein in her translucent skin. As she looked at her Annie knew that she would never again experience the powerful emotions that swept through her body. This was her child, and she would fight tooth and nail for her for the rest of her life.

There was a hush in the room as everyone stopped for a second to watch Annie meet her child.

'You fight,' Annie said to her daughter. 'Don't you dare leave me.'

'We need to take you down to theatre now,' Raphael said gently, and Annie knew that her brief moment with her baby was over. 'I'll be there with you.'

'No, Raphael,' Annie said, mustering the last of her strength. 'You go with our daughter. Please. I'll be all right.'

'I don't want to leave you on your own.' He looked after his departing child, obviously torn.

'She needs you more than I do. Besides, Kate is here. Come and tell me as soon as there is any news. Promise?'

He leaned over and brushed the top of her head with his lips. 'Everything is going to be all right. I'll be back as soon as I can.'

When Annie next opened her eyes, it was to find Raphael looking down at her. Fear clutched her chest but before she could speak, Raphael smiled.

'They stopped the bleeding. They had to put an intra-uterine balloon in but it will be removed shortly. You are going to be OK.'

Dazed, Annie looked around. She had a drip in her arm, but apart from feeling a little groggy she was fine. She licked dry lips and, without asking, Raphael poured a glass of water and, slipping his arm behind her shoulders, lifted her slightly so that she could drink. The water was enough to ease Annie's throat sufficiently to speak.

'Where is she? Is she all right? I want to see her.'

'Hey, take it easy, Annie. She's upstairs in Intensive Care. They have her on a respirator, but she's doing well. Our daughter is beautiful.' Annie saw the wonder in his deep brown eyes. But she needed to see her child for herself. That was the only way she could believe that she was all right. She pushed the sheets aside just as Julie entered the room. Annie had worked with Julie many times before and knew the experienced midwife well.

'And just what do you think you are doing?' Julie said, lifting Annie's legs and popping her back into bed.

'I want to see my child, Julie,' Annie said. 'Then I'll come back to bed. I promise.'

'No way,' Julie said firmly. It was a different side to the midwife, one that Annie hadn't seen before, but, then, she hadn't been a patient before. 'You are not leaving this bed. Not until I say so.'

Annie looked across at Raphael. She had to see their daughter. She just had to.

'Raphael, please. Tell them I can go upstairs. Only for a moment. I'll do as I'm told after that.'

Raphael looked at Annie. His eyes softened. 'I'll take responsibility,' he said. 'We'll take the drip with us and put her in a wheelchair. She's so stubborn, if we don't take her she'll be up there as soon as we aren't looking, anyway.'

Julie looked indecisive, but before she could protest further, Raphael was helping Annie out of bed.

'I don't need a wheelchair,' Annie protested, but then as her legs buckled she had to lean on Raphael for support.

'It's a wheelchair or nothing,' Julie said. 'Just give me a mo' to fetch one.'

Annie didn't have the strength to argue. Besides, she didn't want to wait a moment longer to see her baby. Only when she saw her for herself would she truly believe what Raphael had told her.

But it was almost more than she could bear when she finally saw her tiny baby. She was almost hidden from view by wires, her face covered by the ventilator that was breathing for her, and Annie felt cold with dread. More than anything in the world she wanted to hold her daughter. Transfer the strength from her own body to that of her child. Let her know that she was there.

'Remember, it looks worse than it is,' Raphael said, resting his hands on her shoulders. 'The lines and wires are there to monitor her as much as anything.'

Annie nodded. She knew all that, of course she did. Plenty of her mothers over the years had had babies that required time in Special Care. But it was one thing telling a mother not to be frightened by the paraphernalia of Special Care and quite another when it was your baby lying there. So small and so helpless.

She slipped a hand through the hole in the incubator and slipped a finger into her daughter's minuscule hand. Her heart filled with wonder as she felt the small fingers close around hers.

'Hello, darling,' she whispered. 'This is your mummy.

Everything is going to be okay. But you have to fight.' Turning to Raphael, she could see his anguish in eyes. 'I want you to tell me everything the paediatrician has told you. I don't want to be protected, so keep nothing back from me.' She meant every word. Whatever terror gripped her, she was going to stay strong. Her baby needed her and until she was out of danger... She pushed the thought away. One step at a time.

'As you can see, she is being ventilated. Her lungs aren't fully developed yet, so she'll probably stay on it for a few days at least. They are also giving her surfactant to help her breathing.'

'What about...?' She could hardly bare to say the words, but Raphael guessed what she wanted to know.

'We won't know whether there are any complications— if she's suffered any—until later, Annie. She has to get through the next few days first.' He laid a hand on her shoulder and squeezed. 'Come on, let's get you back to bed. I'll come back up here and stay with her while you sleep.'

'I can't leave her,' Annie whispered.

'You are going to need all your strength in the next few days. And she is going to need her mother fit and healthy.'

'How can I sleep when she is fighting for her life?' But even as she said the words Annie felt a wave of fatigue wash over her. She was so tired.

'You can't stay here, Annie. The nurses need to work on her. But you can come back later, when you have had a rest. You lost a great deal of blood earlier.' He looked at his watch. 'It will be morning soon.'

Reluctantly Annie let Raphael take her back to her room and help her back into bed. 'You will wake me if there is any change, no matter how small?'

'Of course.'

'And you won't leave her?' She clutched his hand. 'I know you must be tired, too.'

'I won't leave her,' he promised. 'I'll watch over her while you sleep.'

Knowing he would be true to his word, Annie closed her eyes and gave in to sleep.

It was getting light when Annie next opened her eyes. As the memory of the night before came flooding back, she panicked.

Her baby. She needed to see her baby. Where was Raphael? Why wasn't he here to let her know what was happening? If he was still in Special Care, did that mean something had happened? Knowing that if she called for a nurse they would try and prevent her from getting out of bed, she pushed the bed covers aside and reached for the dressing gown Kate had packed for her. Then on legs that felt like rubber she slipped upstairs and into the special care nursery.

She found Raphael in a chair by the side of the incubator. He was leaning forward, gazing into the incubator and talking quietly in Spanish. Annie stood silently listening. Although she couldn't understand the words, she knew by the timbre of his voice that he was suffering too.

He must have felt her standing behind him because he turned. Annie drew a sharp breath when she saw his face. He looked gaunt with fatigue, his eyes were shadowed and there were lines on his face that Annie had never seen before. Clearly he hadn't left their baby's side, not even to change or shave. He had told her that he would watch over their baby and he had. There was no doubt he cared about his daughter, but would he feel the same way if she turned out to be less than perfect?

'There's no change. I was going to come and see you,' he

said. 'The nurses were supposed to ring up as soon as you were awake.'

'They didn't know. I slipped out when no one was looking. I know the night sister well and she would have tried to stop me. I didn't want to take that risk.' She bent over the cot. Her daughter was still on the respirator and there were wires everywhere. But she was alive. That was all that mattered.

Raphael stood next to her.

'Have you thought of a name? We should name her.'

Annie felt fear claw her throat again. Why was he so keen? Was he about to suggest that they had her baptized—just in case? She shook her head.

'I would like to call her Angela, after my mother.' She took a deep steadying breath and clenched her hands so hard that the nails dug into her palms.

Raphael put his arms around her and held her close. For a moment she resisted, then as he whispered her name she couldn't help herself. She clung to him as she gave in to her grief and fear.

'Angela. Little Angelica. It is a good name,' he murmured into her hair.

And then she was only vaguely aware of Raphael leading her away from the cot and into the staff room. The nurses, seeing her distress, quietly stood up and left them alone. Raphael sat in one of the easy chairs and, still holding her, pulled her onto his lap as if she were a child. She wound her arms around his neck and cried until eventually her tears subsided to hiccups.

She hid her face in his chest. She felt safe there, as if nothing bad could ever happen as long as this man held her. He slid a handkerchief under her bowed head and she took it gratefully, using it to dry her face then blow her nose noisily.

Eventually she sneaked a glance at his face, knowing, but not caring, that she must look a mess.

'I'm sorry,' she said. 'I don't usually cry like that, at least not in front of people.'

As he looked down at her with warm brown eyes she suddenly realised she was still curled up in his lap. Embarrassed, she struggled to her feet, but he put a restraining arm around her waist.

'You must not apologise. Not everyone can be strong all the time, and this is a terrible time for you. But you are not alone. Not any longer. I am here with you.'

He sounded more Spanish, almost as if emotion had robbed him of his hitherto perfect English. But he was suffering too. This was a child he had also longed for. But what if Angela didn't pull through? There was nothing to stop Raphael walking away—and she wouldn't try to stop him. Once again she realised how little she actually knew about this man. She loved him, there was no doubt about that, but if he chose to walk away, she would let him.

She rested her head back on his chest and felt him rest his chin on top of her head. They sat there for a while longer, not saying anything, each one alone with their thoughts.

Eventually Annie eased herself out of his arms. 'I'm going to have a shower and get dressed so I can spend the rest of the day with Angela. Then you could go home and get some rest yourself. You must be exhausted.'

'I'm used to not sleeping.' He smiled up at her.

'No argument,' Annie said firmly. 'I want you back here later this afternoon awake and alert. Neither of us will be any use to Angela if we are falling asleep on our feet.'

Raphael looked surprised. He raised an eyebrow at her and a small smile tugged at the corner of his mouth.

'You must be feeling better, *cariño*, to be wanting to boss me about.'

Annie's heart melted at the look in his eyes. How she wished everything could be different. If only Raphael could love her, nothing would be impossible.

'Go,' he said, tipping her gently off his lap. 'There is something I need to tell you. But now is not the right time. Soon, I hope. When our child is safe, we will talk. But for now let us do what we have to.'

CHAPTER TWELVE

KATE finished packing the box of fruit, home-made jam and crusty rolls she had bought down at the farmers' market earlier that morning. Although she knew Annie wouldn't feel hungry, she hoped she'd be tempted by the snacks. Chloe was due to pick her up shortly so that the two women could go and see Annie together. They wouldn't stay long, just long enough to let Annie know that they were there if she needed them.

Poor Annie. The next few days, even weeks would be awful for her. But all they could do now was hope.

She thought about what she had found that morning when she'd been showering, and wondered what to do. See a doctor, obviously, although the lump was bound to be nothing. If only Rob wasn't away, she could have discussed it with him. Put it in perspective. She'd told herself a hundred times already that it was probably only a cyst, but the small voice in her head wouldn't go away. What if it wasn't? What then?

The slamming of a car door announced Chloe's arrival.

'Are you ready?' Chloe asked as she came into the kitchen. 'Yum, is that some of the Trevellyans' fab cheese?' she said, pinching a piece and popping it into her mouth. Then she looked at Kate sharply and frowned.

'There hasn't been bad news from the hospital, has there?' she asked anxiously.

'No, the baby's doing okay. If she had taken a turn for the worse, someone would have phoned us.'

'What is it, then? You're looking a bit tired.'

Kate laid her hands on the worktop. She didn't want to burden Chloe with her worries, but she hadn't counted on her friend's intuition.

Chloe came across and laid an arm across her shoulder. 'Kate, I can see something's wrong. You know you can talk to me about anything. Is it Rob? Are you two having problems? Or Jem?'

'No, Jem's fine. He's at football practice. And Rob and I are getting on fine. More than fine, in fact. He's so good to me, and fun to be with. I'd forgotten what that was like.'

'Mmm. He is lovely. And Jem seems to get on with him—unless there are problems there? Or is it Nick? Has he said something to upset you?'

Kate realised that Chloe wasn't going to give up. She knew something was wrong and was clearly determined to get to the bottom of it. The young midwife was the closest thing she had to a best friend. One of the few people who knew the truth about Jem. And Nick.

'I felt a lump in my breast this morning when I was showering,' Kate finally admitted. 'I know it's probably nothing but…'

'But you're going to get it checked out,' Chloe finished for her. 'God, Kate, you must be scared stupid. So the sooner you see someone the better. Have you spoken to any of the doctors? What about Rob? Does he know?'

'Rob's away and it's Saturday so, no, I haven't seen anyone. I only discovered it this morning and I had to go to the farmers' market and I want to see Annie. I'll make an appointment to see Oliver next week.'

'Just like you, Kate, to put the needs of others before your own. You're always taking care of other people and forgetting about yourself. But for once I'm not going to let that happen,' Chloe said firmly. 'Oliver is doing the Saturday morning surgery. I'm positive he'll see you today.'

Chloe ignored Kate's protests about not wanting to bother anyone. She was right, of course, it wasn't an emergency and another day or two wasn't going to make any difference, but she dialled the number of the surgery anyway and asked to be put through to Oliver.

'Hello, darling. Yes, everything's fine. It's Kate. She needs to see someone. Straight away. I mean not in front of any life-and-death emergencies, but today, nevertheless.'

Kate couldn't hear the response on the other end of the line.

'She'll be there,' Chloe said firmly, before disconnecting the call and turning to Kate. 'He can see you at the end of surgery. About twelve? That way we can still go and see Annie if you want.'

Kate gave in, knowing it was useless to argue. 'I promised her I would. So if it's okay with you, I'd like to go as planned. But I had no idea you could be so bossy.' She smiled to show there was no malice in the words. 'You're always so mild-mannered with your patients.'

Chloe smiled back. 'I suspect it's the only way I'll get you to do as you're told.'

Suddenly Kate felt frightened.

'God, Chloe. What if it is cancer? What about Jem? I couldn't bear to leave my son alone. And Polly, the new GP. I persuaded her to come back to Penhally and said I'd be here to support her. She'll be here any day now. Now all this...'

Chloe hugged her fiercely. 'Slow down, Kate. Everything's going to be all right. Remember we have some of the best doctors in the world between here and St Piran's. And as you said, it could be nothing. Maybe just a cyst. Let's just wait and see what Oliver has to say.'

Kate knew that Chloe was right. There was no point in worrying until she had to. And right now she had a patient to see. Annie needed her support.

After checking on Angela, Annie returned to her room for a shower. She kept it short, anxious not to be away from the special care nursery too long.

When she emerged feeling almost human, it was to find Chloe and Kate sitting on her freshly made bed, waiting for her. The sight of her two friends broke the control Annie had been so desperately clinging to. Kate opened her arms and Annie let her hold her as she gave in to the anguish and fear of the last few days. It seemed that Kate was always there whenever Annie needed someone. In the absence of her mother, who was desperately trying to get a flight back to the UK, Kate was the next best thing.

Annie wiped her eyes and managed a shaky laugh. 'For someone who hardly ever cries, that's all I seem to have been doing lately.'

'Hey,' Chloe said gently. 'We all need to let go sometimes. And these are exceptional circumstances. How is she, anyway?'

Annie brought them up to date. There wasn't really that much to tell. The next few days would be critical. 'If Angela survives…' Annie choked on the word but took a steadying breath before continuing, 'Then the next hurdle will be whether her brain has been damaged.'

Kate reached out a soothing hand. 'Everyone is rooting for you both,' she said softly. 'How is Raphael holding up?'

'He's been wonderful,' Annie admitted. 'He's hardly left her side. But he's agreed to go home for a bit as soon as I get back up.' She tried a smile. It was weak, but the best she could manage. 'I don't suppose anyone could bring me some clothes from home? I could ask Raphael, I suppose…'

'Tra-la.' Kate smiled, holding up a small case. 'We called by your house on our way in—I held onto your key last night. I think you'll find everything there. I don't think you can trust a man in these circumstances. He might remember the top, but forget the trousers!'

'You're a love,' said Annie gratefully, and, taking the bag from Kate, rummaged around. 'Bless you, you remembered everything—even my deodorant.'

Kate whipped out another carrier bag. 'I brought you something to eat as well. I popped down to the farmers' market this morning and selected some goodies to tempt you. It's my guess you haven't had anything for some time.'

Annie felt her throat close at the gesture. It was so typical of Kate and Chloe and she really appreciated her friends' support.

'I'm sorry, sweetheart, but I'm going to have to get back. I have a patient who is due to deliver very soon and I promised I'd go and see her,' Chloe said apologetically. 'But I'll pop in later if I get the chance.'

Chloe looked at Kate. 'Call me later?'

Kate nodded. Annie thought she looked tired. There were lines of tension around her mouth she hadn't noticed before.

'Thank you both so much for coming. I know you both have your own lives to be getting on with. And I want to get back upstairs, anyway,' Annie said.

'Hey,' Kate said. 'What are friends for? You know you can call me any time.' She kissed Annie on the cheek. 'Take care. I'll see you soon.'

Annie returned to the special care ward to be given the welcome news that Angela had been taken off the respirator. Instead, two tubes had been inserted into Angela's nostrils and she could see her baby's face clearly for the first time. Her breath caught as she gazed down on the beloved features of her child. Angela's lips were like seashells washed in the ocean, her miniature nose perfect. She has Raphael's hair, Annie thought, taking in the dark hair that covered her head. Carefully she inserted a hand into the incubator and stroked the downy skin of her baby.

She knew then that she would stand between her child and a tank or a tidal wave or a stalking tiger. She would lay down her life without a moment's hesitation over and over again if she had to, but right now she could do nothing for her child. Nothing except wait and watch over her. She became aware of a presence behind her and she didn't have to turn to know it was Raphael.

'If I lose her…' Her voice cracked and she had to take a deep breath before she could continue. 'If I lose her, I don't know what I'll do. I can't imagine wanting to go on.'

She felt his hand on her shoulder and then he turned her so that she was facing him. Placing a finger under her chin, he tilted her head, forcing her to meet his gaze.

'Don't say that. Never say that. You are stronger than you think. And anyway, I told you I will not let anything happen to her.' His voice was low and urgent, his need to convince her evident in every syllable. Annie desperately wanted to believe him. She dropped her eyes to his achingly tender mouth before slowly raising her eyes to his. Through her fear she could see her pain reflected in his eyes. He too needed comfort, but Annie couldn't offer him any.

'*Cariño,*' he said, his voice a river of anguish. '*Te quiero con toda mi alma.* I love you with all my soul. You and our daughter are my heart, my soul, my future. All I ever want and all I will ever need.' Annie's heart thumped lurched.

Had he really said he loved her? Could he mean it?

He took her hand and placed it on his chest. She could feel the pounding of his heart through the thin fabric.

'Do you feel that?' he demanded.

Despite her grief, Annie felt a small smile tug at the corner of her mouth. It was such a Latin gesture. She nodded, the emotion welling up inside her preventing her from speaking.

'As long as my heart keeps beating, I will not let anything happen to you or our child.'

But however much she wanted to believe him, she couldn't. It wasn't in his power to promise anything. Least of all that their child would live.

Kate slipped off the examination couch and picked up her blouse, sliding her arms into the sleeves. Oliver waited until she had finished and was settled in the chair opposite him before he spoke.

'There is a lump there. I can feel it the upper left quadrant. As you said, it could be nothing, a cyst perhaps, but I think we should get it checked out all the same.'

Kate could read the concern in his brown eyes. He was being matter-of-fact, but she could read him like a book. He didn't believe it was a cyst and neither did she.

'Does Rob know?' Oliver continued. 'Can he go with you to the hospital? It's Saturday but I might be able to get one of the surgeons to come in and see you. They'll probably want to do a fine needle biopsy and a mammogram.'

'Rob's away this weekend. He's gone up north to see his mother. I would have gone with him if it hadn't been for Jem.' She stood up and went to look out the window. The day, which had started off dull and threatening to rain, had turned into one of those perfect days. In the distance she could see the tips of the waves as they rolled to shore. There were quite a few boats out as well, a mixture of fishing trawlers and yachts. Kate wished she were out there with them, far away from talk of lumps and biopsies and far away from the terror of what it would mean for her son if she turned out to have cancer. She thought about Annie. Her hopes and fears tied up with the tiny life she had given birth to, and all the other people, not just in Penhally Bay but all over the world who would be facing the same uncertainties and fears as she was.

'I can wait my turn like everyone else,' Kate said. 'A day or two isn't going to make much difference.'

'Are you sure you don't want me to phone Ben? He'll know who you should see.'

'No,' Kate said heavily. 'I don't want to jump the queue. It's not fair to every other frightened woman out there. Besides, by the time my appointment comes through, Rob will be back.'

'There's only a week waiting time for urgent appointments,' Oliver said. 'And I'm going to grade yours as urgent.'

Kate smiled wanly. 'Okay,' she said. Just then there was a knock on the door and Nick stuck his head around it.

'Oh, Oliver. I'm sorry. I thought you had finished seeing patients.' Then he noticed Kate and he looked surprised. 'Kate! I didn't think you were in today. Is there something up with one of your patients?' His eyes narrowed. Something in her and Oliver's expression seemed to alert him that Kate's presence was unusual.

'I just had something I wanted to talk over with Oliver,' she said hastily. Well, it was true. But let think Nick it was about a patient.

'There's nothing wrong, is there?' he asked. He walked over to the desk and crouched down next to Kate. 'You would tell me if there was something wrong, wouldn't you?' Kate felt her heart tighten at the obvious concern in his eyes. Whatever problems they might have had, were *still* having, she knew that somewhere deep down inside Nick cared about her, even if it was as just a friend. But that didn't mean she was ready to share her worries with him. He had made it clear often enough that he wasn't prepared to offer her more than the professional support of a colleague. And one thing Kate couldn't bear was for him to feel sorry for her.

She laughed, but the sound was hollow even to her own ears.

'What possibly could be wrong, Nick, that I couldn't cope with on my own?' She didn't mean the words to have such a bitter quality to them, but she couldn't help herself. The one thing she truly wanted from Nick, acceptance of the child they shared, he wasn't able to give her.

'If you're sure?' Nick said, straightening. He sounded less than convinced but Kate knew him well enough to know that he wouldn't probe. One thing you could say about him was that he respected her privacy. He turned back to Oliver, who was watching the exchange quietly. Kate wondered if he had picked up on the tension that seemed to be a permanent feature between her and Nick these days. 'I wondered if you fancied a round of golf this afternoon?' he asked. 'Dragan and Ben are up for it if you are.'

'Sure,' Oliver said. 'I think Chloe has plans for this afternoon, so I'm free.'

'How is Annie?' Nick asked. 'Has anyone spoken to her?'

'I saw her this morning,' Kate said. 'She's okay. Raphael is with her.'

'Raphael? Dr Castillo?' Nick said, looking puzzled.

Oliver and Kate exchanged a smile. Good grief, Kate thought, Nick could be so dense sometimes, completely failing to see what was right underneath his nose.

CHAPTER THIRTEEN

A WEEK after their baby had been born Annie and Raphael sat in the easy chairs the staff had provided and watched over their child. The lights had been turned low, although the nurses and doctors still tended their tiny charges with the same dedication and attentiveness that they did during the day.

Annie rested her eyes, thinking back to what Raphael had said. He had called her his heart and his soul. But surely these were just the words of a man in emotional turmoil to the woman who was locked there with him? She still couldn't believe that he meant them.

'Maybe she'll be a piano player,' he said suddenly into the silence. 'She has your long fingers.' He picked up Annie's hand in one of his. 'Such beautiful hands.' Annie looked down at her hands in surprise. She had never thought of her hands as being beautiful before, but perhaps he was right. Her fingers were long and shapely.

'Why did you come back?' she asked. 'You know, the night Angela was born after we…' She tailed off, blushing furiously, but she wanted to know. Everything had happened so fast it was only now that she had begun to wonder.

He turned towards her, his eyes glowing in the semi-darkness. 'I came back because...because I realised something important. When this is over, I'm going to do everything to win you properly. Make you believe me when I tell you that I want to marry you. Because I love you.'

Annie started to say something but he stopped her words with his fingertip.

'I want us to start over. Do everything as it should have been. How it was meant to be.'

Annie felt something deep down inside her blossom at his words. Could she dare to believe that he meant what he was saying? And did he truly understand what he was saying?

'Don't. Please, Raphael. Don't say any more.' She flinched at the naked pain in his eyes, but forced herself to go on.

'I can't have any more children. You must know that. Angela was miraculous enough. If we marry, you will be signing yourself up to a lifetime of childlessness.' Her voice broke on the words. 'If...' she faltered, but forced herself to go on. 'God forbid, but if Angela doesn't pull through, there will be no more children.'

'I would be signing myself up for a lifetime with the woman I love,' Raphael said firmly. 'The woman without whom life has no meaning—a dark and empty place. Don't you know that when I am with you my life is full of light? I told you before and I will tell you again and keep on telling you until you believe me—you are all I need.'

'You would give up everything for me?' Annie whispered, hardly daring to believe he meant what he was saying.

'I would give my life for you if I had to.' He crouched by her side. 'I have been so foolish. Can you ever forgive me? How could I have ever believed even for the smallest second—' he held out two fingers millimetres apart '—that you were anything except the strong, loving, honest woman you are?'

'Because you believed it once before and she betrayed you,' Annie said, unable to bear the self-reproach in his eyes. 'I can understand.'

'I know I don't deserve you. I am full of mistakes…' Annie hid a smile. His English only ever suffered when his feelings ran high. 'But if you marry me, I will spend the rest of my life proving I am worthy of you. If you want to adopt a little brother or sister for our sweet daughter, I would be happy too.'

Annie still wasn't sure. He might mean it now, but later, in years to come, he might come to regret having married her, and that was one thing she would never allow. She would rather let him go—even if it broke her heart—than see him become resentful of her. But before she could formulate the words there was the sound of an alarm going off at Angela's cot. Within seconds the incubator was surrounded. Annie looked at Raphael, terrified.

Quickly the paediatrician attached Angela to a machine again and after a few agonising minutes the monitor stopped bleeping as Angela's breathing returned to normal.

After listening to Angela's chest, the paediatrician turned to Annie and Raphael.

'I think your daughter has patent ductus arteriosus, or PDA as we call it. As you both are probably aware, the blood circulating in the foetus doesn't go through the lungs but bypasses the lungs via an artery. Normally this artery closes itself soon after birth, but in pre-term babies such as yours, it sometimes fails to close.'

Raphael nodded. 'I've seen it before.'

'We've been giving her drugs for a day or two to try and close it that way, but that doesn't seem to have worked…'

'So you'll need to do it surgically,' Raphael finished for him.

'But she's so small,' Annie interjected.

Raphael turned to Annie and took both of her hands in his. He looked at her steadily, his brown eyes calm.

'It's her best chance,' he said. 'The surgeons are used to operating on babies of Angela's size. We have to trust them to do what's best for her.'

Annie looked at her daughter. Lying in her cot, all alone attached to tubes and wires. Her child was totally dependent on her parents making the right decision. Annie felt so helpless. What if they made the wrong one? 'But what if…?' Annie couldn't bring herself to finish the sentence.

'Look at me, Annie,' Raphael demanded. Annie dragged her eyes away from her baby. Raphael's eyes burned with his need to convince her. 'Only you have the right to make the decision. I can't. But I love her, too. You have to trust me about this. Please.'

There was no doubting his pain. There was no doubting his love for their daughter. And she did trust him. They were together in this and would always be. Annie realised that never again would she be alone. She would always have Raphael to share impossible decisions with.

'Okay,' she whispered, 'I'll sign the consents.'

Annie and Raphael passed what seemed like hours while their daughter was in surgery, in almost complete silence. Annie laid her head on Raphael's lap and he gently stroked her hair. They waited in the relatives' room just along the corridor from theatre. Every now and again Raphael would ask Annie if he could get her anything. Water? Coffee? But she always shook her head. She knew she couldn't possibly swallow anything until she knew Angela was out of surgery. Eventually they heard footsteps coming down the corridor.

Annie sat up, her heart in her throat, knowing that the moment of truth had arrived.

Raphael got to his feet and pulled Annie up and into his embrace. 'Whatever it is, be strong, my love. I am with you.'

The surgeon stepped into the family waiting room, a broad grin lighting up his face. It was the news they had both been desperately longing for. The paediatric surgeon explained that Angela had come through the surgery well and he expected her to make a full recovery. She was currently in Intensive Care but they could see her if they wanted. If they wanted!

Dr Nick Tremayne sat deep in thought. Something was up with Kate. He couldn't quite put his finger on it, but something was worrying her, he would bet his life on it. He crossed over to his consulting-room window and looked out. The perfect weather had turned again. The rain was falling in thick slabs, perfectly matching his gloomy mood. He didn't know why, but seeing Kate with her new partner made him feel uncomfortable. Not that it was any of his business. He should be glad she had found someone who could offer her a life free of complications. But, damn it, he hated seeing the way Jem responded to Rob. The way the growing boy seemed to look up to him, almost as if he had accepted that Rob was the father he had never known. And why should that bother him? Shouldn't he be glad that his son had a good man as a role model in his life? Rob was a decent man. Nick knew that. And it wasn't as if he could offer the child anything, no matter how much Kate had tried to convince him. Perhaps if he'd known that Jem was his son much much earlier. Perhaps then he could have found a way to be a father to him. But it was too late now. Every time he looked at the child he remembered that he had been unfaithful to his beloved wife, Annabel. What kind of man was he?

He sighed with exasperation. How had he managed to make such a mess of it all? He couldn't see a way to make things right.

A soft tap on the door and then Kate popped her head around. She was still beautiful, he thought. The years had been kind to her. Why couldn't he let her go and make a proper life for herself? Why did the thought of her being with someone else drive him crazy? It wasn't as if he had anything to offer her.

'Just to let you know that Chloe is doing the antenatal clinic on her own this afternoon and I'm taking the afternoon off. So she might need some help from you.'

Nick was surprised. It was unlike Kate to take time off, especially when she knew it would leave her colleagues short-handed.

'Is everything all right, Kate? There's nothing up with Jem, is there?'

'No, Jem's fine. He's at school. It's just I have something I need to do this afternoon.'

'Can't it wait?'

He could see the exasperation in Kate's eyes.

'It's not as if I ever ask for time off, Nick,' she said frostily.

Of course, she was right. If anything, she had put the patients' needs before her own for years. He knew that. It was just that he sensed she was keeping something from him. And he wanted to know what it was. But one look at the determined set of her mouth told him it would be useless to pry. He had given up all rights to Kate's personal life and they both knew it.

'Of course,' he said. 'Forgive me.' He thought he saw a flicker of disappointment in her eyes, but just as quickly it was gone. It seemed that he was forever destined to disappoint this woman.

'I'll see you tomorrow, then,' she said before closing the door behind her.

Kate perched on her chair, trying not to show how nervous she was. In the seat next to her, Rob looked as ill at ease as Kate felt. He had insisted on coming with her to St Piran's. At first Kate had tried to dissuade him, she was so used to doing everything on her own, but then relented. Rob cared about her. Why face something so difficult on her own when he so clearly wanted to be there to support her? He had waited outside while Dr Bower had performed a fine needle biopsy and then waited some more while Kate had a mammogram. The hour they had waited to be called into see the surgeon for the results was the one of the longest in Kate's life.

The surgeon, Dr Bower, an older woman Kate had met before through work, seemed to take her time looking through Kate's notes before removing her glasses and placing them carefully on the table. Kate was dimly aware of Rob reaching across and taking her hand. He gave it a reassuring squeeze and she was thankful she had let him come with her.

'I'm sorry, Kate,' Dr Bower was saying, 'but the tests have come back positive. The lump is cancerous. The good news is that the mammogram suggests that we have caught it at a very early stage. I'm fairly confident that we can get away with removing the lump without having to resort to a mastectomy, but I won't be sure until we have you on the table. If there is any sign that the cancer has invaded the lymph nodes then we might be facing a different scenario. In that case, a mastectomy may still be an option, followed by chemotherapy and radiotherapy. As I said, I don't think that's what we are facing here, but I think it's best that you know the worst possible outcome. One way or another, I suggest we get you in for the procedure as soon as possible.'

Kate felt her world tip and slide. Of course she had known that it could be cancer, but she hadn't allowed herself to believe it. The pressure of Rob's hand on hers grew stronger but she was barely aware of it. She had cancer. She could die. Her son could be left motherless, and—a sick feeling washed over her—fatherless. How could life be so unfair?

'Are you sure?' she managed through a mouth that felt as if it was stuffed with pebbles, it was so dry. 'I mean—I'm sorry, of course you're sure. We wouldn't be having this conversation if you weren't.'

'I know it's a shock,' Dr Bower said sympathetically. 'But as I said before, it's good news that we caught it so early. You'll want some time to take it all in, but I really want to schedule you in for theatre, possibly the week after next.' She consulted her diary. 'I have a slot in my diary for a week on Monday. Would that suit you?'

Kate could only manage a nod. Her mouth was still too dry to speak. What was she going to tell Jem?

Kate managed to hold it together until she and Rob were back in his car. But when Rob silently put his arms around her and held her close, the tears came. Rob let her cry while he stroked her hair and murmured soothing words of comfort. He waited until her sobs subsided.

Kate removed herself from his arms, miserably aware of her tear-stained cheeks and swollen eyes. She blew furiously on the handkerchief Rob held out for her.

'I'm sorry, Rob, to land you in all this. I don't think it's what you expected when you took up with me.'

'I took up with you, as you put it—' Rob smiled '—because you are the most wonderful woman I have ever met. I would rather be with you than anywhere else in the world. But I want you to listen to me.' He swivelled around in his seat and took Kate's hands in his. She felt the warmth of his touch ease away some of the chill that had been seeping through her body since Dr Bower had given her the diagnosis.

'Dr Bower said that they caught it very early and survival rates from breast cancer have improved enormously over the last few years. That is what you need to remember.'

Kate looked at his dear, kind face. He always made her feel so protected and loved. Why couldn't she feel about him the way he so obviously felt about her?

'I know,' she said. 'But all I can think about is Jem. There is a chance when they do the biopsy at the time of surgery that they'll find it's more advanced. What will happen to him if…?' She took an uneven breath. 'If the worse comes to the worst? I have to think about that. I'm all he has…I can't imagine what it would do to him to be left alone. He's still so young.' Her voice broke and she couldn't help the tears from falling once more.

Rob pulled her back into his arms. 'It's all right. You'll see. Everything will work out fine.'

But Kate knew it wasn't all right. Bad things happened. And even Rob couldn't promise her that everything would be all right. No matter how much she wanted to believe him.

In the following days, as their daughter got gradually stronger, Annie let herself think about what Raphael had said. In the days after Angela's surgery they hadn't spoken much. When Raphael wasn't with them he was back at work, putting in a full day before returning to the ward to sit with them both.

Annie wondered if, now that their child was out of danger, he regretted his words the night of Angela's surgery. But she wouldn't be the one to speak of it. If he had changed his mind, or in the cold light of day realised he didn't love her, she would accept that. In time the pain would ease and whatever happened she would always have her beloved daughter. It would be a few weeks yet before they would be able to take Angela home, but the nursery, with its sunshine-yellow walls and crib stuffed with soft toys, was ready and waiting for her.

Kate had been to see Annie often, as had the other members of Penhally Bay Surgery, and Annie had been overwhelmed by their love and support.

She leaned back in her chair as her child suckled. It had been a great joy to find that it was still possible and Annie revelled in the feel of her baby's skin close against hers.

Annie looked up to find Raphael standing looking down, his face filled with wonder. Her heart started racing. She knew without a shadow of doubt that she would never love anyone the way she loved him. When she had met him she had felt as if she had found the other half of her soul. And she still felt that way. She couldn't imagine a life without him. Not seeing him. Perhaps one day hearing that he had met someone else? But she also knew that she loved him too much to wish anything for him except happiness. Even if that life didn't include her. She loved him so much that she knew she could let him go. Even if it broke her heart.

'You look beautiful,' he said. 'How can I ever thank you for giving me the most precious gift in the world?'

He knelt by her side and touched her face with a gentle finger, before dropping his head and kissing the top of their child's head.

Annie felt her throat tighten. She wanted to imprint everything about him into her heart. Every facial feature, every expression, so in the months or years to come she would have her memories even if she didn't have him.

She replaced Angela in the incubator. She was only allowed to hold her for short periods, but she savoured every opportunity.

Raphael remained kneeling and reached a hand up and pulled her back down into the chair. Annie was uncomfortably aware of curious heads turning in their direction as the nurses stopped what they were doing to watch.

'I have something I want to ask you,' he said hoarsely. 'I was going to wait until we brought our baby home for good. But I can't sleep for not knowing what your answer would be.'

Annie studied him. He looked exhausted. The last few days of working while spending every moment with their child had taken their toll. There were dark shadows under his eyes and lines around his eyes that Annie hadn't seen before.

'I must know,' he said his voice tense. 'Do you think you could ever love me?'

Annie looked at him in wonder. Didn't he know? Hadn't he guessed how she felt? Without waiting for a reply, Raphael continued. 'From the moment I met you, I knew you were different. But I tried to tell myself it was impossible to fall in love with a woman I had only known so briefly. I couldn't let myself believe it. I wanted to contact you. I thought about it often, but I didn't. I thought it was better to keep my image of you alive and not risk having it smashed. And I still hoped there was a chance that I would win the court case for access to Sebastian on appeal. So I didn't listen to my heart. I let you go.'

Annie opened her mouth to speak, but he stopped her

words with his finger. 'Please. I have to say this. Whatever happens, I have to tell you.'

Annie waited for him to continue, acutely aware of the tiny shivers of delight and hope darting through her.

'Then when you told me you were pregnant, I thought that it was fate, but I couldn't let myself hope. I needed to know that it was my child and if it was, I needed to know that I couldn't lose her. The thought of losing another child drove me crazy. But when I saw you again, as I got to know you, I realised that I hadn't made a mistake about you. You were everything I ever thought you were. Everything I had ever hoped to find in a woman. Kind, caring, beautiful and loyal.' He looked a bit sheepish for a moment as he realised that the staff as well as most of the patients were riveted to every word he was saying. Annie felt a smile spread over her face.

'I love you. I love you more than I thought it was possible to love a woman. I want to marry you. I want to spend the rest of my life making you happy, making you smile. I want us, you me and Angela, to be a family. It doesn't matter where. Here or Spain. All that matters is that I am with you.'

'Can I speak now?' Annie asked when he came to a halt. Her heart was singing. She couldn't wait to put him out of his misery.

'I love you too, Raphael Castillo. I have loved you since the moment I saw you. And there is nothing that would make me happier than to marry you.' She could see the triumph in his eyes as he took in her words. She let him pull her to her feet, dimly aware of the sound of clapping and cheering. But as she tilted her face to his she knew that finally she had everything she had ever dreamed of.

EPILOGUE

ANNIE walked down the aisle her hand on her father's arm. The church where she had first met Raphael had seemed to them both to be the logical place for their wedding. She passed Raphael's mother, who was holding Angela in her arms. Little Maria was pressed close to the older woman's side. From the moment she and Raphael had returned to Spain with their daughter, Maria had become Angela's self-appointed guardian. She and Raphael had decided to look into the possibility of adopting Maria. Although it was early days yet, the young girl's father had raised no objections and it looked as if in time they would have two daughters. And maybe in a couple of years they would investigate the possibility of adopting another child. But all that was in the future, Annie thought as Raphael turned to watch her approach. His eyes darkened as he looked at her and Annie blushed, knowing that he was thinking of their wedding night.

Since he had proposed they had taken it slowly, getting to know the little things about each other and falling deeper in love every day. They hadn't made love, even though it had almost driven them both crazy. They had agreed to wait until they were married and Annie felt a heat low in her abdomen as she thought about the night to come. They had also agreed that they would live in Spain for the time being. It made sense. Annie had no plans to go back to work until Angela was a little older and the last thing little Maria needed was more disruption. They would go back to the UK often on holiday to see her parents and friends and, of course, they would come to Spain to see them too. She heard a little cry as Angela stirred from her nap. Annie caught Raphael's eye as she stood beside him and prepared to make the vows that would bind them together for the rest of their lives. In his eyes she found just what she was looking for. Right now she had everything she had ever wanted. Right here in this church.

COUNTDOWN
TO BABY

BY
GINA WILKINS

Gina Wilkins is a bestselling and award-winning author who has written more than sixty-five books. She credits her successful career in romance to her long, happy marriage and her three "extraordinary" children. A lifelong resident of central Arkansas, Ms Wilkins sold her first book to Mills & Boon in 1987 and has been writing full-time since. She has appeared on the Waldenbooks, B. Dalton and *USA TODAY* bestseller lists. She is a three-time recipient of the Maggie Award for Excellence, sponsored by Georgia Romance Writers, and has won several awards from the reviewers of *Romantic Times*.

For Sally—she of the untapped wisdom.

Chapter One

The slippery seven-pound boy squirmed in Cecilia Mendoza's arms. Pink legs flailed with his irritation at being shoved out of his warm, liquid cocoon and into the openness and light of the clinic birthing room. A series of shrill screams issued from his toothless mouth, and his scrunched face was beet red with fury.

Cecilia thought he was absolutely beautiful. With hidden reluctance, she transferred the child into the arms of his exhausted but eager mother. The stocky young father hovered close by, his ruddy face split with an enormous, proud, and just a bit nervous, smile.

Pushing her own emotions to the back of her mind, Cecilia concentrated on her job as a certified nurse midwife, turning her attention to the routine follow-up procedures of this blessedly complication-free delivery. Her workday was almost over. She couldn't go straight home, unfortunately, because of the reception for Lillith Cunningham, the new public relations director for the Foster Midwifery Clinic and the Bingham Midwifery School, both affiliated with the regional hospital in Merlyn County, Kentucky. The reception was to begin at six. Cecilia wasn't particularly looking forward to the event, but she felt obligated to drop in.

She could contemplate her feelings of wistfulness, envy and frustration later, when she was alone in her house, longing for a child of her own. As her thirty-eighth birthday loomed closer, she couldn't help wondering if she would ever know the joy of holding her own baby.

Geoff Bingham's bedroom smelled of freshly applied orange-oil wood polish and a hint of woodlands-scented air freshener. As he precisely knotted an expensive red silk tie around the neck of his tailored white shirt, he wondered if he was only imagining the slightly musty scent of a long-unoccupied room beneath the more pleasing fragrances.

His efficient housekeeper made sure his condo was always clean and welcoming when he returned from one of his many long business trips, but sometimes the place still felt foreign to him. Like just another of the series of hotel suites and corporate apartments he slept in during his travels—when his demanding job allowed him to sleep, of course.

Picking up the hand-tailored jacket that had been laid out on his bed, he shrugged into it as automatically as a mechanic might don his blue cotton work shirt. As far as Geoff was concerned, this fifteen-hundred-dollar suit was merely a business uniform, no more indicative of his true personality than his immaculately polished wing-tip shoes. The party for which he was dressing was just another business meeting to him, at which he would smile and mingle and shake hands with the smooth skill he had spent the past ten of his thirty-two years developing.

Squeezing the tight muscles at the back of his neck with his left hand, he could only hope the reception for the hospital's new public relations director wouldn't last long. All he wanted to do was get this over with, come back to his citrus-scented condo and crash in the den with a beer, some chips and his trea-sured Taylor guitar. An evening of quiet solitude sounded very good to him right now. But he would do his duty. He always did.

"So, Geoff." A florid-faced man in a suit that was too tight across the belly clapped him on the back with enough force to make him almost stagger. "How long are you in town for this time?"

With the benefit of a decade of practice, Geoff held on to his pleasant smile, which was, to him, as much a tool of his trade as a hammer was to a carpenter. "Looks like I could be around for a while this time."

"That's good to hear." Bob Howard slapped Geoff's back again. "Maybe we can hit the golf course. Not this weekend, I'm afraid. The wife's sister is coming for a visit, and I'm expected to entertain my moron of a brother-in-law."

That was one thing Geoff could identify with. Family obligations. His entire life revolved around them. "Maybe some other time."

"I'll give you a call."

Geoff could think of a couple dozen things he would rather do than spend an afternoon golfing with Bob Howard—root canals and ditch digging among them—but since Howard's bank was a major financier for Bingham Enterprises, he spoke warmly. "I'll look forward to it."

Howard moved on, and Geoff took advantage of the moment of peace to take another bracing swallow of his lemonade. Around him various members of his family—his father, his grandmother, his sister, his cousins—worked the crowd attending the reception for the new public relations director for Merlyn County Regional Hospital.

The hospital had been founded by Geoff's grandparents and was still family controlled, along with their other local and international business interests. The Binghams took their responsibilities to the corporation and to the community very seriously. And to the rest of the family, of course.

Even Geoff's late, wild, uncle Billy's illegitimate offspring—the ones he had acknowledged, anyway—had certain expectations thrust upon them, whether they wanted them or not. Two of those cousins, Dr. Kyle Bingham and Hannah Bingham-soon-to-be-Mendoza, were in attendance at this affair, doing their part to promote the hospital and its upcoming public relations campaign.

Geoff's gaze lingered on Hannah, who was several

months along in her pregnancy. She had very recently announced her engagement to Eric Mendoza, a rising young executive in Bingham Enterprises. The couple looked radiantly happy, and the engagement had been approved by Geoff's father and grandmother.

In their opinions, Hannah needed someone to help her raise the child she had conceived in an ill-advised affair several months ago, and young Eric needed a wife to help him further his career. This marriage was the ideal solution, as far as they were concerned.

It wouldn't be long, Geoff feared, before they turned their attentions back to him. Ever since his thirtieth birthday two years ago, they had been pressuring him to find a suitable bride and start producing more Binghams.

While Geoff had no problem with the idea of fatherhood, the prospect of marriage did not appeal to him at all. As it was now, his free time was almost nonexistent. The opportunities were extremely rare for him to do whatever he felt like doing without taking anyone else's needs or wishes into consideration. In his opinion, a wife was simply someone else who would claim a right to his time and attention.

Maybe he could subtly redirect the family's matchmaking efforts to his sister Mari, he mused. After all, she was thirty-four and firmly established as an M.D. and director of the Foster Midwifery Clinic and the Bingham Midwifery School. Sure, she was busy with her duties and her plans for the biomedical research center she dreamed of founding here in town, but she was no busier than Geoff, whose primary job was to secure funding for those grandiose plans and to keep the other Bingham Enterprises interests viable in an increasingly tough international market.

Someone walked by nibbling on a fat, juicy-looking chocolate-dipped strawberry, reminding Geoff he hadn't eaten in a while. He glanced toward the refreshments tables, where a small crowd of attendees munched on summer party fare. His gaze lingered on a beautiful brunette in a flame red dress.

Cecilia Mendoza. A prominent midwife at the clinic, Eric's sister was an extremely attractive woman Geoff had admired several times but had never actually met.

Maybe he would sample the treats before he made his escape from this boring affair.

The reception was held in the atrium of the administration and education building on the hospital campus. Four stories high, the fully enclosed atrium was a haven of glass, greenery, statuary and fountains. Wrought-iron tables, chairs and benches were scattered artfully around the stone floors. Greenery cascaded from the balconies of the floors above, leading the eye to the angled glass roof high above their heads. Accessed by gently rising ramps, another balcony circled the main atrium, holding more tables and chairs and providing a second level for entertaining and activities.

There was very little empty space, Cecilia noted as she entered the atrium from the back hallway that led into the main clinic building. When Mari Bingham arranged an official event, few members of her staff or the surrounding business community failed to make an appearance.

This affair had been billed as an informal after-hours welcome for the new PR director. Cecilia was a bit late because she had taken the time to change out of her wilted scrubs and into a bright red sheath dress she'd chosen to counter the weariness of a long day's work. Sleeveless and scoop-necked, it fit closely to her hips, then flared out just a little and fell to her knees.

She had reluctantly swapped her comfortable walking shoes for a pair of black high-heeled sandals, and her feet were already protesting. Several tendrils of dark hair had escaped the upswept style she had worn for convenience, tickling the back of her neck and her freshly made-up cheeks when she turned her head to greet friends and business associates who had already gathered around the refreshments tables.

In deference to the heat of a July evening, the caterers served frosty lemonade, iced raspberry tea and light snacks—chilled shrimp, crisp vegetables, tiny sandwiches, fresh fruits and flaky pastries. Cecilia looked longingly at the food. She had worked through her usual lunchtime—the McAllister baby having chosen just then to make her appearance—and she was hungry. But since she had never quite mastered the art of eating, mingling and conversing all at the same time, she settled for a clear-plastic tumbler of lemonade and a single chocolate-dipped strawberry, which she barely had time to eat before a deep, masculine voice spoke from close behind her.

"I don't know about you, but I wish they'd served

pizza and cheeseburgers. It would take a whole platter full of these little munchies to fill me up.''

Uncertain if he was talking to her, she turned her head to make sure. She found herself looking straight into the clear hazel eyes of Geoff Bingham, a top executive of Bingham Enterprises and brother to the administrator of the clinic where Cecilia had spent her entire career as a certified nurse midwife.

She identified him immediately, of course—few people in these parts would not—but she had never actually spoken to him before. ''I think it would be hard to gracefully eat pizza and cheeseburgers standing in a crowd of dressed-up people,'' she replied in the same light tone he had used. And then she smiled. ''But it does sound good.''

Geoff studied the selection of finger foods spread on the tables and shook his head. ''It all looks very nice, but there's no real food here. I've got to talk to Mari about putting out buckets of chicken or stacks of burritos or something for the next official event.''

Cecilia couldn't help but laugh at the image of this restrained and proper crowd munching on chicken legs and burritos. ''I'm sure that's going to happen.''

His gaze drifted down to her mouth. ''So, do you have any recommendations for a guy who's very close to starvation?''

He was definitely flirting with her, and she wasn't too tired to appreciate the attentions of such a handsome and charming man. It had been too long since she had been studied with such open masculine approval—and not in an insulting way, she decided, but decidedly flattering. This brief exchange would give her something to smile about later while she was sitting alone in her house with her feet up and a cup of coffee beside her.

She glanced at the tables again before answering him. "I don't see anything particularly filling here, but I can recommend the strawberries. The one I had was delicious."

He reached past her to pluck one of the chocolate-dipped berries from a serving platter. His arm almost, but not quite, brushed against her with the movement. Close enough to make her pulse trip a bit, in a very pleasant way. She couldn't help watching as he took a bite of the fruit, and she found herself moistening her own lips with the tip of her tongue.

Goodness, but this was one fine-looking man.

"You're right," he told her, his voice low and intimate, as if they were the only ones present in this crowded room. "This is good. Want a bite?"

The blatant entendre earned him a look of reprimand, and then a smile she made no effort to repress. "Thanks, but I've already had one."

"A woman of great willpower, I see."

Cecilia gave him a look from beneath her eyelashes. "When I choose to be."

His left eyebrow rose. "So…"

"Geoff. Hey, Geoff, good to see you." A balding man whose suit hung loosely on his bony physique peered over the tops of half glasses as he spoke, seemingly unaware of Cecilia's presence.

Recognizing the newcomer as a prominent local business owner, and guessing Geoff was there specifically to mingle with potential investors in Mari's planned biomedical research center, Cecilia tactfully slipped away. She was still smiling when she joined a group of her co-workers in another corner of the room.

"Was that Geoff Bingham you were flirting with over there?" Vanessa Harris, a registered nurse, instructor, and Cecilia's closest friend in the clinic, asked.

"Unless you know some other rich, movie-star-gorgeous guy that might have made an appearance here today," Cecilia quipped in return.

"Well, did you slip him your phone number?"

"Gee, I would have, but you know my policy. I never date men who are prettier than I am."

Vanessa laughed, and, after a moment, Cecilia joined in. As much as she had dreaded this reception, it was surprisingly enjoyable. Amazing what a few minutes of flirting with a handsome man and laughing with a friend could do to turn around a trying day.

"Have you met the new PR director yet?" Vanessa asked in a low voice.

Cecilia stopped casting what she hoped were discreet looks toward the man still standing near the food tables and turned back to her friend. "No. Have you?"

Vanessa's nod made her trademark large hoop earrings sway against her cheeks. "This afternoon."

Tall and lushly rounded, Vanessa was a striking woman who would stand out in any crowd, even if it weren't for her penchant for brightly colored clothing. She wore her black hair cropped close to her head. Her nearly black eyes glittered with a sharp wit and avid interest in her surroundings, and her flawless, chocolate-toned skin was taut and smooth. Having noted the faintest hint of developing laugh lines around her own brown eyes and full mouth, Cecilia could only hope she would look as good when she was forty-five.

Vanessa's attractiveness wasn't all Cecilia envied. Her friend was also the mother of four delightful children—two boys and twin girls, all under twelve. Vanessa was even lucky enough to have found one of those rare men who was deeply committed to his family and would probably stay with them through thick and thin, unlike so many of the men Cecilia had encountered.

"What did you think of Lillith Cunningham?" she asked, trying to put her growing obsession with children and motherhood out of her mind for the remainder of the evening—or at least until she got home.

"She's interesting," Vanessa replied. "Kind of artsy looking, you know? Flowing clothes in bright colors, jingling jewelry. No doubt she comes from money, but she's got a nice smile, so maybe the wealth hasn't gone to her head."

"Mari wouldn't hire a snob to promote the clinic," Cecilia said, confident that she was right. Dr. Mari Bingham certainly fit the description of a woman who had been raised in wealth and privilege, but she still knew how to work hard and mingle comfortably with people of all circumstances. Anyone who wanted to adequately represent the Foster Midwifery Clinic, with its huge diversity of patients and associates, would have to possess the same qualities.

"You're probably right. Mari's a good judge of character—most of the time," Vanessa added in a mutter.

Their conversation was interrupted when Milla Johnson, a young midwifery student, greeted them quietly. Pretty and competent, Milla was one of the shining stars of the midwifery school, and Cecilia had grown quite fond of her. She couldn't help noticing that Milla looked a bit tired this evening, despite what appeared to be a fresh application of blusher and lipstick.

Milla was definitely showing the effects of the strain of her demanding job, in addition to the worry of a malpractice lawsuit that Cecilia considered little more than an unfair nuisance by a couple determined to blame their own shortcomings on someone else. Milla, in this case.

"Have you had anything to eat lately?" she asked the younger woman in rather maternal concern. "You look a little pale."

"I'm fine," Milla replied, trying to smile. "It's just been a long day."

"Tell me about it," Cecilia agreed with a crooked grin, pressing a hand to her back to indicate her own weariness. "We're well into a Merlyn County baby boom, aren't we?"

Milla chuckled wearily. "I think the population of Binghamton almost doubled in the past week alone."

"We've sure got a boatload of Binghams represented here tonight," Vanessa murmured in a bit of a non sequitur as she surveyed the crowded room. "There's dear Miss Myrtle and Mr. Ron. And Mari and Geoff. You know this event's a big deal if they brought him home for it. Then there's Hannah, of course, I suppose she counts as a Bingham. Don't she and your brother look happy, Cecilia?''

Cecilia smiled mistily across the room to where her handsome and utterly adored younger brother, Eric, stood attentively next to a lovely, and very pregnant, Hannah. The couple were so visibly in love—and so excited about the child they would soon welcome into their lives.

Eric was another exception to Cecilia's general theory that most men weren't interested in long-term family obligations. There was no question in her mind that Eric's commitment to Hannah and her baby would last a lifetime.

And as happy as she was for her brother, she couldn't help envying...

''Oops. Almost missed a Bingham,'' Vanessa added cheerily. ''Dr. Kyle is posed broodingly on the other side of the atrium, looking like he stepped off a *GQ* cover. He is one fine-looking young man, isn't he?''

Cecilia's smile deepened. ''If you happen to appreciate blond hair, blue eyes, a pretty face and a perfect body. And who doesn't, right, Milla?''

Her formerly pale face now bright pink, Milla murmured an answer, then made an excuse to move away. Something about seeing someone she needed to speak to.

With a slight frown, Cecilia watched Milla hurry away. Like others who worked closely with them, she hadn't missed the sparks between the young nurse and

Dr. Kyle Bingham. But something other than a possibly complicated attraction seemed to be haunting Milla, and, worrier that she was, it concerned her. "Does it seem to you that Milla's been acting oddly lately, Van?"

"Who wouldn't be, with that stupid lawsuit hanging over her? But she'll be okay, don't you worry. Mari and the legal staff will take good care of her."

"I'm sure you're right." Telling herself to let the experts worry about Milla's problems, Cecilia glanced discreetly at her functional, easily readable stainless steel watch. "Wonder how soon before we can make an escape? I'm ready to get home and crash."

"I'll try not to take that as a comment on my sparkling companionship."

Smiling, Cecilia shook her head. "Like Milla, I'm just tired. It really has been a long day."

"I'm about ready to head home, myself. George is supposed to have the kids fed and homework supervised, but you know how it goes. I'll probably have to check to make sure it all got done. And I want to read Damien his bedtime story tonight."

Vanessa couldn't have known, of course, that her lighthearted words would go straight to Cecilia's heart. Though Vanessa knew Cecilia wanted children of her own, she had no idea just how strong that longing had become.

It was with some relief that Cecilia was able to change the subject of the conversation. "I think someone wants to speak to you," she said, nodding toward a young nursing student who was trying to get

Vanessa's attention. "Looks like a lively discussion is going on over there."

Vanessa sighed. "I'm sure there is. That group is always getting into a debate about something—and I always seem to get called in as referee."

"Mama Vanessa," Cecilia teased. "Go take care of your chicks. I'm going to try to score another chocolate-dipped strawberry."

"Okay. Catch you later." Vanessa moved to the group of nursing students and was soon engaged in an animated conversation with them.

Cecilia worked her way slowly across the crowded atrium, pausing several times to chat with co-workers. She made sure she spoke to enough people to leave no doubt that she had attended the gathering—standard office politics. On the other side of the room, her brother and his fiancée were surrounded by well-wishers. She managed to swap smiles and waves with them, but she made no effort to join them. As a rising young executive in the Bingham corporation, Eric had his own politics to practice this evening.

And, speaking of Binghams...

She smiled when Geoff stepped in front of her again. "Still looking for a cheeseburger, Mr. Bingham?"

He chuckled. "Actually, I'm hungry enough now for a thick slab of steak and a huge baked potato. These little finger foods aren't going to hold me any longer."

"I know what you mean. I haven't had time to eat since breakfast this morning."

"So, how about it? Want to go find a steak?"

She blinked. "Um...now?"

"Of course. We're both hungry. We've dutifully made our appearances at this official reception thing, and there's no reason for either of us to stay any longer. So, if you have no plans for the remainder of the evening, I would be honored if you would join me for dinner."

She could hardly believe that Geoff Bingham was impulsively asking her out within a few minutes of meeting her. Heck, she couldn't even say they had met, officially. She was quite sure she hadn't even told him her name. "We haven't even been introduced."

His grin deepened, pushing intriguing creases into his lean cheeks. "We haven't, have we? Of course you already know I'm Geoff Bingham, and I know you're Eric Mendoza's sister, Cecilia. You're a valuable member of the midwifery team here and highly respected by everyone who mentions you. I'd like to get a chance to know you myself."

So he did know who she was. Maybe, she decided, he just didn't like eating alone. Maybe he was using her as an excuse to get out of this reception—being the gentleman by feeding a hungry guest, being a good executive by getting to know one of the subordinates in the organization, getting better acquainted with the sister of the man who was marrying one of his cousins. All sorts of rationales could apply. The question was, did she want to accept?

Rather surprisingly, considering her earlier weariness and eagerness to get home, the answer was yes.

Maybe she was simply trying to postpone going

home alone—again—to contemplate her life and her future. Maybe watching Eric and Hannah from across the room made her aware again of her own depressing lack of a social life, if she discounted a few disastrous blind dates—which she did. Or maybe she simply liked the idea of spending a couple of hours with an attractive, charming and interesting man.

Deciding she had no reason at all to turn him down, she smiled. "Would you mind if I order chicken instead of steak?"

Satisfaction gleamed in his clear hazel eyes. "That can definitely be arranged."

Chapter Two

If he had known when he'd dressed for the evening that he would end up dining with a beautiful brunette, he wouldn't have been so reluctant to attend the reception, Geoff mused as he studied Cecilia Mendoza across a cozy table a short time later. Melinda's was busy this evening, as it was most weekends, but a combination of clever table arrangement and discreet lighting gave them a sense of privacy as they studied the menus by candlelight.

At Cecilia's suggestion, they had left the reception separately, driving their own cars to the restaurant. He had assumed the suggestion was based at least partly on discretion, since the gossip lines in the clinic were as active as in any tight-knit work environment. He had to admit it had been clever of her.

Geoff had had the foresight to call ahead as he'd

left the hospital so that a table had been waiting for them, avoiding the usual lengthy wait for seating. He didn't often wield his influence as a member of one of the wealthiest and most prominent local families, but this had been one of the rare occasions when it had been irresistible to do so. If Cecilia had been impressed, she hadn't let it show, which was something else he liked about her.

"I think I'll have the trout," she said, laying her menu aside.

"Change your mind about the chicken?"

Her smile brought out tiny dimples at the corners of her mouth. Geoff couldn't keep from staring at them as she replied, "Actually, everything looks so good it's hard to decide. It's been quite a while since I've had the chance to dine here."

He dragged his gaze back up to her eyes. "Then I'm glad you were free to join me tonight."

Located in an old firehouse, Melinda's was a steak and seafood restaurant with a menu and a wine list that compared favorably to anything in the state, as far as Geoff was concerned. He liked the history of the place, the redbrick walls decorated with framed black-and-white vintage photographs from Merlyn County's colorful past, the polished brass pole left over from the old fire station, the huge carved oak bar that made up the entire back wall of the popular lounge downstairs.

Geoff's family had always come here for special occasions, such as birthdays and anniversaries, and the management had always given them preferential treatment. During the past few years, he had dined in some of the most renowned restaurants in the world, but Melinda's would always feel like home to him.

Having placed their orders with the server who had been hovering discreetly nearby, Geoff focused on his companion again. "I'm told the clinic has been very busy lately."

Her smile turned wry. "You're told correctly. We've decided there's a major baby boom going on in Merlyn County. And there's more and more demand for midwifery services, partially due to the shortage of obstetricians in the county."

"How are the new students performing? Is the school doing its job properly?"

"Absolutely. I would put our school up against any in the country."

Pleased by her unmistakable loyalty to the company, Geoff nodded. "Enough about business—let's talk about you."

She gave him a look that warned him she wouldn't fall easily for the usual trite lines, but he hadn't really been feeding her one. He was interested in finding out about her. Something about the contrast between her politely restrained manner and her sexy flame-red dress intrigued him as much as her lovely face and curvy figure attracted him.

It had been much too long since he'd had time to spend an evening with an intriguing woman, he concluded. He had been so busy being the dutiful son and employee during the past ten years that he had almost forgotten how to be spontaneous and impulsive. He had tried so hard to be like his hardworking and upstanding father and not like his wild and irresponsible uncle that he had almost forgotten how to be himself. He had begun to suspect that there was a little of both his father and his uncle inside him.

It was the latter side that he called upon when he leaned slightly forward and gave Cecilia his most winning smile. "What do you like to do when you're not delivering babies?"

"I'm an avid reader and gardener. I enjoy hiking and bird-watching in the mountains."

"How do you feel about football?"

She lifted her wineglass to her lips and studied him over the rim. "I am positively passionate about football. Especially when it comes to University of Kentucky football."

His interest went up a couple more notches. "A woman after my own heart."

"I'm not after anyone's heart, Mr. Bingham," she said, setting her glass on the table. "Hearts are very high-maintenance organs, and I barely have time to take care of myself."

He laughed. Now that was a sentiment he could agree with. With each passing moment he was becoming more pleased that he had followed his impulses and asked Cecilia Mendoza to join him for dinner.

Cecilia had always believed that the nicest pleasures were unexpected ones. Dining with Geoff Bingham definitely fell into that category. He was very good company—articulate, funny, attentive when she spoke. All skills picked up during the course of his job, she was sure, making him an ideal companion for a leisurely meal.

She couldn't help chuckling as she compared this

outing to the last time she had gone out on a dinner date. At Vanessa's urging, she had reluctantly agreed to a blind date set up over the Internet. After all, there were so few available men Cecilia's age in this area, and with her long hours at the clinic, she didn't have many opportunities to meet other singles.

The date had been a dismal failure, a total waste of time on both sides. He hadn't been at all interested in hearing about her work—just the opposite, actually, since he freely admitted that the idea of childbirth "grossed him out." And his description of midnight frog gigging—his favorite sport, apparently— had done the same for her.

"What's so funny?" Geoff asked, looking up from his nearly finished steak.

She hadn't realized she had laughed out loud. "Nothing. I'm just enjoying the meal."

He glanced at her plate and then at his own. "Maybe I should have ordered the trout. My steak's good, but it doesn't make me laugh."

"Let's just say it's been too long since I've been out for a nice meal with a charming companion," she said, reaching for her wineglass. "I've been eating alone entirely too much lately."

Geoff's expression turned wry. "I almost wish I could say the same. I have very few opportunities to spend any time alone. Seems like I rush constantly from one meeting or reception or dinner party to the next. I can't even tell you the last time I had a chance to crash in front of the TV with a pizza for an entire evening."

"You don't enjoy your work?"

"Actually, I do, for the most part. But I think I'm

going to start scheduling a bit more free time in the future.''

She nodded. ''Good plan. Spend too many hours working and too few relaxing and you'll end up burned out and suffering from stress-related health problems. I've seen it entirely too many times.''

''Maybe you should take your own advice. From what I hear, you're one of the hardest workers in the clinic.''

She wondered who had been talking about her to Geoff. His sister, perhaps? While it sounded as though the conversation had been complimentary, it still made her uncomfortable to think about being discussed in her absence. ''Yes, well, like you, I've been giving some thought to my personal life lately.''

As much as she loved her work, it was no substitute for a family or for the child she wanted so badly.

''You're not planning on leaving the clinic, are you? Mari would have a cow if you even suggested it.''

She laughed at his wording, then shook her head. ''I'm not leaving the clinic. I love my job. I just need more.''

She changed the subject before he could ask what that ''more'' entailed. ''Tell me about your latest trip. I heard you were in Italy.'' She wondered how she felt knowing he had been the subject of a few discussions, too.

If it bothered him, he didn't let it show. He merely nodded to confirm the rumor. ''Milan. I met with some scientists and international venture capitalists about investing funds and expertise into our biomedical research center.''

"Did the meetings go well—or can you say?"

"I can't really give any details at the moment, but I can say the family was satisfied with my progress."

Cecilia toyed with a fork-size piece of tender salmon. "Your family seems to be more than satisfied with your work. They always sound so proud when they speak of you."

She noted that his smile was just a bit crooked. "That's what I've been trained for all my life—to make my family proud."

Was that a trace of restlessness she heard in his voice? She doubted that Geoff had been given much choice about joining his family's business. Were there times when he wished he could have pursued his own path?

Cecilia knew all about family obligations. After all, she had pretty much put her own life on hold for several years to care for her mother. She had set aside dating and traveling and experimenting because she felt she owed it to her mother, and because she had wanted to give her much younger brother a chance to finish his education and get started in his own career.

But now their mother was gone. At twenty-six, Eric was successfully established with Bingham Enterprises, blissfully engaged to the woman he adored, and expecting a child he would love with all his heart. Cecilia was thirty-seven and still recovering financially from the daunting medical bills she had hidden from her brother. Her social life was pretty much nonexistent, and having her own child was a dream that seemed farther out of reach with each passing month.

"What's wrong?"

She glanced up from the food she had suddenly lost

interest in to find Geoff watching her from across the table, his clear hazel eyes entirely too perceptive. She felt as if he could read her thoughts in her own brown eyes, and even though she knew that was foolish, she glanced quickly away, pretending to concentrate on her meal again. ''Nothing's wrong. Why?''

''You stopped smiling.''

She smiled again and tried to make it look completely natural. ''No serious talk tonight. I won't allow it. Tell me about Milan—and make me see it in my mind.''

Proving himself to be as skilled with words as he was with a smile, he entertained her for the next twenty minutes with stories of his travels. His descriptions were so clever it was almost as if she could see the classic architecture, almost smell the spices and flowers, almost hear the music and voices, almost taste the exotic air. Maybe she would never have a chance to visit Milan for herself, but she would leave this restaurant feeling as if she had been treated to a brief glimpse of the faraway city.

Within minutes her smile was entirely genuine again. And all because of Geoff.

Funny how Geoff had fantasized earlier about spending the evening alone with his guitar. Instead, he found himself doing everything he could think of to delay his return to his empty rooms.

''Are you sure you don't want dessert?'' he asked when they could spend no more time toying with their empty plates.

Still wearing the soft smile his word-pictures had evoked, Cecilia shook her head. ''I couldn't eat another bite. But feel free to order something for yourself.''

He had no interest in dessert, either. As delectable as the pies here were, they couldn't draw his interest away from the woman across the table from him.

It seemed he was in the mood for spicy rather than sweet this evening.

Somewhat reluctantly he paid the tab and escorted her out of the dining room. The strains of music drifting from the downstairs lounge gave him an idea for prolonging the evening. ''The band sounds good tonight. Unless you're in a hurry to get home, why don't we have a drink and listen for a little while?''

She barely hesitated before agreeing. ''That sounds like fun.''

Immensely pleased with himself, he led her in. Melinda's lounge was a popular weekend date destination, and both the dance floor and the numerous cozy tables were almost full. Geoff thought it was another example of how magical this evening had been so far that a particularly nice table opened up just as they entered.

An efficient waitress took their orders almost as soon as they sat down. Cecilia asked for white wine, and Geoff requested the same.

The band—a group of talented local thirty-somethings—played a mix of adult contemporary and country pop numbers, the most popular genres for the usual crowd here. Geoff tapped his foot in time with a lively rendition of ''Boot Scoot Boogie.'' Energetic dancers two-stepped and line danced on the polished wood floor.

Geoff could two-step with the best of them, but he

was rather hoping a nice, slow number would be next.
The thought of holding Cecilia Mendoza in his arms
was enough to make his foot tap faster.

She seemed to be enjoying watching the dancers.
An amused smile flitted across her lips as she focused
on one rhythmically challenged couple in matching
turquoise western shirts and ill-fitting jeans.

Taking advantage of the opportunity to watch her
without her noticing, he admired the way the flickering candlelight and colored dance floor lights
gleamed in her dark hair. Wispy tendrils had escaped
her upsweep to sway against her cheeks and flirt with
the tops of her shoulders. He would like to see her
hair down. Even more, he would like to see it spread
across his pillow.

She chose that moment, of course, to glance his
way, making him hope his thoughts were well concealed. "The band is good, aren't they?"

"Very good," he agreed, though he hadn't heard
a note since he'd started gazing at her.

She leaned a bit closer to him so he could hear her
over the music and surrounding conversations.
Though he could hear her perfectly well when she
made another comment about the music, he scooted
his own chair a bit closer to hers when he replied.

She lifted an eyebrow when his knee brushed hers.
"You aren't getting fresh, are you, Mr. Bingham?"

He grinned and ran a fingertip slowly down her
smooth bare arm. "I was sort of thinking about it."

"Well, let me know when you decide."

"Are you telling me it's okay if I do get fresh?"

She gave him a smile that heated his blood to a

low simmer. "I suppose you'll just have to try it and see."

Obligingly enough, the band slipped into a slow number, the country arrangement of "I Don't Want to Miss a Thing." As of that moment, it was Geoff's new favorite song.

He stood and held out his hand. "Dance with me?"

Though she placed her hand in his and rose obligingly enough, she murmured, "I'm not much of a dancer, I'm afraid."

Somehow he doubted that, considering the graceful way she moved, the gentle sway of her hips. But he couldn't care less about fancy steps or choreographed moves—he just wanted to get his arms around her.

It felt as good to have them there as he had predicted.

Funny that he hadn't realized until now how small she was. He would guess her to be a good seven inches shorter than his own six feet, so that even the strappy, heeled sandals she wore brought the top of her head just to his chin. Her figure was slender but nicely curved, making his hands itch to wander and explore. He kept them discreetly placed for public dancing, but he couldn't help fantasizing a bit....

"It's been forever since I've danced," Cecilia murmured.

"It's been a while for me, too." The double entendre was unintentional—but accurate, nonetheless. When another couple crowded them, bringing Cecilia more closely against him, he was forcefully reminded of just how long it had been since he'd spent any quality one-on-one time with an attractive woman. It took some effort for him to keep his body from embarrassing him like a randy teenager's.

They spent the next hour dancing and talking. Flirting. Having fun. Geoff could almost feel the last traces of work-induced tension seeping from his muscles. He sensed the same thing in Cecilia as her smiles warmed and softened.

It was inevitable that other people there recognized them with apparent surprise and curiosity, but other than acknowledging greetings, Geoff ignored everyone but his companion. Cecilia did the same, exchanging the occasional smile or wave, but subtly discouraging further approaches.

She was good at that, Geoff decided. Politely reserved. It was a skill his late mother had perfected and that Geoff had worked to develop to preserve some semblance of privacy in his hectic and very public life.

Though he paid little attention to gossip, his prominent family having been the subject of all too much of it during the years, he wondered if it bothered Cecilia that they were attracting so much notice. Tongues would probably wag tomorrow about Geoff making time with one of the midwives from the clinic. He was cynical enough to know that a few would turn the question around. "Didja' hear that Cecilia Mendoza was making a play to snag the Bingham's bachelor son?"

Such idle talk didn't concern him, but maybe Cecilia took it more seriously. Then again, maybe not. After all, she must have known when they agreed to dine here that plenty of people would recognize them and speculate.

He had the feeling that Cecilia was self-confident enough not to be overly concerned at what other people said about her. He admired that about her. It was only one of the things he admired about her, he mused, his gaze lingering on her lush mouth.

Cecilia was reluctant for the evening to end, and it was clear that Geoff felt the same way. She couldn't remember the last time she'd had such a pleasant outing. She certainly couldn't recall the last time she had danced this much. Even if her feet were throbbing in the heeled sandals she hadn't expected to wear this long, it was well worth the discomfort.

It was a heady feeling knowing that Geoff found her attractive. Too often lately she had felt routine-bound and uninteresting, her days consumed with work, her home life unfulfilling. She was so often surrounded by young nurses and young mothers, who often treated Cecilia with a deference usually reserved for much older women. It was a sign of their respect for her and her career, of course, and she acknowledged that. But their attitudes sometimes made her feel older than thirty-seven.

Now a man at least five years her junior was looking at her with desire and admiration in his eyes. A very attractive, successful, interesting and respected man, who must meet dozens of beautiful and fascinating women in his travels.

She didn't expect this to go anywhere, of course. Nor did she particularly want it to. After all, Geoff was a Bingham—and she certainly didn't want to be involved in *their* lives. It concerned her enough that her brother was marrying one of the notorious Binghams—even though Hannah was only loosely connected to the clan.

Still, Cecilia thought, as Geoff's strong arms went around her for their final dance, it had been nice to enjoy his company for a few stolen hours.

He held her more closely this time. His cheek rested against her hair. The band played Lonestar's "Amazed," the lead singer crooning the words into the mike. Whenever she heard the song in the future, she would remember this dance and the deliciously shivery sensations running through her.

Geoff was a skilled dancer who made it very easy for her to follow his lead. A smooth turn brought them even closer together, her breasts brushing against his chest, their thighs touching as their feet moved in unison. She felt a tug of response deep inside her, a dull ache that she acknowledged as pure physical desire. It had been much too long since she had indulged that side of herself.

The song ended eventually. Inevitably. Geoff held her for just a moment after the last note faded away, and then he stepped back. "I suppose we should go," he said as he escorted her back to their table. "It's getting late, and I know you must be tired."

She was a bit tired, actually, and her feet were killing her, but she was tempted to ask him to stay a little while longer. Instead, she merely nodded. "It is getting late."

He stayed close by her side as he walked her out. Cecilia could almost feel eyes watching them leave, and she knew there would be talk tomorrow. She didn't particularly care.

From her early childhood as one of the town's few

residents of Hispanic descent at that time, she had accepted that people thought of her as different. People had talked when her father died in a senseless whitewater-rafting accident when Cecilia was still in elementary school. They had whispered when her mother bore an out-of-wedlock son when Cecilia was eleven. Maria had raised both children on her own because Eric's no-good father hadn't stayed around to help.

Maria had lived quietly, but somewhat defiantly, working as many as three jobs and asking for no help from anyone except Cecilia, who had served almost as surrogate mother to her baby brother. Though she'd had little spare time to devote to her children, Maria's strength and self-sufficiency had set an example for both Cecilia and Eric to pursue their own goals without being overly influenced by anyone else.

The gossip had started again when Cecilia had impulsively married at nineteen, a marriage that had lasted barely two years. Six years her senior, Gary McGhee had swept her off her feet and into his arms, promising her everything she had ever dreamed of— a loving partner, an encouraging supporter, a caring father for the children she had wanted even then. Someone to take care of her, for a change.

She had discovered quickly enough that what he had really wanted was someone strong to take care of *him.* An adoring young wife who wouldn't mind putting her own dreams aside so she could serve as his personal cheerleader while he drifted from one get-rich scheme to another.

She had finally accepted that Gary was all talk and that she had made a mistake to believe any of it. She had come to the decision that she would rather pursue her own goals by herself—like her mother—than to give them up for someone who would never appreciate the sacrifice.

And now people were talking about her family again as her brother prepared to marry a woman who carried another man's baby. A woman who had, herself, been an illegitimate child of notorious bad-boy Billy Bingham.

Knowing how deeply Eric loved Hannah, and what a good father he would make for her child, Cecilia didn't care if the gossips talked until their tongues deflated. It was no one's business but Eric's who he married or why. Just as it was no one else's business if Cecilia wanted to enjoy Geoff Bingham's company for a few delightful hours.

Let them gossip, she thought with a private smile. These memories would be hers to savor for quite some time.

"You're smiling again," Geoff observed, turning at her car door to study her in the yellow glow of the parking lot lights.

"I had a lovely time," she told him, tilting her smile up for him.

"So did I." Ignoring anyone who might see them, he lowered his head and brushed a quick kiss against her cheek. As relatively innocent as the gesture was, it still made her knees go weak to feel his lips against her skin.

Geoff lifted his head, and though he was still smiling, there was a new heat in his eyes. "Sorry. I couldn't resist."

"Did you hear me protest?"

"No." He bent toward her again. "So maybe you wouldn't mind if I—"

She moved quickly out of his reach. A disregard for gossip was one thing, but her deeply entrenched sense of privacy prevented her from making a complete spectacle of herself. "This is a little too public for my taste."

He pushed his hands into his pockets as if to demonstrate that he wouldn't touch her again without permission. "Would you allow me to see you home? Just to make sure you get there safely?"

Though she wasn't sure her safety had much to do with the offer, she took a moment to think about it. She supposed there was no harm in allowing him to follow her home. The fifteen-minute drive would give him the satisfaction of making a chivalrous gesture— and her the chance to think about whether she wanted to invite him inside when they got there.

She simply nodded and turned to slide into her car.

By the time she drove into her driveway, she had conducted a full, somewhat heated debate with herself about how she wanted the evening to end. Should she politely thank Geoff again for dinner, then send him on his way? Or should she ask him in for a nightcap and then see what happened?

Just how far was she willing to suspend reality this evening?

Chapter Three

Geoff parked his expensive, new-looking sports car behind the economy sedan Cecilia had bought used four years ago—another sign, she mused, that their lives couldn't be more different. And then he moved toward her, his face shadowed, his lean, strong, yet somehow elegant body silhouetted by security lighting.

Even the way he walked fascinated her, she thought as she watched him approach. He held his head high and his shoulders squared—an innate air of confidence that probably came with being born a Bingham. It wasn't arrogance she sensed in him, exactly—more an expectation of being accepted and respected, a feeling that had been lacking in her own background.

This man could have spent the evening anywhere he wanted—and with anyone—but he had chosen to spend it with her. She couldn't deny that it was a huge boost to her feminine ego.

He stopped in front of her. "Nice neighborhood."

"Thank you. I enjoy living here."

It was an older neighborhood, filled with aging houses—and aging residents, many of whom had lived here since Cecilia was a little girl. The teenage girl next door was the youngest resident of the neighborhood since moving in with her grandparents a year ago.

Tall, stately trees guarded the sides of the narrow street, their branches nearly touching over it. Neat yards and flourishing flower beds gave testament to the pride her working-class neighbors took in their homes.

Cecilia had inherited her small white-frame house when her mother passed away three years earlier. Though she had protested, Eric had insisted on signing his half over to her—in gratitude, he had said, for her putting her own life on hold to care for their mother while he completed his education and embarked on his career.

Cecilia's name was the only one on the deed now, but she still considered it Eric's home, too. He made a point of keeping up the routine maintenance for her—such as painting the siding and shutters and flower boxes last spring—and he ate lunch with her every Sunday.

At least, he had until very recently, she corrected herself with a little ripple of sadness. Now that Eric was about to be married and was establishing his own family, some of the old routines had to change, Sunday lunches being one of them. As much as she welcomed Hannah into the family, Cecilia couldn't help regretting a little that her role as the most important woman in Eric's life had come to an end.

Now she wasn't the most important person in anyone's life, she had found herself thinking during the middle of several long, lonely nights. Though she had never been the type to indulge in self-pity, she was human enough to wish some things had turned out differently for her.

"Have you lived here long?"

Pulling herself back to the present, she replied to Geoff, "Since I was very young. This is the house where my mother raised Eric and me."

Geoff nodded, his face still obscured by the shadows of the warm summer night. "You must miss her very much."

"Yes, I do."

"I miss my mom, too."

The simple and palpably sincere statement brought a lump to her throat. She remembered Geoff's mother—a beautiful, classy, kind-hearted woman who had been known as a tireless contributor to local charities. At only forty, Violet Bingham had died of a massive heart attack. That was almost ten years ago. Cecilia had been a relatively new employee of the clinic, but even then she had seen how the tragedy had devastated the family and the community.

People who knew him well said that Geoff's father, Ron, would never get over the loss of his young wife. Cecilia had always considered it a shame that handsome, charming, still-vibrant Ronald Bingham should spend the rest of his life alone.

Maybe it was the moment of bonding or maybe it

was the thought of the empty rooms waiting for her that made her say, "Would you like to come in for coffee? Or if you're too tired, I—"

"I would love to come in for coffee," he agreed before she could even finish the sentence. "I'll just go lock my car first."

Hoping she wasn't making a gigantic mistake, Cecilia turned toward her front door.

Trying to be subtle about it, Geoff studied Cecilia's home curiously when he followed her inside. The love of bright colors revealed by the red dress she had worn this evening was echoed in the decor of her living room. The sofa looked new—a splash of bright graphics on a deep-red background. The few wood pieces were old—a mix of refinished and fashionably distressed antiques.

On the walls hung framed prints of impressionistic paintings. The jewel-toned throw pillows scattered about the furniture had probably been hand crafted. It was a room that had been decorated by someone with excellent taste and limited funds. He liked it better than many expensive and professionally decorated rooms he had been in.

He made note of the framed photographs grouped on the mantel. Most of them were of Eric, from infancy through adulthood. Eric lying on a bear rug, blowing out three candles on a birthday cake, posing in Boy Scout and baseball uniforms, beaming in cap and gown. A dark-eyed brunette who could only be Cecilia's mother appeared in a few of the photos, looking stiff and camera-shy. Cecilia was pictured even less, either because she didn't like being photographed or didn't care to display pictures of herself.

It was obvious that she adored her younger brother. Geoff was quite sure that his own sister had no similar photographic shrine to *him*. He and Mari had always gotten along well enough, though they had been too busy and focused on their careers to connect much during the past decade. Since their mother's death, actually.

Violet had been the glue that held her family together. Their grief over her loss had caused them to drift apart, throwing themselves more fully into their activities to dull the pain.

Cecilia motioned toward the couch. "Have a seat. I'll put the coffee on."

He placed a hand on her arm. "I have a confession to make."

Her eyebrows lifted in question. "What?"

"I don't really want any coffee."

She tilted her head to study his face, her expression hard to interpret. "Is that right?"

"I don't even like coffee."

"So you came in because…?"

"Because I wasn't ready for the evening to be over."

The admission certainly didn't seem to surprise her. Nor did it appear to perturb her. She had to have known when he'd followed her home that the moment would come when she would have to decide how she wanted their evening to end.

Maybe she had made that decision when she invited him in. She glanced at his hand where it rested on her arm and then looked back up at him through her thick, dark lashes. The smile that played on her lips was neither shy nor hesitant, but the smile of a woman who knew what she wanted. And tonight, it seemed, she wanted him.

"Then maybe we can make it last just a little while longer," she murmured, sliding her free hand up his chest.

His pulse rate sped up in anticipation. "Just for a little while," she had said, making it clear that she wasn't expecting more from him than this one night. She was no starry-eyed ingenue who would take his attentions too seriously. No hungry, wannabe socialite hoping to secure a country-club future by snagging a most-eligible bachelor.

Perhaps that was why he'd had such a good time with her tonight. She'd had no expectations, no demands of him. He hadn't been trying to sell her anything or charm anything out of her, and the same had been true in reverse. He had been free to be himself— to eat what he'd liked, to talk without overanalyzing his words, to laugh and dance and sometimes sit quietly and listen to the music.

Damn, it had felt good. He wanted to hang on to that feeling for a bit longer. He released her arm only to slide both of his own around her. "I suppose you've been told that you have beautiful eyes."

She gave him a look that was a mixture of amusement and reproach. "You've been refreshingly natural all evening. Don't start spouting corny lines now."

He laughed, though it hadn't really been a line. She *did* have beautiful eyes. And an absolutely amazing mouth. And a body that seemed to have been tailored to fit nicely against his.

"Okay," he promised. "No corny lines."

She seemed to give that vow a moment's thought, and then she shook her head and slid her arms around his neck. "Oh, the heck with it. Tell me more about my eyes."

He was still grinning when he covered her mouth with his.

He had been fantasizing all evening about tasting her full, soft lips. He discovered now that imagination couldn't compare to reality when it came to kissing Cecilia Mendoza.

Though he had bent down to her, she stood on tiptoe to meet him. The position brought her even more snugly against him, making him intensely aware of the womanly fullness of her breasts and hips. Geoff had always appreciated curves, having never been a fan of the fashionably underfed look.

He no longer tried to hide the effect she had on him. They weren't in public now, and he felt free to be completely honest with her. If she didn't know how much he wanted her by now, then she simply wasn't paying attention.

He surfaced from the kiss long enough for them both to draw quick breaths of air, and then he dove in again. As waves of pleasure swept through him, he found himself thinking about how glad he was that he had changed his mind about spending the evening alone with his guitar.

No woman should reach the age of forty without having at least a few reckless adventures to remember, Cecilia figured. And since she was getting rather close to that particular milestone, this was one adventure she simply could not resist.

Kissing Geoff was a revelation. Who would have thought any man could make her feel so much with no more than a couple of deep, skillful kisses? She was typically a bit slower off the mark, so to speak. But then, it had been quite a long time since she had participated in the sport.

She could feel the heat in her face when he finally drew back. Her hair was beginning to slip its restraints, lying against her cheeks and tickling the nape of her neck. She knew she must look flushed and disheveled, but still Geoff gazed at her as though he found her beautiful. And while she knew she wasn't, really, it still felt nice to have him look at her that way.

His smile was crooked, and his voice satisfyingly gravelly when he said, "I should warn you that I feel another corny line coming on."

She cleared her throat. "I'm getting close to spouting a few myself."

"As much as I would like to hear any outrageous compliments you choose to make about me, maybe it would be better if we move the conversation to another location. We could at least sit down. Or, if it's getting too late, you could walk me to the door...."

Another gentlemanly way to offer her an out if she had any doubts. He really was a nice guy, Cecilia thought as she slid her fingers into the back of his neatly brushed hair. She couldn't help thinking how nice it would look tousled around his handsome face.

Because he held her so tightly against him, she knew their kisses had affected him as deeply as they had her. Yet his lightly spoken words had been intended to ease any tension their passionate kisses might have created between them. Geoff wanted her to feel comfortable with him, the way she had at the restaurant earlier. He was obviously trying to reassure her that he was putting no pressure on her, that she was fully in control.

While she appreciated his consideration, she almost wished he would sweep her off her feet so she didn't have to make any decisions. It was an uncharacteristic thought, and one she quickly suppressed, since she was admittedly a control freak who wanted the final say in all areas of her life.

"Maybe you would like to see the rest of my house," she said, giving him a smile designed to let him know exactly what the invitation included.

"There's nothing I would like more," he assured her huskily.

She took his hand. His fingers closed eagerly around hers.

Because there was no way she could have known anyone would be joining her in her bedroom that evening, it must have been a lucky impulse that had made Cecilia change her sheets and put out fresh flowers from her garden before she left for work that morning. She enjoyed coming home to a clean house after a long day in the clinic, and tonight the faint whiff of the flowers only added to the romantic haze she had slipped into.

The small Tiffany-style lamp on her nightstand was connected to a timer so she didn't have to walk into a dark room after working late. The lamp glowed softly now, throwing gentle illumination over the 1930s-era dark pecan bedroom furniture and the hand-pieced quilt she used as a bedspread. Period accessories gleaned from flea markets and antique shops decorated the vanity and double dresser, and more family photos hung on the walls. Numerous soft, colorful throw pillows turned the room into an old-fashioned, comfy boudoir, complete with a bentwood rocker tucked into one corner.

This was Cecilia's haven, the place where she hid out to read and daydream. Though the decor had changed, it was the same room she'd had as a girl, never having the desire to move into the rooms that had been used by her mother or her brother. She rarely brought anyone in; even Eric had stepped foot in her room only a handful of times, and then only to make various repairs.

It took an enormous leap of faith for her to invite Geoff Bingham into her private space. For a woman who generally took as few risks as possible in her life, this was pretty huge on the adventure scale.

Maybe he sensed her sudden attack of nerves. He turned to her and gave her a smile that was both gentle and endearing. "It's not too late to walk me to the door."

"I know, but the thing is, I don't want to do that yet."

"Can't say it's what I want you to do, either," he murmured, his smile crooked again.

Drawing a deep breath, she walked her fingers up his chest. "Tell me again about my eyes."

"They are—" he lowered his head to speak against her lips "—amazing."

She let herself drift into the kiss, into the moment. She'd had a few great kisses in her life—some that she would have described at the time as spectacular—but there was something different about kissing Geoff. She couldn't think of a word that wasn't clichéd or trite or simply inadequate, but there was definitely something….

Apparently he found time to work out during his travels. Beneath the conservative businessman's clothing was a lean, solid, nicely muscled body. She had noticed that during their first slow dance. Her observation was confirmed when she slid his jacket off his shoulders and tossed it over the rocker. Even through his shirt, she could see that his shoulders were wide and his stomach flat. What she *couldn't* see, she mused as she went to work on his tie, was whether his chest was smooth or furry. Tanned or pale.

Only moments later she was able to confirm that he was lightly tanned and that there was only a smattering of dark hair down the center of his chest. Drawing his shirt slowly down his arms, she tried to anticipate how it would feel to be pressed against that very nice chest, with nothing between them except desire.

She couldn't wait to find out.

Holding her gaze with his own, he slipped his hands behind her. A brush of cool air followed her zipper down her back, and then her dress pooled around her bare feet. She couldn't really remember kicking off her sandals, but then the details of this night were beginning to blur into a haze of sensation. She had given up on rational thought a long time ago—maybe even the first time Geoff had smiled at her.

Unfortunately, her intuition hadn't warned her to don sexy lingerie beneath the red dress. She was still wearing the serviceable beige bra and matching panties she had worn to work. Before she had time to regret the choice, the problem had become moot; Cecilia barely had time to reflect on how suspiciously good Geoff was at removing women's undergarments before she found herself in his arms again. With nothing between them but desire.

It felt even better than she could have imagined.

As he lowered her to the bed, she came very close to telling him that she never did things like this. That it was so unlike her to bring a man she had just met into her bed. She bit the words back because they sounded so overused. So difficult to believe—even though in this case they were so absolutely true.

She could only hope he somehow understood without being told that this was a special evening. A brief visit to fantasyland.

Reality intruded momentarily when he retrieved a plastic package from his pants pocket—did he *always* carry condoms or had he hoped to hook up with someone tonight?—but she pushed the question to the back of her mind to ponder later.

He kissed her eyelids. "Have I mentioned that I have a thing for big brown eyes?"

"I—" She was forced to clear her throat before she could speak. Apparently the fact that they were practically glued together in her bed wasn't affecting his voice the way it was hers, though it was certainly affecting other parts of him dramatically enough. "I think you have."

His lips trailed across her cheek. "Did I tell you how much I like the dimples at the corners of your mouth?" he asked, then pressed a kiss just there.

She felt those dimples deepen. "I don't think you have mentioned that."

The tip of his tongue swept across her lower lip, causing a shiver of reaction. "Consider it said."

She could only nod this time.

Scooting downward a bit on the bed, he nibbled a line from her chin down her throat to the top of her shoulder. "Should I keep listing the parts of you that I like best? Because I warn you, it could take the rest of the night."

Arching into his explorations, she closed her eyes and threaded her fingers into his hair. "I just happen to be available all night," she managed to say.

He lifted his head from his downward path just long enough to flash her a wickedly beautiful smile. "I can't tell you how glad I am to hear that."

The outrageous idea came to her while she was making coffee the next morning. It hit her with enough force to make her stumble, almost dumping coffee grounds on the spotless linoleum floor.

She placed a hand on a countertop to steady her while she took a moment to wonder if she had just slipped over the edge of sanity. Surely she must be crazy to even consider what she suddenly found herself contemplating.

Dimly aware of the sound of the shower running in the back of the house, she knew she had only a few minutes to gather her composure—and, perhaps, her courage—before facing Geoff.

It was still early on this Saturday morning—not quite 8 a.m. She'd woken first, a bit startled with the realization that she wasn't alone in her bed. Resisting the opportunity to watch Geoff sleep—and he had looked as delicious with tousled hair and a shadow of beard as she had thought he would—she had slipped out of the bed and into the shower.

By the time Geoff had roused, looking a bit embarrassed that jet lag and a strenuous night had caused him to sleep so heavily, Cecilia had already donned a T-shirt and shorts, pulled her hair into a loose braid and applied judicious touches of makeup. Urging him to take his time in the shower, she had promised to have breakfast ready when he came out.

Hastily dumping coffee into the filter, she turned on the coffeemaker and set out cereal, fruit, milk and yogurt on the kitchen table. Remembering Geoff's choice of steak and potato for dinner last night, she wouldn't be surprised if he preferred a bacon-and-eggs breakfast, but this was what she had on hand.

She should probably wait until after they had eaten before broaching the proposition that had hit her with such staggering force. He would need the energy, she thought wryly, when he bolted in panic from the crazy woman he had awakened with this morning. Could she really expect him to react any other way?

But did she have any logical choice but to ask him? How else would she know if it was even within the realm of possibility?

Geoff came into the kitchen then, and her heart tripped—whether from nerves or a surge of raw attraction, she couldn't have said. Probably both. He looked younger, somehow, with his hair still damp and his white shirt open at the collar and rolled up on his arms. He hadn't shaved, and the scruffiness only added to that sexy-young-rebel look that was so deceptive for the button-down businessman she suspected him to be.

She swallowed and rubbed her palms on her khaki shorts, suddenly feeling every day of the five years she had on him. Though she didn't usually have issues with vanity—no more than any other woman, anyway—she found herself hoping those extra years weren't immediately visible.

Geoff smiled, only adding to his extraordinary appeal. He brushed a light kiss across her mouth. "Looks good."

"I hope you like fruit and cereal."

He chuckled as he glanced at the table. "Oh, yeah. The food looks good, too."

A silly blush warmed her cheeks. Heaven only knew when she had last blushed that way, she thought with a shake of her head. She had to get herself under control. If a simple flirtatious compliment turned her into a giggling schoolgirl, how could she begin to talk to him about certain much more serious—yet undeniably awkward—matters?

"Sit down. I'll pour the coffee," she said, turning toward the coffeemaker. And then she stopped and whacked her forehead with the palm of her hand. "Oh, darn. I forgot. You don't drink coffee."

He laughed and patted her shoulder on his way to the table. "No. But feel free to have some yourself."

"I drink too much coffee, anyway. It's my one

vice." And because that sounded like such a foolish statement after last night, she blushed again.

She tried to hide it by turning her back to him and opening the refrigerator door. "I have juice. Apple or grape. Eric loves fruit juices, so I try to keep plenty on hand."

Stop babbling, Cecilia. She really did have to get a stronger grip on her emotions this morning.

"Apple juice sounds good. Thanks."

They finally settled at the table—she with her coffee, he with a glass of apple juice.

"Looks like it's going to be a nice day," Geoff remarked, nodding toward the window over the sink. His light tone indicated that he was trying to start a casual conversation. Maybe he sensed that she was tense this morning. If so, he probably attributed it to morning-after jitters, maybe after-the-fact misgivings.

He had no clue, of course, what was really making her so nervous. If he did, he couldn't have looked so calm.

Trying to put on a show of being completely relaxed, she responded to his comments in kind and toyed with her breakfast, making a pretense of enjoying it. Actually, her throat was so tight she thought she might choke if she tried to eat much.

When he had finished his meal, Geoff pushed his plate aside and laced his hands on the table. "Okay," he said, leveling a look at her. "What's wrong? Second thoughts about last night? Regrets?"

"No. As uncharacteristic as it was for me, I don't regret anything that happened last night."

His smile turned gentle. "I never doubted that the night was hardly routine for you."

And now she worried that he was misinterpreting her admission that she wasn't exactly a party girl. "It isn't as if I'm making too big a deal out of what happened between us last night," she assured him hastily. "I mean, I am a thirty-seven-year-old divorcee."

He reached out to cover her hand with his. "It *was* a big deal, Cecilia. One of the best nights I've had in a very long time."

She laced her fingers with his. "For me, too."

"So what's the problem?"

"I'm sort of afraid of ruining everything now."

"Not possible."

"You haven't heard what I want to ask you yet."

Though she saw a touch of wariness enter his eyes—poor guy, she couldn't blame him, considering how awkwardly she was handling this—he managed to keep his expression politely encouraging. "What do you want to ask?"

She drew her hand from his and reached for her coffee cup, relieved to see that it was steady when she lifted it to her lips. After a bracing sip, she began, "I'm thirty-seven years old."

"Yes, so you said."

"I was married once. A long time ago. It didn't work out."

"You mentioned that, too." He sipped his juice, eyeing her curiously over the rim of his glass.

She was really making a hash of this. Clearing her throat, she tried again. "The thing is, I've never had an overwhelming urge to remarry. I love my home and my work and I would rather be contentedly single than unhappily married."

''We agree on that point. My family's been nagging me to marry for years, but to be honest, I simply have no desire to do so at this point. I just don't want to be responsible for anyone else's happiness and welfare.'' He still looked a bit wary as he clearly spelled out his position.

Realizing the direction his thoughts were taking, she laughed a little and held up her hands. ''Relax, Geoff. I'm not asking you to marry me. As pleasant as our night together was, it hasn't turned me into a starry-eyed romantic with foolish dreams of happily ever after.''

Though he looked marginally relieved, he seemed contradictorily perturbed with her choice of adjectives. ''Pleasant?''

''*Very* pleasant,'' she clarified a bit impatiently. She had almost forgotten to make allowances for the male ego during this impromptu proposition.

''So what is this request you have of me?''

She drew a deep breath, then blurted the words before she lost her nerve. ''I want you to help me make a baby.''

Chapter Four

Geoff wondered for a moment if an unexpected night of passion had somehow damaged his hearing. Surely Cecilia hadn't just said what he thought she had said. "You want me to do *what?*"

He watched as she moistened her lips with the tip of her tongue, a gesture that seemed uncharacteristically nervous from this woman who had appeared so self-confident and composed the night before.

"I want a child," she repeated. "I want to be a mother. And since my prospects of that are getting slimmer as time passes, I'm ready to do whatever is necessary to make that dream come true for me."

She locked her slender, capable hands on the table in front of her as she spoke, her gleaming white knuckles giving further evidence of the tension she was trying not to show.

Geoff shook his head. Wasn't this his luck? He had been telling himself that last night had been a rare gift—unplanned, uncalculated, uncomplicated. A brief foray into the wild side for wild Billy Bingham's straitlaced and compulsively responsible nephew. And now it turned out that the woman he thought he'd charmed into bed had her own reasons for ending up there.

"You're looking at me as though I've grown another head," Cecilia said ruefully. "I know this has taken you by surprise."

"You could say that again."

Her fingers twisted even more tightly. "The thing is, this subject has been on my mind a lot lately. Every day I deliver other women's babies, and every day I wonder whether I'll ever have one of my own. I would be a good mother. I'm mature and responsible and patient. I practically raised Eric, since my mother worked all the time, so I know what I would be getting into. The preschool day-care center at the clinic would give me a chance to see my child often during the day. I'm ready physically, emotionally and financially—as much as I can be, anyway. I don't want to waste any more time."

"So have you, um, thought about adoption?" he asked, still trying to assimilate what she wanted of him.

"I've considered adoption, but it's still rather difficult for a single working woman to be approved, and private adoptions can be terribly expensive. Besides, I would really love to have a child of my own. The artificial insemination process is, again, so expensive that it would be hard for me to afford it. The best option for me seems to be the old-fashioned method.''

"With me." It sounded so improbable when he said it that he couldn't help wondering again if he had completely misinterpreted her request.

Her cheeks were a bit pink, but she held her head high. "It occurred to me this morning that it wouldn't hurt to ask you. After all, we got along very well last night, and we've already taken the biggest step."

His frown deepened. "I used protection last night."

"Yes, I know. Um, do you always carry a couple of packets with you?"

Now it was his turn to be self-conscious. "I got them out of my car. After you invited me in. Just in case we—"

Hell, this conversation wasn't about defending *his* motives. "So when you asked me in last night, you were planning to—"

"No!" Her eyes wide, she cut him off sharply. "I didn't plan anything that happened last night. I thought I would make an appearance at the reception and then come home—alone—for a grilled cheese sandwich and an evening with a mystery novel. When you asked me to dinner, I expected a nice meal and then a polite good-evening in the parking lot. And when I invited you in, it was an impulse, based on the lovely time we'd had at Miranda's. You said you didn't want the evening to end—and I didn't, either."

He couldn't help being skeptical, despite the ring of sincerity in her voice. Having been raised in a wealthy and influential family, he had learned long ago that all too many people had hidden motives when it came to their dealings with him.

She began to frown, as if his thoughts had been apparent to her. "I'm really making a mess of this, and I apologize for that. I know it seems outrageous of me to even suggest something like this after knowing you such a short time. As I said, it's something I've been considering, and when this opportunity popped up—well, it just seemed like I would be foolish not to at least ask if you would consider helping me out."

He stood and walked to the coffeemaker, where he slipped a mug off the nearby holder and filled it to the brim with the dark, hot brew.

"I thought you didn't like coffee."

"I seem to need the caffeine jolt. I'm having a little trouble thinking clearly this morning. And, besides, it's too early for scotch."

She waited until he had returned to his seat and had taken a bracing sip of the coffee—which wasn't bad, considering—before she spoke again. "You probably think I have ulterior motives in making this request of you. That's a natural assumption, of course. I should have expected—anyway, I know a man with your connections has to be careful. I want to assure you that I've been entirely straightforward about my goals.

"I want a child, but that's all. I would be willing to sign anything you draw up waiving any claim to money from you for any reason. I am fully prepared to support my child both financially and emotionally. I can't say the child will be raised with a lot of extra money, but I can provide all the necessities and an occasional luxury without any help from anyone else.

To be honest, I prefer it that way at this stage in my life.''

He set his coffee mug on the table with a thud. ''So, basically, what you want is for me to create a baby with you, then simply go away and leave you alone to raise the kid with no input from me.''

She shifted restlessly in her chair. ''You make it sound rather cold when you put it that way.''

''You think?'' He knew he sounded curt, but what could she expect after blindsiding him this way?

Looking defensive, Cecilia glared across the table at him. ''You needn't make it sound as though I've insulted you by asking you to be the father of my child.''

''Maybe I think you have.''

''Just the opposite, I would say. You're intelligent, attractive, healthy—all qualities I would be pleased for my child to inherit.''

''And yet you think I'm the kind of man who would make a child and then walk away from it without a backward glance.''

''It isn't as if there aren't plenty of other illegitimate Binghams living in Merlyn County,'' she shot back.

Geoff watched through narrowed eyes as Cecilia's face paled in response to the echo of her own words, then went bright pink. ''None of those children are mine,'' he said after letting her squirm for a few long moments.

''I'm sorry,'' she said stiffly. Placing both hands flat on the table, she pushed herself to her feet. ''This was obviously a huge mistake. Please forget I said anything. And don't feel obligated to call me again after you leave, not even for courtesy's sake. Let's just pretend our date ended before breakfast.''

He rose more slowly, keeping his eyes on her face, which she was doing her best to hide behind a silky curtain of dark hair. ''So you've changed your mind about trying to have a child?''

''I didn't say that. I'm just going to have to explore other options.''

Other options being another man to father the baby she apparently wanted so desperately that she'd been willing to risk this embarrassment with him, he realized abruptly. And it said something about his state of mind that thinking of her approaching another man—any other man—with her offer bothered him almost as badly as the fact that she had thought he would go along with her scheme.

''Look, Cecilia, I can tell how important this is to you. Maybe there's something I can do to help. I mean, you work in a place that specializes in fertility treatments. Sure, artificial insemination can get expensive, especially if it takes a few times to produce results, but I'm sure something can be worked out. Installment payments, maybe. Or a bank loan. In fact, I can—''

''No!'' She tossed her hair back to give him a glittering look. ''No,'' she repeated more quietly. ''Thank you. I can handle this.''

Which meant another man again, he thought with a scowl.

''This is really getting awkward. Please, Geoff, just forget it. Actually, I have a lot of things to do today, and I wouldn't want to keep you away from the things I'm sure you have to do. Besides, my brother pops in sometimes on weekends to help with a few maintenance chores, and it would be very uncomfortable for me if he were to find you here.''

In other words, here's your hat.

Hustling him out the door, she babbled nervously the whole time about what a lovely evening she'd had, and how much she had enjoyed getting to know him and maybe they would see each other in passing at the hospital sometime. Unspoken was the addition, ''But not if I see you first.''

Moments later Geoff stood on her front stoop staring blankly at the door that had just been firmly closed in his face. It appeared his impromptu date with Cecilia Mendoza had just come to an abrupt, strange and seemingly permanent end.

All in all, it had been one of the more humiliating episodes of Cecilia's life. No wonder Geoff had looked at her as if she had lost her mind. She must have sounded like an idiot.

She should have expected him to react as he had. Undoubtedly he now thought of her as a desperate, aging woman looking to secure a comfortable retirement by duping a wealthy young man into fathering her child. He probably hadn't believed her for a moment when she'd said she wanted nothing more from him.

To top it off, she had inadvertently insulted him by comparing him to his notoriously womanizing grandfather and uncle, even though all the talk she had ever heard about the Binghams indicated that Geoff and his father were both complete straight-arrows.

If she were absolutely honest, she would have to

admit that she rather admired Geoff for his instinctive reaction to that comparison. She had become so cynical about men that she had automatically assumed it wouldn't particularly bother him to have no part in an illegitimate child's life.

That was certainly the way his elder relatives had behaved. Rumor had it that Gerald and Billy Bingham had fathered kids all across the county without staying around to be responsible for them. She knew of at least four of Billy Bingham's offspring, her future sister-in-law among them, and Billy hadn't bothered to marry any of the mothers or to be directly involved in his children's lives.

The men in her own family certainly hadn't set any higher example. Eric's father hadn't stayed around to help raise his son. In fact, Reuben had shown no interest in his child at all. He had left before Eric was born and had never made any effort to get back in touch.

Her own father had loved his child, but had continued to pursue his daredevil sports until he'd gotten himself killed. Only within the last few years had Cecilia acknowledged the grief-stricken anger at him that she had carried since. A resentment she was sure her mother had shared, though they had never spoken of it.

As for the man Cecilia had married, it had turned out that he didn't really want children at all, despite what he'd said to the contrary. A child would have interfered with his own immature need to always be the center of attention.

So maybe Geoff was different from so many of the other men Cecilia had known. He had made it apparent that he wasn't interested in being married right now, but she thought he'd also made it clear that if and when he had children, he intended to do so the traditional way. It would certainly be expected of him by his family—and hadn't he told her that he always did what his family expected of him?

She sighed. Oh, well, it hadn't hurt to ask. She would never hear from him again, of course, but she hadn't expected that, anyway. She would spend the rest of the weekend cleaning her house, doing some reading—and giving serious consideration to her plans for motherhood.

Maybe Geoff had given her an idea, after all. Maybe she could swing a loan, mortgage the house, perhaps, to finance fertility treatments. It was definitely a possibility.

She wasn't sure she could ever get up her nerve to make that embarrassing proposition to another man— not that she knew any other reasonable prospects at the moment, anyway.

Too bad about Geoff, though, she thought with another long, regretful sigh.

Geoff sat on his sofa with his guitar across his lap and stared down at the strings, wondering why he had suddenly forgotten how to play. He'd been turning to the guitar in times of stress since he was fourteen, taking pleasure in old Beatles tunes that had been written before he was born. Songs his mother had loved.

Today he couldn't even remember the tunes. His mind was still filled with the echo of Cecilia's voice as she had asked him to father her child.

Despite all the suspicions that had poured through his mind—all the precautions that had been programmed into him almost from birth—he had finally come to the conclusion that she had been completely honest with him. She'd wanted nothing more than what she had asked of him. He simply couldn't believe anything else of her.

She wanted a baby. He supposed he could understand that. Most women did seem to want children, and he imagined Cecilia's biological clock was clamoring pretty loudly at this point. But did she really think he was the kind of man who could walk away from his own kid? A man like—

Like his uncle Billy.

Grimacing, he set the guitar aside and stood to pace. How many times during his late teens and early twenties had he secretly wished he could be more like his father's wild and footloose brother? While Geoff had been bound by smothering rules and regulations, spending his weeknights studying and his weekends working in the family businesses to "build his character," Uncle Billy had been bouncing from one party to another, one beautiful woman to the next.

Billy had tried occasionally to draw his nephew into the fun, urging Geoff to rebel occasionally, to slip away and forget about family expectations, at least temporarily. But, as much as he might have been privately tempted, Geoff had been too tightly bound by the sense of obligation that had been impressed upon him from birth.

He had done everything that was asked of him—and more—without complaint, watching his uncle's exploits with a vague wistfulness. When Billy died piloting one of his expensive airplanes, the family had sadly pointed out how wise Geoff was not to have been influenced by his uncle's wild ways. Hadn't they always predicted that Billy would come to a bad end? While Geoff had taken their lessons to heart, he had grieved for the man who had always been the happy clown among the somber, respectable Binghams.

While his beloved mother had lived, he'd have cut off his arms before he caused her any disappointment or distress. After her death, he'd felt he owed it to his father and sister to cause them no more worry or grief. He had rebelled in only two relatively minor ways since: the big motorcycle he kept in the condo garage, to the great disapproval of both his father and his grandmother; and his refusal to go along with their efforts at finding him a suitable match.

He thought again of the longing look in Cecilia's eyes when she had spoken of the child she wanted so badly. He wished there was something he could do to help her. His awkward offer of financial assistance certainly hadn't impressed her.

It wasn't hard to guess what his uncle would have done. Billy would have happily provided his services in Cecilia's bed until her objective was accomplished, and then he would have moved on to the next adventure without a backward glance.

He knew what his father would say about Cecilia's request. Ron would accuse Geoff of making an error in judgment getting intimately involved with a clinic employee in the first place, even for one night. After another lecture about the expectations of upholding the Bingham name, Ron would remind him about the number of people who would take advantage of him.

He would question the motives of a woman of limited financial means who just happened to choose a man with money to sire her child. And he would predict disaster if Geoff were foolish enough to fall for her scheme.

Was there any way he could combine Billy's daring and Ron's caution and still find a way to help out a new friend?

Cecilia was digging weeds out of the herb garden in her tiny backyard when she heard someone call her name. She swiped the back of one dirty hand across her perspiration-beaded forehead and twisted to look over her shoulder.

"Oh, hi, Brandy," she said to the teenager standing on the other side of the low wooden fence that separated Cecilia's yard from the one next door. "How's it going?"

"Okay. Can I come over?"

"Sure." Cecilia rose, grimacing when her leg and back muscles protested being in a kneeling position for too long. Apparently she had needed a break anyway. "Want some lemonade?"

"Sounds good."

"I'll get us some. We can drink it out here."

Brandy was waiting for her when she came back outside carrying a tray that held two plastic tumblers of lemonade and a plate of oatmeal-raisin cookies. The sixteen-year-old redhead sat in one of the four wrought-iron spring chairs grouped around a small round wrought-iron table. The stone patio on which the furniture was arranged was surrounded by plantings and potted plants and shaded by several large old trees.

Eric had built that little patio for her a couple of years ago, and they had both enjoyed it since. She often ate outside on pretty days.

After handing Brandy her lemonade, Cecilia settled into one of the spring chairs, looking around in satisfaction. There were so many things she liked about her little house, and this tidy backyard was one of her favorite features. It had been a wonderful place to play as a child, to daydream and swing during the daytime, and to gaze at the stars at night.

"Your yard looks good," Brandy said, her gaze following Cecilia's.

"Thank you." Turning her attention back to her guest, Cecilia suddenly frowned. "What happened to your face?"

Brandy shrugged, and one strap of her pink tank top fell off her skinny shoulder. Her shaggy red hair tumbled into her face, which was why Cecilia hadn't immediately noticed the purple bruise that darkened the girl's left cheek. The smattering of acne that marked the girl's skin looked even less attractive in combination with the bruise.

Brandy's green-gold eyes shifted, and she appeared to study the plate of cookies very closely before making her selection. "Played a game of catch and didn't get my glove up fast enough. Caught the ball with my face."

"Ouch. That must have hurt."

"Nah. No big deal. Who was that guy who was here this morning?"

Cecilia swallowed. "Um...guy?" she parroted, stalling for a moment.

"Yeah. I heard a car door and I looked out my window and I saw him drive away in that totally sweet car. It wasn't your brother, was it? He didn't get a new car?"

"No," Cecilia admitted. "He's a man I know through my work."

It was true enough, and all she intended to say to a curious sixteen-year-old. "I haven't seen you around much during the past few weeks. Busy summer?"

"Yeah, kind of. What with my job at South Junction Burgers and my boyfriend and all."

Ah, yes. The boyfriend. Cecilia had seen him a time or two with Brandy, and she hadn't been particularly impressed by the swaggering, wannabe tough guy. From a few brief conversations, she knew Brandy's grandmother worried about the intensity of the relationship, but Maxine Campbell was still being rather hesitant in setting boundaries for the girl.

Another example of a child whose father hadn't bothered to hang around, Brandy had moved in with her grandparents a year ago when her mother's substance abuse had become a problem that could no longer be ignored. Cecilia had befriended the girl then, and she genuinely liked Brandy, but she knew there had been some adolescent problems in the Campbell household.

"I haven't seen your friend Lizzie all summer," she commented, thinking of the chubby, giggly blonde who had been Brandy's shadow for months. "Is she out of town?"

Brandy shrugged again. "Nah. She's kind of pi—er, mad at me."

"I'm sorry to hear that."

"She's all, like, jealous or something because I've been too busy to spend much time with her lately. Jeez, I don't know how she thinks I got enough hours to work almost every evening and spend time with Marlin and hang out with her, too. I told her maybe we could go shop or something when Marlin plays basketball at the Y on Monday nights, but she's all, like, that's not enough. Just as well, I guess. Marlin don't really like her, anyway. He says she's too all about herself—and obviously he's right."

Although Cecilia knew how intense teenage romances could be, it still concerned her that Brandy seemed to be obsessed with Marlin to the point of dropping her friends. She would hate to see the girl make the same mistake she had—rushing into an ill-fated teenage marriage, ending up a disillusioned young divorcée.

"You know, boyfriends come and go while you're young, but your friendships can last a lifetime," she said, almost cringing at the triteness of the remark. "Maybe you should…"

"Now you sound like Grandma," Brandy cut in irritably. "She's always trying to tell me I spend too much time with Marlin. Well, I don't care. Me and Marlin are going to get married as soon as I graduate. There won't be any more boyfriends for me."

"Oh, Brandy, I'm sure you think that now, but you're still too young to know what will happen in the next two or three years. Don't try to grow up too fast."

"I'm old enough to know what I want," Brandy insisted, sounding as though this was a familiar, and increasingly frustrating, argument for her. "No offense, Cecilia, but I don't want to end up like you, living alone and working all the time. It's okay for you, but I want a man and a family of my own. And I'm not going to let anyone come between me and Marlin, because he's the only one who really understands me."

Flinching at the words that cut much too close to her own vulnerabilities, Cecilia tried to concentrate on the danger signs hidden in Brandy's words. Something was worrying her about Brandy, and even though the girl was openly defiant of anyone who tried to give her advice, Cecilia couldn't help feeling as if she needed to say more.

But before she could think of the words, Brandy looked beyond her. "Looks like *your* boyfriend's back," she murmured.

It took Cecilia a moment to figure out what the girl had just said. And then, with her heart in her throat, she looked quickly around to find Geoff Bingham standing on the stone pathway that led around the side of the house, gazing at her over the chain-link fence.

Chapter Five

"Hi," Geoff said, his eyes locked with Cecilia's, his expression hard for her to interpret.

Hoping he hadn't overheard Brandy's comments, Cecilia set her lemonade glass on the table. "Um…hi, yourself."

"I thought I heard voices back here. Is this a bad time?"

"No. I was just having a visit with my neighbor. Brandy Campbell, this is my, er, friend, Geoff Bingham."

"Nice to meet you, Brandy."

Brandy jumped to her feet, automatically hitching at the low-riding denim shorts that hung precariously on her bony hips. "I gotta go, anyway. Marlin will be here pretty soon. We're going to the arcade so I can watch him play video games."

Which didn't sound particularly entertaining to Cecilia, but she was too busy wondering why Geoff had come back to spend much time contemplating Brandy's choice of entertainment. "Um, yeah. See you later."

"'Kay." Brandy checked Geoff out quite thoroughly as she sauntered past him. "'Bye."

"'Bye, yourself." He watched her head for the house next door, then turned back to Cecilia. "I hope I didn't interrupt anything important."

All too aware of her yard-work dishevelment, Cecilia resisted an urge to reach up and smooth her unraveling braid. "No. I was just taking a break from weeding. Would you like some lemonade?"

"Yeah. Sure."

Standing and picking up her tray, she nodded toward the back door. "Let's go inside."

Whatever he had come to say, she thought it best not to discuss it out here, where there was the possibility of being overheard. He moved to open the door for her, and it was impossible for her to walk past him without her shoulder brushing him. Even that brief, rather impersonal contact made her pulse rate increase.

So much for convincing herself that she had already put last night behind her.

Setting the tray on the counter, she heard Geoff close the back door. She wasn't able to look at him just yet, so she busied herself by opening a cabinet and reaching for a glass.

Geoff rested a hand on her arm. "Cecilia?"

"Yes?"

"I don't really want any lemonade."

"You don't like lemonade, either?" she asked, referring to his comment about the coffee the night before.

"I like lemonade. I just don't want any right now."

She closed the cabinet and turned to face him, his hand still resting on her arm. "I didn't expect you to come back today."

"I didn't expect to be back," he admitted.

"So why...?"

"I wanted to talk to you."

She felt her cheeks warm. "If you've come to discuss the proposition I made to you earlier, it isn't necessary. I told you to forget about it."

"Have *you* forgotten about it?"

"If you mean, have I realized that I made a mistake discussing it with you, the answer is yes. It was an impulse that I should have stopped to think about before blurting it out to you. If I had, I would have realized what a crazy idea it was."

"So you aren't going to try to...well, to conceive, after all?"

She lifted her chin. "I didn't say that. If I'm ever going to have a child, I'll have to do something about it very soon."

"With someone else."

Her cheeks burned hotter. "Despite my indiscretion this morning, my reproductive choices are personal. I would rather not discuss them with you any further."

He eyed her moodily. "Do you have someone else in mind?"

"Geoff!"

"Well, do you?"

Jerking her arm away from his grasp, she whirled

to pace. ''No. But I'm not giving up on my dream.
If it means mortgaging my house for treatments or
hanging out at singles bars or whatever I have to do,
I will have a child. I can't accept that I won't ever
be a mother.''

She wasn't sure what, exactly, she had said to bring
a scowl to his face and an edge to his voice. ''It
sounds as if you've made up your mind.''

''I have.''

He nodded. ''Then so have I.''

She studied him in confusion. ''What do you
mean?''

''I've decided to help you.''

There was something decidedly surreal about
calmly discussing the making of a child as if it were
just another business transaction, Cecilia thought a
very short while later. She and Geoff had moved to
the living room to continue their conversation. As she
had led him in, she had tried to hide the fact that her
knees had gone suddenly weak when he had announced so abruptly and unexpectedly that he had
decided to help her conceive a child. Now she wondered if he had referred to his earlier offer to help her
financially with the process of artificial insemination
or in vitro fertilization, rather than a more, um, active
role in the conception.

''When you said you've decided to help me, what
exactly did you mean?'' she asked, deciding that the
best way to clear up the confusion was simply to ask.

Geoff had settled onto the end of her couch closest
to the chair she had chosen for herself. Clean shaven
and casually dressed in a green polo shirt and pressed

khakis, he looked relaxed enough sitting there facing her, but she could see the faint lines of strain around the corners of his mouth, indicating he wasn't quite as casual about all this as he seemed.

He leaned slightly toward her as he spoke. "I've done a lot of thinking about what you said this morning. You said you aren't sure you want to marry at this stage in your life—and I understand that completely. As I told you, I've been under a lot of pressure to get married, and it doesn't interest me now, either. I just don't want to make myself answerable to another adult when it already seems like I spend my whole life trying to please too many people."

"That makes perfect sense to me. I've felt that way many times."

He nodded. "So you understand that my first reaction when you made your request this morning was negative. It seemed as though you were asking me to take on the responsibility for two more people—a child and its mother."

That brought her chin up. "I thought I made it clear that I take care of myself—just as I intend to take care of my child."

Geoff held up a hand in a conciliatory gesture. "I said it seemed that way at first. The more I thought about it, the more I decided I believed you when you said you had no ulterior motives."

She wasn't sure if she was pleased that he had come to that conclusion or still rather insulted that he'd ever doubted her. "You decided correctly."

"I'm prepared to help you get what you want, but not quite the way you outlined it this morning. I have a couple of conditions of my own."

She frowned warily. "I told you this morning that I'm prepared to sign anything you want. Have your attorneys draw something up, if you like. I don't want a penny of your—"

He shook his head and held up a hand again, looking impatient this time. "Just listen, okay?"

Clenching her hands in her lap, she nodded.

Geoff rested his forearms on his thighs as he leaned even closer to her, his expression grave. "Women aren't the only ones with biological clocks, you know. I wouldn't mind having a kid, either, preferably while I'm still young enough to throw a ball or go for a hike or teach my child to swim and ride a bike. And since I'm in no hurry to marry—and I don't see that changing in the foreseeable future—your idea sounds like a solution for both of us."

She could feel the tension mounting inside her as she considered the ramifications of his words.

"I don't want to make a child and then walk away from it, in fact, there's no way I'm going to do that. But what I would consider is a joint custody arrangement. We have a child, and we raise it together...sort of."

"That isn't—" she cleared her throat "—that isn't at all what I had in mind."

"I know. You were hoping to raise this child completely on your own. I think I've made it clear I'm not interested in that sort of arrangement. But think about it, Cecilia. I'm offering the best of both worlds. A father for your child—an active father, not just a sperm donor. Financial assistance. Someone to turn to when you need to talk about a problem."

"But I—"

"I wouldn't interfere with your personal life," he assured her quickly. "And I'm still going to be on the road a lot—that's the nature of my job—so you'll still have the bulk of the day-to-day responsibilities of child rearing. But I can promise that any time you need me—any time my child needs me—I'll move heaven and earth to be there."

Her fingers knotted, causing her knuckles to ache with the strain. "I don't know, Geoff. What you're suggesting means you and I would be involved, at least in some ways, for a long time."

"Eighteen years, at a minimum," he agreed evenly, and she noticed that his left hand went to the back of his neck in the gesture she already recognized signaled his tension. This wasn't easy for him, either, she realized. "When you think about it, it's not really much different from divorced parents who come to an amicable agreement about joint custody. It's actually better for us, because we'd skip the ugly fighting and breaking-up phases and go straight to the point where we work out a plan that's best for our child."

Our child. The words seemed to echo in the room, and for the first time it felt as though they were discussing more than a hypothetical possibility. This was real, she thought dazedly—or it could be. He was offering her exactly what she wanted, though certainly with a few complications she hadn't expected. And now she wondered if she had let impulse lead her into making a huge mistake.

"Well?" Geoff prompted, studying her face as if trying to read her thoughts.

She gazed back at him and suddenly found herself

picturing a little boy with Geoff's clear hazel eyes and thick, brown hair. A little boy who would probably love to have a dad—just as Eric would have given anything as a boy to have a father in his life, she realized abruptly.

Maybe she had been selfish in wanting to deny her baby a father. And yet she doubted that Geoff would be as actively involved as he rashly predicted in the excitement of the moment. Once the novelty of the idea wore off and the reality of diapers and colic and tantrums and daily worries set in, Geoff would probably disappear—as had the men in her past. As he'd said himself, he traveled a lot, anyway, so she wouldn't have to worry about him being too visible in her life. And she would have the baby she had dreamed of for so long.

She couldn't deny that Geoff's genes were certainly arranged in a spectacular pattern, she thought, eyeing him with a silent sigh.

"This is the only deal I can offer," Geoff said when she continued to stare at him. "We compromise—or we forget the whole thing."

Finding her voice, she asked quietly, "You really think I would be a good mother? The kind of mother you would want to raise your child?"

For the first time since he'd appeared on her pathway, he smiled. "I have no doubt that you will be a wonderful mother. You helped raised Eric, didn't you? He certainly turned out okay."

Geoff seemed to know every one of her weaknesses. A compliment about her little brother was guaranteed to work with her every time.

Maybe she should be worried that he seemed to

know her so well after so short a time. But the truth was she felt strangely the same way about him. For some reason they understood each other. Had from the beginning. Their friendship was new, but it had gotten off to a wonderful start. And suddenly it didn't seem like such a bad idea to be friends with her child's father.

"I, um, suppose you want to think about this a bit longer. Before we actually commit to anything, I mean," she said.

"I'll be in town for about another month, and then I'll have to take off on business again. I'm not sure when I'll be back. So unless you want to wait until my next trip home—"

"I'm tired of waiting," Cecilia said with feeling. "It feels like I've been waiting forever."

Geoff stood and walked slowly toward her chair. "You realize, of course, that it sometimes takes a while to get results with this sort of thing."

She rose to gaze up at him. "Yes, I'm aware of that."

"I tend to be an overachiever when I'm working toward a goal. Single-minded, almost."

"I've been accused of being the same," she admitted, tilting her head back as he moved even closer, so that he towered over her.

He lifted a hand to her cheek, his thumb tracing the line of her jaw. "Just so you'll know, I'm willing to give this my best effort. As often as possible—as many times as it takes."

Her smile felt a bit shaky. Uncharacteristically shy. "That's very noble of you."

His other hand rose so that he was cupping her face

between his palms. He leaned so close to her that she could feel his breath ruffling her hair when he murmured, "I just wanted to reassure you that you've picked the right guy for the job."

Before she could tell him that she had already reached that conclusion for herself, his mouth was on hers.

The heavy wooden door to Geoff's condominium loomed in front of Cecilia later that evening. Because of the impressive security in the building, he knew she had arrived, but she hesitated before ringing the bell. It felt like her last chance to change her mind and make a dash for sanity, but when it came right down to it, she just didn't want to go.

She had been perfectly willing for Geoff to simply stay at her place earlier. She would have prepared a meal for them—spaghetti, maybe, or a quick casserole—followed by…well, by the first step in their get-Cecilia-pregnant campaign. But Geoff had vetoed that plan, insisting, to her surprise, that he would cook for her, instead. At his place.

He had explained that he wanted this night to be special. Cecilia had wondered then, as she wondered now, if he had really been giving her time to rethink her decision. To change her mind, if she wanted. By having her come to his place, he was giving her the option to leave whenever she wanted.

She smoothed her hands down the sides of the mid-calf-length black knit skirt she had paired with a sleeveless top in a purple-and-black geometric print. Her freshly washed hair was pinned up into a neat roll, and she had applied her makeup very carefully.

Quite a contrast to her disheveled and rather grubby appearance earlier, she decided in satisfaction.

He'd caught her off guard earlier, but this time she was prepared. No more stammering or blushing. Her intention now was to act like the mature, competent, confident woman her carefully groomed exterior proclaimed her to be. She was a woman with a plan, and she would not allow last-minute qualms to get in her way.

Squaring her shoulders and holding her chin high, she reached out to ring his bell with a proudly steady hand.

Geoff opened the door. One look at him standing there in a crisp white shirt and beautifully tailored dark slacks made her mouth go dry. And now her hands were trembling. So much for calm and composure, she thought with a silent sigh of exasperation.

He gave her a smile that made her heart race even faster. ''You look beautiful.''

With an inward struggle for composure, she said, ''Thank you.''

Stepping back, he motioned her inside. ''Come in. Dinner's almost ready.''

She looked around with discreet curiosity as she entered his home. She had never visited one of these exclusive condominiums before. From the spectacular mountain view to the obviously professionally decorated interior, the condo spoke of money and social status. It was a very different setting from her modest little middle-class house, but she still preferred her own home.

There was something rather cold and impersonal about Geoff's condo. It felt like...well, like a hotel room, she decided, glancing at a vase full of neatly arranged, hothouse flowers.

Because etiquette demanded it, she said, "This is very nice."

"Thanks. But to be honest, I've had very little to do with it. I'm not here enough to put much of myself into the place."

Glancing again around the cream-on-cream room with its elegant touches of gleaming woods, polished brass and green-veined marble, she asked curiously, "What would you change if you could put yourself into it?"

Geoff raised his eyebrows as if he'd never actually asked himself that question before. "I, um, well, I guess it would look a bit more like your place."

She was tempted to roll her eyes. "You would fill your fancy condo with secondhand furniture and handmade decorations?"

"I would try to make it look like a home," he corrected her, "and not just a designer's showcase."

She smiled at him. "I'm pretty sure that was a compliment."

"It was meant to be."

A timer buzzed in another room. Geoff turned in that direction. "I'd better take care of that."

"Can I help?"

"You can keep me company while I finish up."

She followed him into a black granite and stainless steel kitchen that looked as though it belonged in a magazine dedicated to gourmet cuisine. This room, at least, showed signs of use. Pots simmered on the six-burner stove, utensils were scattered on the counters, and something had been spilled on the stone floor.

Geoff spotted the spill at the same time she did. He grabbed a paper towel and bent to wipe it up. "I tend to be sort of messy when I cook," he said as he straightened.

"Whatever you've prepared, it smells heavenly."

He opened the oven door. "Rosemary chicken, rice with almonds and peas, orange-glazed carrots and crusty wheat rolls. I bought the rolls, by the way. They're the heat-and-serve kind."

"Everything sounds delicious. Are you sure there's nothing I can do?"

"You can grab that basket of rolls and follow me."

He led her into a small but elegant dining room, and once again she was struck by how much trouble he had gone to for her this evening. Candles burned on the table and on an antique sideboard she'd have given her eyeteeth for. Mounds of fresh flowers had been arranged in crystal bowls. The table was perfectly set with snowy linens, white china and gleaming silver.

A housekeeper? she wondered. Or had he done all of this himself?

Geoff moved to hold her chair for her, and she was romantic enough to be touched by his efforts. It was a scene set for seduction, made even more special because it hadn't been necessary. The outcome of this evening was pretty much a sure thing—and would have been even if their meal had consisted of burgers from a fast-food drive-through.

Geoff seemed completely comfortable during their meal. The perfect host, charming, witty and relaxed. Oddly enough, Cecilia grew more nervous as the evening progressed. Because he had gone to the trouble of providing brandied fruits for dessert, she accepted a dish, but she could eat only a few bites.

"Is something wrong, Cecilia?"

She looked up from her barely touched fruit to give Geoff a smile that she hoped looked more natural than it felt. "Not at all. I'm just getting full. Dinner was excellent, by the way. You're a very good cook."

"Thank you. My repertoire is a bit limited, but my mother made sure I knew my way around a kitchen. Even though we had cooks and housekeepers while I was growing up, Mom said everyone should be able to prepare a meal, sew on a button and run a vacuum cleaner."

"Your mother was a very practical woman."

"Yes, she was. It was important to her that Mari and I would not grow up spoiled, even if we were fortunate enough to have a privileged upbringing. She was determined that we would understand exactly how lucky we were, so we spent every Christmas helping her with her charity projects. Working in soup kitchens, delivering food baskets and toys to homes that were little more than drafty shacks, visiting nursing homes and hospital wards."

"We had a tradition in our family, too," Cecilia mused. "We each contributed money from our allowances and paychecks to donate to the homeless shelter each Christmas. We usually had a rather modest holiday, ourselves, but Mother wanted us to understand that there were always people who had less."

"Your mother must have worked very hard to support you and your brother."

"Too hard," Cecilia admitted with a sigh. "It seemed as if she was always working. After my father died so young and Eric's worthless father took off before Eric was even born, Mother decided she couldn't depend on anyone ever again. Except me, of course. By the time I was twelve, I was responsible for Eric's care. I fed him, bathed him, dressed him, read him his bedtime stories, tucked him into bed. I'm sure that's why I still tend to be overly maternal with him, giving him entirely too much advice and too many unsolicited opinions."

"I have a feeling he is more appreciative of your concern for him than resentful."

"Most of the time, yes. He lets me know when I cross the line into meddling—not that I always take the hint," she added with a faint smile.

"Who took care of him while you were in school?"

"A series of baby-sitters and day-care providers. The best care Mother could arrange for him."

"I want to assure you that you'll never have to work that hard to support our child. I'll make sure of that."

Cecilia set her dessert fork down abruptly, making no further pretense at eating. "I told you, I'm not after your money. That has absolutely nothing to do with my reasons for asking you to help me."

He already had a hand up to appease her. "I wasn't implying anything about your motives. I simply wanted to remind you again that I'm not anything like Eric's father. I won't leave you to shoulder the financial burdens alone, and my child won't have to grow up with the knowledge that his father had no interest in him."

Cecilia shifted restlessly in her chair. "I suppose I

have been a bit selfish in that respect. I know the ideal
situation is to provide two caring parents for a child.
But I've already explained that the clinic day-care
center will let me be more visible and active than my
mother was able to be with Eric. And the child will
have Eric and Hannah and their baby for extended
family. An uncle, an aunt and a playmate.''

''Now he—or she—will also have a devoted father.
Another aunt. A grandfather and a great-grandmother.
Family he'll share with Eric's child, of course, since
Hannah is my cousin. It's a bit convoluted, but I believe we can make this work. I know it isn't what you
had in mind originally, but surely you can see it's
better for everyone involved, especially the child.''

''Once I get past my knee-jerk reluctance to share
my baby with anyone, I do see the advantages,'' she
admitted.

His smile could almost be described as sweet—if
such a flowery adjective could be applied to a man
so undeniably virile and masculine. ''I won't ever try
to take your child away from you, Cecilia. We're partners in this adventure, not competitors. And *I'll* sign
anything you like to set your mind at ease about
that.''

She gave a self-conscious little laugh. ''Stop reading my mind. I suppose it does concern me a bit that
our social and financial circumstances are so different.
It gives you advantages that I can't help but be nervous about.''

''I won't abuse your trust in me,'' he vowed again.
''I'm sure we'll have some disagreements about child
rearing—we're both the independent and assertive
types, or we wouldn't be so successful in our respec-

tive careers—but we'll work everything out to our mutual satisfaction. I can negotiate and make compromises when I'm working toward something important.''

"So can I."

He held out a hand to her. "Then we're agreed. Our baby is going to have two parents who will always put his—or her—interests ahead of their own.''

She laid her hand in his. "So you think we're doing the right thing?''

His fingers closing warmly around hers, he smiled a bit crookedly this time. "Beats the hell out of me. I just know it feels right now.''

"You could sound a little more confident.''

He chuckled. "I don't have a crystal ball, Cecilia. We don't even know that we can have a child together. All I know is that I'll be the best father I can be and that you'll make a great mother. If you're still certain this is what you want—''

"It is," she cut in quickly. "It's all I've wanted for a very long time.''

"Then let's go for it.''

She inhaled deeply, then released the breath in a long sigh. The decision had been made. There was no going back now. She could hardly believe that she was finally taking steps to make sure her most cherished lifelong dream could come true.

Chapter Six

Cecilia might have worried that nerves would interfere with their lovemaking this time. After all, it was different when there was a goal other than simple pleasure at stake. If Geoff had been at all tense or awkward, she would have understood and forgiven him.

Instead, he seduced her as if it were the first time again. As if nothing mattered more to him than her pleasure. As if there were nowhere in the world he would rather be, nothing he would rather be doing than making love with her on this summer night.

His kisses went from gentle to passionate, his movements from practiced to impetuous. He was an amazing lover—generous, thorough, patient. Even when he was obviously driven by an overwhelming need for climax, he made sure she found her own release before he gave in to his.

Lying sated and exhausted beside him afterward, she wondered at his control. Was everything he did always so calculated? Even his seemingly impulsive decision to help her conceive had come after a day of thought and consideration, during which she would bet he had deliberated every angle and potential repercussion. This was very likely the most rebellious and nonconformist action he had ever taken, and even in that he had made it clear that he intended to be fully responsible for and committed to the child they were making.

"Geoff?"

The arm behind her tightened a bit as he drew her more snugly against him. "Mmm?"

He sounded half-asleep. As lazy and satisfied as she was. She couldn't help smiling a little before asking, "What will your family think about this?"

He lifted his head from the pillow, casting a glance downward at their nude, intimately entwined bodies. "About *this*?"

She giggled. "I meant about you having a child with me. If you intend to claim the child as your own—"

"Which I do."

She nodded. "So what will they think about you having a baby with Eric's sister? One of their employees. A woman who, by the way, is considerably older than you."

"You keep mentioning your age. Does it really bother you that you're thirty-seven and I'm thirty-two? It's not that great a difference, you know. And they are, after all, only numbers."

"I know. But I can't help but think your family won't approve."

"I won't lie to you, Cecilia, they're going to think I've lost my mind. At first. As I've told you, they want me to get married. Start a family in the traditional way. They don't understand why I won't let them fix me up with a nice girl with the right connections. They'll understand my wanting a child— after all, I've been raised to appreciate the value of family—but they won't believe I'm going about it the right way."

It was what she had expected, of course, but still…

"Don't worry about it," he said, then brushed a kiss across her forehead. "They'll come around. If there's one thing my grandmother loves, it's babies. And Dad will be tickled to be a grandfather, even if it isn't exactly the way he had envisioned. To be honest, he has begun to wonder aloud if he's ever going to have grandkids."

"Still—"

"Cecilia. It's my life. My choice. For once my family will just have to accept that. And they will."

Once again she thought she heard the faintest trace of rebellion in his voice, as if this was the first time in a very long while that he had risked openly defying his family. As if he rather enjoyed the prospect.

"And if you do find that nice girl with the 'right' connections that you want to marry?" she couldn't help asking, keeping her voice carefully neutral. "What do you expect her to think about you having a child?"

"I have no interest in getting married, can't think of anyone I would want to marry, but if it should ever happen that I meet someone I feel that way about, she'll just have to accept the decisions I made before I met her. The same holds true for you, you know. You may well meet someone, yourself...."

She was shaking her head before he even finished speaking. "Not likely. I'm too...well, I won't say old, but too set in my ways to be interested in marriage now. I like making my own decisions. Handling my own problems. Setting my own priorities."

"Some of that will change when you have a child."

"True. But I'll still be in charge of my own household."

"Your marriage must have been a very unhappy one."

She hadn't realized she had revealed quite so much. "Yes, it was. But I'm not bitter or angry. Just realistic."

He shifted to lean over her, his expression both grave and tender at the same time. "Any man who would make you unhappy—who was not respectful of your needs and your dreams, who tried to break your valiant and independent spirit, who didn't value you for the strong, capable woman you are—was not worth the time you wasted with him."

She grinned and slid her arms around his neck. "You know what? You are absolutely right."

A gleam of satisfaction and renewed desire warmed his beautiful eyes. "I usually am," he murmured as he lowered his head to hers.

Cecilia refused to spend the night. It was quite late when Geoff escorted her to his door. "Are you sure you won't let me follow you home?"

"I'll be fine," she assured him. "I've got the kind of job that often takes me out in the middle of the night, remember?"

"You could call me when you get there—just so I'll know you're safe."

She wrinkled her nose. "Don't start practicing your fathering skills on me, Geoff. I'm quite capable of taking care of myself."

He laughed and looped an arm around her shoulders for a quick hug. "I've never met anyone quite as stubbornly independent as you—with the possible exception of my sister. So will we see each other tomorrow?"

"I have plans for lunch, but I'm free tomorrow evening. Unless you have other plans?"

He shook his head. "How about taking in a movie? I haven't seen any of the big summer blockbusters this year. It's been forever since I've been to a theater for some popcorn and a couple of hours of mindless entertainment."

She chuckled. "Actually, I did sort of want to see that new superhero film. Eric loved it, but his taste in film is sometimes questionable, so it could be awful."

"Let's go find out, shall we? I have to admit, I was hoping to see that one, too. Have I mentioned I had a serious comic book addiction as a kid?"

"No, you didn't."

"My mother finally sent me to a twelve-step program to break me of the habit. She called it school. I learned to appreciate other types of literature, but I kept a stash of comics hidden under my mattress."

"No girlie magazines?"

"I eventually worked my way up to those," he confessed, looking not the least embarrassed. "I outgrew them both about the time I was able to grow a mustache. But I still have a soft spot for the comics. So I'd like to see the movie, even though it will probably make a mess of the original story, as those films so often do."

"Then, it's a date." And then, because that sounded too cozy for the relationship they had agreed upon, she said quickly, "Well, not a date, exactly, but a plan. I mean…"

"It's a date," Geoff interrupted firmly and pressed a kiss on her still-parted lips before opening his door. "Drive carefully, Cecilia. I'll call you tomorrow to arrange a time."

She drove home in a haze of bemusement that her life had changed so drastically in the past twenty-four hours. And her state of mind was so mixed up that she wasn't sure which was harder to believe—that she had a date with Geoff Bingham or that she could even now be carrying his child.

"Are you sure there's nothing I can fix for you while I'm here, CeCe? Didn't you say you've got a squeaky hinge in the bathroom that's been driving you nuts?"

Cecilia smiled lovingly across the dining table at her brother, who, along with his fiancée, had joined her for Sunday lunch. Eric had called her CeCe from the time he had learned to speak, and it was certainly too late to try to change that habit now. She wouldn't be at all surprised if his child called her "Aunt

CeCe.'' Oh, well, she supposed she could live with that as long as Eric looked this happy, she mused, watching the adoring look he gave Hannah.

"I took care of the squeaky hinge myself. A little shot of oil was all it needed."

Eric frowned. "What about the step that was coming loose on the back porch?"

"I found a hammer and a nail, and I fixed it myself. I have paid attention to a few of your maintenance lessons, you know."

Hannah laughed. "Looks as if you aren't quite as indispensable as you think, Eric. Your sister is perfectly capable of looking after herself."

"She always has been," Eric admitted. "I just like to delude myself occasionally into thinking that she needs me."

"I will always need you," Cecilia assured him. "Just not necessarily as an on-call handyman. You have your own life now, and it's about to get very busy," she added with a meaningful glance at Hannah's rapidly expanding tummy.

Resting a hand on the bulge, Hannah sighed a little. "None too soon, as far as I'm concerned."

Cecilia smiled. "Between the wedding and childbirth classes and setting up your household, the next eight weeks are going to pass more quickly than you can imagine. It won't be long at all before you're holding that baby in your arms."

And maybe, if she was lucky, she would hold a baby of her own before this time next year, she thought wistfully.

"So, CeCe, Hannah and I were thinking about going to the park this evening to hear the bluegrass band that's scheduled to perform. Would you like to join us?''

''Thank you, but I have other plans,'' she said, busying herself by scooping another spoonful of peas onto his plate. ''Here, have some more of these. You never eat enough vegetables. You'll have to keep an eye on that, Hannah. I swear he would live on junk food and candy if we let him.''

Eric cleared his throat. ''I am an adult.''

''So eat like one.''

Hannah laughed again.

''What plans do you have this evening?'' Eric asked, turning the conversation back to Cecilia.

She should have known her ploy to change the subject wouldn't have worked. Eric was like a dog with a juicy bone when his curiosity was aroused. ''I'm going to a movie.''

''Alone?''

''Eric,'' Hannah murmured, ''your sister would tell you her plans if she wanted you to know them.''

''Hey, if she can monitor my diet, I can ask a few questions about her life,'' he retorted. ''Who're you going to the movie with, CeCe?''

She sighed. Might as well answer him, she told herself in resignation. The way gossip spread through this town, he would hear it eventually, anyway. ''Geoff Bingham.''

Hannah's eyes widened. Eric looked startled. ''Geoff Bingham? You mean it was true that you two had dinner together after the reception Friday evening? I thought that was just a case of mistaken identity.''

"How could you possibly have heard about that already?"

"Oh, you know. Someone saw you and told someone else who told— But that isn't important. I didn't even believe it."

"Well, it's true," Cecilia admitted. "Geoff was hungry at the reception, and so was I, so we had dinner together at Melinda's."

"And tonight you're seeing a movie together."

"Yes. Neither of us had plans for the evening, so…"

No way was she telling her brother what she and Geoff were really up to. There would be time enough for that when—*if,* she corrected herself cautiously— it became a fait accompli. After it was too late for Eric to try to change her mind, which she had no doubt that he would do.

"What's going on?" Eric asked bluntly. "You're dating a Bingham? Aren't you the one who warned me about getting involved with one of them?"

"For heaven's sake, Eric." Feeling her cheeks warm, Cecilia cast a quick, apologetic look at Hannah, who looked more embarrassed than offended. "You know I'm delighted that you're marrying Hannah."

"Of course. Once you got to know her you saw how wonderful she is. And, of course, she wasn't really raised a Bingham, since she was a teenager when she found out that Billy Bingham was her father. But Geoff—he's a Bingham to his neatly polished wing-tips. I wouldn't have thought he was your type at all."

"I'm not marrying him, Eric, I'm simply taking in

a movie with him," she replied. Among other things, she silently added.

Eric didn't look particularly reassured. "But—"

"Goodness, the baby certainly is active this afternoon," Hannah said suddenly, pressing her hand to her tummy again. "Feels as if there's a jazzercise class taking place in there."

To Cecilia's great relief, and obviously exactly as Hannah had intended, that drew Eric's attention away from his sister's social life. He had to reach over to feel the baby's movements, which led to more talk about prenatal care and delivery preparations, which led again to the plans for the simple wedding that would take place very soon.

Cecilia knew her brother had allowed himself to be distracted. He hadn't forgotten her impending date with Geoff. He confirmed that suspicion as he and Hannah prepared to walk out the front door a little while later.

"Watch yourself with Bingham this evening, you hear?" he warned his sister after kissing her cheek. "The guy practically oozes charm. He's the family politician and has a way of getting anything he wants."

"Don't worry. I know exactly what Geoff is like," Cecilia replied lightly. And since Geoff's wants at the moment were closely aligned with her own, she hoped sincerely that Eric was right about Geoff always getting his way.

Still looking a bit fretful, Eric allowed Hannah to tow him away, leaving Cecilia to get ready for another interesting evening with Geoff.

* * *

Geoff found himself approaching Cecilia's front door with a spring in his step that made him feel strangely like an eager teenager. After a rather tense day, an evening in Cecilia's warm, pleasant and undemanding company sounded awfully nice.

And speaking of teenagers…

He raised a hand in greeting to the redhead who had just hurried out of the house next door in response to an imperative horn blast from a long-haired boy in a battered brown pickup truck spotted with patches of gray primer. The girl quickly returned Geoff's wave, then jumped into the truck, which was peeling away from the curb almost before she could close her door.

So much for the social niceties of modern teenage dating, Geoff thought with a glance at the small bouquet of flowers in his hand.

Cecilia seemed delighted by the offering. "These weren't necessary, but thank you," she said, burying her face in the fragrant blooms for a moment.

Grinning, Geoff motioned toward the house next door. "Guess I could have just pulled up to the curb and blown the horn. Seemed to work for your neighbor."

Cecilia sighed and shook her head. "Marlin refuses to get out of his truck when he picks Brandy up for their dates. She says it's because her grandparents don't like him, but that behavior certainly doesn't endear him to them."

"Is he the one who gave her the shiner?"

Cecilia seemed startled by the question. "Her bruised cheek, you mean? She told me she did that while playing a game of catch. She didn't get her glove up fast enough.''

"Mmm.'' It hadn't looked like a softball injury to Geoff, but he supposed Cecilia knew what was going on next door better than he did. "Ready for the movie?''

"Just let me put these in water,'' she said, turning quickly with the flowers. "You can wait in the living room. I'll be right back.''

Closing the front door behind him, he caught her arm to detain her for a moment. Before she could ask what he was doing, he planted a long, firm kiss on her lips.

"That was just to hold me over until later,'' he murmured when he released her.

Her expression held just a hint of reproach. "You are a fresh one, Mr. Bingham.''

"Want me to stop?''

With a smile brilliant enough to make him blink, she murmured, "Don't you dare.''

He was grinning when she turned to walk away, adding a seductive swish of her hips to her movements. He really liked this woman.

There were only two movie theaters in the immediate area—downtown Binghamton's old-style movie house, the Bijou, which offered a selection of new and classic family films, and a more modern four-screen metroplex in an adjoining town. Geoff took Cecilia to the latter, since that was where the superhero film was playing.

There was a good-size crowd at the theater on this nice summer evening, and once again there were a few who obviously recognized both Cecilia and Geoff. Once again they exchanged nods of greeting without getting entangled in conversation. Cecilia couldn't imagine what the gossips were making of her second public appearance with Geoff, but she wouldn't worry about that for now.

They shared a buttered popcorn during the movie, their hands brushing with almost suspicious frequency as they reached for popcorn at the same time. Funny how Geoff always seemed to be hungry at the same time she was, she thought with a glance at his blandly innocent profile.

When the popcorn was gone, he abandoned subterfuge and simply took her hand in his, entwining their fingers in a loose, warm clasp. He sat closely enough that their knees brushed, and even through the fabric of his jeans and her chinos, she felt the impact of the contact.

It was a good thing the action-packed and plot-thin film required little thought or attention, Cecilia decided. Geoff had her so addled that she couldn't even remember the names of the characters.

Even though they had both agreed their relationship was temporary and based on a specific purpose that had little to do with romance, he still seemed to enjoy these nice gestures. Flowers, dates, holding hands. A charming man, this Geoff Bingham—the family politician, she reminded herself.

Still, she couldn't help but enjoy his attentions. What woman wouldn't?

As the film came to an end—finally—Geoff lifted their hands to his lips, brushing a kiss across her knuckles. "My place or yours?" he murmured into her ear.

"Mine's a bit closer," she whispered back, as anxious as he seemed to be to be out of the public eye.

The credits rolled and the theater lights came up, and Geoff pulled Cecilia to her feet. "Let's see how fast we can get there."

It sounded like a good plan to her.

Chapter Seven

Because of the usual rush for the exits, it took Cecilia and Geoff a few minutes to get into the aisle. They had almost reached the back of the rapidly emptying theater when Cecilia noticed a very pregnant young woman still seated about halfway down one of the rows of high-backed seats. The woman was doubled over, apparently in pain, while an anxious-looking young man sat beside her, talking to her.

Cecilia had to stop. Stepping around one of the theater employees who had entered to pick up trash between screenings, she walked sideways down the aisle to get closer to the woman while Geoff waited curiously behind her.

"Is everything okay?" she asked the woman, who was moaning quietly in a way that had Cecilia's midwifery instincts kicking into overtime.

The young man, whom she would guess to be about twenty-two, looked around quickly. "Katie—my girlfriend—isn't feeling good. Maybe she shouldn't have eaten so much candy during the movie."

Cecilia bent down to check the pregnant woman—girl, she corrected herself when the extremely pale Katie looked up at her. This mother-to-be couldn't be older than seventeen. "Where does it hurt?"

Katie's brown eyes swam in tears. "Everywhere."

"When is your due date?"

"Next month. The fifteenth."

Three weeks away, Cecilia figured rapidly. "My name is Cecilia Mendoza, and I'm a nurse-midwife. Tell me about the pain. Is it steady or does it come in waves?"

Looking relieved to have an expert at hand, Katie whispered, "It hurts all the time, but it comes in waves, too. They start in my back and move around to the front. I...I don't think it was the candy."

"I don't think so, either," Cecilia murmured, watching as Katie stiffened against another sharp pain. "How long has this been going on?"

"About...about an hour. Maybe a little more, wasn't it, Rusty?"

"I told her we could leave if she didn't feel good, but she wanted to see the end of the movie," Rusty said defensively. "She said it might be a long time before we'd get a chance to come to another movie because of the baby and all."

Geoff leaned closer to Cecilia. "Should I call an ambulance?"

Because Katie had already doubled into another contraction, Cecilia nodded. "Tell them to hurry."

Geoff already had his cell phone to his ear when Cecilia turned back to Rusty. "Let's see if we can get her to the aisle. I can't get to her now to see what's happening."

Bobbing his sandy head in assent, Rusty got on one side of Katie, grabbed her arm, and yanked upward. Wincing, Cecilia placed a hand on his shoulder. "Gently."

"Oh. Yeah, sure. So you think she's like in labor or something?"

Katie let out a moan that ended as a near wail.

"I think it's a definite possibility," Cecilia replied.

"Oh, man."

Staggering to her feet, Katie took a few halting steps, then cried out again. "It really hurts, Miss Mendoza."

They were attracting attention now, as the theater employees stopped their tasks to gawk at them. Geoff moved forward. "Here, let me help."

Without further hesitation, he bent to sweep Katie into his arms. "Where do you want her?" he asked, not even appearing to strain beneath the weight of the heavily pregnant young woman.

At least this theater was pretty much empty for the moment, she thought—and could stay that way until after the emergency crew had arrived, she decided abruptly. "Let's just lay her in the aisle. Randy, sit cross-legged so we can rest her head in your lap. Geoff, let the manager know what's going on so they can clear a path for the emergency crew. Were you given an estimated time of arrival?"

"There was a multicar wreck on the mountain highway on the other side of the county," he replied as he helped arrange Katie as comfortably as possible. "The dispatcher said there could be a delay. Want me to get my car? We could probably get her to the clinic faster than the ambulance."

Cecilia bit back a grumble. Poverty-stricken Merlyn County was a victim of difficult financial times, and emergency services had suffered in the resulting cutbacks. Having a state-of-the-art medical facility was a blessing, but they had to get the patients there first, she thought with familiar frustration.

She watched as Katie bowed upward, a ragged cry escaping her taut lips. "I don't think that's a good idea. I'd rather deliver a baby here, if necessary, than in the tiny back seat of your car."

"D-deliver?" Rusty stammered. "You mean the baby's coming *now?*"

"I won't know until I check." She spoke calmly, reassuringly. "Geoff, maybe you'd clear the employees out of here on your way to notify the manager? I think Katie would be more comfortable without spectators. And see if you can find some towels—paper, if necessary," she added as a dark, wet stain spread rapidly across the front of Katie's light-colored maternity jeans.

Geoff met her eyes for a moment, mutely acknowledging the seriousness of the situation, and then he efficiently took charge of the scene.

The theater manager, a stocky, auburn-haired woman in her forties with kind eyes and a brusque manner, appeared with a blanket and a couple of towels. "I heard what's happening. I keep these in my office for emergencies. I'm holding the showing of the next film until the ambulance arrives.''

''Thank you.'' Cecilia draped the blanket over Katie, who was weeping quietly now between racking, near-constant contractions. ''Things seem to be moving very quickly. I'm a midwife, so I can handle things in here if you'll take care of everything out there.''

''No problem.'' The manager leaned over Katie. ''You listen to this lady, honey. She'll help you till the ambulance gets here.''

Writhing and panting, Katie still managed to nod in response to the manager's maternal advice. ''Yes, ma'am.''

After dashing through a curious milling crowd to the nearest bathroom, where she did the best she could to wash up with plenty of soap and warm water, Cecilia hurried back into the theater to find Katie still moaning, Rusty looking even queasier, and Geoff doing his best to keep both of them from panicking.

''You're being very brave, Katie,'' Cecilia encouraged, reaching beneath the modestly draped blanket. ''I'm going to take these wet clothes off, okay? If you can lift up for me, I'll arrange these towels beneath you—the best we can do by way of a sheet for you to lie on. We'll keep the blanket draped over you so no one will see anything except me.''

Katie was arching again, her hands flailing. ''I don't care. Just make it stop hurting so bad.''

''Lift your knees, sweetie. I'm going to do a quick check to see how far along you are.''

''Oh, man,'' Rusty muttered, and he had gone so

pale and glassy-eyed that Cecilia wondered how long it would be before he hit the floor in a faint.

Geoff, on the other hand, was perfectly calm. He knelt beside Katie and took her restless hands in his, looking directly into her eyes.

"Katie, do you remember that my name is Geoff?" he said, speaking loudly enough to be heard over her moans. When she nodded, he continued, "Cecilia delivers babies every day, so she knows exactly what she's doing. I want you to hold on to me and squeeze my hands if it helps when you feel pain. Rusty's going to wipe your face with the damp paper towel I just handed him, aren't you, Rusty?"

"Uh, yeah." Apparently grateful to have something useful to do, Rusty wielded the towel with more enthusiasm than finesse.

"Oh, my goodness," Cecilia said a few moments later. "This baby is in a real hurry to get here."

She suspected that Katie had been in labor longer than the hour or hour and a half she had admitted. Had the girl really been so eager to see the film, which Cecilia hadn't even considered very good? Or had she been too young and inexperienced to recognize the signs as something more than the usual discomforts of late pregnancy?

"When was your last prenatal checkup, Katie?"

Katie was too busy to answer, her face contorted as she squeezed Geoff's hands hard enough to make him wince a little. Cecilia gave him a quick smile of encouragement before looking to Rusty for an answer.

Rusty cleared his throat, his eyes darting nervously. "It's been a few months. We don't have insurance, see, and we couldn't afford to go running to the doctor all the time. Everything was fine last time she went, so we thought it would be okay to wait."

Cecilia bit back an exasperated sigh. Money couldn't have been the only obstacle to prenatal care, since the clinic provided income-based services when lack of insurance was a factor. More likely they lacked transportation or time or simply the incentive to make the appointments. She had seen all too many deliveries complicated by lack of adequate prenatal care.

At least Katie seemed to be reasonably healthy. Her pulse was steady and strong, and she was already completely effaced and almost fully dilated, so the delivery should be relatively uncomplicated. Cecilia saw no signs of drug abuse or other health concerns— but, damn, she wished that ambulance would get here. Delivery in a theater aisle was bad enough. But doing so with absolutely no medical supplies available was even more difficult.

"Aah," Katie cried out, her entire body contracting in pain. "It hurts, Miss Mendoza. And I need to push."

Rusty blanched as pale as his white tennis shoes and began to sway. Cecilia gave Geoff a look before turning back to her duties.

"Rusty," she heard Geoff say a bit sharply. "Stay with us, you hear? Katie needs you to be strong now."

"I'll—" Rusty cleared his squeaky voice, speaking a bit more clearly next time. "I'll be strong," he promised. "I won't let you down, Katie."

"Good man," Geoff murmured, and then he smiled down at Katie again. "Just concentrate on holding that baby in your arms, okay? You've got a lot of help here."

It didn't surprise Cecilia in the least that both Rusty and Katie seemed to find reassurance in Geoff's steady, confident manner. To be honest, she felt much the same way.

"You were absolutely amazing this evening." Geoff gave Cecilia a dazzling smile as he spoke, making her heart beat a little faster in reaction.

"I was simply doing my job," she demurred.

"No, it was more than that. You kept those kids calm, even when they were on the verge of panic. And considering the circumstances, you delivered that baby as easily as if you had all the clinic facilities at your disposal."

Self-conscious about the praise Geoff had been heaping on her for the past hour, she tucked a strand of hair behind her ear. "It helped that the ambulance arrived before the baby did."

"By all of ten minutes."

She gave a brief, tired laugh. "True. But at least I had some professional assistance at the end."

Snuggled beside her on her couch, Geoff kissed her forehead. "I still thought you were amazing."

She rested her head on his shoulder. "You were pretty cool and collected yourself. The way you talked so reassuringly to Katie and Rusty. The way you kept her focused on you when the contractions were so strong. You sounded like a professional doula—a trained birthing coach."

Geoff chuckled. Lifting his right hand, he flexed

the fingers a few times. "Let me tell you, that girl's got a grip. My fingers are still numb."

"You're a very handy man to have around in an emergency."

Dropping his hand to his knee, he turned his attention back to her. "So, do things like that happen to you often? How many babies have you delivered unexpectedly like that?"

"Counting this one?"

"Yes."

"One."

His eyebrows shot up in surprise. "No kidding? That was the first time?"

"Contrary to what you see on television, babies aren't often born in theaters or elevators or cabs or airplanes. I mean, sure, it happens—obviously—and I've known colleagues who made emergency deliveries before, but that was a first for me."

He pressed another kiss on her forehead. "You handled it beautifully."

"Thank you. But as I've already said, it's my job. I simply did what I'm trained to do. Even though I have to confess that I don't want to have to work under those circumstances again anytime soon. A dirty theater floor—no antiseptics or hot water or even a pair of gloves...."

She shuddered. No, she didn't want to go through that again. She was grateful that the paramedics had arrived before the baby, being on hand with medical supplies and IVs to take charge of Katie's care while Cecilia had wrapped the screaming, apparently healthy baby boy in a sterile blanket. Somehow Rusty had survived the ordeal without passing out, a feat for which Geoff had praised him generously.

Rather than being annoyed by the delay of their movie, the crowd in the lobby had broken into applause when Katie and the baby had been wheeled to the waiting ambulance. So much for making a discreet exit, Cecilia had thought as she and Geoff had made their way to his car through a barrage of questions and congratulations.

They'd only arrived at her house a short while earlier, collapsing onto the couch as soon as they'd walked in. Their simple movie date had turned into an exhausting and emotionally draining event, Cecilia mused, and they both needed a little time to recharge.

Geoff seemed to still be preoccupied with their adventure. "Do all newborn babies look like that? All gooey and wrinkled and sort of purple?"

"Pretty much."

"Oh. I thought maybe their kid was just... homely."

Amused, Cecilia tilted her head back to smile at him. "Actually, he was a rather pretty baby."

"If you say so."

"He looked like his mother, I think."

"Fortunate, considering that his father was pretty goofy looking."

She felt almost guilty for laughing. "You're terrible."

"Maybe I wasn't seeing him at his best."

"Obviously you weren't."

Settling more comfortably into the cushions, Geoff tightened his arm around Cecilia's shoulders. "That baby's got a tough road ahead of him. His parents are just kids themselves. Chances are slim they'll stay together—or that his mother will even finish high school.''

''Children born to teenage mothers are much more likely to live in poverty, less likely to have health insurance, less likely to get an adequate education, and more likely to become teenage parents themselves. But...well, maybe things will work out for Rusty and Katie and their son. I hope so, anyway.''

Geoff seemed to think about that for a while. And then he sighed and said, ''It's been a long day.''

''Did you work today?''

''Worse. I had lunch with my dad and my sister.''

Raising her eyebrows, she kicked off her shoes and tucked her feet on the couch behind her. ''I thought you got along well with your family.''

''Oh, we get along. Everyone was just sort of grumpy today.''

''Grumpy?''

''Yeah. Mari couldn't get her mind away from work. All she could talk about was the lawsuit—''

''That is worrisome,'' Cecilia murmured. ''Poor Milla doesn't deserve that hassle.''

''It's hardly good for the clinic, either. It's bad enough that all the rumors about the biomed center are threatening our endowments from local investors. Just talking about fertility research—not to mention such controversial subjects as stem-cell research— makes some people so skittish they're afraid to even be mentioned in the same context. This lawsuit couldn't have come at a worse time.''

''There's always a frivolous lawsuit of some sort against a hospital, especially when obstetrics are involved. It's why so many doctors and hospitals have gotten out of the delivery business. Not that I have to explain the daunting rise in malpractice insurance to you."

"Hardly. That's the sort of business discussion that's been taking place in my family since I was old enough to join them at the dinner table."

"Mari's under a great deal of pressure in her job. She's allowed an occasional grumpy day." As for herself, Cecilia was perfectly content being a valued employee of the corporation rather than trying to fill an executive position, as her brother dreamed about doing. Her passion was delivering babies, not crunching numbers or studying spreadsheets or developing long-term business plans.

"Yeah, but there's still something more nagging at Mari. I heard her talking to Dad about a growing drug problem in the county. One that's affecting the clinic."

Cecilia nodded glumly. "It's something we're all becoming concerned about. Controlled substances—especially powerful and addictive painkillers such as Orcadol—have become increasingly available through the black market here in the county. We're seeing an increase in drug-addicted mothers and in delivery complications. The number of stillbirths is up, as well as other infant medical problems. It seems as though the crisis has been intensifying during the past few months, particularly. I know Detective Collins has been hanging around a lot lately, trying to track down where the women are getting the drugs."

"Well, that would certainly explain part of Mari's bad mood. I don't know if you're aware that she and

Bryce Collins were pretty seriously involved at one time. They broke up when he tried to force her to choose between him and the career in medicine she had always dreamed of. Fortunately, in my opinion, she chose medicine. Their breakup was unpleasant and painful, and they've hardly been on the best of terms since. In fact, Collins is pretty much a jerk about the whole thing. Even after all this time, he's still bitter and angry with Mari. If I find out he's been giving her trouble—''

''I really wouldn't know,'' Cecilia said hastily. ''I stay so busy and focused with my patients that I tend to fall out of the loop when it comes to any other department. I'm always the last to hear any official news—or even run-of-the-mill gossip—which is rather ironic, considering that my brother is a rising executive in the corporation.''

''And I'm usually in some other city, so I'm hardly in the loop myself. But I could tell that both Mari and Dad are completely preoccupied with business right now. In Dad's case I think it has something to do with the new public relations director.''

''Lillith Cunningham? I haven't met her yet, but I've heard she's nice.''

''I like her, and I know Mari's very fond of her. Dad seems to think she's a little kooky. He's very skeptical of some of her ideas. I hope he doesn't make things too difficult for her.''

''Your father seems like a very reasonable and practical man who puts the best interests of the company first.''

''You can say that again. Especially since my

mother died, my father lives and breathes Bingham Enterprises.''

''My brother was coming very close to doing the same thing. I've nagged him for ages about finding a balance between work and a personal life. Fortunately, I think Hannah and the baby will take care of that. He'll always be a dedicated employee, but now he'll have more in his life. As it should be.''

''This from the woman who just admitted she's so focused on her work she doesn't even keep up with office gossip?''

She smiled wryly. ''True. But don't forget I'm working on changing that.''

''I've hardly forgotten. And speaking of working on our little project...'' He shifted so smoothly that she found herself on her back beneath him almost before she realized his intentions.

Her weariness suddenly evaporated. Smiling up at him, she slid her arms around his neck. ''Does this mean you've recovered your energy?''

''I do believe I have.''

Pulling his mouth down to hers, she smiled against his lips. ''Strangely enough, so have I.''

The echoes of their groans of satisfaction had barely faded away when Geoff spoke into the darkness of Cecilia's bedroom a long time later. His voice was still gravelly. ''Cecilia?''

She couldn't seem to find the strength to form coherent words. ''Mmm?''

''Our baby's going to be beautiful.''

Melting into his arms, she smiled mistily into his damp shoulder. She had no doubt that Geoff was right—as he claimed to always be.

Chapter Eight

"Your suspicions were correct, Mrs. Hoover. You are definitely pregnant."

The thirty-six-year-old African-American woman sitting at the end of an exam table broke into a tearful smile in response to Cecilia's announcement. "I can't believe it. We've been trying for so long. And now to find out we've been successful…"

Her husband, a tall, lanky laborer in his early forties, looked torn between elation and trepidation. "How long till we can stop worrying about something going wrong?"

Because she knew Rebecca Hoover had suffered two miscarriages in the past, followed by several years of being unable to conceive, Cecilia understood his anxiety. "I can't offer any guarantees, of course, but everything looks good so far. I'll be working very closely with Dr. Kyle Bingham, who's an excellent pediatrician. We're going to monitor both your wife and the baby very closely, and do everything we can to make sure we deliver a healthy child in about seven months.''

She spent the next fifteen minutes outlining the plan of action for those next seven months. They talked about nutrition, vitamins and a checkup schedule, and then touched on some areas they would discuss in more detail later. By the time they left, the Hoovers seemed a bit calmer and determined to do everything within their power to make this pregnancy a successful one.

They had a tense few weeks ahead of them, Cecilia mused as she made some quick notes in Mrs. Hoover's file. As she had said, there were no guarantees, but she had a good feeling about this pregnancy. Of course, there was always a chance of complication when a first-time mother was over thirty-five.

Mrs. Hoover was a year younger than Cecilia.

Nervously moistening her lips, she closed the file. She was healthy, she assured herself. She ate well, took vitamins, exercised regularly. It was practically commonplace in some areas these days for women to wait until their late thirties and early forties to bear children. There was no reason at all to think she couldn't successfully conceive and carry a child. And considering Geoff's youth and fitness and, er, stamina, she couldn't imagine any problems in that respect.

It was sometimes still mind-boggling to her that she thought of him so casually—and so intimately. Considering that she had only met the man a few days ago, events were moving almost faster than she could comprehend. It was exciting but, to be honest, rather terrifying.

"Hey, Cecilia, I'm starving. Got time for lunch?" Vanessa had poked her head in the exam room to ask the question, big earrings swaying.

"Yeah, sure. I've got a half hour till my next appointment. Did you brown bag?"

"Tuna salad on a croissant. How about you?"

"Turkey on whole wheat." Standing, Cecilia moved toward the door. "And strawberry yogurt for dessert."

"Wanna trade? I've got chocolate-chip cookies."

Chuckling, Cecilia shook her head. "Thanks, but I'll stick with the yogurt."

She needed the calcium, a consideration she saw no need to mention since she didn't intend to go into further explanations. There would be time enough to fill Vanessa in when a pregnancy test produced a positive result. It wasn't going to be easy, since Vanessa was going to have a zillion questions, but of all Cecilia's friends and acquaintances, she knew Vanessa would be the most accepting.

Of course, Eric would support her decision, too, she assured herself. She had no doubt that he would be a loving and visible uncle for her child. But that wouldn't stop him from expressing his opinion about her decision to have a baby—specifically, Geoff Bingham's baby—without discussing the idea with him first.

Because Vanessa was pretty much in the very center of the loop when it came to workplace gossip, it shouldn't have surprised Cecilia at all when her friend said, "Tell me what's going on between you and Geoff Bingham."

They had just settled at a comfortable table for two in the atrium, a table tucked cozily into a plant-filled corner that offered some conversational privacy. Cecilia had barely had time to unwrap her sandwich. She set it down rather abruptly, not sure she could swallow just then. "What do you mean?"

"I know you had dinner with him after the reception Friday. A group of nursing students went to Melinda's that evening and they saw the two of you together. It was all over the clinic the next day."

Which explained how Eric had heard about it. It said something about Cecilia's absorption with Geoff that evening that she hadn't even seen the nursing students, though she'd recognized several other Melinda's patrons. She gave Vanessa the same vague explanation she had offered her brother. "We were both hungry, so we decided to have dinner together."

"And the movie last night?"

"You heard about that, too?"

"Honey, you delivered a baby in the movie theater, with Geoff Bingham's assistance. Did you think I *wouldn't* hear about it?"

Cecilia hadn't been quite that deeply into denial. The ambulance personnel had recognized both her and Geoff, of course, and the young parents, who had been brought to this hospital, had certainly known the names of the couple who had delivered their child.

Cecilia had been fielding questions and congratulations about the delivery all day—even being called for comment by a reporter for the local newspaper, the *Merlyn Mage*. She had given few details to the reporter, claiming client confidentiality as a hasty excuse to keep herself out of the headlines, but she knew there would be an article about the movie theater "premiere." Especially since Geoff Bingham had been involved.

"So...two dates with Geoff in one weekend. Sounds promising."

"We aren't dating, exactly."

"Oh. What *are* you doing?"

Cecilia focused very hard on the soda can in front of her. "Just hanging out. He's out of town so much he hardly knows anyone around here anymore. We enjoy each other's company because there's no real pressure. He's not trying to raise money from me—because, of course, I have none to donate—and I get a chance to spend a few pleasant evenings with someone who's only peripherally involved with the clinic, so there's very little shop talk."

Vanessa seemed downright disappointed by the practically of her friend's explanation. "Sounds pleasant. What a shame."

Cecilia smiled and shook her head, relieved that Vanessa's curiosity seemed somewhat appeased, but knowing she was going to have a lot of explaining to do eventually.

"So what's he like?"

"Geoff?" Cecilia picked up her sandwich again. "He's very nice. Charming, actually. Eric described him as the family politician, which sums him up pretty well, I suppose."

"So, you don't see a chance of anything long-term developing between you?"

Other than parenthood, no. But Cecilia said

merely, "If you're talking about marriage, all I can say is be serious. We couldn't be any more different. Besides, he'll be taking off again in a few weeks— Boston and then London, I think he said—and I have a very busy life right here."

Vanessa swallowed a bit of tuna salad sandwich, washing it down with a sip of bottled water. "Might as well take advantage of his company while he's here. How often do you have a chance to spend time with a gorgeous, rich young stud?"

"Not very often—obviously."

"So, how is it? In general, I mean."

Cecilia felt a stupid grin spread across her face. "All in all—it's great."

Vanessa sighed dramatically. "Just as I suspected. Oh, well, we old married ladies just have to be content with fantasizing."

"As if you'd rather have anyone other than George."

At the mention of her pudgy, balding and incredibly sweet husband, Vanessa giggled. "True. But that doesn't stop me from daydreaming about Denzel Washington occasionally. The occasional romantic fantasy never hurt any woman."

Cecilia supposed that was true—as long as the woman never let herself get so carried away with the daydream that she lost sight of the difference between fantasy and reality.

She was relieved when Vanessa was suddenly distracted. "Look, there's Detective Collins snooping around again. I hear he's been asking an awful lot of questions about our security protocols for controlled substances."

"The Orcadol epidemic again. He seems convinced he's going to find some leads here."

"I don't know, something about the way he's been skulking around here is starting to get my back up. Especially the way he watches Mari—as if he thinks she's deliberately interfering with his investigation or something. Just because she's too busy to be at his beck and call...."

A discussion about the drug crisis ensued, both Vanessa and Cecilia expressing concern about the toll it was taking on the young people in a community already burdened with poverty and illiteracy. By the time they had discussed several ideas for combating the problem through public awareness campaigns, they had finished their respective sandwiches and had to get back to work.

Determined to put thoughts of Geoff out of her mind—or at least, push them to the back of her thoughts—Cecilia headed for the examining rooms to visit with yet another expectant mother.

Geoff was having a bit of trouble concentrating on his work. He had no difficulty pinpointing the source of his distraction. The image of Cecilia Mendoza's pretty smile was too clear in his mind to leave him in any doubt.

Remembering the state of exhaustion he'd been in when he'd finally left her house last night, he chuckled and shook his head. He wasn't at all sure he would survive the next couple of weeks, but as the old saying went, at least he would go out with a smile on his face.

A disembodied voice came from a speaker on his

rarely used desk. "Mr. Bingham, your father is on line two."

He lifted the receiver to his ear. "Hey, Dad. What's up?"

Ron Bingham's voice was a rich baritone that suited his distinguished appearance. Still trim and fit at fifty-four, he had a full head of salt-and-pepper hair and a neatly trimmed beard and mustache. Geoff had been told for as long as he could remember that he had inherited his father's clear hazel eyes.

"I thought maybe you would like to have lunch today. Seems like you and I have hardly had a chance to see each other except in passing or in a crowd since you got into town."

There was a restless tone in Ron's voice that Geoff had been hearing more frequently lately. As Mari and Geoff became busier and more involved in their own lives, giving them less time to spend with their father, and as Ron passed over more of the responsibilities of running the family business to his offspring, Geoff wondered if Ron was feeling a bit at a loss.

Ron had always planned to retire with his beloved wife—leaving them free to travel and work in their spectacular gardens and continue their community activities. Violet's untimely death had left her grieving widower to face a future alone, and he made sure to grumble at every opportunity about the lack of grandchildren to spoil in his spare time.

Geoff had no doubt that Ron would be delighted to welcome Geoff's child into the family, especially once he recovered from the shock and skepticism. In fact, Geoff thought his father would be delighted with

Cecilia as the grandchild's mother if Ron had a chance to spend some time getting to know her.

Thinking it would have been nice if she could have joined them for lunch, Geoff said, "Sure, Dad. Lunch sounds good. I haven't had a chance to look up all day and I could use the break."

"Great. We can catch up. You can tell me when you found time to sneak into midwifery classes."

"When I did what? Oh. You heard about the theater incident."

"Yes. I heard you helped deliver a strapping baby boy. Nice job, son, but must you take business from our clinic?"

"Trust me, I'd have been delighted to send her to the clinic. But her baby apparently has a thing for action films. Kid's probably going to be a stunt man or something."

Ron laughed. "I can't wait to hear all the details. Including how you ended up being at the theater with Eric Mendoza's sister. I didn't even know you two were acquainted."

Geoff was already planning a carefully edited description of his friendship with Cecilia when he hung up the phone with a promise to meet his father in half an hour.

It was after 7:00 p.m. by the time Cecilia climbed out of her car that evening. Geoff had some sort of meeting with investors that night, so they wouldn't be seeing each other.

She should probably be looking forward to an evening alone to read and catch up on some chores around her house. She wasn't usually the type to want to spend every evening doing something or seeing people. Usually, after a long day of dealing with people at the clinic, she was perfectly content to spend a few hours in peaceful solitude.

She had just unlocked her door when a commotion from next door made her pause. She could hear Brandy's voice, shrilly raised in anger, and then the slamming of her neighbors' back door.

Another fight between Brandy and her grandparents, Cecilia thought with a sigh. Probably about Marlin again. It was Brandy's custom to sulk in her grandparents' backyard after one of those confrontations. Sometimes Cecilia went out to talk to her, trying to calm her and help her see the older generation's side of things.

Tonight she really just wanted to close herself into her own house and pretend she hadn't heard anything. After all, she had her own problems to think about. Brandy would probably rather Cecilia mind her own business, anyway.

And then, hearing an angry sob coming from the neighbors' backyard, Cecilia sighed. She would go inside and put up her purse, then see if there was anything she could do to help Brandy.

Poor Maxine, Cecilia thought as she stepped into her house. It had been difficult for the older woman to become a mother again after so many years. Especially since Brandy had been raised so haphazardly, resulting in a teenager who was bright and articulate but often rebellious and defiant.

She had just set her purse down when her telephone rang. Tempted to let the machine pick up, she decided instead to answer, just in case it was an important call. "Hello?"

"How was your day?"

Just the sound of Geoff's deep voice made some of the tension seep from her muscles. She felt a smile replace the worried frown her neighbors' problems had caused. "Long. Busy. But not bad. How was yours?"

"You just summed mine up pretty well. Long. Busy. Not bad."

"I thought you had a business thing tonight."

"Yeah. It starts at eight. I was just trying to work up some enthusiasm for the event."

"From the expression in your voice, I take it you're having a hard time doing so."

"Impossible. Can't stand a couple of the jerks I'll be dining with. But that doesn't mean I won't be on my best behavior while I try to convince them that fertility research is a worthy cause for their charitable donations. And somehow convince them that the crazy rumors about the most controversial plans Mari has on her agenda are mostly just that—rumors. I wish I could figure out who's spreading all the talk about Mari lately. We Binghams have always been targeted for gossip—some admittedly legitimate but much of it spurred by petty jealousies—but, from what little I've heard since I've been in town, it seems particularly vicious lately."

"Poor Mari. She looked so tired and worried when I saw her this afternoon. I admire your sister a great deal, Geoff. I'm sorry she's going through such a difficult time."

"I know she would appreciate your concern."

"If only Detective Collins could make some headway with his investigation so he would stop getting underfoot. At least that would be one annoyance off Mari's shoulders."

"Maybe I should have a little discussion with Detective Collins," Geoff growled.

"He is conducting an official investigation, Geoff. And there really is a serious drug problem in Merlyn County. We had another addicted pregnant woman come in today with serious medical complications. As annoyingly persistent as the detective is, I hope his efforts will pay off by cutting the supply of black market drugs that are wreaking so much havoc on our community."

"You're right," Geoff conceded reluctantly. "I shouldn't let my personal bias against Mari's ex-boyfriend interfere with necessary police business. I just wish he could do his work without causing Mari so much stress."

"Yes, so do I."

"Do you have any big plans for the evening?"

Cecilia thought of the teenager sobbing so angrily next door. The crisis that was none of her business, actually, but in which she felt obligated to get involved. "No. No big plans."

"I envy you. Actually, I'd like to be there with you. We could have a nice, quiet pizza-and-television night. Or I could bring my guitar and serenade you."

"You play guitar?"

"Contrary to what my sister might tell you, yes, I do play guitar. Mostly oldies—Beatles tunes, especially. My mother was a Beatles fanatic. Other kids heard lullabies at bedtime, I heard 'Hey, Jude.'"

''What about 'Golden Slumbers'? That's a Beatles tune that makes a very nice lullaby.''

''You're a Beatles fan?''

''Of course. They were brilliant songwriters and musicians. 'Norwegian Wood' is one of my all-time favorite melodies.''

''And one of my favorite songs to play.''

''Then you'll definitely have to play it for me.''

''A woman after my own heart. And, yes, I know,'' he added, laughing. ''You aren't after anyone's heart. But I still think you're very cool.''

She was cool, Cecilia thought as she hung up the phone a few moments later when Geoff reluctantly disconnected so he could prepare for his business meeting. It wasn't exactly a flowery or poetic compliment—and he had definitely been speaking tongue-in-cheek—but still she found herself beaming with pleasure.

She really wasn't after Geoff's heart, she assured herself, but she suspected he had already taken over a little corner of hers.

Cecilia rarely took an entire day off work, but she had scheduled Tuesday as a stay-at-home day. She had accumulated two weeks' vacation from the clinic, and she preferred taking it a day or two at a time rather than all at once. With the support of her supervisors, she had arranged her summer schedule so that she wouldn't be away from her patients for very long, yet would still have periodic breaks.

Though she had made no secret of her plans for the day, even mentioning them to Geoff, she wasn't expecting company Tuesday morning. It was with both surprise and curiosity that she heard what sounded like a motorcycle pulling into her driveway, followed by the musical peal of her doorbell.

Climbing down from a stepladder in the tiny front bedroom of her house, she automatically smoothed a hand down her hot-pink T-shirt and denim shorts. Her hair was up in a loose ponytail, and she had applied just a touch of makeup that morning—a habit too strong to break even when she planned a day at home alone. Could this be a delivery of some sort? She wasn't expecting anything, but she supposed it was possible.

Checking the security window before unlocking the door, she reached quickly for the dead bolt. "Geoff," she said a moment later. "What are you doing here?"

He smiled, and she had a moment to reflect on how unfair it was that he could look so breathtakingly handsome even with his hair all tumbled and wearing a plain gray T-shirt, faded, worn jeans and scuffed boots. "You said you were going to spend the day doing home maintenance projects. Since I didn't have any pressing business, I thought I'd give you a hand, if that's okay with you. I'd have called first, but it was sort of an impulse."

She looked behind him toward the big black-and-chrome motorcycle sitting in her driveway, a black-and-silver helmet dangling from the handlebars. "You came on that?"

"Yeah. I don't get a chance to ride it much, and it needs to be taken out occasionally to keep it purring. Maybe you want to go for a ride later? I've got a second helmet strapped to the back."

"Er, uh, thanks, but I'll probably have to wash my hair or something this afternoon."

Geoff laughed. "You sound like my family. Don't tell me you're afraid of my bike."

"I'm just not really the motorcycle type."

"Maybe you'll give me a chance to change your mind about that."

Cecilia truly doubted that was going to happen. She didn't even like the idea of Geoff careening around on that dangerous-looking machine. Pushing some painful old memories to the back of her mind, she held the door wider.

"Come in," she said, turning her back on the motorcycle. "Can I get you anything?"

"I didn't come to be entertained." He closed the door behind him. "I came to work. What's on the agenda?"

"Painting. I just finished taping off the front bedroom."

"Painting, huh?" He looked momentarily doubtful, then nodded. "Okay, lead me to it."

Planting her hands on her hips, Cecilia tilted her head to study him. "Have you ever actually painted a room before?"

"I scribbled on my bedroom wall with felt-tip markers when I was five. I thought it looked pretty good myself, but my mother wasn't as enthusiastic about it."

She couldn't help laughing. "You must have been a handful."

"Actually, I was a model child. I just indulged in small rebellions every once in a while."

"I think you still indulge in the occasional rebellion,'' she murmured, thinking of the motorcycle. Not to mention his present arrangement with her.

''Me? Nah. I'm still a model child.''

Smiling, she took his arm and tugged slightly. ''Come on, I'll show you how to paint a room the proper way.''

He put a hand on her wrist and tugged her into his arms, covering her mouth with his for a long, hungry kiss. She was practically panting by the time it ended.

''Now,'' he said, looking rather proud of himself, ''I'm ready to learn how to paint.''

After that mind-emptying kiss, Cecilia just hoped she remembered how.

Chapter Nine

Geoff followed Cecilia down her hallway at a bit of a distance. He liked watching her walk, her slender legs nicely showcased by her denim shorts. She glanced over her shoulder, caught him watching her, and gave him a look. Totally unrepentant, he grinned back at her.

The room she led him into was small, no more than ten by ten. She had taken out all the furniture, if there had been any to start with. The windows and baseboards had all been carefully outlined with blue masking tape. Plastic sheeting covered the wood floor. A bucket of paint sat in the center of the room next to a paint tray, a couple of rollers and some brushes in assorted sizes. "Looks like you know what you're doing."

"I've done a lot of painting. I can't afford to hire

someone to do something I'm perfectly capable of doing myself. Eric offered to help next weekend, but this room's so small, it won't really take long. If there's anything else you would rather be doing, I can handle this alone.''

"Nope. There's not a thing I would rather be doing than painting this room.''

"You expect me to believe that?''

"Okay, maybe there is one thing I'd rather be doing. But since you're busy in here, I suppose that will have to wait.''

He liked it when she gave him those dryly chiding looks. Which must be why he kept doing or saying things to earn them. "So what color are we painting?'' he asked before she could come up with a response to his entendre. "The same off white that's in here now?''

"No.'' She bent to remove the lid from the can, revealing the pale green paint inside.

Not quite a pastel, he decided. More of a soft, moss green. "Nice.''

"I was thinking this would be a good color for a...well, for a nursery. I like something different than the usual pinks, blues and yellows.''

"A nursery.'' Geoff reached up to massage the back of his neck as he looked around the room again from this new perspective. "Uh, yeah, green's nice.''

She seemed to be staring rather fiercely at the paint. "I know I'm getting a little ahead of myself, but the room needs to be painted, anyway, and this is a color that will work just as well in a guest room if we don't—well, if our plans don't work out. If they do,

I thought I would use light maple woods with green, butterscotch and cream accents for the nursery.''

"I would have thought you'd prefer bold, primary colors.''

"Because of the rest of my house, you mean? I admit, I do have a weakness for bold colors, but I think a nursery should be relaxing. Peaceful. And the earthy colors I have in mind should create that effect.'' She straightened abruptly. "Not that you're at all interested in my decorating plans. Really, Geoff, if you would rather go ride your motorcycle, I—''

"Cecilia.'' He rested a hand on her arm. "I'm interested. Let me help.''

Her smile was tentative. "I'd like that.''

Brushing a kiss across her lips, he drew back and glanced again around the room, picturing a maple crib against the far wall. "Where do we start?''

Cecilia picked up a paint roller and held it out to him. "That paint goes on these walls. It's a fairly simple process. Try not to get it on your clothes.''

It was fairly simple, actually. And unexpectedly pleasant. Working side by side with Cecilia, rolling paint on the walls of the room that might one day hold their child. Sharing warm smiles, talking about inconsequential matters. Stopping for the occasional stolen kiss.

It was nice. Almost…domestic, he thought, and promptly dropped the paintbrush he had been wielding for a few finishing touches. Paint splattered his jeans and his right boot, then puddled beneath the brush on the plastic sheeting. "Great.''

"Oh, my. You made a mess.'' Cecilia was obviously making an effort not to laugh at him.

"Yes, I did."

"Fortunately, the paint washes off with soap and water. I don't think it will stain your jeans if you launder them quickly."

"What about skin? Does it wash off skin with soap and water?"

"Yes. Why? Did you get paint on your—Geoff!" She stared in disbelief at the paint he had just smeared on her arm with his fingertip. "Why did you do that?"

"Call it an impulse." It must have been the same impulse that made him reach out and place a dot of paint on the tip of her very cute nose.

She reached up to slap his hand. "Have you lost your mind?"

"Sorry." He rested a hand on her cheek. Since he had just deliberately squeezed the bristles of the wet paintbrush, he left a perfect green print on her smooth skin. "Sometimes I just can't help myself."

Her chocolate-brown eyes were huge. "Um, did you just leave paint on my face?"

"Yes. And green is definitely your color."

"I cannot believe you did that."

"Well, since I got paint all over me...."

"But *I* didn't put it there."

"That's true. I suppose I owe you an apology."

"Apology accepted." She patted his cheek, leaving a wet, sticky residue behind. "You know, actually, green looks quite good on you, too."

He laughed. "Oh, lady, are you in trouble now."

"Don't even think about—"

Before she could finish the sentence, he had her on her back and on the floor, plastic sheeting crinkling beneath her. Laughing, she squirmed beneath him as he tickled her with scattered kisses and neck nuzzles. "You crazy man," she said in gasps. "This is *not* the way to paint a room."

"I think it's a great way to paint a room." He kissed her again, fancying that he could taste her sweet smile. With maybe a slight hint of paint thrown in, he thought, grinning against her lips.

The humor carried them out of the guest room/ nursery into Cecilia's bedroom. They were still playing and laughing when they stepped into the shower to wash off the paint. But as the warm water cascaded over them and their soapy hands began to wander, the laughter and banter faded.

He crowded her against the tiles, dipping his head to cover her mouth with his. She was so small, delicately boned, yet strong and capable. As comfortable climbing a ladder as she was cradling a fragile newborn in her arms. What man wouldn't want a woman like this to be the mother of his children?

Oops. Wrong word. Children implied a long-term commitment, not a one-time partnership.

Deciding not to think beyond this day—not even beyond this moment—he pulled her closer. Her arms went around him, and it pleased him that she seemed as eager to be close to him as he was to be close to her.

Their wet bodies fused. The kiss went deeper. Became almost hot enough to cause the shower water to steam around them. He lifted her against the wall, bringing her mouth within easier reach, and she wrapped her legs around him.

Humor had been completely replaced now with

hunger. His need was so great his knees were weak with it, forcing him to brace Cecilia against the shower wall.

He wanted her. Desperately. It had nothing at all to do just then with any agreements or plans they had made, but everything to do with her warm smiles, her beautiful eyes, her generous heart and dry sense of humor. The only goal he had in mind just then was mutual satisfaction. And in that quest Cecilia seemed to be a very willing partner.

"Are you sure you won't take a ride with me?"

Cecilia looked over her shoulder for a moment to answer, drawing her attention away from the last of the painting supplies she had been cleaning. "I'm absolutely certain. But promise me you'll be careful on that thing."

He smiled and leaned over to kiss the tip of her nose, which was now scrubbed free of paint. "Careful is my middle name."

"Yeah, right," she muttered, thinking of their exploits in the spare room. And in the shower. And then in her bed.

"You'd better put those clothes in the wash as soon as you get home—or have your maid or housekeeper or whoever take care of them," she added, suddenly doubting that Geoff Bingham did his own laundry. "As it is, I'm going to be scrubbing paint out of my shorts for a while—thanks to your roving hands."

He looked more proud of himself than apologetic. "If those shorts are ruined, I'll buy you another pair. Heck, I'll buy you a dozen. That will give me a chance to ruin a few more with my, er, roving hands.''

She found it hard to hold on to her smile when he talked about buying her anything. Even though she knew he was joking, reminders of the difference in their financial standing didn't strike her as particularly funny.

He stepped up behind her and kissed the back of her neck, which she had bared by pinning her damp hair into a loose roll. ''Any other chores I can help you do around here?''

She wasn't sure she would survive any more of his help. ''No, thank you. You didn't have to work today?''

Helping himself to an apple sitting in a bowl on the counter, Geoff shook his head. ''I've decided I deserve an occasional day off, myself. After all, I worked until late last night, if you count a business dinner as work, which I do.''

Cecilia wiped her hands on a paper towel and reached for the teakettle, deciding she would prepare herself a cup of herbal tea. She was making a deliberate effort to cut back on coffee, which would be good for her health—and for the child she hoped to carry. ''How did it go last night?''

''Not bad. Maybe we soothed a few concerns about some of the craziest rumors buzzing around. I've got to admit Lillith Cunningham did a good job working the crowd. Not that you'd get my dad to admit that.''

''He's still resisting her?''

''He still thinks her ideas are too impractical. She's talking now about using my grandmother as a spokeswoman for the medical facilities. He thinks that's just foolish.''

Cecilia took a moment to think about that idea. ''Actually, that's not a bad suggestion. No one would be a more knowledgeable or passionate spokesperson than Myrtle Bingham. After all, she's the one who founded the Janice Foster Memorial Midwifery Clinic and Women's Health Center. And she's obviously the perfect representative for the Myrtle Northrup Bingham School of Midwifery. Who better to talk about the need for readily available quality prenatal and delivery facilities?''

Geoff swallowed a bite of apple. ''Actually, I thought it was an idea with potential, myself. If my grandmother wants to take that on, I'd say more power to her. She's still healthy and vibrant and sharp as a tack, and I've always believed that staying active goes a long way toward keeping her that way.''

''So what's your father's objection?''

''I'm not sure, exactly. Lillith just seems to rub him the wrong way.''

''Odd. Do you want a cup of tea?''

''Do you have any juice?''

''In the fridge. Help yourself.''

Geoff opened the refrigerator and pulled out a bottle of grape juice. As he poured it into a glass, he said, ''You know, I was thinking....''

''Always a frightening prospect,'' Cecilia murmured, dunking a tea bag into a mug of boiling water.

He grinned. ''Smart alec. Anyway, what do you thinking about joining my family for dinner tomorrow night? Grandmother's having us at her house.''

Her hand froze in the process of stirring her tea.

Dinner with Geoff's family? "Thank you, but I think I'd better pass."

Leaning against the counter, he lowered his glass to look at her. "Why?"

"I just think it would be…awkward. You haven't told anyone what we're trying to do, have you?"

"No, of course not. That's strictly between us, for now. I just thought you might enjoy spending an evening with my family. I know they would enjoy your company."

"If you don't mind, I'd rather not this time. I actually have a couple of things to do tomorrow evening at the clinic. I'm helping out with a Lamaze class, and there's always a ton of paperwork to catch up on."

He didn't look particularly satisfied by her decision, but he didn't push. Probably because he knew it wouldn't have done any good. "All right. Maybe some other time before I leave town."

She didn't want to think about him leaving town. Or about spending an evening with his father, sister and grandmother, who would be bound to wonder what was going on between the midwife and their fair-haired boy.

Thoughts of Geoff didn't actually interfere with Cecilia's work on Wednesday. But they stayed very close to the front of her mind all day as she saw patient after patient in her regular, busy appointment schedule.

She'd had such a wonderful day with Geoff on Tuesday. Who would have thought she could have so much fun painting a room?

"You've dilated to two centimeters, Angie. I wouldn't be at all surprised if we see that baby by the end of the day tomorrow."

"I sure hope so. My back is killin' me."

Geoff had hung around for the remainder of Tuesday evening, and they had indulged in the pizza-and-television quiet time he claimed to have been craving. She liked veggie pizzas and he preferred pepperoni, so they'd ordered a half-and-half. She liked watching the home and garden channel and he preferred the news channels, but it turned out they both liked the history channel, so they'd found an interesting documentary there that they had both enjoyed.

Funny how well they had gotten along from the beginning, she mused. There seemed to be no silent competition between them, no need for them to have their own ways or prove they were right. That was more than she had ever accomplished with her ex-husband, who saw every disagreement as a challenge he had to win.

"I'm very proud of you for giving up cigarettes for your baby's sake, Jolene. I know it's been hard for you, but your daughter will appreciate it."

"It has been hard, but when you told me all the bad things cigarette smoke could do to my baby, I knew I had to quit. Low birth weight, developmental disorders, asthma and other respiratory complications—I couldn't live with any of those possibilities. I've known for a long time that I should quit, but my baby gave me the best reason to finally do it."

"The important thing is, you made your health and that of your unborn child's a priority, and I commend you for that. Stay strong, okay?"

"For my baby's sake, I will."

Parenthood involved sacrifice, and Cecilia was as prepared to make them as any of the eager mothers under her care. She sometimes had trouble identifying with the women who weren't willing to give up—or at least make the effort to give up—the bad habits that were detrimental to their unborn children.

This Orcadol crisis, for example. It simply broke her heart every time she came into contact with someone so deeply addicted that the drugs became more important than anything else.

Which was why she had mixed feelings about the impending confrontation that seemed to be building between the clinic director and the perhaps-over-zealous detective assigned to the Orcadol case. As much as Cecilia admired Mari Bingham, she hoped Mari's old, hard feelings toward Bryce Collins were not blinding her to the importance of his work. Cecilia knew how protective and defensive Mari was about the medical facilities she had devoted her entire life to, but if anyone here was involved with the black-market drug ring, the truth must be exposed.

It wasn't as if Bryce was accusing Mari of protecting drug pushers, after all. More likely their old wounds were preventing them from communicating effectively.

"So it's okay if I keep getting my hair dyed while I'm pregnant? I sure would hate to have to be half blond and half brunette for the next few months."

"Yes, Lacey, you may keep dying your hair as long as you let your hairdresser know to take reasonable precautions with ventilation. There's no medical evidence that hair dye causes any problems in pregnancy.''

"Man, I'm glad to hear that. It was hard enough having to give up drinking a beer at the bowling alley on Friday nights. But I'd have really hated to give up my hair dye.''

It had been a pretty good day so far, Cecilia mused as she moved on with a smile to the next patient. Busy, but not particularly difficult. As long as she concentrated on her work and not on her relationship—or whatever it could be called—with Geoff, she could function quite normally.

When she did steal a few moments to think of Geoff between tasks, she ended up staring into space, reliving a few special moments and dreaming of what might come....

She checked on a patient in a birthing room, still at least an hour away from delivery. There was a real party going on in that room, with the father, two grandmothers, a maternal aunt and an eager big sister all awaiting the birth. Comparing that scene to her first delivery that morning—a fourteen-year-old girl accompanied only by a rather detached foster mother—Cecilia thought about how the presence of a supportive and welcoming family made the whole process so much more joyous.

For the first time, it occurred to her that Geoff might want to be present when their child was born. He had made it clear enough that he intended to take an active role in his child's life. He was approaching parenthood the same way Cecilia was, which she could understand, but she couldn't help wondering how much more complicated his participation would make things for her. Especially when it came to *his* family....

She was still surprised that he had invited her to join him this evening at his grandmother's house for a family dinner. That was taking their partnership into sticky territory, as far as she was concerned. It would be much better to make explanations later, after they had accomplished their goal, than during the process. Not that they would tell anyone they were trying to have a baby, of course, but everyone would assume she was dating Geoff with another purpose in mind— maybe even marriage—and she didn't want to deal with that misconception.

Oddly enough, it seemed easier to explain a pregnancy resulting from a passing affair than to face speculation about why Geoff Bingham was spending so much of his rare time in town with her.

But it really had been nice of him to invite her, she reflected with a slight smile. Nice to think that he hadn't yet grown tired of her company.

"Cecilia, you're wanted in birthing room two. Looks like things are started to get underway in there."

"Thank you, Crystal." Trying to put her own concerns out of her mind for a while longer, Cecilia smiled at the younger woman and made an effort to penetrate the cloud of melancholy that seemed to surround Crystal these days. "How is Ryan, Crystal? Is he going to play T-ball this year?"

Usually, questions about her six-year-old son were guaranteed to bring a smile to Crystal's face. This time, her eyes looked instantly stricken, instead. She recovered quickly, masking her emotions behind the rather sullen expression she had been wearing lately, to the concern of many of her co-workers. "Ryan's with his father right now," she mumbled.

"Still? Oh, I thought…"

Cecilia could have sworn she saw a sheen of tears in the younger woman's eyes as Crystal turned abruptly away. "You'd better hurry to room two. Mrs. Vargas is anxious to see you."

Watching Crystal hurry away, her shoulders hunched, her posture unmistakably defensive, Cecilia decided that her associates had good reason to be concerned about the woman. Something was very definitely wrong there. Maybe she should talk to Vanessa, who had such a knack of dealing with the younger employees. Maybe Vanessa would have better luck with Crystal.

Pushing away the ever-present paperwork that would still be waiting for her after this much-anticipated baby made its debut, Cecilia also mentally pushed away her personal concerns. She had a job to do.

Cecilia had only been home for a few minutes that evening when her doorbell rang. It couldn't be Geoff, she thought with a puzzled frown. Tonight was his family dinner, and she thought she had made it clear that he couldn't change her mind about accompanying him.

Setting down the chicken breast she had been preparing to broil for her dinner, she hurried into the living room to answer the door.

A delivery truck sat in her driveway, and the driver

stood at the door, a pleasant smile gracing his florid face. "Cecilia Mendoza?"

"Yes?"

"I have a delivery for you. Would you sign here, please?"

"Yes, of course." She used the stylus he offered her to awkwardly sign her name on the electronic screen—a skill she had never quite mastered in her usual handwriting. She couldn't imagine what this delivery could be. It wasn't a flower truck, she thought, watching as the delivery driver opened the back of the vehicle.

The box was big enough to require a wheeled dolly. She watched in wide-eyed curiosity as the driver guided it onto her porch and through her front door. "Where would you like it? It's not particularly heavy, just awkward."

"Just leave it here in the living room. You're sure this is for me?"

He chuckled. "Yes, ma'am. Has your name and address written right here on this tag. Have a good evening, Ms. Mendoza."

"Thank you." Closing the door behind him, she turned to study the box for a moment. And then she ran to find a knife with which to slice through the wrapping tape.

Her heart jumped right into her throat when she saw the contents of the box. There was no card, but then, none was needed. She knew exactly who had sent this gift.

Fighting back a quick rush of tears, she ran an unsteady hand across the back of the small, beautiful maple rocker. The seat was covered with a gingham cushion in the exact shade of green she and Geoff had applied to the walls of the room she hoped would become a nursery. This rocker was absolutely perfect for holding a baby. And it was even made of the very wood she had said she wanted to use.

He really shouldn't have done this, she thought, unable to resist sinking into the cushioned seat and rocking a little. It was such an extravagant, unexpected gesture. One that could make her fall entirely too hard for him. The kind that could endanger the carefully objective perspective she was trying to maintain during their temporary affair.

They didn't even know that their efforts would be successful. Though there was no medical reason that she knew of preventing her from conceiving, there was still a very strong chance that these three weeks of effort would be fruitless, and who knew when—or if—they would try again. The disappointment of that would be bad enough, but it was going to be even worse if she was foolish enough to let her heart get broken in the process.

Chapter Ten

Geoff had tried not to mind when Cecilia turned down his dinner-with-the-family invitation. She'd been afraid it would be awkward, but he really didn't agree with that fear.

She already knew his family, at least in passing. Because of the clinic, they had plenty of topics for conversation. It wasn't completely unprecedented for him to bring a date to dinner, though admittedly it had been a while. No one would have wondered why he'd be interested in spending time with an attractive, interesting woman while he was in town.

It certainly would have saved him the ordeal of having his grandmother fixing him up with a lovely young woman who was the granddaughter of one of Myrtle's ladies-who-lunch friends. Although Myrtle had enthusiastically described the twenty-six-year-old

attorney as a paragon of modern young woman-
hood—beautiful, intelligent, ambitious and person-
able—Geoff had no interest in meeting her, much to
his grandmother's exasperation.

"I'm not going to be in town much longer, anyway," he had reminded her. "I leave for Boston in
less than a month."

"But you'll be back. And as you take over more
of your father's responsibilities, you'll be staying in
town more." She was as quick with a retort as always. "It is time for you to think about starting your
family while you're young enough to enjoy them,
Geoffrey. And while your father and I are around to
enjoy them, too," she had added with a shake of her
finger.

Geoff had chuckled and kissed his grandmother's
softly lined cheek. "Emotional blackmail doesn't
work with me, you should know that. And besides,
you're going to be around for a long time yet."

The truth was, he thought as he drove his car into
Cecilia's driveway Thursday evening, he simply
wasn't interested in meeting his grandmother's
friend's granddaughter. For the usual reasons, yes. No
inclination to get caught up in a matchmaking scheme
that would only lead to bruised feelings all around
when he failed to cooperate. That same old reluctance
to sacrifice any of his cherished freedom.

But there was another reason that he didn't care
about meeting the single lawyer. He was enjoying Cecilia's company so much that he didn't want anything
to interfere with their time together.

Holding a small package in his hand, he climbed
out of his car with a smile on his face that was be-

coming increasingly familiar whenever he was about to see Cecilia. The smile turned to a frown when he heard a rather disturbing commotion coming from the house next door.

He glanced instinctively that way, spotting the rusty pickup he'd seen before parked in front of the house. Though overgrown shrubbery prevented him from seeing anyone on the shadowy porch, the voices were coming from there.

They sounded young. A male who was obviously angry—irate, even. And a girl who seemed to be speaking in sobs. He remembered the redhead with the bruised face that he had seen with Cecilia. Brandy? The one Cecilia had explained was being raised by her grandparents next door.

Were the grandparents home now? Were they aware that their granddaughter's boyfriend was throwing an obscenity-laced tantrum on their front porch?

A muffled thud might have been a blow, or a push followed by a fall. The sound was accompanied by a choked cry that made him toss the package he'd been holding onto the hood of his car and move purposefully toward the house next door.

Before he'd crossed Cecilia's lawn, a door slammed, and the battered pickup peeled out of the driveway, gunned so violently that the tires smoked on the asphalt. Brandy ran down the porch steps into Geoff's view, crying and calling after the departing truck. "Marlin, wait! Don't go, please!"

"Is there anything I can do to help?" Geoff asked her, raising his voice to be heard over her sobs.

She hadn't seen him prior to his speaking. She jumped and whirled toward him.

Her face was red and tear streaked, her eyes wild beneath her tumbled red hair. ''What?''

''Is there anything I can do for you?''

''No.'' She swiped at her streaming eyes with the back of one hand, calling his attention to the fading bruise on her cheek.

Softball injury? He seriously doubted it. ''Look, Brandy, I heard that lot yelling at you—''

''It was my fault,'' she said quickly, defensively. ''I said some things that made him mad. He's got a quick temper, but he's not a bad guy.''

He suspected that he would accomplish nothing by verbally attacking her jerk of a boyfriend. ''Are your grandparents home?''

''No.'' Drawing a ragged breath, Brandy turned dispiritedly toward the door. ''I'll be okay. I'm going in to wait for Marlin to call. He'll calm down pretty soon, and he'll be sorry he yelled at me like that. He's really a great guy. I love him a lot.''

He wished he could think of something profound to say. Some wise words to get through her infatuated defensiveness and bring her to her senses. But all he could think of was, ''Brandy, no one has the right to curse at you like that. And he damned sure doesn't have a right to put his hands on you in anger. If he has hit you, or shoved you—''

''You don't even know him!'' Brandy snapped, hunching her skinny shoulders in an unmistakably closed posture. ''Just leave me alone, okay?''

Sighing, Geoff held up both hands and stepped

back, signaling surrender. He watched as Brandy ran up the steps into her grandparents' house.

Okay, he'd blown that big-time, he thought in disgust. Instead of convincing Brandy to give Marlin the boot, he had probably sent her right back into his abusive arms.

Maybe Cecilia would have a better idea of what to do. He turned back toward her house, remembering to retrieve the package from the hood of his car.

In response to his knock, Cecilia opened the door with a smile that went a long way toward restoring his good mood. And then she pulled him inside, tugged his head down to hers, and gave him a kiss that nearly fried his brain circuitry. There wasn't an inch of him that wasn't hard by the time they finally broke apart for oxygen.

"What—" His voice cracked, and he had to stop to clear it before continuing. "What was that for?"

"For the rocker," she said, her eyes glowing as she smiled up at him.

"You already thanked me for the rocker, on the phone."

"Now you've been thanked in person."

"In person is definitely better," he murmured, and pulled her into his arms again.

He managed to end the kiss this time before it flared completely out of control. He was within a heartbeat of taking her right there on the entryway floor. His arms were around her, their bodies plastered together. He'd have sworn he was holding something else when he came in....

Clearing his thoughts with a slight shake of his head, he reached down to scoop up the package he had dropped sometime during the first kiss. "I forgot. I brought you something."

Suddenly she was frowning. "Another gift? Really, Geoff, that wasn't necessary. I mean, the rocker was already too much. You mustn't keep—"

"Maybe you should see what it is before you start fussing."

Looking decidedly wary, she accepted the bag and peered into it. And then she smiled and pulled out a small, colorful tin. "It's tea."

"Herbal. It's made of rose leaves and some other stuff from the garden that's supposed to taste good when you steep it all in boiling water. My grandmother loves it—and its caffeine free. Much better for you than all that coffee you drink."

Her smile was just a bit embarrassed by her automatic assumption that he had brought her something expensive. "It looks good. I'll try a cup tonight. Thank you."

"Something smells delicious."

"Dinner's almost ready."

"Need any help?"

"You can stand there and look pretty while I finish up."

"Very funny." But he was smiling when he followed her into the kitchen.

Cecilia had just set the food on the table when Geoff suddenly smacked his forehead with the heel of his hand. "I almost forgot."

"What?"

"Your neighbor. Brandy." He quickly told her what he had overheard when he'd arrived at her house. "Your, um, warm welcome sent it completely out of my head. She's over there by herself now, if you think you should check on her."

Concerned, Cecilia moved to the kitchen window and peered out. "Her grandparents must have just gotten home. I see their car in the carport now."

"Good. Then they can talk to her."

"Oh, they'll talk to her. They'll tell her what a loser Marlin is, and she'll get mad and yell back at them. Then she'll storm out to the backyard and sulk for a while. And tomorrow she'll be with Marlin again, letting him treat her like dirt because she has convinced herself he's her soul mate."

Geoff scowled. "I've got to tell you, Cecilia, I think the guy's doing worse than treating her badly. I think he's physically abusing her."

Her stomach muscles clenched. "You mean—"

"I mean, I don't believe for a minute that she was hit in the face by a softball. I think she was hit by a fist. And I'm pretty sure he either hit her or shoved her again tonight before I could get over there."

"Surely Brandy wouldn't keep excusing Marlin if he was actually hitting her."

"You haven't seen any other bruises or injuries?"

Cecilia thought about the question for a moment and then grimaced. "There have been a couple of bruises. And she sprained her wrist last month. She said she fell. But she's the active type who's always doing something physical like roller skating and climbing and swimming at the lake. I thought she was just a bit accident-prone."

She stopped and sighed. "I guess I wasn't really

thinking at all. If I had been, I would have recognized the signs.''

''From what I've read, abused women are very adept at hiding the truth from their friends and family. Covering, making excuses, taking the blame.''

Cecilia still felt like an idiot. ''I've seen it more than a few times in my job. You would be surprised and disgusted by the number of men who don't stop punching their wives or girlfriends even during pregnancy. And the women almost always have a cover story—running into a door or falling off a porch or, well, getting hit by a softball. Or if they're confronted by the truth, they make excuses for the jerks. The poor guy was just under stress or worried about money or being treated badly at work. Or maybe he'd had a little too much to drink and he wasn't really in control of his actions, but he's always so sorry later.''

''Brandy claimed this quarrel was all her fault. She said things she shouldn't have and Marlin got mad. She was obviously ready to crawl to keep him from leaving.''

''I just can't understand why she's so desperate to hang on to him. I've tried to convince her that she doesn't have to have a boyfriend to make her happy, but she has an almost neurotic fear of losing him.''

''From what you've told me of her background, she's looking for someone to belong to. Someone who puts her first. It's a shame she can't find that with her grandparents rather than with some boy who doesn't appreciate her.''

''I'll talk to her grandmother tomorrow. Maybe a family counselor can help them. And I'll try talking to Brandy again, though I'm not sure it would do any good. She thinks of me as her grandmother's unmarried neighbor. She likes me well enough, but she thinks I'm too old to understand teenage love affairs. Nor is she interested in modeling herself after me. According to her, my life is boring—all work and very little play, in her opinion. She doesn't understand when I tell her how much I love my work.''

"Maybe you should take her to work with you someday. Let her see what a vital and fascinating job you have.''

"If I thought it would accomplish anything, I would do that. But I'm not sure showing her my work would convince her that she should listen to me rather than Marlin.''

"It couldn't hurt for her to watch a woman who's competent, highly respected and fully in charge of vitally important situations.''

She couldn't help but be pleased, of course, by the way he described her. "Maybe I will see if she's interested in shadowing me one day. She'll be a senior in high school in the fall and she really should be considering her career choices. Whenever I've asked, she's merely shrugged and said she was still thinking about possibilities, but it couldn't hurt for me to give her an up-close look at one option.''

"There's always a need for young people to train for health care careers. Especially in nursing, I understand.''

Cecilia nodded. "In some areas of the country, nurses are in critically short supply. And there's a growing demand for midwives, with so many doctors shying away from obstetrics practices.''

"It will be good for her to see that work can be

challenging and enjoyable. From what I've always heard, the clinic is a pleasant place to work. Friendly co-workers, happy new parents, lots of cute babies.''

Cecilia lifted her eyebrows as she studied him across the table. ''Maybe *you* should shadow me at work one day. Have you ever actually spent any time in the birthing center?''

''Well…no, not much. My job has always been in other areas, so when I'm in town I'm usually in my office at Bingham Enterprises. Are you telling me it's not a happy place to work?''

''Obviously, I enjoy working there, but it isn't a theme park. In any medical setting, you'll find stress and tension and an occasional tragedy. Especially lately, we've—''

Realizing abruptly that she was being somewhat too candid with a man whose family controlled the workplace she was describing, she decided a bit more discretion was probably in order. ''All in all, it's a wonderful place to work. I wouldn't want to go anywhere else.''

His gaze was locked on her face. ''What did you start to say about the clinic before you suddenly remembered that I'm a Bingham?''

She sighed lightly. Was she really so transparent that anyone could read her thoughts or had Geoff gotten to know her a bit too well during the past few days? Six days, to be precise, she thought with a vague sense of wonder that a week ago she hadn't even known him.

''Cecilia?''

''I've told you it's been a particularly tense time lately,'' she reminded him. ''Everyone's nervous about the lawsuit—we can't help but think about how vulnerable we all are to such actions as we go about our work. It's a busy time, deliverywise, so we're all working pretty long hours. The drug crisis affects all of us in one way or another as we deal with addicted mothers and affected newborns. Detective Collins watching our every move doesn't help. One of our nurses is going through some sort of personal crisis, and she has been so jittery and tearful that it can't help but affect the people around her."

"And the stress Mari's been under can't help but affect everyone, either. Tension always seems to work its way down from the top."

"We all understand that Mari has a lot to deal with."

"Maybe I should talk with her. See if there's anything I can do to help her out."

"I wouldn't want her to think anyone in the clinic has been talking about her."

"Give me some credit for discretion, will you? I'll simply say that I've noticed she seems stressed. Your name will never come up."

"Thanks. I, um, guess your family's beginning to wonder where you've been for the past week?"

He shrugged and reached for his water glass. "I doubt it. Everyone's busy, and I usually entertain myself when I'm in town."

"So they don't know about…"

"Us?" he inserted smoothly when she hesitated. "I haven't said anything in particular, but Dad and Mari both know I was with you Sunday evening when you delivered that baby at the movie theater. Word of that sure got around."

"Especially after the article appeared in the *Merlyn Mage*," she muttered.

"Well, don't worry. No one's making a big thing of our seeing each other. My family likes you. They aren't surprised I enjoy spending time with you. That's why I wanted you to join us last night at my grandmother's. We'd have had a pleasant dinner together, and you'd have spared me another evening of my grandmother trying to fix me up. This time she was pushing me to meet the granddaughter of one of her friends."

Cecilia found it difficult to smile in response to the ironic humor in his voice. She didn't find his grandmother's matchmaking efforts nearly as amusing as Geoff did. Maybe because she strongly suspected that Myrtle Bingham would never include Cecilia's name on her list of desirable brides for her beloved grandson.

Not that she wanted to be on the list, she assured herself. Hadn't she just asserted that she was perfectly content without a man in her life? That she was not like Brandy, so needy and insecure that she would sacrifice her own dignity to obtain the illusion of love? Though she longed for a child, she was content in every other way with her own company, her own accomplishments.

As for Geoff, he couldn't have made it more clear that he had no interest in settling down. In his own words, he saw a wife as someone else to answer to, someone else he would be obliged to keep satisfied and content.

He didn't seem to view a child in the same way, which reinforced Cecilia's suspicion that he thought of a child as a novelty. A form of slightly rebellious entertainment—like his motorcycle. Or an outlet for his creativity and self-expression—like his guitar.

She envisioned his role in their child's life as the noncustodial parent who made grand appearances with gifts and play dates and out-of-the-ordinary fun, while she would be the full-time nurturer, caregiver and disciplinarian. She could live with those roles. She knew plenty of people who had grown up under similar parental circumstances and had turned out just fine. If she didn't think Geoff would be a good part-time father, she would never have agreed to his terms in this partnership.

It would all work out, she promised herself. But in the meantime, she would just as soon not talk about his family's efforts to arrange a suitable marriage for him.

She promptly changed the subject, bringing up a local campaign to raise funds to spruce up some of the historic buildings in downtown Binghamton. The Merlyn County Public Library, for example, which was located in a renovated white clapboard house that provided five stories of books when the basement and attic were included in the tally. The library was always in need of upgrades and maintenance. The arts-and-crafts and bluegrass festival being discussed by community activists would became an annual event if successful and would be designated as a fund-raiser for the library and other local facilities.

"I think it's a great idea," Geoff said. "I've always said we need an annual festival of some sort to celebrate the area's history and unique character."

Relieved to have found a topic that interested him,

Cecilia kept the remainder of their dinnertime conversation centered on community affairs, rather than their own. All in all, she decided, it was a much safer topic.

Geoff insisted on helping Cecilia clean up the kitchen after they had eaten. The task took only twice as long with his help, she thought wryly. The way he kept distracting her with increasingly lengthy kisses, it would be a miracle if they got all the dishes into the dishwasher before he dragged her off to bed. Or maybe she would be the one doing the dragging, she thought after one particularly arousing close encounter.

He lifted his head from hers with a wicked grin. Only then did she realize that both his hands were beneath her knit top, his palms warm on her back. "I think the kitchen's clean enough, don't you?"

Mentally consigning the rest to a later time, Cecilia smiled. "Yes, I think it is."

Pulling her closer, he murmured, "Then maybe you and I could—"

His suggestion was cut short by the shrill ring of the telephone. Cecilia sighed deeply, tempted to let it ring. It probably wasn't an important call, she tried to convince herself. Maybe a telemarketer.

But when the phone rang again, she gave Geoff an apologetic look, extricated herself from his grasp and moved to the kitchen extension. "Hello?"

Her expression was even more apologetic when she hung up a very short time later. "Geoff, I'm sorry, but I—"

He nodded and cut in. "I heard enough to figure out that you've been called to work."

"Looks like I have a delivery to make. I saw this client earlier today, and I was pretty sure she would give birth at any time."

"A home delivery?"

"No. I'm one of the more traditional midwives on staff. My clients tend to prefer more standard deliveries with medical facilities close at hand—and so do I. Women who choose home deliveries or water births or other nontraditional methods are generally guided to other midwives."

"And yet you're still available for the occasional movie-theater delivery."

"We do what we have to do," she replied with a smile and a shrug.

"You need a lift to the clinic?"

"I'd better take my own car. This is a first baby, and she's in the early stages of labor. It could take several hours yet—perhaps all night. I can nap at the clinic if necessary."

Looking a bit disappointed but resigned, Geoff nodded. "Then I'll head on home."

She nodded reluctantly.

"Do you have plans for the weekend?"

"Not really. I have a birthing seminar to conduct tomorrow evening, which will last until around seven, but I'm not expected back at the clinic until Monday morning."

His smile returned with blinding intensity. "Just what I was hoping to hear. I'll pick you up at seven-thirty. Pack light—and don't eat dinner."

"Pack?" She blinked. "Where are we going?"

"Not far. You'll be less than an hour away from the clinic if you're needed. So what do you say? Want to sneak away for a weekend?"

A weekend with Geoff. Away from the clinic, the phone, the neighbors' problems. "I would like that. What do I bring?"

"Shorts, a bathing suit and a toothbrush. I've got everything else covered."

"A bathing suit?" Few women over thirty-five considered bathing suits their favorite type of leisure wear, and she was no exception.

His grin turned wicked. "Unless you prefer skinny-dipping."

"I'll bring a suit."

Putting on an exaggeratedly disappointed expression, he heaved a sigh. "Okay. Then I'll see you at seven-thirty tomorrow. I hope everything goes smoothly with your delivery tonight."

"Thank you."

She saw him out and then grabbed her purse and car keys. She was definitely going to have to make an effort to put Geoff and his mysterious plans for the weekend out of her mind for the next almost twenty-four hours, or she would never be able to concentrate on her work.

Chapter Eleven

Cecilia was having lunch in the atrium with Vanessa on Friday when her brother stopped by their table, looking so handsome and professional in his dark suit, white shirt and blue tie that she couldn't help beaming with pride.

He nodded to Vanessa, then spoke to Cecilia. "I thought I might find you here."

"Is there something you need, Eric?"

"Yeah. Hannah and I are going out to eat tonight. Someplace nice—Melinda's, maybe. We'd like you to come with us."

Cecilia moistened her lips. "Thanks, sweetie, but I can't tonight. I have other plans."

"Oh." He wasn't used to hearing that. After a moment he nodded and said, "Then how about if we do it tomorrow night, instead?"

Resisting an impulse to squirm in her seat, she said, "No, I can't tomorrow night, either. Actually, I'll be out of town for the weekend. You and Hannah go ahead and have your nice dinner. I'll call you as soon as I get back."

"Out of town?" Eric parroted blankly.

"For the weekend?" Vanessa murmured.

She lifted her chin. "Yes."

Eric planted his fists on his hips. "You didn't say anything to me about going out of town. Where are you going? Who are you going with?"

Cecilia glanced around, hoping they wouldn't be overheard. "I'm just taking a couple of days off. I'll have my cell phone with me, and I'll only be an hour away if anyone needs me."

"Surely you're not going away with—"

"Eric." She put a hand on his arm, squeezing to get his attention. "I'd rather not announce my personal business to anyone within hearing distance, if you don't mind."

He subsided to a disgruntled mumble that would carry no farther than their table. "You're going with Geoff Bingham?"

She should have known she couldn't pull this off in secret. "Yes. And I shouldn't have to remind you that I'm old enough to make my own decisions about my weekend plans without clearing them with you first."

"Doesn't mean I have to like it," Eric muttered.

"No, it doesn't," she agreed evenly.

Still frowning, he asked in the same quiet tone, "So where is this thing with you and Bingham headed, anyway? I mean, are we going to end up married to cousins?''

Vanessa propped her elbows on the table and rested her chin in her hands, apparently interested in that answer herself.

"No," Cecilia said firmly. "That is an extremely unlikely possibility. Geoff and I are friends, and we've both been working very hard lately. We need some time off for relaxation, and we've enjoyed spending that time together. That's pretty much the extent of it.''

She told herself it wasn't really a lie, since she had summed up the relationship quite well—except for the making-a-baby part she had chosen not to mention. If Eric was this freaked out by her going away for a weekend with Geoff, she couldn't imagine how he would react when she told him she was pregnant with Geoff's child. But she would face that hurdle when—if—it became necessary.

"Since I'm obviously not going to change your mind about this, I'll just tell you to have a good time." He leaned over to brush a kiss against her cheek. "Don't forget to call me when you get back, CeCe.''

"I won't forget. Enjoy your nice dinner with Hannah.''

She watched her brother walk away, still shaking his head in disapproval. And then she drew a deep breath and turned back to Vanessa. "Shut up.''

Vanessa lifted her eyebrows. "I haven't said anything.''

"You don't have to. That dopey grin says it all.''

"What happened to your policy of not dating men

who are prettier than you are? Not that I'm saying he is, of course.''

"Are you kidding? He's gorgeous."

"You're hardly plain yourself, kiddo."

"Thank you. But you're my friend and you're hardly objective."

"Perhaps. Anyway, I think it's really great that you're having a good time with—'' she lowered her voice to a stage whisper "—you know who."

"You, um, don't think less of me for going away for a weekend with a man I've only known for a week?"

Vanessa seemed surprised by the hesitant question. "Come on, Cecilia. You're a mature woman. You've been married. It's not like Geoff's a total stranger you know nothing about. I'd say as long as you've both been clear from the beginning what you expect from each other so we don't have any broken hearts in the making, there's no reason at all why you shouldn't have a little fun."

Cecilia sat back in her chair, satisfied with her friend's blessing. For a moment she was tempted to tell Vanessa everything. But that was a bit more than she was prepared to share.

"Geoff and I have both made it perfectly clear what we want from each other," she said, instead. "No hearts are going to be broken."

"I'm glad to hear that."

Was that just a hint of warning in Vanessa's voice—a touch of concern despite her support?

Cecilia glanced at her watch. "I'd better get back to the madhouse. I've got an appointment in fifteen minutes."

"Me, too. And Cecilia?"

Gathering her things, Cecilia responded absently.
"Mmm?"

"Have a great weekend, okay?"

She smiled. "Thanks, Van. I intend to."

It was an impulse that made Cecilia change into a
bright red sundress when she got home from work.
Maybe because she'd had on a red dress when she'd
met Geoff last week, though this one was more casual. The spaghetti straps bared her arms and shoulders, while the ruffled vee bodice gave just a hint of
cleavage. She wore hoop earrings for a gypsy touch
and chose more comfortable sandals than she'd worn
last week.

Maybe she was a bit overdressed, she mused as she
pinned her hair into a loose roll, but she enjoyed
dressing up occasionally after spending so much of
her life in scrubs and casual clothes.

She decided it was worth the effort when Geoff saw
her. After giving her a kiss that nearly melted her into
the floor, he raised his head to ask huskily, "Have I
mentioned that I like the way you look in red?"

"I think you just made that clear. You look awfully
good yourself," she added, admiring the way his
white shirt and well-tailored khakis showed off both
his tan and his athletic physique.

He nodded toward the red wheeled bag sitting
nearby. "Is this all you're taking?"

"Yes." She picked up her purse. "I'm ready."

A grin spread across his face. "You have no idea
how glad I am to hear that."

It was a nice evening for a drive. Clear and not

quite as hot as it had been. Piano music played quietly from the CD player, proving a pleasant background without impeding their lively conversation. It was always a bit surprising to Cecilia how much they could find to talk about even when they'd only been apart for a few hours.

''Are you going to tell me now where we're going?'' she asked when they had been on the road for just over half an hour.

''My family owns a vacation cottage on the far side of Ginman's Lake, close to the river. It's a place we go when we want to get away from the phone and the social calendars, yet we're still nearby if we're needed. I think you and I can have a nice, relaxing weekend there.''

''It sounds very nice. How much farther?''

''Ten minutes. It's only a forty-minute drive from your house.''

Which meant she could be at the clinic in half an hour if necessary, she figured.

She hoped it wouldn't be necessary.

The Bingham ''cottage'' was hardly a modest little vacation house, she observed when Geoff drove down the long gravel driveway. Constructed of rock and glass and sitting on a secluded lot that fell off to the lake in the back, the two-story house was bigger than her own home. Everything was so tidy and well maintained that she was quite sure they kept a groundskeeper on full-time retainer. ''This is lovely.''

''I haven't spent much time here since my mother died, but Dad comes fairly often for a fishing weekend.''

Carrying their bags, he led her inside. She noted

immediately that the heavy wood and overstuffed upholstered furnishings bore not a trace of dust. The main room was two stories high, surrounded by an upstairs balcony that probably led to bedrooms. The back wall was covered with closed draperies, but she would bet it was made of glass to showcase the lake view.

One wall was made up entirely of built-in bookcases to display books, family photos, electronic equipment, board games and knickknacks. A swinging wood door on another wall probably opened into the kitchen. The room was sweetly scented by the fresh flowers arranged in several scattered vases.

"Obviously you had someone prepare for our arrival," she commented.

"Mmm. Come with me and I'll show you the upstairs."

Tagging obligingly behind him, she climbed the curving staircase and stepped into the first door on the left. It was a bedroom, of course, with a big iron bed in the center of the back wall and a dresser, armoire and nightstands made of distressed pine. The fabrics were in nubby golds and browns, and a thick rug was spread on the oak floor.

It was a warm, inviting room, and it wasn't hard for Cecilia to imagine snuggling with Geoff in that big bed. The image alone was enough to bring a light flush to her cheeks.

"Maybe you'd like to freshen up while I take care of a few last-minute details downstairs," he suggested. "I hope you're hungry."

"Are you kidding? I'm starving."

He smiled. "Give me fifteen minutes."

"I suppose I can wait that long—barely."

"I'll meet you at the bottom of the stairs."

She took advantage of the time to wash up in the big attached bathroom that was decorated in the same warm colors as the bedroom. She tidied her hair, unpacked a few toiletries and applied a fresh touch of lipstick. When fifteen minutes had passed, she made one last quick check in the mirror and left the room.

As promised, Geoff waited for her at the foot of the stairs. He smiled as he watched her walk down, his expression so appreciative that she couldn't help smiling in return. He held a white rose in his hand; he offered it to her when she reached the bottom step.

Touched by the gesture, she lifted the bloom to her nose to appreciate its scent. Only then did she notice that the draperies at the back of the room were open now, revealing a scene that made her breath catch in her throat.

Taking her hand, Geoff led her toward the glass wall. It was almost dark now, the sky a rich purple, the big, spreading trees casting long, deep shadows. The lake beyond the property, set into a deep valley surrounded by wooded Kentucky mountains, looked like a sheet of purplish-gray glass. A boat dock and fishing pier were accessible from the house by way of a long, sloping rock walkway with metal railings for safety.

But it was the stone patio just behind the house that held Cecilia's attention when she and Geoff stepped outside through a sliding glass door. Anchored by a big rock barbecue pit at one side, the patio was lined with inviting benches and big wooden planters that held Japanese maples, large lacy ferns and mounds of summer flowers. Multicolored paper lanterns glowed from wires strung overhead, illuminating a round wrought-iron table in the center of the patio.

The table had been set for two with china, crystal and silver. Silver-domed serving dishes, silver candlesticks and a floral centerpiece added elegance to the setting. Champagne chilled in a silver bucket. Soft music played from hidden speakers.

It was so blatantly, over-the-top romantic that Cecilia could feel her knees start to weaken. No one had ever done anything like this for her before. The only evening that had come close was the night Geoff had cooked for her at his condo—the night they had celebrated their decision to have a child together.

Bracing a hand on the back of a curvy wrought-iron chair, she looked at him through a sheen of tears. "You really have to stop doing things like this."

He trailed a fingertip down her bare arm. "Why?"

Because you'll make me fall for you. "Because you'll spoil me."

"I rather enjoy spoiling you."

"Still...."

Without waiting to hear further objections, Geoff moved to the table and lifted the champagne bottle from the ice bucket. Moments later he handed her a flute filled with the fizzing beverage.

"To our child," he said, touching his glass to Cecilia's. "May she be as smart and beautiful as her mother."

"Or may he be as handsome and charming as his father," she countered, then lifted the flute to her lips. She would only drink a few sips—just in case—but this was most definitely a toast she wanted to acknowledge.

He held her chair for her, then insisted on serving her. The meal was perfection—a salmon-and-pasta salad kept cool by ice in the bottom of the clever serving dish, crisp asparagus spears, fruit salad. He'd gone to a lot of trouble to have someone prepare all this so that he'd needed only a few minutes to add the finishing touches. That gesture alone illustrated how completely different their lifestyles were.

She wondered if it would be confusing for a child to have one parent with so much money and status and the other parent who lived quietly and on a careful budget. A tiny part of her worried that the child would be more impressed by Geoff's extravagant gestures than Cecilia's steady reliability. But she wouldn't make this a competition, she vowed. Her child would just have to learn that money wasn't the most important thing in life.

It was fully dark now, and the lanterns glowed against the starry sky. Tiny white lights were strung in the potted trees on the patio. She would have to do something like that on her much-tinier patio, she thought. She liked the fairyland look.

"You've been quiet this evening," Geoff commented. "Tired?"

"A bit overwhelmed, I think."

"Which means?"

"I'm just not accustomed to such grand gestures. The expensive dinners, the rocking chair...all of this."

"Don't forget the herbal tea," he murmured.

"I'm serious, Geoff. Do you always do things like this?"

"What do you mean by always?"

She sighed, frustrated by his obtuseness and her own inarticulateness. "I mean, do you shower so much attention on all the women you…well—"

"Try to make babies with?" His voice was just a bit too measured now. "I can't answer that, since it's never happened before."

"Still, it isn't necessary to…well, to court me. I mean…"

"Cecilia." He didn't look or sound angry, but something in his tone let her know he found absolutely no humor in this particular topic. "I enjoy spending time with you. Yes, there's a purpose in our being together, but there's no reason we can't make the next few weeks special."

Now she felt terrible. Geoff had gone to so much trouble to make this a perfect evening, and here she was questioning his motives. Just because most of the men in her past had turned out to be all flash and no substance didn't mean she should judge Geoff by their standards.

But experience made a pretty darned good teacher, she thought as she tried to ignore the ripple of foreboding that went through her. She would be incredibly foolish to forget all the hard-earned lessons she had learned along the way.

Propped on one elbow, Geoff lay in the big iron bed watching Cecilia sleep. Moonlight streamed through the open bedroom window, bathing her in a soft light that suited her creamy skin. Her dark hair tumbled around her, and he remembered once wondering how it would look spread across his pillow. He was delighted that he'd had the chance to find out.

She must be tired, he thought, his gaze lingering for a moment on the purply smudges beneath her long eyelashes. She had talked about how busy they'd been at the clinic lately, and how much stress they'd been working under.

She had been up most of the night delivering the baby that had interrupted their last evening together. She'd told him the baby hadn't arrived until nearly two a.m. She needed a couple of days of rest and relaxation.

They'd had a very pleasant evening. After finishing their dinner, they had taken a leisurely stroll down the path to the water, where they'd sat for a while on the benches built into the sides of the fishing pier. Letting a companionable silence fall between them, they had listened to the water lapping against the pier and the bank.

Away from the lights of town, the stars had twinkled brilliantly above them, reflecting in scattered-diamond patterns on the surface of the lake. Hidden in the trees surrounding them, frogs and night birds had entertained them with an enthusiastic concert.

It had been a magical evening, as far as Geoff was concerned. He was so comfortable with Cecilia, so relaxed. Not only did she seem to have no particular expectations of him, she actually seemed uncomfortable when he went to extra trouble on her behalf.

He remembered her warning that he was in danger of spoiling her. Had it been so rare for her to be pampered? He knew she was close to her brother and that Eric took care of her home-maintenance needs, but she seemed to be almost entirely unaccustomed to nice gestures from anyone else.

Were all the men she had known—including her ex-husband—total idiots? Hadn't they realized that Cecilia was a very special woman, someone who gave so much to others that she well deserved to be indulged occasionally herself? If so, it was no wonder she'd been a bit wary of his motives.

She'd asked if he always made romantic gestures toward the women in his life. Truth was, he *had* done things like that for other women. He enjoyed planning nice evenings, got a kick out of watching a woman's eyes light up in surprise and pleasure.

But it had been a long time since he'd made the effort for anyone. And there was something different about the way he felt when he did something special for Cecilia. Maybe because she expected so little from him. Maybe because there was something different about Cecilia herself.

She was the first woman he had ever considered having a child with. Maybe because she was the first woman who'd ever asked him to, he thought with a smile. But also because she was the first woman he had ever seen as a suitable mother for his child. Darned near perfect, as a matter of fact.

He reached out to smooth a strand of hair away from her cheek. She murmured something in her sleep and nestled more deeply into the pillow. He wanted to lean over and kiss her, but he was afraid he would awaken her. She needed her rest. If he'd had to, he would have lain awake all night watching over her to make sure nothing interfered with her sleep.

This new level of protectiveness was different, too. Especially considering that he'd met few women more unmistakably capable of taking care of themselves.

He felt his smile turn slowly to a frown, and he wasn't sure exactly why. It seemed to have something to do with the strength of his feelings for Cecilia—feelings that were beginning to seem too intense considering the parameters of the relationship they had agreed to. While he'd thought it would be convenient to be good friends with his child's mother, this felt like more than friendship. Unnervingly more.

The odd feelings would pass, he assured himself. Neither he nor Cecilia wanted this situation to get all sticky and complicated. With the possible addition of a child, she liked her life just the way it was, and he felt the same way about his.

Just because she looked so absolutely right in his bed didn't mean he wanted her to become a permanent fixture there, he assured himself.

Funny. He usually made pronouncements like that with a bit more conviction.

Chapter Twelve

Cecilia must have needed time away from her usual routines even more than she had realized. Though Geoff's weekend place was less than an hour from her home, it felt much farther.

Rather than waking at sunrise and going nonstop all day as she usually did, she and Geoff slept late Saturday, then woke to a slow, delicious bout of love-making. They had a late breakfast, then walked down to the water to swim and sunbathe and be lazy until heat and precaution against too much sun sent them back inside.

She discovered something new about Geoff that afternoon. The man was a fanatic about games. Scrabble, Monopoly, Yahtzee, Parcheesi—he didn't seem to care which game she selected as long as they played. And as long as she made it a true challenge.

He loved to win—and he gloated unrepentantly when he did—but he was a good loser, accepting defeat with grace and humor.

She couldn't remember the last time she had played games like this, since Eric wasn't much of a player. Nor could she remember laughing so much in one afternoon—laughing until her sides ached and tears rolled down her cheeks in response to Geoff's foolishness.

They fired up the barbecue for dinner, threading chicken and vegetables onto skewers and roasting them slowly over the coals. They ate outside again, taking their time, talking about nothing more serious than the taste of the food and the merits of the music playing quietly on the unseen speakers.

Cecilia made a specific effort to keep things light, casual. The way it had been between them all day. She didn't bring up his romantic gestures—or allow herself to wonder how much of that was for her benefit and how much just from habit. She didn't talk about the clinic and the problems there. She didn't mention Geoff's impending business trips.

She didn't even discuss their hopes for a baby, since even that seemed like too serious a topic for this utterly relaxed day.

It was nicer this way. No past. No future. No plans or expectations. It was so delightfully different from her usual carefully planned and scheduled routine. And she intended to enjoy every single moment of it.

Geoff was the one who finally brought reality into the fantasy. They had gone back outside in the late afternoon when some of the heat had dissipated, and they were taking a stroll through the woods surrounding the house, watching birds and enjoying an occasional spectacular view from the hilltops. He turned to lean against the trunk of a tree as she enjoyed a particularly nice scene of the lake dotted with sailboats and fishing boats, with fluffy white clouds overhead and the blue mountains in the distant background.

"So when do you think we'll know?" he asked unexpectedly. "Whether we've hit a home run, I mean."

She took a couple of beats to shift mental gears. Keeping her gaze focused on that calming horizon, she said, "I assume you mean whether we've been successful in making a baby."

"Yeah. When should we know?"

"A couple of weeks, I suppose. Some of the new tests give results very early."

"So we could have an answer before I have to leave town?"

Now he had brought up two serious subjects practically in the same breath. She turned to face him. "Possibly. Of course, there's a very good chance that it will be negative. The odds against conceiving so quickly are fairly high."

He made a show of flexing his biceps. A light breeze ruffled his hair, making him look young and fit and so appealing her mouth went dry. "Don't forget who you're dealing with—Mr. Macho. When I'm faced with a challenge, I conquer it. I go about it the same way I play Monopoly. I play to win—no mercy, no acceptance of defeat."

Trust Geoff to compare making a baby to playing

a board game. And to make light of a topic that was so important to her that she wasn't even allowing herself to think about it this weekend.

She desperately wanted that test result to be positive. Of course she did. Once that goal had been achieved she could get back to her own life, and Geoff to his. No more juggling her work schedule and her evenings with him. No more awkward explanations about what they were doing together. No more grand romantic gestures. No more lazy days of swimming, laughing and eating beneath the stars.

And if she kept thinking along those lines, she was in danger of bursting into tears right here in front of Geoff.

"I suppose we'd better head back to the house so we can start dinner," she said.

He caught her arm when she would have started in that direction and pulled her against his chest. "I think dinner's going to be a little late this evening," he murmured against her mouth.

She wrapped her arms around his neck. "Is it now? And what if I'm hungry?"

"I certainly hope you're hungry," he said with a wicked grin. "I know I am."

Not even for a moment did she think he was talking about food. Raising her lips to his, she let herself enjoy the novelty of making out with a good-looking man on a shady mountain hillside.

She could go back to being sensible and practical Cecilia later, she promised herself. She would allow herself just one more night in fantasyland. And then it was back to the real world.

* * *

The real world was sometimes an incredibly hectic place. A week and a half after Cecilia and Geoff returned from the weekend house, she found herself in the middle of chaos at the clinic. Three women in labor at one time—somewhat unusual even in the middle of the Merlyn County baby boom. A full waiting room, including a few women who'd brought their unruly children with them. A woman who was probably going to be transferred through the connecting glass hallway to the hospital for a cesarean section, since her labor was not progressing well.

The entire staff was operating at a full run. Cecilia passed Mari, Vanessa, Milla, and Kyle during one full-out dash down the long hallway, and everyone looked as harried as she was beginning to feel. She didn't know what was going on between Milla and Kyle, but the tension between those two lately was becoming almost palpable. Whether it was smoldering attraction or growing antagonism, she couldn't say, but there was definitely something building.

Crystal Hendrix, the nurse whose personal problems were beginning to interfere noticeably with her work, looked more edgy than usual, her eyes shadowed, her hands unsteady. Cecilia couldn't help wondering if the planets were in some sort of weird misalignment or something.

Was *everyone* going through personal crises at the same time? Maybe that would explain her own totally atypical behavior of the past couple of weeks.

To make the situation even more tense, Detective Collins was back, lurking around like a gray-eyed predator watching for signs of weakness. He seemed determined to pester Mari with a few dozen new questions about the black market drug trade, but Mari simply didn't have time to deal with him.

Cecilia nearly collided with the detective herself as she rushed from an examining room to check on the status of a client who was in the transition stage of labor. Murmuring a barely civil apology, she sidestepped around him. She knew the man had an important job to do, but couldn't he understand that this was a terribly inconvenient time?

She thought longingly of her weekend vacation with Geoff, which now seemed so very far in the past. She'd been so busy since their return that her time with him had been all too brief. Even last weekend had been filled with professional meetings for both of them, two deliveries that had called her back to the clinic at inconvenient times, and other obligations that had seemed to have little purpose except to keep them apart.

She should get used to that, of course, since he would be leaving town before much longer, but she already found herself missing him. At least they had made the most of the time they'd had to spend together.

Forcing thoughts of Geoff to the back of her mind, she concentrated fiercely on the tasks at hand.

She was looking for Mari, for consultation about a new patient, when she overheard a snippet of heated conversation between the doctor and the detective. She had followed Mari to her small, cluttered office, where the door was always open to anyone who needed her. But Cecilia wasn't the only one who had been looking for Mari, apparently. Bryce Collins was already there.

Posed in a tense face-to-face confrontation, they didn't see Cecilia when she stepped into the doorway. She ducked quickly back into the hall just as Mari said, "Damn it, Bryce, can't you see how busy we are? I don't have time for this."

"Make time," he snapped back, his voice so hard that Cecilia instinctively flinched.

"How many times do I have to tell you that I know nothing about black-market drug suppliers?"

"Until you make me believe it. Something's going on in this clinic. Somebody here knows exactly where those drugs are coming from. And since you're in charge around here, *Dr.* Bingham, it's hard to accept that you're completely oblivious."

After what might have been a gasp, Mari said, "Surely you aren't suggesting I've been deliberately holding back information from the police."

"I'm not suggesting anything—I'm telling you that something is damned suspicious around here—and that a lot of the signs are pointing right at you. You have been pretty desperate to raise large amounts of cash for your new research facility, haven't you?"

This time it was Cecilia who gasped. She hadn't meant to eavesdrop, but she hadn't been able to avoid hearing that rapid-fire exchange. Surely Detective Collins wasn't flat-out accusing Mari of being involved in drug trafficking. Was the man completely off his rocker?

Even if Mari had broken his heart in the past, he had to know what an insane suggestion it was that Dr. Mari Bingham, to whom nothing was more important than this clinic and its patients, would have anything to do with something so evil and destructive.

Cecilia should probably make a hasty retreat, since this conversation was absolutely none of her business. But she really needed to consult with Mari, and she was beginning to believe Mari would appreciate the rescue. Besides, Cecilia was feeling a strong urge to rush to Mari's defense against this unfair attack, even though she knew Mari was fully capable of standing up for herself.

But a distraction came in the unlikely form of a young woman with wildly spiked blue hair and a pierced eyebrow. A new receptionist at the clinic, Heather was certainly an attention getter. Nodding to Cecilia, who had stepped somewhat abashedly back out of the way, embarrassed to be caught eavesdropping, Heather rushed to Mari's office door.

"Sorry to interrupt, Dr. Bingham, but we've got a situation developing out there in the waiting room. Some crazy woman is throwing a fit, saying she's hurtin' and she needs some Orcadol. She doesn't have an appointment or anything, but she said she got it here last time, and she needs it again. She's so strung out that none of us can make any sense of anything she says, so we think you'd better come."

Cecilia grimaced. She could just imagine what Bryce Collins would make of *that* jumbled summons, considering that he already thought Mari had something to do with illegally supplying the powerful and addictive painkiller.

She stepped into the doorway, determined to do what she could to deflect his attentions. "Mari, when you're free, I need to consult with you on a new patient. Late-stage pregnancy with a risk of preeclampsia."

Mari pushed a hand through her hair, then squeezed the back of her neck in a gesture that made her look even more like her brother than usual. "Thanks, Heather, I'll be right out. And, Cecilia, I promise I'll find you as soon as I'm available."

"Thank you." Cecilia turned to the officer then, her voice chilly when she asked, "Can I show you out, Detective Collins?"

He looked at her with narrowed eyes. "I know the way."

She nodded, then crossed her arms and waited, making it clear that she thought he was in the way of business. Heather also hovered nearby, looking curiously from Cecilia to Mari to the scowling detective.

Collins exhaled sharply, then pointed at Mari. "I'll be back. And if I find out that you're involved in this in any way, you can bet I'll do my job and haul you in."

Avoiding his eyes, she moved toward the doorway. "Just go away so I can do *my* job."

He stalked off, leaving the three women to glare after him.

"Mari, if there's anything I can do…" Cecilia began awkwardly.

Mari gave her a weary smile. "Thanks, Cecilia, but I can handle Bryce. Now, Heather, let's go take care of the crisis in the waiting room."

It looked like rain. Skimming down the highway on his motorcycle after escaping from a long, mind-numbingly boring day at the office, Geoff studied the dark clouds gathering over the mountains in the distance. He would bet that was a storm building on the horizon.

But in the meantime, he could enjoy the ride as he tried in vain to convince himself he wasn't counting the minutes until he could be with Cecilia again.

He wondered if he was coming down with something. Did the flu cause a person to walk around in an addled state or muddle his thoughts until he wasn't sure what was real anymore? How else could he explain his odd behavior of the past week and a half, ever since he had reluctantly brought Cecilia home from the cottage weekend?

He seemed to be waking with a new sense of expectancy each day. Rather than his usual rather grimly determined morning routines and obligations, he was singing in the shower, spending more time planning nice things to do for Cecilia than thinking about the business concerns that usually occupied nearly every waking minute of his days.

Odd, that, considering the limited nature of their partnership. Maybe it was because he was confident that the relationship was temporary that he could enjoy it so much, he rationalized. Maybe he saw his time with her as...well, as an emotional vacation of sorts. A chance to have a great time with a beautiful, sexy woman without worrying about where it would all lead.

Or maybe it was flu.

He slowed as he approached the city park. Although it was a weekday, there were still a few families taking advantage of the facilities on this steamy July afternoon.

One particular family caught his attention as he

cruised past. The man was tall with brown hair, the woman shorter with darker hair. She was a bit heavier than Cecilia, but the couple still looked oddly familiar. A small child bounced between them, an energetic boy of perhaps three.

Maybe he and Cecilia could bring their son to this park, he mused. They would laugh as he went down the slide and applaud when he navigated the monkey bars. And maybe that boy would have a little sister to play tag with and to—

Realizing where his thoughts were taking him, he shook his helmeted head. He and Cecilia weren't starting a family in the traditional sense. Their plan was to have a child together without sharing anything else in their lives. Cecilia had made it very clear that was all she wanted from him.

It was all he wanted, too. Right? The joy of a child without the drudgery of marriage?

And yet—drudgery seemed like such an inappropriate word when applied to Cecilia. She was so fascinating. So intriguing and challenging. And yet so restful. He thought it could very well take a lifetime to get to know every facet of her.

She fit with him in a way no woman had before her. He couldn't imagine anyone suiting him better. Not that he was looking for anyone better suited, he assured himself quickly. Everything was just fine for him the way it was.

He had his family, a successful career, and he could soon have a child to satisfy his natural desire to procreate. What more could he want. Right?

To be fair, the accident wasn't caused by his distraction with thoughts of Cecilia. Even with his mind so jumbled, he had followed every rule of the road, obeyed the speed limits, had come to a full stop at every intersection. Unfortunately, the driver of a rusty old sedan wasn't as careful. Either he didn't see the stop sign or didn't see the motorcycle, but he sped into the intersection at the same time as Geoff.

Geoff saw the car at the moment before impact. It gave him barely enough time to lay the bike down so that he didn't slam directly into the side of the big car.

As pain ripped through his left side, he only hoped his reaction hadn't been too little, too late.

The pace at the clinic was finally slowing a bit. Cecilia had already delivered healthy twin girls. The C-section was underway in the hospital. The hysterical Orcadol addict was on her way to rehab—though not without causing a major scene first. The waiting room was only half full now.

Maybe she would survive the day, after all, she thought as she pressed a hand to her aching back. It had been touch and go for a while there.

She still hadn't had a chance to talk to Mari. She checked on her next mother-to-be, who was, perhaps, a couple of hours away from delivery. Leaving her in the capable care of her husband and doula, Cecilia made another effort to have a quick conference with Mari. She still needed the consultation, of course, but she also wanted to see if Mari had recovered from the upsetting incident with Detective Collins.

She turned a corner into the hallway that led to Mari's office. As she walked that direction, she saw Mari step out, accompanied by a young man wearing an orderly's uniform. With her back partially turned to Cecilia, Mari pressed a stack of what looked very much like prescription slips into the young man's hand. He stuffed them unceremoniously into his pocket, turned and disappeared into the stairway at the other end of the hall from where Cecilia stood.

That had certainly looked odd, Cecilia thought, pausing in her steps for a moment as Mari moved back into her office.

And then she frowned and shook her head. She blamed Detective Collins for planting even the tiniest seed of doubt about Mari in her mind. There was no reason at all to find anything suspicious about that exchange, no matter how it might have looked to....

Hit suddenly by an eerie feeling of being watched, she glanced over her shoulder. Detective Collins lurked behind her at the very end of the hallway, arms crossed over his solid chest, one shoulder propped against the wall.

His gray eyes locked with hers, and his expression made her wonder if he suspected *everyone* at the clinic of being a drug pusher. Was he following her? Or watching Mari's office? She had no doubt he had seen the exchange between Mari and the orderly.

Probably because she was tired and grumpy, she took a step toward him with the intention of asking exactly what he thought was going on at the clinic. Before she had taken a second step, he turned and disappeared around the corner.

She was tempted to chase him down and ask her questions, anyway. Some remnant of common sense made her stop, take a deep breath and remind herself that belligerent confrontation was probably not the wisest way to deal with an overly suspicious officer of the law.

She turned back, instead, toward Mari's office. She would let her intuition tell her if Mari was acting in any way different than usual—though she still didn't believe there was even the tiniest bit of merit in Bryce Collins's accusations.

Mari was buried in paperwork. She looked up with a weary smile when she heard Cecilia in the doorway. "I haven't forgotten about you, Cecilia. It has just been an incredibly hectic day."

"For all of us," Cecilia agreed. "Our consultation can wait until tomorrow morning. I'll have some test results back by then. I'm quite concerned about this patient. She's determined to have a midwifery delivery, but I tend to think we should be considering an early cesarean section. I'd appreciate your opinion."

"I'll clear some time just before lunch, if that's convenient for you. We'll look over the file and the test results, and then we'll schedule a time when I can examine her for myself."

"Yes, that will be fine. Um, Mari—"

Before Cecilia could mention her strange encounter with Detective Collins in the hallway, the phone almost hidden beneath the papers on Mari's desk buzzed loudly.

Mari sighed deeply. "Hold on." She picked up the receiver. "Yes?"

A moment later she sat straight up in her chair, her expression shocked. "He did *what?* Is he all right? Okay, I'll be right there."

Slamming the phone back into the cradle, Mari jumped to her feet. "Cecilia, I'm sorry, but I have to go. Can you keep things running around here? I'm supposed to be in the conference room in ten minutes, but it looks like I'm going to be delayed.''

"Of course. I'll spread the word that you've been called away.''

"Thank you.'' Mari was already hurrying toward the doorway. "I won't forget about our consultation tomorrow, but I really have to go now. My brother has been injured in a motorcycle accident.''

Cecilia felt her heart leap straight into her throat. Holding on to the doorway to steady herself, she lifted a hand to her suddenly tight throat. "Is he going to be all right?'' she called after her rapidly departing supervisor.

Mari replied without looking back. "Yes, I think so. I just need to go see him.''

Mari disappeared around the same corner Detective Collins had vanished around earlier. Cecilia was left standing in the hallway, her heart pounding so hard against her chest that she could hardly breathe.

She had no right to hurry after Mari to Geoff's side. He needed his family now, not his temporary...what? Fling? Lover? Neither term seemed to fit.

Putting both hands to her temples, she tried to collect herself. She had a baby to deliver. She had to put her emotions aside. And more importantly, she had to resist the impulse to abandon her responsibilities and rush to Geoff, even if it almost killed her.

Chapter Thirteen

Geoff climbed out of his car very carefully Thursday evening. The walk from the car to Cecilia's front door seemed a bit longer than usual as his aching muscles protested every step.

Confident that he looked fine, scrapes and bruises hidden for now beneath a blue shirt and khaki slacks, he held himself straight and rang the doorbell. Thanks to his helmet, there were no injuries to his head or face, but the truth was, he'd been damned lucky today.

Cecilia opened the door. Something in her expression made the smile he had donned for her benefit fade away.

"I, uh, guess you heard," he said when she only stood there, staring mutely up at him.

"I heard." She moved aside so he could enter.

He might have reached out to her then to give her his usual kiss of greeting, but her body language was perfectly clear: "Stay back."

She closed the door behind him, her movements very deliberate. "I take it you aren't seriously injured?"

He supposed there was concern in the question. She had spoken so mechanically that it was hard to tell. "A few scrapes. There was no reason for me to even go to the emergency room, but the cops insisted."

She nodded. Her arms were crossed in front of her now, and her dark eyes were so shuttered that he saw no expression in them at all. "I'm glad you're okay."

He raised his left hand to the back of his neck, then immediately regretted the habitual gesture. He lowered the arm very carefully back to his side, feeling his scraped elbow throb in rhythm with his heartbeats.

Perhaps she was angry with him for some reason. There was only one way to find out for sure. "What's wrong, Cecilia? Are you annoyed because I didn't call you? Because I knew you were busy, and my cell phone was smashed in the wreck, and I wasn't really hurt, anyway...."

Deciding he sounded like a babbling idiot, he shut up.

Cecilia seemed to rouse from her reverie then. Blinking a few times, she tucked a strand of hair behind her ear. "I worked late this evening, delivering a baby who decided during the latter stage of labor to take his sweet time coming out. I haven't been home long enough to start dinner. How about if we order pizza again? Or if you want to head on home and soak in a hot bath, I'll understand."

Because she sounded suspiciously hopeful when she made that suggestion, he asked, "Do you want me to leave?"

Her look of surprise in response to the blunt question was patently false. "No, of course not. I just thought you'd—"

"I don't need a hot bath," he said, deciding to pretend as though everything was completely normal until she relaxed enough to tell him what was going on. "Pizza sounds fine. In fact, I'll order. What kind do you want? Veggie?"

"Sure. Okay. Veggie."

She was definitely not acting like herself, he thought as he placed the order. Should he pressure her to tell him what was wrong or give her time to volunteer the explanation?

He decided the latter was probably the best plan. He never liked being nagged to talk when something was bugging him. So he really should give Cecilia some space.

But, being the impatient sort that he was, he barely made it back across the room before he asked, "So, did you have a bad day at work?"

"Not bad, particularly. Hectic."

"You must be tired." Could that be the explanation? Simple exhaustion. If so, he had just the remedy. A night of lazy pampering would do them both good.

"Yes, a bit."

He lowered himself gingerly onto the couch, then patted the cushion on his right side. "Then let's just kick back and relax and you can tell me all about it."

She made no move to sit down. "Actually, I think

I would like some coffee. Do you want something? Juice, maybe?''

He stifled a sigh, telling himself again to be patient and let her take her time. "I'm okay for now. Thanks."

She was gone for quite a while. She must be harvesting the coffee beans, he decided wryly. She was certainly brewing it so long it should be strong enough to walk back into the living room by itself.

She finally reappeared, carrying a steaming mug cradled between both hands. She seemed to be taking care not to meet his eyes. He waited until she had taken a seat—notably not beside him on the couch, but in one of the chairs. And her body language was no more open or encouraging now than it had been when he had first arrived. "You're going to have to tell me what's wrong eventually, you know."

"There's nothing wrong, Geoff. I told you, it's been a long day. There was a rush on our services. A strung-out drug addict made a scene in the waiting room. Detective Collins made an absolute pest of himself, even coming out and accusing Mari of knowing something about black-market drug trafficking. It was all I could do to keep from kicking him out of the clinic myself then, even though it certainly wasn't my place to do so."

"It couldn't have helped your day when you heard I had stupidly wrecked my bike," he said, trying to imagine how he would have felt if something similar had happened to her. He didn't even want to think about that.

She scowled down into the coffee. "No. That didn't help at all."

Suddenly realizing exactly what she had said before he'd brought up the accident, he straightened sharply on the couch, muttered a curse when his whole left side throbbed in reaction, then said, "What was that about Bryce accusing Mari of drug trafficking?"

"I said he practically accused her. He didn't come right out and say those words, but he said he doesn't believe she's telling him everything she knows. He even implied that her ambition to raise money for the medical research center could make her receptive to drug money."

"I'll pound his face in," Geoff said between clenched teeth as a wave of fury rushed through him.

She answered a bit sarcastically, "Oh, that will help. You and Mari can request adjoining jail cells."

He made an effort to get his rarely seen temper under control. "I'll call our lawyer tomorrow and see what I can do about keeping Collins away from Mari."

"Maybe you had better ask Mari what she wants you to do first. She might not appreciate you rushing to her rescue without telling her. And she probably wouldn't be at all pleased that I've been reporting to you about what I accidentally overheard Detective Collins say to her in the privacy of her office."

"All right, I'll talk to her. I'll tell her I've heard he's been on her case and ask her how she wants me to handle it. I can't believe that guy would still be nursing such a grudge against her that he would let it interfere with his professional objectivity. There's no way he can honestly believe she would get involved in that kind of sleaze."

"Of course not. No one who knows Mari would believe such a thing."

"How did she take it? Tell me she slugged him."

Cecilia shook her head. "Of course she didn't slug him. She managed to contain her temper—and her dignity—very well."

"She should've slugged him," he muttered.

"I never realized you had such a violent side to you."

"Only when someone messes with someone I care about." And it occurred to him suddenly that he would be just as belligerent toward anyone who was making trouble for Cecilia.

Because he wasn't sure she would want to hear that right now, he said only, "Collins has really gone over the line. He couldn't have a scrap of evidence that Mari is involved in anything suspicious."

Cecilia started to say something, but stopped when the doorbell rang. Geoff wondered what it was she'd started to tell him. Something she knew about the investigation? Some reason, no matter how unlikely, why Collins may have set his sights on Mari. Making a mental note to ask her later, he watched as she set her coffee cup on the table beside her chair. "That will be the pizza. I'll get it."

He held up a hand to keep her in her seat while he rose, exerting all his strength to keep her from seeing how much the movement pained him. "I ordered. I'll get it."

She looked as though she was going to argue, but she must have known it would do no good. Settling back into her seat, she subsided into the same moody silence as before, to Geoff's exasperation.

* * *

Cecilia was struggling to act naturally with Geoff this evening, but she didn't try to delude herself that she was being successful at it. The truth was, she didn't quite know what she was feeling. Numbness seemed to be the closest description.

She looked down at the half-eaten slice of pizza on her plate, doubtful that she could swallow another bite. She wasn't usually the type to overreact so dramatically to a trying day, but this day had been more than ordinarily stressful.

"Tell me the truth, Cecilia. Are you angry with me?"

She couldn't meet his eyes when she answered. "No, of course I'm not angry."

It wasn't quite a lie, she assured herself. She wasn't angry with him…exactly. More perturbed with him for risking his life and scaring her so badly, which was so unreasonable of her that she didn't know how to explain it to him.

"Then what's wrong? Did something bad happen with one of your deliveries?"

"No. I've already told you how hectic my day was. Nothing specifically upsetting, just a series of complications."

And that, she thought, was the biggest lie she had told him yet. Of course there had been a specific incident that had upset her today. Hearing Mari say that Geoff had been involved in a motorcycle accident had shaken Cecilia all the way to the core.

She had managed to control her emotions while she'd completed her workday, even smiling and speaking cheerfully during the prolonged but uneventful delivery of the Claussen baby boy. And then, after tapping the hospital grapevine to discover that Geoff had already been released from the emergency room, she had come home and pretty much fallen apart.

Just remembering that period of secret anxiety between watching Mari rush away and hearing that Geoff's injuries had only been minor ones made Cecilia's chest start to ache again. Finding that she simply couldn't sit still any longer, she pushed her chair back abruptly and sprang to her feet. "I need some more lemonade. Can I get you anything while I'm up?"

She waited barely long enough for him to decline the offer before she rushed into the kitchen. Maybe if she had just another few minutes to collect herself...

Geoff didn't give her those minutes. He followed her into the kitchen, then stood blocking the door, his arms crossed, his expression grimly determined.

"I've tried to be patient," he said, his voice quiet but firm. "I thought you would eventually get around to telling me what's bothering you this evening. But it isn't working. You're not giving me any clues. What's going on, Cecilia?"

"I told you, I'm just—"

"Tired," he finished in unison with her. "But that doesn't cut it. It's more than that."

She reached for a paper towel and wiped at an imaginary spot on the countertop, just to give her unsteady hands something to do. "I don't—"

"Cecilia." He had moved to stand very close behind her. "If it isn't your work that's upsetting you, it must be me. And the only thing I've done today is get involved in a minor motorcycle accident."

Saying nothing, she crumpled the paper towel in her hand.

"Are you annoyed that I didn't call you? Or have someone else call you? I explained why I didn't. And besides, when I mentioned that someone should let you know what happened, Mari told me you were with her when the emergency room nurse called her— without my knowledge, I might add. Mari told me she had let you know it wasn't a serious accident."

"Yes, she said she thought you would be fine."

"So you weren't worried about me."

"Not worried?" Feeling something snap inside her, she threw the paper towel on the counter and whirled to face him. "Not worried? Are you joking?"

He looked surprised by her vehemence. "You mean, you were worried? Even though Mari told you—"

"Mari told me—as she left her office at a run— that her brother had been in a motorcycle accident and while she *thought* he would be okay, she was obviously frantic to find out for herself. That was the last I heard until a few hours later when I finally managed to find out that you had been treated and released."

Now he looked defensive. "I told you I thought you'd been kept informed."

"Right. You told me."

"Look, I didn't realize you would be so concerned. And while I appreciate that you were worried about me, I—"

She glared at him, wondering if he could really be so obtuse. "I just knew that motorcycle was an accident waiting to happen."

That made his eyes narrow. "Now you sound like my father and my sister. Both of them spent a couple of hours yelling at me this afternoon about the bike. Telling me how reckless and irresponsible it is for me to even own the thing, much less take it for an occasional ride."

She lifted her chin. "Maybe I agree with them."

He scowled. "Great."

Though she tried to hold them back, the words spilled from her, anyway. "Well, you do have responsibilities—to your family, who love you and depend on you—and to Bingham Enterprises, where you serve a very important role."

"And to you, of course," he added. "Were you afraid I'd broken my neck before I fulfilled my bargain to you?"

That made her jaw drop. "That is *not* what I was concerned about!"

He lifted his left hand to the back of his neck, grimaced, then dropped the arm to his side again. She had already noticed that he had been favoring his left side all evening. Heaven only knew what sort of scrapes and bruises he was hiding beneath his long-sleeved blue shirt.

When he spoke, his tone wasn't as cutting, but it was still aggrieved. "I really didn't expect *you* to lecture me about obligations and responsibilities. I thought you, at least, understood me better than that."

"I'm sorry," she said stiffly. "I realize I have no right to lecture you about anything."

Just as she'd had no right to expect to be called when he was injured, she added silently. No right to ask him to be careful. No right to know where he was when he wasn't with her. What he was doing. Or who he was with.

This was exactly what he'd made it clear that he didn't want from her—or any other woman. He had said he had too many people to answer to already. Too many expectations to live up to, too many commitments to fulfill.

He wasn't interested in a wife. Not even a long-term relationship. And she had thought that was fine with her. Exactly what she wanted, too.

Or so she had believed.

Because she understood now how unfair she was being to criticize him when she was the one who seemed to be changing the rules, she sighed and shook her head.

"I'm sorry," she said again—only this time she meant it. "I really *don't* have a right to lecture you. You just scared me, that's all. I was already stressed today, and when I heard you'd been in an accident, I guess I just freaked out a little."

She watched as his face softened a bit and his taut shoulders relaxed. "And I'm sorry I snapped at you. I should be grateful that you were concerned about me. And I should have realized you would be."

Still shaking her head, she took a step toward him. "Don't apologize. I'm the one who's been acting unreasonably. I suppose I do need to sit on the couch and relax for a little while, as you suggested earlier. Why don't I serve us both some ice cream—I have your favorite, chocolate—and then we can crash in front of the TV. Unless you need to go?"

"Ice cream and TV sound good to me," he assured

her and then gave her a decent imitation of his usual
lazy grin. "But let's not use the word *crash,* okay?"

The sharp words they had both spoken weren't forgotten, Cecilia mused, but she and Geoff could put
them aside for the rest of the evening. After all, there
wouldn't be many more evenings to spend together
before they returned to their separate lives.

He would probably be relieved to move on, especially after this. She didn't think it would be quite so
easy for her.

Which was all the more reason for her to try to
enjoy the remaining time they had together.

Sitting on the couch at Geoff's right side an hour
later, Cecilia felt a bit of tension ease from her shoulders. They hadn't said much since they had moved
into the living room, but the silence had been companionable. Having eaten their ice cream, they sipped
the herbal tea Geoff had brought her and watched a
new documentary on the history channel. The program was interesting, informative, quietly entertaining—just the sort of calming activity they both
needed.

As the program neared its end, she noticed that
Geoff was beginning to squirm a little—surreptitiously rubbing his left arm and shoulder, stretching
his leg out as if it were cramping.

She set her empty teacup on a side table. "Are you
in pain?"

"No, I'm fine."

She gave him a look that let him know he wasn't
fooling her for a minute.

Geoff made a face. "Okay, I'm a little sore," he admitted. "Kind of stiffening up."

She twisted on the couch to face him more fully. "Just how badly were you hurt? Really?"

"Nothing serious. Really. As I said, it's just scrapes and bruises."

She reached out to unfasten the top button of his shirt. "So you won't mind if I check for myself?"

"Um—" He cleared his throat as another button popped out of its hole. "Just remember, it looks worse than it is."

"I'm a nurse. I know how to assess an injury." She slid the unbuttoned shirt carefully off his shoulders.

Had she not been a nurse, she might have gasped. Fortunately, her training helped her see with one long, searching glance that he had told the truth about the severity of his injuries.

Though the scrapes down his arm and his side were raw and angry looking and the bruises were already turning a rainbow of muddy colors, none of the wounds was serious. He was going to feel like hell for the next week or so—the soreness and stiffness would get worse before they got better—but he would suffer no long-lasting repercussions.

"You got lucky," she said.

He released a breath he must have been holding while she examined him. "I know. Dad blew a gasket when he saw me, but Mari convinced him I would be okay despite appearances. He's not a medical professional, of course, so it looked worse to him than it is."

"Were you given a prescription for pain medication? Because you might need something later."

"Mari tried to give me some pills to take, but I told her I didn't need them. I don't like to take prescription medications unless it is absolutely necessary. I can manage this with over-the-counter painkillers."

She frowned, both because it had been Mari, rather than the E.R. doctor, who had offered the pills, and because Geoff had turned them down. "I don't know, Geoff. You're going to be awfully sore. There's nothing wrong with taking something to make you feel better."

"You know what would *really* make me feel better?"

She looked up from his bruises to his face. His smile gave her a clue what he was going to say when she asked, "What?"

For a man whose left side looked as though it had been attacked by a cheese grater, he moved surprisingly quickly. He pulled her against his bare chest, letting his mouth hover only an inch above hers. "I'm prescribing my own medication."

She slid her hands up his chest, taking care where she touched. "And just what do you prescribe, doctor?"

"You."

She smiled against his lips. "I just happen to be available."

He might have murmured something about being glad to hear it, but since the words were lost in the depths of a spectacular kiss, she would never know for sure. Truth was, she didn't really care.

It was very…interesting making love to a man who had recently been injured, Cecilia discovered. When he had insisted that he was up to the activity even as she expressed her doubts, Cecilia had willingly co-operated.

On one condition, she had added. She would do all the work.

It was quite a challenge. She had to take great care to give him only pleasure and not cause him any pain. Oddly enough, doing so greatly enhanced her own pleasure.

She covered him with gentle, tender kisses. And then she covered him with herself. And when tears rolled down her cheeks as they experienced their release together, she knew it had much more to do with almost losing him that afternoon than with the physical gratification she had found with him now.

It was pain that drove Geoff from Cecilia's bed sometime around midnight. Gritting his teeth, he slipped stiffly from beneath the covers. He was relieved when she didn't stir. Remembering her description of her day, he knew she must be worn out.

He found nonprescription painkillers in her medicine cabinet. Though the dosage was two tablets, he swallowed four.

He really was hurting. He doubted that the four little brown pills would be nearly as effective against his pain as Cecilia's tender loving care had been earlier, but it didn't seem like a particularly good idea to wake her for another dose.

Wearing only a pair of boxer shorts over his sorely abused body, he prowled restlessly through Cecilia's house while he waited for the medicine to take effect. He ended up in the room they had painted together last week.

The nursery.

Looking at the maple rocker that was the only piece of furniture in the green-walled bedroom, he allowed himself a few minutes to savor the memories of that day that seemed oddly longer ago than it actually had been. The laughter. The kisses. The long, arousing shower that had followed their silly play with the paint.

And then his thoughts drifted forward. To the future that might be. He could almost see a crib against the far wall, and a tiny body sleeping peacefully in that crib. He could picture Cecilia lifting the baby from the crib and settling into the rocker for a middle-of-the-night nursing. And he saw himself, standing in the doorway to watch.

But no, that wasn't right, he thought with a shake of his head. He didn't belong in that particular scene. He wouldn't be here for feedings and baths and bed-time stories and first smiles. That was the agreement they had made. He would be the part-time parent, the one who popped in for weekend and holiday visitations, while Cecilia would handle the day-to-day responsibilities he had said he didn't want.

Hadn't this evening proved he was right about having someone else to answer to if he got seriously involved with a woman? After being chewed out by his family just for trying to have a little fun on his bike, he'd had to endure pretty much the same from Cecilia. Another lecture about his obligations to family and business. More wounded looks that had made him feel guilty for being in an accident that hadn't even been his fault.

So why did he find it sort of nice that she had been so frightened on his behalf?

''Geoff?'' Cecilia's sleepy voice came from the hallway behind him. ''Are you all right?''

Turning away from the empty wall where he had just imagined a crib to be, he responded. ''Yes, I'm fine. Just a little sore.''

He snapped off the nursery light as he went to meet her and to assure her again that he was okay—physically, at least. Emotionally—well, he seemed to be a little shaky in that area this evening.

Chapter Fourteen

Cecilia was on her way to Mari's office for the scheduled consultation Friday morning when she crossed paths with Vanessa. Because it was so unusual to see Vanessa frowning, Cecilia had to take a minute to stop and ask what was wrong.

"Everything is just so crazy around here lately," her friend complained. "Have you noticed it, too, or is it just me?"

"Trust me, it's not just you. I've been wondering if the planets are misaligned."

"Wouldn't surprise me at all."

"Is there anything in particular that's got you scowling now or just a series of events?"

Vanessa made a face. "I've been dealing with a mess in the medical supply room. Everything's rearranged. I couldn't even find the Orcadol. Someone put all the bottles in the wrong place."

Cecilia frowned and spoke quickly, "Orcadol is missing? Should we notify Detective Collins?"

Vanessa shook her head, making her enormous earrings swing wildly. She held both hands up in a calming and rather pleading gesture. "Lord, don't get the detective all worked up again. I didn't say anything was missing, just misplaced. The new security measures seem to be working well enough to satisfy even Detective Collins. The filing system, on the other hand, definitely needs some work."

It still concerned Cecilia that Orcadol had been incorrectly shelved, but she told herself Vanessa had the situation under control. She was just oversensitive about the subject, she supposed, after what she had overheard between Collins and Mari. "I'm on my way to a consultation with Mari. It shouldn't take too long. Want to grab lunch afterward and have a nice, long gripe session?"

"You bet I do. Find me when you're free."

Cecilia nodded and moved on toward Mari's office. Mari looked up from her usual mountain of paperwork with a smile. Obviously, judging from her expression, she was having a better day than yesterday.

"Thank God it's Friday," she said as Cecilia took a chair beside the desk in response to a wave from Mari's hand. "Those words have never seemed more appropriate than they do this week."

"I know what you mean. Vanessa and I were just saying something to that effect. It's been a madhouse around here."

"Speaking of which—I'm sorry I ran out of here like a crazy woman yesterday."

"I understood. You were worried about your

brother.'' Cecilia had pretty much been a crazy woman herself after that, though she had done her best to hide it.

Mari nodded gravely. ''Yeah. I hate that motorcycle, and Geoff knows it. It's a miracle he didn't break his fool neck.''

Were you afraid I'd broken my neck before I fulfilled my bargain to you? Cecilia could hear the echo of Geoff's resentful question in her mind, and it still irritated her.

''I'm glad he wasn't seriously injured'' was all she said to his sister.

Mari's face softened. ''Me, too. As annoyed as I get with him at times, I still love the guy.''

Cecilia was becoming increasingly concerned that she did, too. And that possibility terrified her almost as badly as Geoff's motorcycle.

''Did you see him last night?'' Mari asked casually. ''He seemed anxious to let you know he wasn't seriously injured.''

So maybe he *had* thought she'd been kept informed. It made Cecilia feel somewhat better that he had at least thought of her. She answered very casually. ''Yes, he came by my place for dinner. He looked battered, but generally in good shape.''

''Bet he's sore today.'' Mari sounded more amused than perturbed. Typical sibling, Cecilia thought with a slight smile. Mari had ''I told him so'' written all over her.

There was a bit more compassion in Cecilia's reply. ''I'm sure he is.''

''So you and Geoff have been seeing quite a bit of each other during the last few weeks, haven't you?''

Also typical big sister. Nosy.

"We're friends," Cecilia said with a light shrug. "He's been at loose ends while he waits for the next business jaunt, and it turns out we share a fondness for pizza and the history channel."

She had been making similar explanations so frequently during the past few weeks that it came naturally to her now. She hadn't even had to stop to think about how to respond without piquing his sister's interest.

Mari looked a bit disappointed by the prosaic response. "He does love the history channel. And he rarely finds anyone willing to watch it with him."

"Same here. Now, about this new patient I saw yesterday…"

Confident that she had adequately deflected Mari's curiosity—at least for now—Cecilia kept the conversation on business for the rest of the meeting.

She would leave it to Geoff to make explanations if a pregnancy test yielded positive results at the end of the month.

Geoff doubted that it was entirely coincidence that he ran into Eric Mendoza in the hallway of Bingham Enterprises Friday afternoon.

"I heard about your accident yesterday," Eric commented. "How are you feeling today?"

"Like I got hit by a Buick," Geoff answered wryly. "I've got some fresh-squeezed orange juice in my office. Want a glass? Or I could have someone bring you a cup of coffee."

The quickness with which Eric accepted reinforced Geoff's suspicion that he was in for a brotherly interrogation. "Orange juice sounds good, thanks. CeCe's the coffee fanatic in our family."

"CeCe?"

Eric shrugged as he followed Geoff into the spacious office. "I've called her that since I was a toddler. She raised me, you know. Our mother was always away at one job or another and Cecilia, who's eleven years older, was my substitute mom—except for the two years she was married when I was between eight and ten."

"She still seems to have very maternal feelings toward you." Geoff handed Eric a crystal goblet of ice-cold juice.

Eric accepted it with thanks, took a chair, then remarked as Geoff sank into his own chair, "You seem to be moving sort of stiffly today. Pretty sore, huh?"

"You can say that again." Geoff opened a drawer in his desk, pulled out a bottle of ibuprofen, shook a couple into his palm and washed them down with orange juice.

"So how's your bike?"

Geoff grimaced. "It's in ICU at the Harley shop. It's a mess, but fixable."

"So you're keeping it?"

"Of course I'm keeping it. I love that bike."

"Never had one, myself. CeCe would've had a nervous breakdown if I'd even suggested it."

"She does seem to have a rather marked aversion to motorcycles."

"I guess they remind her too much of her dad. Understandable, I suppose."

Geoff leaned back in his chair, studying the younger man's somber face. "What do you mean?"

Eric's dark eyebrows lifted, an expression that reminded Geoff forcibly of Cecilia. The Mendoza siblings were certainly a good-looking pair. "CeCe hasn't told you about her father?"

"No, she hasn't really mentioned him. I know he died when she was young."

"Yeah. He died in a freak whitewater accident. Capsized and broke his neck on a submerged boulder."

Geoff winced as he remembered his ill-tempered comment about Cecilia being afraid he had broken his neck before he fulfilled their bargain. "I, uh, didn't know that."

"Apparently, he was a real daredevil. Always doing something dangerous, keeping his wife and daughter worried about him. He raced motorcycles, nearly got himself killed on them a couple of times before the kayaking accident."

Damn it, why hadn't she told him? This information explained so much about the way she had reacted when she heard about Geoff's accident.

"She doesn't like to talk about her dad. Neither did our mother. I don't know a lot about Cecilia's father, but I know neither one of them ever fully recovered from his death."

Not only had Geoff unwittingly brought all those painful memories back, he'd even snarled at her when she had shown concern for him. He wished he had known all this sooner. He felt like a heel.

"So," Eric said after draining his glass, "when are you leaving town again?"

Was that a hint? "In a week or two. The arrangements are still sort of tentative."

Eric nodded. ''I suppose you'll be glad to get back to a big city. You must be getting pretty bored with the limited entertainment Merlyn County has to offer.''

''No, actually I haven't been at all bored.''

''Mmm.'' Eric gave him a long, measuring look. ''I haven't seen much of my sister lately. I understand she's been spending a lot of her spare time with you. Anything I should know about?''

Geoff tried to keep his expression unreadable. ''No.''

Not yet, anyway.

But he didn't blame Eric for asking. If some guy with unclear motives came sniffing around Mari, Geoff would want to know if there was anything to worry about. He was still considering finding Bryce Collins and making a few not-so-veiled threats.

He and Eric talked about business for a few minutes. Geoff asked about Hannah, and then Eric took his leave, obviously having more questions to ask but not sure how to phrase them. Geoff was left to pace his office, business completely forgotten as he considered the things Eric had told him about Cecilia.

Cecilia had only been back from lunch for an hour when she was summoned to a telephone. Patting the knee of a young woman who was in the early stages of labor, she promised to check back in soon. And then she found a quiet corner in which to take her call. ''Hello?''

''Hello, CeCe.''

The nickname was the one only her brother used,

but the deep, amused voice was Geoff's. "You've been talking to Eric."

"Yes. It was a very…illuminating conversation."

"That sounds rather unnerving."

"Don't worry. He didn't tell me anything that would embarrass you."

"That's a relief." Cecilia glanced at her watch. As much as she enjoyed talking with Geoff, she had a lot to do. "How are you feeling?"

"Fine. But I need a favor from you."

"A favor? What is it?"

"I need you to join me for dinner this evening."

She smiled. "That doesn't sound so—"

"At my grandmother's house."

Cecilia sank into the nearest chair. "Oh."

"It's sort of a command performance. My grandmother heard about the bike wreck, and she wants to see for herself that I'm okay."

"That's certainly understandable. But—"

"I need you there, Cecilia. Someone has to protect me."

"Why do you need protection from your grandmother?"

"She'll be much less likely to yell at me about the motorcycle if you're there. Not to mention that she could hardly try to fix me up with all her friends' granddaughters if I have a date."

"I don't know, Geoff. I'm really not very comfortable with the idea of having dinner with your grandmother. What's she going to think about us—being there together, I mean?"

"She'll think I've brought one of my nice friends

along to entertain her. She'll be delighted. My grandmother loves entertaining.''

''But I—''

''Did I mention that I'm pretty sore today? I'll hide
the bruises, of course, but my grandmother's sure to
notice how stiff I am unless there's something to distract her.''

The man was shameless.

When she didn't immediately respond, he sighed
lightly into the phone. ''Don't worry, Cecilia, I won't
pressure you into going if you would rather not. It
isn't as if you owe me any favors.''

Completely shameless! Of course she owed him a
favor. A rather big one, at that.

''All right. I'll go.''

''Great.'' He seemed to have absolutely no remorse
about pretty much blackmailing her into accepting.
''I'll pick you up at seven.''

''Yeah,'' she grumbled as she hung up the phone.
''Great.''

Why, oh why, had she let him talk her into this?

Geoff arrived at Cecilia's house a bit earlier than
seven o'clock. As it was, he'd had to make himself
kill a little time before leaving his condo. His eagerness to be with Cecilia was a bit daunting, since it
seemed so uncharacteristic.

He could list plenty of things that were different
about this relationship from the casual and temporary
affairs he had enjoyed in the past. The way he
counted the minutes he was away from her. The way
he savored each one he spent with her. The way he
woke thinking of her every morning. Hell, the way

he found himself grinning at nothing in the middle of a busy afternoon.

He'd been accused of being a little slow when it came to relationship issues, but even he could figure out that there was more than simple friendship involved in his feelings for Cecilia.

Even his eagerness to have him join her at Myrtle's was a little suspect. He usually tried to keep his girlfriends away from his matchmaking grandma. While the excuses he had used with Cecilia about deflecting Myrtle's attention were all legitimate, they didn't fully explain his compulsion to invite her. Cecilia seemed to fit with his family. He and Myrtle would both enjoy having her there.

This was definitely getting complicated. Especially when he considered how reluctant he was to think about leaving town again in a couple of weeks. For the first time he would be leaving behind someone other than family whom he would greatly miss.

He wasn't expecting to spot Cecilia standing in the front yard next door to her house, involved in a visibly tense confrontation with Brandy and the notorious Marlin. Keeping his eye on that scene, he climbed slowly out of his car.

He couldn't hear the words, but he heard the voices—Marlin's arrogant and furious, as usual, Brandy's tearful and pleading, also as usual, and Cecilia's firm and authoritative. Geoff hesitated, unsure whether to get involved or stay right where he was for now.

The decision was made for him when the argument turned violent. Marlin must have said something about leaving, because Brandy launched herself at him, obviously trying to hold him there. He shoved her, making her fall backward on the grass. Cecilia immediately rushed forward, and Marlin whirled, one arm cocked back as though to strike her.

Brandy cried out, "Marlin, *no!*"

Forgetting his sore muscles, Geoff sprinted in that direction. If that thug laid a hand on Cecilia...

Some last-minute shred of common sense—or maybe a glimpse of Geoff charging toward him like an enraged bull—made Marlin drop his arm and turn toward his truck. Geoff caught up with him at the door of the ugly vehicle. "You must be Marlin."

A scowl darkening his rather greasy face, and a bully's cowardice reflected in his eyes as he faced the man who was older, taller and in peak condition— except for a few recent dings and dents, Geoff thought ruefully—Marlin responded wittily. "Yeah. So?"

"My name is Geoff Bingham." Pausing a beat to let the significance of the last name sink in, Geoff added, "I'm a friend of Cecilia's, and of Brandy's. And if I hear that you've laid a hand on either of them, I will make your life a living hell."

Marlin blanched a bit, but he tried not to lose his blustering defiance. "You can save your threats," he snarled, jerking open the driver's door of the truck. "'Cause I don't plan to see either of them ever again."

Brandy broke into wails as Marlin drove away. Geoff moved to assist Cecilia in helping the girl to her feet.

"I thought he was going to hit you," Brandy told Cecilia.

"I thought so, myself, for a moment," Cecilia said,

brushing a strand of red hair away from Brandy's tear-dampened face. "Of course, if he had, I'd have been forced to pound him into the ground."

Brandy hiccuped in surprise at Cecilia's unexpectedly fierce response. "You…you would?"

"Honey, I've told you before. No man—or overgrown brat of a boy—has a right to put his hands on you in anger. Ever. And I promise you, no guy is ever going to do so with me. Not twice, anyway."

"Why do you think he backed off?" Geoff tried to keep his tone as light as possible under the circumstances. "Bullies are all cowards under the surface. If they can tell someone's going to fight back, they swagger off."

"He said he wasn't ever coming back," Brandy said, sounding forlorn.

"Actually, he probably will—the next time he needs a cheering section. Or a punching bag," Geoff said bluntly. "You're the one who's going to have to be strong and send him away. Even if it means calling the cops to escort him off the property."

"He really can be sweet, if he could just learn to control his temper."

Geoff tried to hide the impatience that would serve no purpose at all in helping get through to her. "Brandy, you're an attractive, intelligent girl. You don't have to put up with being treated the way he treats you. You deserve better."

Brandy looked from Geoff to Cecilia again. "I thought I loved him. And maybe I still sort of do, but when I saw his face when he turned on you, well, he looked like a stranger. A scary one."

"You were seeing who he really is, Brandy,"

Cecilia told her firmly. "And I agree wholeheartedly with Geoff. You deserve better."

Brandy drew a deep, unsteady breath. "Yeah. Maybe."

"Remember the talk you and I had last week?" Cecilia asked, brushing a hand over the girl's hair again. "When I told you about that very nice counselor at the clinic? Her specialty is talking to girls and women who have been involved with abusive men. She can help you understand why Marlin thought he could treat you that way and help you see why you deserve so much better. You're hurting inside, sweetie, and she can help you. Will you let me make an appointment for you?"

"I don't know. I'd feel funny talking to some stranger."

"I know the counselor Cecilia's talking about, Brandy. She's very nice. *I* would talk to her in a New York minute if I had a problem I needed help solving."

Brandy looked at Geoff then, first with skepticism and then with slow consideration. "You would? Really?"

"Really." It occurred to him that she was accepting his input because he was a confident-sounding male. Because she still lacked the confidence to trust her own judgment. Perhaps counseling could give her the self-assurance she needed to prevent her from falling back under Marlin's control—or that of some other abusive man in the future.

"Why don't you go back in the house and wait for your grandparents to come home," Cecilia suggested. "Lock your doors, and if Marlin comes back, don't let him in. No matter what he says, Brandy. Because he *isn't* sorry and he doesn't love you. Not if he's so willing to hurt you.''

Shoulders slumped, Brandy twisted her hands in front of her. ''He won't be back tonight. He's too mad, and he wants me to be miserable without him for a night or two. It's what he always does.''

''Good. Instead of being miserable, you can enjoy your new freedom. Call Lizzie and go buy a new outfit without worrying about whether Marlin will like it. Smile again, Brandy. You're only seventeen. Enjoy it.''

''Let me walk you to your door.'' Geoff crooked his arm and gave Brandy a smile.

She looked at his arm, at his face and back at his arm again. And then, very tentatively, she laid her fingertips on his forearm.

He bade her good-night at the door, advised her again to talk to the counselor, then waited until he heard the door lock behind her before he turned back to Cecilia.

He had quite a few things to say to her, but not here. ''Are you ready to leave?''

''Yes.''

Only then did he notice that she was dressed for dinner in a sleek black-and-white summer pantsuit. ''You look very nice.''

She smoothed her hands down the front of her outfit in a nervous gesture. ''Thank you.''

Belted into his car and on the road to his grandmother's house, Geoff wondered how to start yelling at Cecilia without sounding like Marlin. ''You do realize that interfering in domestic-violence situations is extremely dangerous, don't you?''

''I heard Marlin screaming at Brandy again, and I just couldn't stay out of it. I went running over there without stopping to think about it.''

''And it almost got you punched by the little punk. You should have called the police.''

''He didn't punch me,'' she pointed out. ''And if he had, he would have found himself in more trouble than he ever expected. As my brother would tell you, I'm not as delicate as I might appear. I was married for two years to a guy who thought being male gave him some sort of natural superiority. He kept pushing it a little further until I packed my bags and told him to go to hell.''

''I'm not questioning your spunk, Cecilia. You've proven enough times that you have plenty of that. But the fact is, you're a small woman, and he had four inches and a good thirty pounds advantage over you. He could have hurt you.''

The thought of Marlin's fist connecting with Cecilia's face made Geoff's hands white-knuckled around the steering wheel. ''Damn it, Cecilia, you should have called the police. Putting yourself in that situation was—''

''Reckless?'' she murmured. ''Irresponsible?''

He started to retort, then bit back the words. Okay, he got the allusion. He had asserted that she had no right to judge or criticize his actions; he had no more right to yell at her for her decisions. It was just that…

''You scared me,'' he admitted.

''Imagine that.''

He gave a deep sigh. ''Okay. Point taken.''

Though she didn't respond, a sideways glance let him see her rather smug smile.

After another moment he spoke again. "Brandy's still got some major problems, you know. She's still liable to take Marlin back when he comes around again, playing the victim and telling her how nobody else understands him."

"I know," Cecilia said with a sigh. "I'm not expecting miracles. I just want to try to get her some help."

"I hope she appreciates it someday."

"If she could only figure out that she doesn't need a man to make her happy and fulfilled. I'm hoping that if she gets nothing else out of the therapy sessions, if I can talk her into going, she'll come away accepting that."

Geoff didn't know what it was about that speech he'd heard before from Cecilia that particularly bothered him this time. Okay, sure, he could accept that she didn't *need* a man. She had certainly proven that.

But that didn't mean she couldn't accept a man into her life as a partner, did it? An equal. Someone who valued her, respected her, acknowledged her strength and offered his own when hers wavered. Just as she would do for that fortunate man if she—

If she loved him.

It was the first time the word love had entered his thoughts in connection with Cecilia. At least consciously. And it shook him all the way down to his nervous-bachelor toes.

Chapter Fifteen

As nervous as Cecilia had been about the dinner with Geoff's grandmother, it was a surprisingly pleasant and stress-free evening. From the moment she stepped into Myrtle Bingham's marble-tiled foyer, she was welcomed like an old friend of the family.

Myrtle was eager to hear all the latest news from the clinic, and Cecilia tried to oblige during dinner in the quietly elegant dining room. She left out most of the problems they had been experiencing at the clinic lately, of course, but she had plenty of anecdotes that kept her hostess entertained.

Cecilia thought that she could certainly be excused for feeling as if she were dining with a legend. After all, Myrtle was the one who had founded both the midwifery clinic and, later, the school. The hospital and future research center had both evolved from her early vision of quality health care for this poverty-stricken area.

Myrtle had also been active in funneling some of the Bingham fortune into the public library, the popular public recreation center and other facilities that were so widely used by the residents of Merlyn County. Surprisingly enough, there were still people in the area who resented the Binghams. For their money, their influence, the old history of Gerard's business ruthlessness and Billy's ceaseless womanizing.

Myrtle, as she insisted on being called despite Cecilia's initial discomfort with the familiarity, was still active in the community. With the energy of a woman half her age, she worked tirelessly for her pet charities. She seemed to be almost girlishly excited about serving as the spokeswoman for the new hospital public relations campaign.

"Lilly makes things so much fun," she added, a trace of Boston still detectable in her voice after more than five decades spent in Kentucky. "Have you gotten to know her yet, Cecilia?"

"No, not really. I've, um, been rather busy since she was introduced at the reception." She deliberately avoided looking at Geoff as she spoke.

"So has my grandson, apparently," Myrtle said, giving him a look of fond reproach. "I've hardly had a chance to see him since he's been in town."

"Hey, you're the busy one," he reminded her.

"Yes, I try to stay involved in the community. While you, of course, are out crashing your motorbike and scaring your poor family half to death."

Cecilia stifled a smile at the elder woman's prim

rebuke. Geoff squirmed in his seat like a kindergartener in trouble, then obviously regretted the movement. She suspected that he would have winced, but he didn't want Myrtle to see him display any discomfort. It was only because Cecilia had gotten to know him so well that she spotted the telltale twitch in his cheek.

"It was only a minor accident," he protested. "Dad probably exaggerated when he told you about it. You know how he's been lately."

Geoff must have been delighted that his grandmother was immediately distracted. "What has gotten into that son of mine lately, anyway? He's been so cranky."

Cecilia almost giggled. *Cranky* seemed like such an unlikely adjective to be applied to the distinguished and dignified man she knew as Ronald Bingham.

"He's made poor Lilly's job so difficult. He has challenged every idea she has presented."

Geoff shrugged. "She seems to me like the type who can hold her own against Dad—or anyone else." Then he added with a smile, "Much like Cecilia."

"Then they're both women after my own heart," Myrtle said firmly.

Geoff and Cecilia shared a quick smile across the table—one that Cecilia realized Myrtle had observed with a smile of her own.

"Cecilia's not after anyone's heart, Grandma. She claims they're much too high-maintenance organs."

"Oh, I really do like this young woman." Myrtle beamed at both of them. "I hope my grandson will bring you to have dinner with me again, Cecilia."

"Thank you. I would be delighted." But Cecilia wondered if the invitation would still be good if Myrtle knew what she and Geoff had been up to for the past three weeks.

Myrtle escorted them to the door after dinner. She repeated her warm invitation for Cecilia to join them again and then placed a hand on Geoff's arm to detain him for a moment after Cecilia stepped outside. "I like this one, Geoffrey."

He wrinkled his nose at her. "You like everyone who's single and female."

"That's not true. I didn't care for that brassy redhead you were seeing for a while."

"She wasn't brassy. I think the word busty is more, er, amply descriptive of her."

Myrtle lightly slapped his hand. "You are so bad. Now go out there and charm that pretty young lady before she comes to her senses about you and takes to her heels."

"I'm so touched by your confidence in me." He leaned over to kiss her soft cheek on his way out the door.

As he climbed into his car, he thought about his grandmother's words. "That pretty young woman." Granted, Cecilia *was* a pretty young woman, but not quite as young as the women Myrtle had been practically throwing at him for the past few years. Because Cecilia looked younger than she was, Myrtle might not be aware that Cecilia was actually five years older than he.

Not that Myrtle was hung up about such things. It was just that she was so obsessed with seeing a new generation of Binghams in Merlyn County. Of course, she didn't realize that Geoff was already working on that part.

"I like your grandmother."

Rousing himself from his reverie, Geoff smiled at Cecilia. "So do I."

"She's so energetic. So clever and funny. So...so inspirational."

"She likes you, too."

"You have a nice family, Geoff. Our baby will be very lucky to be a Bingham. I just hope..."

"What do you hope?"

"I hope your family won't think less of me—or the baby—because we're going about this...well, the way we are."

His first instinct was to instantly and heatedly deny any such thing. But something held him back. Surely it couldn't be fear that she was right?

His family wasn't like that. Hell, *all* his paternal cousins had been born out of wedlock. His child would be...just another illegitimate Bingham.

He drove into Cecilia's driveway, parked in front of her door, then sat staring blindly out the windshield until she cleared her throat to get his attention. "Aren't we going in?"

"Going in?"

She snapped her fingers. "Earth to Geoff. Are you in there? This is where I live."

"Oh, yeah, right." He looked at her front door and suddenly shook his head. "Listen, Cecilia, would you mind if I don't come in tonight? I hate to admit this, but I'm so sore I can hardly move. I think I'll go home and soak in the whirlpool for a while."

"No, of course I don't mind." She sounded more concerned than disappointed. "Are you sure you'll be okay? Is there anything I can do for you?"

Feeling just a bit guilty for the prevarication—though God knew he was pretty darned sore—he shook his head. "I can handle it. I'll call you tomorrow, okay?"

"All right. If you're sure you'll be okay."

"Positive." He reached for his door handle. "Let me walk you to your door."

"Don't be ridiculous." She laid a hand on his arm to hold him in his seat. "I'm perfectly capable of walking myself inside. You just go take care of those aches and pains."

He ignored the aches and pains long enough to lean over and give her a slow, thorough kiss. "Good night, Cecilia."

Her soft smile let him know how much she had enjoyed the embrace. "Good night, Geoff. I hope you feel better tomorrow."

So did he, he thought as she closed the car door behind her. Because he was feeling pretty lousy right now—and it had very little to do with the motorcycle accident.

He watched her walk to her door, her steps so brisk and confident. So clearly not in need of anyone's escort.

He really needed some time alone to think. Because he seemed to have gotten himself into a situation here that was more potentially life changing than he could ever have imagined.

Although Geoff called Cecilia on Saturday, as he had promised, he didn't come by to see her at all. He was snowed under, he explained, playing golf with his father and some potential investors, followed by a business dinner, followed by a consultation with his father and some of the other Bingham Enterprises executives about the upcoming, though still tenuous, fund-raising trip to Boston.

She had plenty to do to keep her busy while Geoff was otherwise occupied. Housework, shopping, that sort of thing. One thing she wouldn't think about today was that trip to Boston he had mentioned, she promised herself. While she knew Geoff's time here was limited, and that once he left for the next extended business trip their affair would most likely be over, she didn't want to dwell on that just yet.

He had sounded busy, she thought, glancing at the phone. A bit harried. But there had been something more in his voice. Something that sent her intuition into overdrive.

He'd been acting rather oddly ever since they had left his grandmother's house last night, she reflected, wandering aimlessly around her house in search of chores with which to distract herself from his absence. Replaying that lovely dinner in her mind, she couldn't imagine what might be bothering Geoff about it.

Unless seeing her there had made him realize exactly how different they were, after all? Wasn't that something she had been too keenly aware of since the beginning? Geoff had always acted as though the differences in their ages, incomes and social backgrounds didn't bother him, but maybe he'd just never pictured her at his grandmother's table before.

Or maybe she was being paranoid, she told herself

with a scowl, and maybe he was still hurting from his close contact with the pavement.

Still…

It wasn't as if she had ever implied to Geoff that she wanted to be a part of his family. Just the opposite, in fact. She'd turned down several invitations to join them for various occasions, accepting yesterday's dinner invitation only because he had given her little other choice.

She had promised him that she wasn't angling for marriage or commitment. Just a baby. And while her feelings about those things might have undergone a few changes during the past weeks—as well as her feelings for Geoff—she was still resigned to the reality of raising their child alone. As contentedly alone as she could manage, anyway.

She just wished she knew what was worrying him so she could reassure him. Once she managed to reassure herself, of course.

Geoff was called out of town on Sunday. He explained to Cecilia in a quick telephone call that he would only be gone for a couple of days this time, that it was a business fund-raising opportunity he simply couldn't let pass. Something about a science foundation grant for research that had just become available—he'd been rather sketchy in his explanation.

As disappointed as she was that he'd had to leave, and as bewildered as she was by the fact that the trip had come up on such short notice, she told herself she should use this time to get used to his absence. She had a busy schedule of her own. To be honest, having him underfoot would have been inconvenient.

Nice speech, she told herself as she stared glumly into the mirror on Tuesday morning before work. Too bad she didn't believe it.

She was fully capable of living without Geoff in her life. She was even capable of being happy again on her own, as she'd been for the most part before that reception at the clinic. But she missed him. Much more than she had ever expected.

He called her that evening from Maryland, and this time she had no doubt that something had changed in his behavior toward her. For the first time ever, their conversation was stilted, their silences awkward.

She wasn't sure if Geoff simply wanted to end the relationship now or if he was sorry he'd ever gotten himself into it, but from the way he was acting toward her, it wouldn't have surprised her either way. She only hoped she could be composed and dignified when he finally got up the nerve to break it to her.

Sitting in one of the spring chairs on her tiny patio late Tuesday afternoon, she thought back over their time together. She could almost see him standing at her gate on that first Saturday, when he had agreed to help her with her rather quirky plan to have a baby. And she would never forget those summer nights on the much-bigger patio at his weekend house, the leisurely dinners eaten under the stars and paper lanterns. Painting her nursery. Holding hands at the movie theater. Delivering a baby together. Maybe making one together.

That was the one thing that bothered her most—other than how much she was going to miss him, of course. She still didn't know if their lovemaking had led to anything more than memories that would last for the rest of her lifetime. Maybe it was rushing it a bit, but she thought she would try one of the early detection tests tomorrow after work.

She glanced toward the empty backyard next door. Brandy wasn't there this week. Her grandparents had taken her away for a brief vacation before they started the family therapy sessions Cecilia had set up for them. They had a tough time ahead of them yet, but she wanted to believe they would work things out. And that Brandy would find a path that would lead to happiness and fulfillment, not the misery she had been headed for with Marlin.

Marlin hadn't been back. Maybe Geoff had scared him, or maybe he'd just moved on to the next vulnerable victim, but, at least for now, he was staying away from Brandy. Cecilia hoped the girl's next boyfriend would be worthy of her affection. Someone kind and respectful and caring and strong.

Someone like Geoff.

Feeling uncomfortably like a lovesick teenager herself, Cecilia groaned and hid her face in her hands. She would get through this, she promised herself. As soon as she knew for certain whether she was pregnant—and admittedly, the odds were against that—she could concentrate fully on her work again. Her nice home. Her beloved brother and soon-to-be sister-in-law. Hannah's baby, whom they would soon welcome into the family. She would enjoy being an aunt.

Telling herself she had all anyone could ask for, she pushed herself out of the spring chair and headed back inside, trying to convince herself that it was the sunset making her view hazy and not the sheen of tears in her eyes.

* * *

Cecilia walked straight to her bedroom upon arriving home from work Wednesday evening, leaving the package she'd picked up on the way home sitting on the coffee table. Before she faced the stress of taking that test, she wanted to get as comfortable as possible.

She changed from her work clothes into a bright-blue T-shirt and a pair of soft cotton blue-plaid dorm pants. Pushing her bare feet into a pair of white terry slippers, she tied her hair into a loose ponytail.

It wasn't quite 7:00 p.m. yet, but she didn't plan to go out again this evening, nor was she expecting company. Geoff hadn't called today. If he was trying to pull away from her gradually, he was doing a fine job of it. She was coming to terms with the end of their affair, but that didn't mean it wasn't painful.

Maybe she would make herself something to eat before she took the test. A salad, perhaps. Or a bowl of soup.

She was stalling. The truth was, she was still so nervous about taking the test that she needed a bit more time to work up the courage.

It was early. The results might not be reliable, especially if it came back negative. A false negative was more likely than a false positive. But for some irrational reason, she thought she would know whether the results she received were true.

She wondered if she should wait until Geoff was here. Perhaps he would feel that he deserved to find out at the same time she did. But then, he was the one who had abruptly pulled away. She didn't even have a telephone number for him. And she couldn't wait any longer.

She had the test in her hands and had just turned toward the bathroom when the doorbell rang. After a moment of paralysis, she stuffed the box beneath a cushion on the couch and moved toward the door. There were only two people she could think of who might be on the other side. Her brother. Or Geoff.

She opened the door. "Geoff."

His expression was hard to read. There seemed to be a sense of…resolve about him that she didn't quite understand. Was he here to tell her once and for all that it was over between them? "Come in."

"You look very comfortable," he said as he closed the door behind him.

"I wasn't expecting company."

"I should have called you. I've only been in town for a short while. I came here straight from the airport."

"Then you must be hungry. Would you like me to make you a sandwich? A bowl of soup? I haven't eaten myself, actually." She sounded nervous, she thought. Even to her own ears, her voice seemed an octave higher than normal.

"Anything sounds good. While we eat, we can talk. I have a few things I want to discuss with you."

Which was almost as frightening a prospect as taking the pregnancy test, she mused. "Have a seat. I'll see what I have on hand for dinner. And then we can talk."

She wasn't gone long. When she returned after only a couple of minutes to ask him whether he preferred chicken noodle or tomato soup, she found him sitting on the couch with the pregnancy test in his hands.

He looked up when she came to an abrupt stop just

inside the doorway. "You choose odd places to store these things."

She twisted her fingers in front of her. "I, um, was holding it when the doorbell rang. Since I didn't know who it was…"

The rest seemed self-explanatory.

"Were you going to take this test tonight?"

She nodded. "I couldn't wait any longer."

His expression was even harder to read now than it had been before. "I see."

"It's probably going to be negative, of course. It's highly unlikely that I conceived so quickly. I'm prepared for that, but I would like to know for certain."

He nodded. "So how long does it take to get an answer?"

"Just a few minutes."

"Oh."

Now they were both staring at the box. Cecilia abruptly held out her hand. "Let's get this over with. I'll be right back."

"You're going to take it now?"

She answered on a sudden surge of confidence, "Yes. It's probably best if we know the results before we have that talk you came here for, don't you think?"

Geoff hesitated, and then he nodded. "Maybe it would be better to know the results before we talk."

With her heart in her throat, Cecilia turned toward the bedroom.

Ten minutes later they stood outside her bathroom door, staring at each other as the minutes counted down.

"Nerve-racking, isn't it?" Geoff asked, his mouth tilting into a weak semblance of his usual smile.

"You could say that again."

"I know you're hoping for a positive sign."

She would have thought she would be praying for a positive. But suddenly she wondered if that was really what she wanted, after all. Looking surreptitiously through her lashes at Geoff, she wondered if saying hello to a child would mean saying goodbye to the love of her life.

Not that Geoff would be thrilled to hear himself described that way, of course.

"Why, yes," she said, attempting a smile of her own. "Aren't you?"

"I'm not sure."

She felt her eyes widen. Was he choosing this moment to tell her he'd changed his mind about having a child with her? If so, he had really lousy timing. "Um—"

"Do you want to know why I'm not sure?"

She swallowed. "Yes." *Maybe.*

He leaned against the hallway wall, his arms crossed over his chest. And now she thought she could finally read something in his expression. It looked a lot like the nervousness she felt. "I've done a lot of thinking about us during the past five days. About what we've been trying to do."

"And?"

"And...I realized that I've changed my mind. Only I'm afraid it's too late now to change the terms of our agreement."

"You've changed your mind," she repeated flatly. "Well, that's fine. If the test is positive, we can just go back to the agreement I originally suggested. I'll raise the baby alone, and you can go back to the life you had before.''

He shook his head impatiently. ''That's the problem. I don't *want* to go back to the life I had before.''

He moved suddenly, his hands gripping her forearms in a firm hold that was still somehow gentle. ''You know how I told you that I always thought of marriage as a cage? That a wife would be just another responsibility I didn't want to deal with?''

''I—'' She had to clear her throat as a wave of jumbled emotions swept through her. ''I remember.''

''During the past few days it has occurred to me that maybe I've been looking at it all wrong. Maybe it's possible for a wife to be a partner. A friend. A lifelong lover. Someone to share my burdens, not add to them. And someone for whom I could do the same.''

Her heart was pounding so hard in her throat that she had trouble speaking. ''That's...one way of looking at it, I guess.''

His voice was suddenly husky. ''What if I tell you that I don't want the test to be positive if it means saying goodbye to what we've found together over the past three weeks?''

She moistened her lips with the tip of her tongue, reading the sincerity in his eyes. ''What if I were to say I feel the same way?''

His fingers tightened on her shoulders just enough to pull her a bit closer to him. ''What if I tell you that I want to marry you—whatever the results of that test?''

She placed her hands on his chest, exerting just

enough pressure to hold them apart. "That would depend on why you're asking. Because if it's only for the child's sake or out of some overdeveloped sense of Bingham responsibility or if you've decided that you should make your grandmother happy and get married—"

"What if I tell you it's because I love you with all my heart and soul, and I want to make a real family with you?"

After a brief, taut pause, she whispered, "That might make a difference."

He lifted one hand to cup her flushed cheek. "I've been aware for some time that there was something missing in my life. A hole I tried to fill with business successes and occasional minor rebellions—like the motorcycle. And then I saw you at that reception. I know now that leaving you would tear a hole in my life that no amount of work or financial success would fill."

"Are you sure, Geoff? Because we haven't really known each other very long. And you were so positive that you didn't want this."

"I was an idiot. And a coward. And it doesn't matter how long we've known each other. We've hardly done anything the usual way so far, have we?"

She couldn't help but smile at that. "No. I suppose we haven't."

"You haven't answered me, Cecilia. Will you marry me?"

Nerves gripped her again. "We're so different."

"Don't start with the age thing again," he groaned. "How many times do I have to tell you that doesn't matter to me?"

"It might matter to your grandmother and your father if it turns out that I can't produce another little Bingham," she muttered.

"I don't care. We'll adopt. We'll get a puppy. Just say we'll be together."

Her eyebrows rose. "A puppy?"

His mouth hovered just above hers. "Whatever you want. I love you, Cecilia Mendoza. Tell me you'll marry me."

She waited until he had released her from a tender, knee-melting kiss before speaking again, "I won't be a submissive wife. I tend to be the independent type."

He kissed her again before replying. "You'll have to be. I'll still have to travel a lot, at least for the next couple of years. Since I doubt that you'll want to leave your job, we'll probably have to spend some time apart, but we'll make the most of our time together."

This time she was the one who pressed a quick kiss to his lips. "I can handle that."

He drew back, his eyes searching her face. "Is that a yes?"

"It's a yes—if you're absolutely sure. I love you, Geoff. I think I fell in love with you when you smiled at me and offered me a bite of your strawberry at the reception."

This kiss lasted so long that they were both gasping when it ended.

"I can't believe we're engaged," Cecilia said when she could speak again. "Eric is going to faint."

"Think he'll approve?"

"I'm sure he will. What about your father and Mari?"

"They'll be delighted that someone is willing to take me in hand. And since my grandmother already loves you, we shouldn't have any trouble with family."

"Oh, heavens. Speaking of family." Cecilia looked anxiously toward the bathroom doorway.

Geoff took her hand. "Let's look together, shall we? And Cecilia—if it's negative, I'm willing to keep trying to make a baby until we both collapse from exhaustion."

His exaggeratedly noble tone made her laugh, albeit a bit nervously. They crossed the room slowly, and she suspected that Geoff was as nervous as she was when she drew the plastic stick from its holder.

"Well?" he asked, when she took a moment to get her emotions under control.

The look she gave him must have said it all.

"It's positive?"

She nodded. The planets were definitely out of alignment, she thought in a daze, but this time she wasn't complaining.

Looking disgustingly proud of himself, Geoff grinned and swept her into his arms. "Maybe we should keep working at it, anyway—just to make sure."

Her head spinning with the realization that she had just been given everything she had ever wanted—and so much more—she wrapped her arms around his neck. "I love the way you think."

"And I will love you," he murmured, tumbling her onto the bed, "for the rest of my life."

"I'll expect that in writing," she warned.

''A woman after my own heart,'' he whispered as his hands and his lips began to roam.

This time, she didn't bother to argue with him.

*   *   *   *   *

A sneaky peek at next month...

By Request

RELIVE THE ROMANCE WITH THE BEST OF THE BEST

My wish list for next month's titles...

In stores from 20th September 2013:

3 stories in each book - only £5.99!

☐ Wicked Surrender – Sara Craven, Cathy Williams & Daphne Clair

☐ Taken by the Millionaire – Kate Hardy, Robyn Grady & Nicola Marsh

In stores from 4th October 2013:

☐ Payback Affairs – Emilie Rose

☐ Pregnancy Proposals – Rebecca Winters, Raye Morgan & Brenda Harlen

Available at WHSmith, Tesco, Asda, Eason, Amazon and Apple

Just can't wait?

Visit us Online

You can buy our books online a month before they hit the shops! **www.millsandboon.co.uk**

0913/05

Wrap up warm this winter with Sarah Morgan...

Sleigh Bells in the Snow

Kayla Green loves business and hates Christmas.

So when Jackson O'Neil invites her to Snow Crystal Resort to discuss their business proposal… the last thing she's expecting is to stay for Christmas dinner. As the snowflakes continue to fall, will the woman who doesn't believe in the magic of Christmas finally fall under its spell…?

4th October

www.millsandboon.co.uk/sarahmorgan

1013/MB435

She's loved and lost — will she ever
learn to open her heart again?

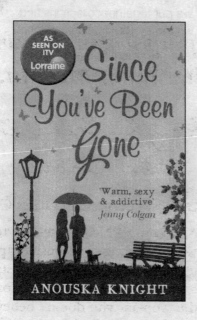

From the winner of ITV Lorraine's Racy Reads,
Anouska Knight, comes a heart-warming tale of
love, loss and confectionery.

'The perfect summer read — warm,
sexy and addictive!'
—Jenny Colgan

For exclusive content visit:
www.millsandboon.co.uk/anouskaknight

Special Offers

Every month we put together collections and longer reads written by your favourite authors.

Here are some of next month's highlights— and don't miss our fabulous discount online!

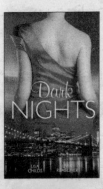

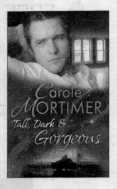

On sale 20th September   On sale 4th October   On sale 4th October

Save 20%
on all Special Releases

Find out more at
www.millsandboon.co.uk/specialreleases

Visit us Online

1013/ST/MB434

Mills & Boon® Online

Discover more romance at
www.millsandboon.co.uk

- **FREE** online reads
- **Books** up to one month before shops
- **Browse our books** before you buy

...and much more!

For exclusive competitions and instant updates:

 Like us on **facebook.com/millsandboon**

 Follow us on **twitter.com/millsandboon**

 Join us on **community.millsandboon.co.uk**

Visit us Online   Sign up for our FREE eNewsletter at **www.millsandboon.co.uk**

WEB/M&B/RTL5